AN UPSETTING UPSTART

The elegant Beau Brummell was the undisputed despot of London society. A lift of his eyebrows and a barbed phrase from his cutting tongue could ruin a reputation and doom a young girl's dreams.

The arrogant William Summers was the most commanding captain in the Royal Navy, used to having his every order instantly obeyed and his every desire speedily satisfied.

Neither of them had ever known defeat. But neither had ever met a lady like Jeannie McVinnie—who dared defy them both in a dazzling display of independence that made one of them bow his beautifully coifed head, and the other lose his haughty heart. . . .

CARLA KELLY lives in Springfield, Missouri. She is a public relations writer for a local hospital.

SIGNET REGENCY ROMANCE
Coming in July 1996

Candice Hern
An Affair of Honor

Allison Lane
The Impoverished Viscount

Emily Hendrickson
The Debonair Duke

Mary Balogh
An Unacceptable Offer

Mrs. McVinnie's London Season

by
Carla Kelly

A SIGNET BOOK

SIGNET
Published by the Penguin Group
Penguin Books USA Inc., 375 Hudson Street,
New York, New York 10014, U.S.A.
Penguin Books Ltd, 27 Wrights Lane,
London W8 5TZ, England
Penguin Books Australia Ltd, Ringwood,
Victoria, Australia
Penguin Books Canada Ltd, 10 Alcorn Avenue,
Toronto, Ontario, Canada M4V 3B2
Penguin Books (N.Z.) Ltd, 182–190 Wairau Road,
Auckland 10, New Zealand

Penguin Books Ltd, Registered Offices:
Harmondsworth, Middlesex, England

First published by Signet, an imprint of Dutton Signet,
a division of Penguin Books USA Inc.

First Printing, June, 1990
10 9 8 7 6 5 4 3

Had we never lov'd sae kindly,
Had we never lov'd sae blindly,
Never met—nor never parted,
We had ne'er been broken-hearted.

—Robert Burns

1

SHE heard the postman's whistle at her own front door almost before she turned the corner and set her feet toward Abbey Head. Jeannie McVinnie stood still a moment in the roadway. She nodded to the other women, baskets over their arms, who were headed in a purposeful cluster toward the greengrocer's. After another nod and a bow to the minister's new bride, Jeannie twitched her plaid up a little higher about her shoulders and continued on down the street.

She was not the kind of woman who backtracked. Jeannie no longer believed her mother's admonition that to turn back, once having set out, would bring down all manner of misery and bad fortune. She was not superstitious, but still, she would not have retraced her steps.

Beside, Galen was there, and in a grumpy mood. It would do him good to stir from his armchair, where everything was laid out within easy reach, and hobble to the front door. Now that his color was much improved and his melancholy in large part gone, Jeannie felt compelled to force a little exertion upon her father-in-law. He had no cause to chafe about the fit of his wooden leg. The surgeon had declared the amputation a thing of beauty, going so far as to summon his colleagues from the University of Edinburgh to exclaim and proclaim until Galen McVinnie was heartily tempted to unstrap the leg and beat the physics about the head with it.

A walk to the door would do him good, she told herself as she turned her head against the little mist that seemed to rise from the ground. She paused again and considered tramping over the road past the church and toward Gatehouse of Fleet. She discarded the notion; the rhododendrons were not yet in bloom. She would wait for that event.

Jeannie turned again toward Abbey Head. It was a walk of

some five miles, affording ample time for reflection, but not too much. She did not trouble herself about the letter. Undoubtedly it was for Galen McVinnie, late a major of His Majesty's Fifteenth Dumfries Rifles. For the past year as the shocking news had spread farther and farther away, like a pebble tossed into Wigtown Bay, letters had dribbled in.

When Galen could not raise his head off the pillow, Jeannie had answered the first spate of letters, stopping often because she could not see through her tears to write. Calmly she accepted the condolences of Tom's death and the prayers for Galen's speedy recovery.

During those dark days of the Scottish winter, Jeannie McVinnie had come to dread the postman's whistle. It only meant more letters, more explanations. When Galen could sit upright again and his handwriting was steady enough, she gladly surrendered the correspondence to him.

Her father-in-law kept up a series of letters to particular friends, and as the year of mourning wore on, the missives of concern turned into invitations to visit. Only yesterday there had been a note scrawled on quite good rag paper and franked by a lord, requesting his attendance at a regimental gathering in Dumfries.

"It is not very far, Jeannie," Major McVinnie had said, and there was something wistful in his voice that made her turn her head so he could not see her smile.

"Indeed not, Father McVinnie," she had replied, knowing better than to attempt to make up his mind for him. Thomas had been woven of the same plaid; and she had learned early in her brief tenure at marriage not to press the issue.

In the end, last night Galen decided against the gathering. "Jeannie, too many questions," he said as he refolded the paper and laid it aside. "Perhaps some other time."

But she had found him looking at the note again before she escorted him upstairs to bed that night. "Still, I could not leave you here alone, my dear, now could I?"

His words were kind; they were always kind. But more and more, it was that condescending kindness of the strong for the weak. He was measuring her each day, and finding her lacking, even as he smiled. He watched her when he thought she wasn't aware, but she was always aware. And what he saw, he did not like.

The mist lifted and allowed the sunshine to stream through the clouds. Jeannie turned her face toward it. She knew it would be brief. March sunlight served only to keep heart in the body until spring's tardy arrival to the lowlands. She took a deep breath, mindful that already there was something of spring in the air.

"The spring of 1810," she said out loud, as if to allow it official recognition. The spring of 1809 had passed without fanfare, other than to be marked with an X on each calender square, the symbol of one more day got through without Thomas McVinnie.

An hour's brisk walk brought her to the head, crowned by the ruins of an abbey. It was too early in the year for the young ladies of St. Andrews' Select Female Academy to be grouped here and there about the picturesque stones, their heads bent diligently over sketching pads, so she had the place to herself. Even the sea gulls normally in residence were wheeling far overhead on the air currents.

In a moment she had perched herself into the shell that had once formed a window overlooking the bay. She sat still, reflecting, not for the first time, on the quality of Scottish woolens, effective even against cold abbey stones.

Jeannie smiled to herself, remembering again that over oatmeal that morning Galen had looked at the invitation from Dumfries. "I wonder, my dear, if that part of the regiment from Canada—Bartley's company—will be there."

A sea gull, irritated at the intrusion upon the abbey, swooped lower to investigate. Jeannie took one of last night's scones from her pocket, crumbled it, and tossed it toward the bay. The sea gull ignored her for several more moments and then condescended to alight and peck among the stones.

Jeannie sighed and sunk her hands deep in her pockets. Galen McVinnie was restless to go to Dumfries, but he would make no move as long as she remained with him in Kirkcudbright. It was time for her to move along. Galen still had a life to live, even if hers was over.

"And where might I move to, may I ask?" she questioned the gull, which hopped a few steps farther away and regarded her with a red eye.

Mother and father were dead long since. Agnes had dutifully invited her to join them in Edinburgh, but Jeannie knew the size of her sister's house and just as politely declined. Her two brothes served in India. They had invited her to the subcontinent, but she did not relish a long sea voyage. She was not very fond of water.

But it was more than that; she knew it and her brothers knew it. At the end of the long journey, there would be row upon row of officers ready to propose, eager to marry a white woman from Britain, all the more so if she were not hard to look at and moderately endowed. Jeannie McVinnie was not ready to cast herself upon the marriage mart so soon after Thomas' death.

"Surely you will agree, friend bird," she said to the gull, which hopped closer, "that the consideration of one's second husband is possibly a matter for some serious thought. And I choose not to think about it yet. India can wait."

If it was not to be Indian, what, then? She knew she must remarry. It was a cold-blooded reflection that had cost her many a night's sleep. The knowledge that she was destined to marry again, duty-bound, had chased about in her head until she was weary of it. And always by the time morning came, she was fully awake to the fact that she had no desire to sleep in anyone's arms but Tom's, and now it was too late for that.

Jeannie hopped down from the ledge and shooed the gull away with her skirts. It rose in an indignant fluff of white, hissing at her, as she walked closer to the cliff overhanging the bay.

A small boat of indeterminate type tacked across the bay, searching about for a bit of wind to bring it safely in. Jeannie shaded her eyes with her hand and watched it.

I would be a sailor, she thought suddenly, and let the wind blow me where it chose. She sighed. If only I could feel some harmony with the sea.

But she would never be a sailor, or a soldier, or a doctor like her father, or a greengrocer, or a vicar. The only path open to her was marriage. As she stood watching the boat in the bay, Jeannie decided to entertain the notion. Somewhere in the wide world, there must be another man for her. She might not love, but she could like.

"And he needn't be handsome," she told the gull, which had plummeted to earth again, chattering and scolding behind her back. "One cannot have such good fortune twice in a row. He must be amiable, however, and good-natured and polite. A wealthy man would be an excellent thing, too."

The thought made her smile. "Where you expect to find a wealthy man, where none existed before, I cannot imagine, Jeannie," she told herself.

She walked back to the abbey ruins and leaned against the ledge. "And while I am about it, he should be wondrous fond of children and devoted entirely to the finer things in life."

The idea was so improbable that she laughed out loud, noting with surprise that it was the first time in a year she had done so. "Such a paragon I have created," she told the gull. "The wonder of it would be if such a man old enough for me was still safe from Parson's Mousetrap!" It felt good to laugh, and she was still smiling to herself as she set her face toward Kirkcudbright again and the little stone house on McDermott Street.

Mrs. MacDonald was out to market when Jeannie returned. The housekeeper had vowed after breakfast to come home with a joint of mutton, "or die in the attempt, Mrs. McV," she had declared as she put on her hat and battened it down in anticipation of Kirkcudbright's wind.

The subject was a sore one, and Mrs. McDonald was not one to let a topic wither without a good shake. "Although why it should be so hard to get a good joint of mutton in Scotland, I canna fathom. Do our soldiers in Spain eat so much that there's not even a dab left for pepper pot? Explain it to me again, Mrs. McV."

And Jeannie had patiently explained again that wartime causes shortages of the most inexplicable commodities, even mutton in Scotland.

The house was quiet. Mrs. MacDonald was most likely still doing battle with the butcher.

"Is that you, Jeannie?" Galen asked from the next room.

"It is, Father." Jeannie removed her cloak and shook it before the fireplace before draping it over the chair. The smell of damp wool made her wrinkle her nose. "I am coming."

Galen was standing by the window, hands clasped behind his back, a letter in them. She admired his balance, noting with pride that he looked good again, not thin and worn. The military set was back in his shoulders. He turned around and held out the letter to her.

"It is another note from Laird Ross. And he has sweetened the pot, Jeannie." He scratched his head. "Indeed, he is making it impossible for me to refuse attendance at the reunion in Dumfries.''

She took the letter from him, reading it swiftly. She looked up at him, and he smiled into her face.

''Ah, Jeannie, when I see that dimple in your cheek, I know you're not precisely oblivious to the hatching of this plot,'' he declared. ''Thomas used to declare that you had a military turn for strategy.''

They could talk about Thomas now, if they spoke carefully and avoided each other's eyes.

She handed back the letter. ''It would seem, sir, that you are about to be kidnapped.'' She could not resist. ''And led in chains to a trout stream in the north when the reunion has run its course.''

''Yes, a scurvy plot, Jeannie, and one that I am powerless to combat,'' he replied with a grin. ''And Major Ross outranks me. Our majorities were purchased two days apart, so he is my senior. Now, what can I do?''

''Nothing except submit to the rule of authority and go to Dumfries, Father.''

Only do not smile at me like that, she thought. You remind me so of Thomas.

Her return to sobriety brought Galen McVinnie to earth again. ''But, Jeannie, I cannot leave you here alone for the summer. I cannot. I promised Thomas that I would look after you.''

No one could argue with the kindness of Galen McVinnie's words, but there was something in the saying of them that stung like a pin under the fingernail. Was she imagining, or could she almost hear a sigh as he spoke, as if he wished Tom had not extracted such a promise?

''So you did promise,'' she said quietly. ''And you have done such a lovely job of it. I can manage here.''

''Still, it is not right.''

Jeannie saw the signs coming of what Thomas had dubbed the ''great McVinnie dig-in,'' that look of stubbornness and duty that was nearly impossible to argue with. She glanced about her for something to distract her father-in-law, and found it on the mantelpiece.

''Father, is there a letter for me?'' she asked suddenly.

''Yes. I forgot. Clumsy of me.''

went to the mantelpiece and picked up the letter. The

handwriting was unfamiliar. She ran her finger over the paper and immediately knew it was of the best quality. The letter had been franked by a lord. The word "Taneystone" was scrawled across the top. She frowned and looked at her father-in-law, who shrugged and stumped closer.

"It is no one I know." Galen managed a mild joke. "Jeannie, my dear, are you in trouble with the lairds of England? A lowering reflection for a Scottish lassie, I vow."

She shook her head. "I haven't a clue. I suppose nothing will suffice but I must open the thing." She faltered. "I only wish it did not look so official."

Her last official letter had led to her widowhood. She shook off the feeling that threatened her somewhere behind her eyelids and accepted the penknife Galen handed her. She opened the letter and spread out the closely written page. Jeannie motioned her father-in-law closer and held it out to him so they could read it together.

"Captain Sir William Summers, commanding *HMS Venture*, Knight Grand Cross of the Bath."

The title seemed to speak in the quiet room so boldly was it written.

Jeannie looked at Galen.

"I am no wiser," she said. "Would this be a navy man?"

Galen nodded and pointed to the salutation. "He labors under the delusion that he knows you."

She looked down. "My dear Miss Jeannie McVinnie," she said out loud. "Whoever can this be? Let us sit down, Father."

They sat. Jeannie spread the letter out on her lap and began to read.

"My dear Miss McVinnie, I regret I have not written you since the occasion of my reply to your letter five years ago, in which you so kindly inquired about my part in Trafalgar. Has it been five years? I have spent most of that time since engaged in blockade duty, which I need scarcely trouble you with. It is an occupation of astounding tedium and occasional terror. The contrast is regrettable, as it sets our teeth on edge, but what are we do to if Boney will rove about the continent, kicking up his heels?

You were never one to beat about the bush. Let me explain the reason for this letter. I believe you to be aware of George's death two years ago (and of course, you are already well aware of Marceline's untimely passing years ago). George's death surprised all of us, particularly in light of the fact that I have always been considered the family favorite to be tamped down first by the undertaker's shovel or slid off a board into the sea.

Jeannie raised her eyes to Galen's face. "Father, he is so ghoulish!"

Galen rubbed his chin. "Permit me an observation. Navy men tend to be more fatalistic than the rest of us. It must come from tossing about in little wooden tubs and eating weevily biscuit."

"It must be so," Jeannie replied. She addressed herself to the letter again.

You will recall George's two children—Larinda, who has just turned seventeen, and Edward, who is fourteen and now Lord Summers. Larinda has begun her come-out, and I have been ordered to London (I shall explain *this* later!) to act as head of the household. This is the reason for my letter. I am in desperate need of a companion for her, someone to chaperone her to parties and routs and such.

You will recall that my sister, Agatha Smeath, has for years been a quasi-guardian, filling in where I could not, because of the press of war. You remember Agatha and her flibertigibbet ways. She cannot be relied upon to usher Larinda out and about. I need someone of dignified years, considerable countenance, and copious good sense. Naturally, I thought of you.

"Well, I like that," Jeannie declared. "I am not above twenty-four!"

Galen laughed. "Jeannie, remember, we do not know this man. Nor does he know you."

"Then we should not be reading his letter," she said crisply. "I feel like a Peeping Tom. Oh, bother it all! Let me finish. There isn't much more. Where was I?"

In short, I need someone who will not be flummeried by a headstrong chit just out of the schoolroom. My dear Miss McVinnie, I rely on you to drop whatever it is you are currently involved in and hurry to Number 3, Wendover Square, where my sister has engaged a house for the Season.

I await your arrival with considerable interest. It has been twenty years since we have laid eyes on each other, although I have enjoyed your occasional letters over the years. I trust I have improved since our last meeting, although I do not know that I will satisfy your expectations. I certainly never satisfied anyone else's.

I remain yours truly and desperately,

William Summers,
Captain of His Majesty's *Venture*.

Jeannie stared at the letter another minute. "I am no wiser than I was when I began this letter, Galen. How odd! Can you make anything of it?"

Her father-in-law took the letter from her and reread the concluding paragraphs. The crease between his eyes deepened for a moment and then disappeared. He was smiling.

"All right, sir, out with it! He cannot possibly be referring to me."

"Indeed, he is not," Galen agreed. "My dear, this is delicious! I only wish she was here to savor the moment."

"*Who* are you talking about?"

Galen tapped the letter. "This . . . Captain Summers can only be referring to my aunt Jean McVinnie. You never knew her, and more's the pity. Delightful woman, if a trifle outspoken."

"Oh, how unlike the McVinnies I know," Jeannie quizzed.

"Baggage! Seriously, she died—well, it wouldn't have been too long after that affair at Trafalgar that the good captain mentioned."

"Then there really was another Jeannie McVinnie?" Jeannie asked. She looked at the letter. "And she was—"

"A nanny." Galen finished her sentence. "Indeed she was, for five years. When Mother died, she returned here to Kirkcudbright to keep house for Father." He chuckled. "And I don't believe she was sorry to shake the dust of London off her shoes. Bless me if she didn't refer to this very Captain Summers as—oh, let me see, I must get this right—'a thoroughly denatured son of Satan.' "

Jeannie gasped and then giggled.

"And as I recall, that was one of her kinder phrases." Galen leaned back on the sofa, his eyes meditative. "Yes, yes, it was Will, because George was a decided slow-top. My dear, you would have loved her letters home. Come to think of it, they must still be about here somewhere."

Jeannie picked up the envelope and shook out the draft on a London bank signed by Captain Summers. "I suppose this is for the mail coach and posting houses," she said. "Goodness, it is a substantial sum. Does this give us some indication of the degree of desperation?"

"A sea captain stuck in the middle of a come-out," Galen said. "It does make the blood run cold."

Jeannie handed him the bank draft. "I suppose you can write

'void' upon the draft and send it back. You probably should accompany it with a letter, Galen.''

"I am sure that would be best, Jeannie, although . . ." His voice trailed off and then he began to laugh. "Oh, the things Aunt Jeannie used to write about the Summers boys! I would almost give a year of my pension to see the look on William Summer's face if *you* were to show up in Jeannie's place!''

Jeannie smiled indulgently at her father-in-law. Men will have their little jokes, she thought as she returned the letter to the envelope. She retrieved the draft and placed it with the letter on the mantel, where it would remind Galen to reply.

Her cloak must be dry by now. Nodding to her father-in-law, who was still in the grip of a huge good humor, she went into the other room and picked up her plaid.

She was smoothing out the fabric when the idea took hold of her. So Captain William Summers wanted a woman of good sense, did he? And he wanted Jeannie McVinnie, in particular.

She went to the desk and looked at the calendar there. April, May, and June. Was that not the extent of a London Season? It would amount to a few balls, suppers, and parties to occupy her agreeably while Galen McVinnie went to his regimental reunion and trout-fishing in the Highlands.

Jeannie knew that he would do none of these things if she remained in Kirkcudbright. He would remember his promise to his dying son and stay to look after her, even though he longed to be elsewhere. She shivered. Even though you so politely wish me elsewhere, Galen McVinnie.

"You McVinnies are so stubborn," she said out loud. "If you will not do what is best for you, then I must. And surely one Jeannie McVinnie is as good as another.''

She gave the idea several minutes' thought. When nothing surfaced to wave her away from it, Jeannie went to the door of the sitting room. Galen was still there, only he was rereading his well-read note from Laird Ross. He looked up at her and Jeannie made her decision.

"Father McVinnie," she declared, "I have a wonderful notion. Tell me what you think of it.''

2

JEANNIE'S first glimpse of London was disappointing in the extreme. Because of a loose wheel, their entrance in the city had been delayed until dusk. The rain, which had been threatening all day to fall, thundered down, obscuring what little else she could have seen.

Her back ached from the discomfort of sitting upright hour after hour. She longed to curl up in a dark corner and abandon herself to sleep. Food could wait; clean linens could wait; she wanted to sleep.

The mud-spattered coach pulled into the Bull and Hind with a flourish of the horn and a great squeak of water-soaked brakes. It remained only to reclaim her baggage and procure the services of a hackney.

The several hackneys for hire were quickly bespoken for by the other occupants of the mail coach, who danced about in the sodden roadway, raising their hands to attract the attention of the drivers and then leaping back to the curb in time to avoid an accident.

I can never do that, thought Jeannie. I will be forced to stand here until spring at least, or until someone takes pity. She was the only unescorted woman remaining in what was obviously an unsavory neighborhood. That thought, plus a sudden rush of water down the back of her neck, compelled her into the street. She waved her arm vigorously, and to her infinite relief, a jobbing cab stopped.

"And where'll ye be heading, now, miss?" asked the driver.

"Three Wendover Square, if you please," she replied.

The driver whistled. "That's a mighty fine direction, miss," he said, and leaned down from his box. "Now you'll not be offended if I ask ye to show me some money first, will ye? It's a bit of a way to go."

And I look none too prosperous soaking wet, she thought grimly as she dug about in her reticule and salvaged a handful of coins. The driver nodded and tipped his hat to her, and she climbed inside.

Once she was out of the rain, she had to smile to herself, thinking how carefully she had assured Galen that she could manage perfectly well by herself. And so she could, once she had learned to overlook the stares of innkeepers and the bold glances of men drinking in taprooms. Jeannie had spoken to no one in the four days of her journey, save a vicar outside of Leeds, who rode for only a few miles, and a governess on her way to Nottingham. In silence she had ridden, one hand firmly on her reticule and her eyes fastened upon the dreary scenery of late March.

She must have slept then in the hackney, leaning against the window, her hand tight to the strap. The monotony of the rain, along with last night's sleepless sojourn in a noisy, overcrowded inn, sent her into a slumber that she did not wake from until the hackney had stopped and the driver opened the door to admit the rain again.

"Here you are, miss. Watch your step, mind."

Jeannie paid the driver, gathered her sodden skirts about her, and descended to the roadway. Whistling to himself, the driver plopped her bags down beside her, tipped his hat again, and drove into the rainy night.

Jenanie picked up her bags, took two steps toward the house, and then set down the bags again. The doubts that had been niggling at her almost since the moment they crossed the border seemed to loom before her now in monstrous proportion. As she stood peering at the large house through the dark and the rain, Jeannie McVinnie knew, deep in her self-critical Scottish heart, that she had erred.

She also knew that she could not return to Kirkcudbright. Galen had locked up the little house on McDermott Street, and Mrs. MacDonald had left for Skye to spend the spring with her oldest daughter. To cry off now would mean that her father-in-law, gentleman that he was, would be forced to leave his Highland trout stream and the agreeable company of old comrades-in-arms.

ad seemed a clever idea less than a week ago was now lish escapade. Jeannie knew that Scottish humor was a piquant thing. Suppose the English were different? She had no experience among them. Her mouth went dry and her hands felt cold and clammy inside her gloves.

How could I be so stupid, she berated herself. What happened to my perspicacity?

A cart tumbled by, flinging water across her cloak. If I remain here much longer, I will be a fetching sight, she thought. Courage, Jeannie. You got yourself into this so gracefully, now you had better get yourself out.

She squared her shoulders and picked up her bags again, compelling herself to move forward and up the front steps. She knocked on the door, praying that no one was at home even as she saw lights glowing in the windows and heard the mumble of voices within.

The bags felt as heavy as Presbyterian sin, and she set them down again, a little to one side, as she waited for the door to open.

It opened so suddenly that the motion nearly threw her off balance. Jeannie blinked and jumped back as an overstuffed woman in an apron and cap grabbed her by the wrist and yanked her inside.

"We thought you would never get here," the woman railed as she pulled Jeannie into the room. "Lady Smeath is about to fall into a foaming fit, and the captain . . . Oh, God help us!"

Jeannie could only stare, openmouthed.

The housekeeper peered at her and spoke in more kindly tones. "Dearie, take off your cloak. My, you look as if you had traveled miles and miles, instead of only from Bond Street. I suppose it's that kind of a night. Hurry up, now. There's work to be done. That's my dearie."

Numbly, Jeannie handed over her cloak and thought only fleetingly of her bags on the front steps. Whatever address she had once possessed deserted her entirely. She started to say something, but the housekeeper had her firmly in tow and was tugging her up the stairs.

A quick glance at the top of the stairs took in the beautiful rooms, the portraits on the walls, the thick carpeting underfoot. She peeked in one open door as the housekeeper hurried her along. A curly-haired gentleman was struggling with a neckcloth.

"Blast and damn, Pringle," he shouted as she was hurried

past. "Damn and blast! I'd rather be under fire and hip-deep in swash!"

"Aye, aye, Captain. Surely we'll come about, sir."

Jeannie's ears caught the burr of a Scottish voice in that reply, but the housekeeper was racing her down the long hall to another room, where she stopped, out of breath. The housekeeper took a closer look at Jeannie and a frown appeared between her eyes.

"Well, didn't Madame Coutant send you with some thread at least? A pair of scissors?"

Jeannie shook her head and the housekeeper sighed in exasperation. "Those frogs haven't the sense of a pound of butter. Oh, go in. I will get thread."

The woman propelled Jeannie into the room and left her there.

A young girl stood in front of Jeannie, her eyes red with weeping. An older woman sat on the bed. She was dressed in the latest fashion, her dress a perfection of lace and silk, but her face was pale and she appeared on the ragged edge of a spasm. The woman rose laboriously to her feet when she saw Jeannie and drifted toward her as if she had not the strength to navigate to the door.

"You can tell Madame Coutant that after this night, I will no longer suffer her with our patronage. Now, what are we to do about this, I ask you? And I suggest that you have a remedy."

With a languid hand, she motioned Jeannie forward. "Stand still, Larinda, and quit sniveling. We haven't time for cucumbers on your eyes. Let the dressmaker see you. Now, I ask . . ."

Jeannie came nearer and the problem was obvious immediately. The dress was too big, nothing more. Jeannie smiled and reached out to touch the girl on the arm. "I can have this ready in a trice. Don't fret so. Now, take it off, like a good lassie."

The young woman pulled back when Jeannie touched her.

"You are a trifle familiar with your betters," she snapped even as she turned around for Jeannie to unbutton the garment.

Resisting the urge to slap her, Jeannie unbuttoned the dress and pulled it carefully over the young woman's hair, which was already arranged with diamonds and flowers. "Wrap a dressing gown around yourself, my dear," she said. "Ah, here we are."

The housekeeper had returned with a workbasket. Jeannie
␣he dress inside out and reeled off a length of thread.
␣ pinned another seam inside the first one and threaded

the needle. She perched herself on the chest at the foot of the bed and started to sew. She thought about attempting some light conversation, but a quick glance at the young lady—was her name Larinda?—and her stormy eyes and a peek at the older woman's white mouth convinced Jeannie to keep her own counsel. As she hunched over the material, she vowed to leave this unpleasant house, leaving no one the wiser. If they thought her the dressmaker's assistant, that was well and good.

Jeannie bent her head diligently over her work, looking down at the exquisite pink muslin dress across her lap. Her glance caught the tiniest movement of the bed ruffle.

Curious, she stuck the needle in the fabric and picked up the bedspread. Gazing back at her was a little girl, finger in her mouth, dark eyes wide.

"Oh, you precious," Jeannie exclaimed despite the tension that seemed to sit in the room like a fog. "Oh, do come out. I'll not bite. Truly, lassie, I haven't a mean bone."

The little girl smiled around the finger still in her mouth, but she did not move. With a sigh of profound ill use, the housekeeper pulled her out from under the bed, picked her up, and set her against the wall. She wagged a finger at her. "Don't you move a muscle now. We haven't time to spare for crochets."

The little girl's eyes clouded over and for a moment Jeannie thought she would cry. The child took a quick, sidelong glance at Larinda's companion, uttered a shuddering breath that went straight to Jeannie's heart, and remained where she was in the shadow.

Jeannie dragged her eyes back to the dress and continued her tiny stitches. She quickly altered both side seams, clipped off the thread, and held out the dress to Larinda, who snatched it from her.

"Help me," she ordered.

Her lips set in a tight line, Jeannie rose to her feet and snapped the scissors shut in her hand with an audible click. Her head went back and her eyes narrowed. "Say please."

Larinda gasped. The other woman—she could only be Larinda's aunt—made a strangled sound deep in her throat and waved her vinaigrette about like incense while the housekeeper coughed.

"Your impertinence defies belief," the aunt said as soon as

she regained the use of her voice. "Tomorrow Madame Coutant will have a full account of it, and I hope she turns you off without a character."

Jeannie looked around at her tormentor. "Yes, ma'am, you tell Madame Coutant every little detail." She turned an inquiring eye on Larinda, who stood, as if rooted to the spot, still clutching her the dress.

"Please."

The word was softly spoken, but Jeannie heard it.

"Very well."

Larinda held up her arms as Jeannie stood on tiptoe and dropped the gown over the curls and jewels that glittered in her hair. She did up the buttons and smoothed the fabric over Larinda's hips, stepping back for a better look.

"It is too long, but that is all. If you will allow me, I can have that hemmed in a jig and jiffy."

After a glance at her aunt, Larinda nodded.

In a moment, the dress was spread over Jeannie's lap again. Quickly she pinned in another hem and set to work.

The chest was too high to perch upon comfortably, and the pain laced through her shoulders as she leaned forward over the material.

And then someone was sliding a footstool under her shoes. Gratefully she looked over and smiled into the face of a countryman.

He could only be a fellow Scot, with his frank blue eyes, square jaw, and liberal dusting of freckles. He must belong to the voice Jeannie had heard from the captain's room. She looked at him, a question in her eyes.

"The captain will be needing your assistance when you are finished here, miss, if you will be so obliging."

"She is not obliging," burst out Larinda's aunt with a sob in her throat.

"I am very obliging," Jeannie said firmly, and smiled at the light of recognition that her accent brought into his eyes. "I am merely a stubborn Scot."

The man—Summer's valet?—stood where Larinda's aunt could not see his face and winked at her. She smiled back, grateful to know that she was not Scotland's only expatriot in

The man went to the door and stood there until the house-keeper shooed him away.

Jeannie hemmed swiftly, wondering what the captain wanted. He could have no idea who she was. I do not think I will ask him to say please, she told herself, and the thought made her chuckle.

While she worked, the women left the room. Jeannie heard them quarreling in the hallway. Someone stamped her foot several times and there were noisy tears. Jeannie shook her head. Nothing could force her to remain in this disjointed household. Agnes would simply have to open her home in Edinburgh to one more body, for she was going there as soon as she knotted her last knot and saw to whatever it was the captain wanted. It might make for a long spring, but at least it would be a tolerable one.

Jeannie looked up into the eyes of the little girl, who still stood against the wall, finger in her mouth. The child couldn't have been above four years old, if that. She was dressed nicely and her curly hair was caught up into a little bow on the top of her head. Jeannie smiled and beckoned her closer.

After a careful look around, the girl ran across the room and held up her arms for Jeannie to lift her onto the chest. Jeannie laughed and settled the child next to her.

"Stay here and be quiet as a mouse," Jeannie said, "and we'll brush through this without a blot on our souls."

Jeannie finished the hem and shook out the dress. The house-keeper whisked herself back into the room and snatched it away. "I've heated the irons belowstairs. It'll want another press."

Jeannie nodded. The housekeeper motioned her to follow. "I'll send your wage along to Madame Coutant's in the morning, but I expect you'll be wanting something to eat."

The Scottish man in the hallway took her by the arm and appropriated the workbasket from the housekeeper. "Nay, Mrs. White, not so fast. The captain hasn't worn his dress blues since I disremember, and he has a loose button."

Jeannie looked back into the room. The little girl had climbed down from the chest and was backed up to the wall again, her eyes on the aunt and daughter, who had taken up residence in the room again.

'Poor little thing,'' Jeannie said out loud.

The housekeeper pulled herself up sharp. "You're feeling sorry for your betters? I marvel that Madame Coutant keeps you on, for all that your stitches are wondrous small."

"It is a source of some amazement to me, too," Jeannie murmured as the door to the room closed.

The Scotsman sighed. "It's amazed I am that you have kept any position at all, miss." He peered closer at her when she seemed disinclined to comment. "How long have you worked for that dressmaker?"

Jeannie twinkled her eyes at him. "You would be astounded how long I have worked for her."

The Scotsman ventured no further discussion. He led her to the door of the room she had passed in such a hurry on her way to alter Larinda's gown. Jeannie slowed down in spite of herself and the Scot regarded her with some compassion.

"He's not so frightening, Miss . . . Miss . . ."

Jeannie did not choose to enlighten him with her last name. "I would rather suspect that he is worse," she replied as she tightened her lips and searched about for the courage to enter the room.

The Scotsman gave her a little push. "He's rather worse if he's kept waiting, but I doubt that he has ever flogged a seamstress," he whispered as they crossed the threshold together and Jeannie stood face to face with Captain Sir William Summers.

There was nothing about the captain to give her one moment's confidence, Jeannie decided as she looked at him, curtsied, and fought down the urge to bolt the room. He was tall—so tall that she wondered how he could have accommodated himself to life aboard a ship. He had the sort of figure she admired in a man, broad of shoulder and solid. His posture was impeccable, his hair curly and light brown, and receding somewhat from his high forehead. His features were unremarkable. If anything, his nose was too beaky by half and his lips too thin.

She decided that the only thing truly remarkable about Captain Summers was his mahogany tan. He was deeply tanned, a thing surprising, considering that it was early spring. It was the tan of someone always outdoors in good weather and bad. His face was lined in a way that reminded her of the shepherds in the Highlands who spent a lifetime facing continually into the wind.

Jeannie's critical review of Captain Summers stopped with

his eyes, and she decided that nothing could soften the hardness in them. They were the green of the sea, the color of Solway Firth when the tide was in spate. They were regarding her now with an expression that held nothing but irritation and a sort of ill-concealed energy that troubled her.

"I trust that you have satisfied whatever curiosity about me that you may have harbored," he said. His voice was low, but it carried, and Jeannie felt a small shiver traverse the length of her spine.

You, sir, are a big bully, she thought as she raised her eyes fleetingly to his again and then lowered them just as quickly. And you know precisely what I am thinking, don't you?

The notion was disconcerting in the extreme, but it compelled her to look him in the eyes again, even as her legs trembled. His glance had not wavered from her face and she realized with an uncomfortable start that she recognized the look. It was the same measuring stare that a border collie would fix upon a sheep, particularly a sheep contemplating a bolt from the flock.

Jeannie cleared her throat, exasperated with herself. "You have a loose button, sir?" she asked, not daring to raise her voice.

He regarded her another moment in silence until she was sure he could hear the heart beating in her chest. He pointed to a gold button on his uniform front and then clasped his hands behind his back.

Jeannie turned to the Scot beside her. "Could you help the captain remove his coat?" she whispered.

The captain shook his head. "I'll not wrinkle it further. Just come a little closer. Surely you can jury rig a button while I'm still in the coat."

She did not budge. Her feet had turned into blocks of wood.

With a sigh that seemed to come from his shoes, the captain took a step toward her. "You silly baggage," he said, biting off the words. "I only bite when the moon is full and the tide is running."

Startled, she looked him in the eye again, and was rewarded this time with the tiniest glimmer. It may have only been a reflection from the lamp on the dressing table, but it gave her the heart to move.

"Very well, sir," she said, and motioned to the Scotsman beside her. "Pray, what is your name?"

"Pringle," the Scotsman said. After a moment's reflection,

as if he were deciding whether to confess, he continued. "Erasmus Pringle."

"Erasmus?" asked the captain, and the little twinkle in his eyes deepened. "You never wrote that on a ship's manifest."

"Indeed not, Captain," replied Pringle. "But she did ask, sir." A slow flush was spreading up his face.

"And in all the years of our acquaintance, I do not remember when I have ever seen you blush, Pringle," continued the captain inexorably. He rocked back and forth on his heels and addressed his next remark to the ceiling. "Overmuch dissipation such as we are currently engaged in will ruin us both, I daresay."

"Aye, aye, sir," Pringle replied.

"And now, Pringle, if you will," said Jeannie. "I need some thread from that workbasket."

Relieved to change the subject, Pringle handed Jeannie a spool of navy thread and found a needle in the pincushion.

Jeannie threaded the needle and approached the captain. In silence she stood right next to him and felt the button on his coat, breathing in the bracing odor of bay rum and noting the row of medals that marched across his chest. She sewed in silence, acutely aware that he was watching her face the whole time. And he was so close.

In silence she knotted the thread. She glanced in the workbasket that Pringle still held, and then remembered that she had left the scissors on the chest in Larinda's room. She stood on tiptoe, leaned forward, and cut the thread with her teeth.

The captain touched her shoulder to steady her. She should have leapt back the second she finished, but before she was even aware of her actions, Jeannie patted him on the chest and arranged the large, star-shaped medal precisely in the front of his uniform.

"You'll do now, sir," she said. "Now hold still a moment more."

His neckcloth had been bothering her since she entered the room. She reached up and straightened it, pleating the folds until it was entirely to her satisfaction.

"Are you quite, quite through?"

The captain's soft voice cut through the silence like a dagger flung at a distant target. Jeannie froze, her hands still raised to his neckcloth. Slowly she lowered them and put them behind her back like a small girl in a china shop.

"I mean, if you are through fiddling over me, and if Larinda, my beloved niece, has put a momentary curb to her whining, and if my sister, the dragon in gossamer, can be forced to exert herself . . ." He stopped and took a deep breath, standing even taller. "Ah, but I have no business speaking like this. You are dismissed. Pringle, see that she is paid something." He turned abruptly back to his dressing table for another look in the mirror.

He looks as though he does not like what he sees, Jeannie thought. I wonder if he has ever smiled.

She watched as he picked up the handsome peaked hat on the stand by the dressing table and tucked it under his arm. He turned to the door again and eyed her with an expression centered somewhere between exasperation and resignation.

"Are you still here?" he snapped. "And I wish you wouldn't look at me like I am a monkey in an exhibit."

Jeannie's chin went up. Only the greatest force of will prevented her from uttering the retort that rose to her lips.

She was spared the bother of reply. The dragon in gossamer swept into the room, the feathers in her headdress nodding and bobbing.

"Oh, it is too, too bad," she declared in tones more appropriate to the stage at Covent Garden. "Edward has chosen to lie down with a sick headache and cannot accompany us. And this was to be a family dinner at Lord and Lady Dearden's. I am sure I will grow distracted."

"You, madam?" murmured the captain. "Surely not."

"Indeed I will," she declared. And her voice rose another notch even as she dug about for her vinaigrette. "And I feel my heart already beginning to race."

"It wouldn't dare," replied the captain blandly.

Jeannie turned away to hide the smile on her face. She stole a glance at the captain and noticed for the smallest second that twinkle in his eye. She might have been mistaken. The look he fixed upon Lady Smeath was all business. She must have been mistaken.

Without a word, Jeannie followed Pringle into the hall and down the stairs. She felt herself relaxing. In another moment, she would be safely on the front steps again. She could retrieve her bags and hurry away before anyone in the Summers household was any wiser. She would chalk up the whole wretched adventure to experience and never venture beyond Hadrian's Wall again.

The footman stood at the bottom of the stairs. "Your carriage waits at the door, Captain."

Pringle touched Jeannie's arm. "We'll go belowstairs and wait for them to leave, miss. And didn't Mrs. White promise you a bite to eat?"

"Truly, it is not necessary," Jeannie said. Gracious merciful Lord, all I want is out of here.

"Oh, I insist," Pringle said. "You can't go out on this raw kind of night without something to keep you warm."

I can indeed, thought Jeannie. Just watch me.

They entered the hallway, the captain and Lady Smeath close behind. Standing by the open front door was a tall, thin woman who was gesticulating in a Gallic fashion with the butler.

"Blast and damn," said the captain under his breath. "And who is this Long Meg?"

The butler separated himself from the irate woman and came forward in some relief. "Sir, I fear that a great deception has been practiced upon this household," he began, and fixed Jeannie with a basilisk stare.

Jeannie dropped her gaze and noticed for the first time that her bags were resting in a growing puddle inside the door.

She heard a gasp behind her. Lady Smeath shouldered herself forward. "Madame Coutant," she declared, "whatever does this mean?"

"It means that I came as quickly as I could to see to whatever had to be done to your daughter's dress. A regrettable incident, to be sure, my lady, but only think upon all the dress I am called to create at the beginning of the Season."

"I neither know nor care," said Lady Smeath as she stiffened and then looked around until her gaze rested upon Jeannie McVinnie, too. "And who, pray tell, are you?" she asked. She swung around to the dressmaker again. "Madame, do you employ this young person in your establishment?"

It was Madame Coutant's turn to stare. "I have never seen her before this moment, my lady."

"I really think I should be going," Jeannie said as she attempted to edge toward the open door.

Captain Summers grabbed her. "Perhaps you had better

explain yourself, and then I will decide whether to summon the watch.''

Lady Smeath staggered to a chair and sank gracefully into it. ''Please. Not a scene. My nerves could never bear it. Oh, where is my vinaigrette?''

''It is in your hand, Aunt Agatha,'' Larinda said.

''Captain, I can clear up part of this mystery,'' the butler said. ''I suspect she must belong to these bags I discovered when I opened the door to admit Madame Coutant.'' He paused then for dramatic effect, and the captain sighed.

''I took the liberty of opening one of the bags to determine their ownership and found this Bible,'' said the butler as he reached inside and pulled out the book in question.

''You are to be commended in your search for righteousness,'' Captain Summers snapped.

The butler cast him a wounded look. ''Sir, I merely read the inscription upon the flyleaf. It says, 'Jeannie F. McVinnie.' ''

The captain started and tightened his grip on her arm. He pulled her around to look her full in the face. ''You cannot possibly be Jeannie McVinnie,'' he declared with such conviction that she almost believed it herself.

''I am Jeannie McVinnie,'' she insisted.

Lady Smeath gasped and clutched at her chest. ''Is this the woman you thought to foist upon my household? 'She is old and steady,' you told me.'' The feathers in her headdress quivered. ''William, I would never have thought you worthy of such a stunt!'' With hands that trembled, she took the vinaigrette to her nose and sniffed deeply. ''Poor dead George would have been mortified if he knew the depths you had sunk. Although we have wondered—''

''That's quite enough, Agatha,'' said the captain, biting off each word and glaring daggers at Jeannie.

His sister threw up her hands. ''Whoever she is, I am glad that I did not pay her! I leave you, William, to pay for your own doxie. And keep them out of my house.''

Jeannie gasped. ''You walloping great toad,'' she said.

''One more word from you and it will be your last,'' said Lady Smeath in an awful voice, surprising in one so pale. She brushed past Jeannie and the captain and summoned Larinda to follow. ''Come, my dear, this is no place for ladies. Captain, we will await you in the carriage.''

"I will be there in a moment," the captain said.

He did not relinquish his grip on Jeannie. He shook her. "If you have practiced some foul play on the kindest old lady of my acquaintance, you'll be cooling your heels in Newgate."

"I am Jeannie McVinne," Jeannie said.

The captain grabbed her by the shoulders and jerked her forward until they were nose to nose. "Then I am Marie Antionette," he declared.

Pringle coughed and turned away.

Jeannie wrenched herself from the captain's grasp. She fumbled in her reticule and pulled out the money remaining from the bank draft. She grabbed his hand and slapped the money into it.

"This is what remains of the bank note you sent me in Kirk-cudbright, you great big bully! I may be Jeannie McVinnie, but I wouldn't stay under the same roof with you for all the tea in China!"

"William," Lady Smeath called from the front steps.

Captain Summers shoved the money deep in his pocket, his thin lips set in a tight line. "That woman has a voice that could summon dead sailors to the riggings in a hurricane." He glared in the direction she had gone and roared, "When it suits her!" He passed his hand in front of his eyes, and for the tiniest moment, for only for a moment, Jeannie felt sorry for him. "I must be headed on the road to Bedlam, Pringle."

"Aye, aye, sir," the Scotsman replied automatically.

"And you needn't be so damned agreeable!"

"William!"

"I am going, sir," Jeannie declared with all the conviction she could muster.

"Indeed, you are not," declared the captain in tones equally fervent. "Pringle, if you have to sit on her, keep this Jeannie here until I return. And that's an order!"

"Aye, aye, sir!"

"And what about me?" demanded the forgotten Madame Coutant.

The much-tried and sorely put-upon Captain Summers rounded on the dressmaker. "You, Madame, can go to the devil! And quickly, too!" He slammed the door behind him so hard that the chandelier swayed and tinkled overhead.

Silence ruled for a moment while the inmates of the hall looked at one another. Pringle was the first to speak.

"And I thought a London Season would be dull work," he said to no one in particular. "I cannot recall offhand when blockade duty was this stimulating." He offered his arm to Jeannie McVinnie. "Come, Miss McVinnie, or whoever you are. We have a bit of night ahead of us."

3

JEANNIE dabbed her lips with the napkin and pushed the plate a little to one side. "And that is the whole of it, Pringle, believe it or not. If you have any doubts, you can direct Captain Summers' attention to Malcolm Caldwell, my Edinburgh solicitor."

Pringle shook his head and laughed softly. "And there he was insisting you were *his* Jeannie McVinnie."

Jeannie shuddered. "Oh, don't remind me. I harbor a vast suspicion that I may be the first person to ever argue with him."

"You claim that title, Mrs. McVinnie."

She spread her hands out in front of her. "Please believe me, I had the best of intentions. I thought I would serve this household equally as well as my husband's Great-aunt Jeannie." She shook her head. "That was before I met the people in this household."

"A quelling lot. And now you wouldn't stay for the world," Pringle said.

"Nay, I would not," she agreed, "especially after that disagreeable woman called me a . . . well, you know what she called me."

They sat belowstairs in the servants' hall. After eyeing her

suspiciously for the better part of the evening, the butler—
Wapping was his name—had finally taken himself off to bed,
but not before muttering something concerning the evils brought
about by adventurous females.

On another occasion, Jeannie would have been sent into
whoops by Wapping's admonitions. Tom had told her once that
he had been attracted to her from the very first by her great
good sense and air of true maturity. But it was scarcely funny.
She had thrown an entire household on its side and made a
perfect cake of herself into the bargain. The only thing that
remained was to suffer through what promised to be a delicate
interview with Captain William Summers and take the next mail
coach north.

"Perhaps things will appear in a better light tomorrow
morning," Pringle suggested. "The captain had set aside a room
for you, or for Jeannie McVinnie, at any rate. I am sure he
would not quibble if you were to retire for the night."

"You're sure?" she asked doubtfully.

Pringle smiled. "He has a better side, Mrs. McVinnie. A
pity that few ever see it."

"I am sure I shall not," Jeannie exclaimed as she rose to her
feet.

Candle in hand, Pringle led her upstairs again and down the
long hallway. The candle threw shadows on the portraits lining
the walls. The flickering light seemed to animate those older
lords and ladies. Jeannie rubbed her eyes. The portraits almost seemed to be dancing in the agitated light. This would
never do.

They passed a closed door. Jeannie paused and put her finger
to her lips when Pringle turned to her with an inquiry in his eyes.

Someone was crying, little gasping sobs that made Jeannie's
heart turn over.

"It must be that little girl," she whispered. "Oh, Pringle,
who is she?"

"Clare."

"Clare? Clare who?" she asked even as he took her firmly
by the elbow and started her down the hall again.

"Clare is . . . Clare," he said finally, in a tone that allowed
no questions.

"So Clare is Clare," Jeannie said to herself when she had
closed the door to her room and listened to Pringle's footsteps

receding down the hallway. Wapping had placed her soggy bags inside the door. To her surprise, someone had taken out her clothes and hung them in the little dressing room. The bedclothes had been turned down; a bulge at the foot of the bed indicated that a warming pan was spreading its comfort.

Jeannie slowly unbuttoned her dress and let it drop to the floor. She made herself ready for bed, braiding her hair and tucking it into her nightcap. Her eyelids drooped. She wanted nothing more than oblivion until the sun came up. She crawled between the sheets, grateful for their warmth. She sighed, stretched, and closed her eyes.

Sleep did not come. As she lay there in the quiet darkness, she could still hear Clare sobbing. It was a sound so totally without hope that Jeannie put her hand over her ears, wondering if she had sounded like that in those awful months after Tom's death.

But this is none of my business, she thought as she lay on her back in the darkness, her hands clenched into tight fists. I am leaving this house first thing in the morning.

And then, as surely as she knew her own name, Jeannie McVinnie knew she could not just lie there and listen to a child cry. "Jeannie girl, you are an enormous fool," she told herself as she got out of bed and padded to the door, opening it a crack and peering into the hall.

No one was about. After a careful glance around, she tiptoed down the hall to Clare's room and opened the door.

A woman sat nodding in front of the little fire in the hearth. When the door opened, she jerked herself upright and then leapt to her feet.

"There's a child crying," Jeannie said. "I thought perhaps . . ." What on earth did I think? How can any of this be my business, Jeannie thought as she watched the woman's expression change from one of surprise to irritation.

"That is only Clare, and I have my instructions."

There. It was as plain as that. The matter was obviously of no concern to her.

But Jeannie did not move. "Surely your instructions do not mean for you to allow the child to cry half the night?"

The woman smiled in a condescending manner and sat down again. "She never cries all night! In another hour she will be silent."

"Another hour," Jeannie exclaimed. "Surely you cannot be serious?"

"I have my orders," the woman insisted. "You'll have to go."

Without another word, Jeannie left the room. She knew her face was red with humiliation and she could only be thankful for the dark. Why do you not learn to mind your own business, Jeannie McVinnie, she scolded herself. Are you not in sufficient trouble already because you thought to wiggle in where you really weren't invited?

She threw herself back into bed and pulled the covers over her head, wishing she had never heard of Captain William Summers and his ill-regulated, ill-mannered household.

An hour later, she was still no closer to sleep. Somewhere a clock chimed once. As her ears practically hummed in the silence, Jeannie heard a door open. She got out of bed, slid open the door, and squinted in the gloom.

It was the door to the nursery. The nursemaid let herself out and went quietly down the stairs. Jeannie listened, a frown on her face. Clare still cried. Jeannie stood where she was, listening. When the maid did not return, she let herself into the hall again and hurried to the nursery door.

The fire had died and the room was cold. Jeannie shivered and hurried into the next room. The light of the moon shone across the bed where Clare huddled, her legs drawn up to her chest, her hands over her ears, Jeannie came closer and touched the little girl, who started and then opened her eyes wider.

"It is I, Clare," Jeannie whispered. "Do you remember?" She touched the child's cheek and rested her hand on the tousled hair, damp with tears. "Oh, come on. We might as well get in a little more trouble."

Jeannie picked up the child, who made no objection but only settled herself into Jeannie's arms and closed her eyes. She hurried down the hall and back into her own room, where she put Clare in bed and climbed in after her. Without a word, she tucked the child close to her side and put her arms about her.

"No sense in being miserable," she whispered. "Now, go to sleep, Clare Whoever-you-are."

Clare nodded, her dark eyes full of sleep. In another moment, she was breathing steadily.

Jeannie rested her lips on the curly hair for a moment, breath-

ing in the faintest fragrance of bay rum. The familiar odor made
her open her own eyes for a moment, but only a moment.
Clare's warmth was pulling her into slumber with all the effec-
tiveness of a sleeping draft.

Jeannie couldn't be sure what woke her. Clare breathed slowly
and evenly beside her. The room was still dark and surprisingly
cold, as if a window had been opened. She almost turned over
and closed her eyes again when she heard someone else's
breathing.

She willed herself to be silent. As her eyes accustomed themselves to the darkness, Jeannie could discern the outline of
someone poised by the open window, as if he had been caught
in flight.

Gently Jeannie disentangled herself from Clare and sat up.
She forced her voice to remain light even as her fingers searched
the night table for something, anything, to throw.

"Pringle," she called softly as she found a hairbrush and
picked it up. "Did you fear I would slip my moorings? Even
after I gave my word?"

No answer.

She looked again. The figure was too slight for Pringle, and
decidedly so for Captain Summers. Lady Smeath or Larinda
would never have entered her room. That exhausted her
knowledge of the residents of 3 Wendover Square.

"Who are you, please?" she asked finally.

No answer for the longest moment, and then, "Edward."

Edward. Jeannie searched her brain for a moment and then
remembered the son who had taken himself off to bed with a
sick headache. She relinquished her grip on the hairbrush,
wondering if anyone kept regular hours in London and if this
was an even more unusual household than she had reckoned.

"Edward, are you not ill? Didn't Lady Smeath say something
about—"

"I'm not ill. It's only a hum," said the voice. "I've only
just now got back from Vauxhall Gardens, and your room
affords the most convenient entry."

"Is there not a door on this house?" Jeannie asked. "I seem
to recall one." She reached for her robe and, after another
glance at Clare, struck a match to the bedside lamp.

"Oh, there's a door," Edward said, "and the others have
not yet returned from the Deardens', so I know it is not locked."

"Then why did you not use it?" Jeannie asked sensibly, drawing her knees up and wrapping her arms around them. "Is this a London custom?"

"It is in this house," Edward replied. "Besides, there is Wapping and that great monstrous Cyclops of a footman sitting up."

Jeannie laughed softly. "Enough said. He does resemble a Cyclops, now that you mention it. Edward, would you please close that window?"

The boy closed the window, moving silently and swiftly. He glanced at Clare sleeping in Jeannie's bed and then looked over at Jeannie.

"Are you that woman who came to fix Larinda's dress?"

"I am. And I'm leaving in the morning."

He sat down at the foot of the bed and leaned forward impulsively. "Oh, I wish you would not! I hear Larinda practically did a Saint Vitus dance when you told her to say 'please.' I should like to have seen that."

Jeannie shook her head. "Don't remind me. I shall do all within my power to forget this night ever happened. But tell me, Edward, why the window? And Vauxhall Gardens?"

He was silent a moment, looking at her as if he wondered if he could trust her.

Jeannie crossed her heart and held up her hand. "Cross my heart and hope to die, Edward." She could almost feel him relax.

"I never saw a woman do that," he declared. "You see, I can climb up the tree outside the window and get in without anyone knowing I have been gone."

Jenanie could only gape at him and wonder. He was not a tall boy. In fact, he appeared rather small for his age. His shoulders were narrow, his face thin, the moon's shadows digging holes in his cheeks.

"Vauxhall Gardens?" she gently reminded him. "Surely such a place, and by yourself—"

"I only went to watch the Grand Cascade," he said, the note of defiance in his voice ameliorated by the fact that he whispered. "My guidebook describes it as an educational event and one of the wonders of George's England. I merely wanted to see it." He sighed. "Aunt Agatha would never let me be among all those people, even though I tell her and tell her that when the Season is over we'll be back in Suffolk and I will have nothing to show for it."

Jeannie understood. She leaned closer to the boy in the dark. "And your aunt is afraid you will take ill?"

"Exactly so," Edward replied. "She is afraid that I will catch a cold, or get too warm, or have too much fun, I declare! Just because my wretched uncle never had a well moment . . ." He plucked at the bedcover in his agitation and Clare stirred and muttered in her sleep.

Jeannie touched the sleeping child until she was still again. "Oh, Edward," she said, "surely not."

He was only warming to his subject. "Who is to know when we will ever be in London again after Larinda's Season?" He sighed again. "And Aunt Agatha says I will probably not live to be very old."

"Monstrous," Jeannie exclaimed.

Clare moved restlessly in her sleep.

"My health is indifferent," he said, in halfhearted defense of his aunt. His voice was level, monotonous, his words bearing a rehearsed sound to them.

"I doubt that," Jeannie siad. "Particularly if you can climb that tree outside the window." She got out of bed and went to the window and looked down. "Why, it must be all of thirty feet to the ground."

"I never thought of it like that," Edward said. "But I do get headaches, and tire easily, and my stomach is weak. Aunt Agatha says so."

They regarded each other in silence. Edward stood up finally and put his hands behind his back. "I had better go now," he whispered. "I hope you won't say anything. As it is, I look through my guidebook every day and plan all sorts of adventures." He looked down at the floor. "Usually, that's all it is, I just plan. But I did want to see the Grand Cascade."

His words twisted Jeannie's heart into a lump that threatened to rise into her throat. She waited a moment before she could speak. "That must be an excellent guidebook," she managed finally. "Perhaps you could show it to me in the morning. Before I leave, that is."

"Oh, yes. I am planning tomorrow to study the section on the Tower of London." He looked up at her shyly. "I think it must be almost as good as being there. But you won't tell?"

"Cross my heart, Edward." He grinned and stuck out his hand; Jeannie shook it solemnly. "Actually, I was thinking about running away. You see, the Deardens and my mama and Uncle Will were at Vauxhall Gardens tonight. I did not expect them there. I think Uncle Will saw me. Do you think I should run away?" he asked as he backed toward the door. "Uncle Will did, time and time again, my aunt says, and he is a captain. Should I run away?"

"Of course not! Running away never solves anything," Jeannie said, and then had the good grace to blush. She was running away as fast as she could in the morning. But what a pity she could not take Edward with her. "Now, run along to bed before your aunt and uncle return. Think of the trouble you would be in if someone found you here."

Edward nodded, opened the door, and tumbled into Captain Summers' arms.

"Good heavens!" Jeannie said.

Captain Summers held Edward out at arm's length. The boy had gone quite pale.

"I thought I heard someone talking."

Summers lifted Edward off the ground and looked him directly in the eyes. "You were at Vauxhall Gardens tonight, you little wharf rat, weren't you?"

Bereft of speech, Edward could only nod.

Terrified, Jeannie looked at the captain and beyond him. She could hear people coming up the stairs. She put her hand on the captain's arm and tugged on his sleeve like a little child. "Oh, please, sir, if his aunt catches him, think of the trouble."

She couldn't be sure, but she thought she saw that little twinkle in the captain's eyes again. He set Edward on his feet, turned him about, and pushed him in the direction of his own room.

"Run, boy! You and I will settle this in the morning. And now, Miss McVinnie—or whoever you claim to be at this hour—I also have no desire to be caught standing in this companionway. Kindly step aside and close the door, for God's sake."

Smiling in spite of herself, Jeannie did as he said and closed the door behind them.

"This is highly irregular," she said finally when Larinda and her aunt walked down the hall, stood arguing for a moment, and then slammed the doors to their own rooms.

The captain did not reply. Jeannie looked around. He was standing by her bed, looking down on Clare, who lay in peaceful sleep, her hands flung wide across the pillows, her curly hair tumbled about her face. As Jeannie watched, he carefully pulled the hair away from her mouth and touched her cheek with the back of his hand. He stood there a moment more and then directed his gaze at her again.

"Well? What is this?"

"Captain, she was crying, and that harridan of a nursemaid wouldn't do a thing about it."

"You certainly are a managing female," he said, and then straightened up until he was poker-stiff again. "My sister tells me that children should not be indulged."

"Your sister is a fool," Jeannie snapped. She gasped and put her hand to her mouth. "Oh, I do apologize."

The captain touched Clare's cheek again. "No need. You are exactly right." He came closer to her. "Are you beginning to understand why I summoned Jeannie McVinnie?" He bowed. "And you are Jeannie McVinnie. Pringle met me at the door with the glad tiding." He bowed again. "I can only regret my rudeness, but you must own, Mrs. McVinnie, that I was expecting someone rather more stricken in years."

"I can't help that," she said sensibly. "And I will not stay in this house beyond tomorrow morning."

Summers went to the door and opened it. "A wise choice. I wouldn't stay here either, if I weren't under the damnedest set of orders from the First Lord of the Admiralty, who, I regret to say, is the little brother of my sister's late husband. Lord Smeath was only too happy to summon me from the blockade to oblige his sister-in-law. That way he doesn't have to play the escort."

He stepped into the hall. "So, you see, I have no choice, Mrs. McVinnie." He came back into the room. "The way is clear. If you will permit me." He went to the bed and picked up Clare, who stiffened for a moment and then relaxed against his shoulder. He smiled at her and then looked Jeannie in the eyes. "Yes, I can smile."

"I wasn't thinking that," Jeannie faltered.

"Oh, yes, you were." He came closer and whispered in her ear. "It's just that I don't waste them, Mrs. McVinnie. Good night."

"Good night," she said softly. A sudden thought assailed her. "But tell me, Captain, is—"

"Clare my daughter?" he finished. "She might be."

"But . . ." Jeannie followed him down the hall to Clare's room. She opened the door for him and turned back the covers while he settled the child in bed and then kissed her good night.

The captain stood looking down at Clare for several moments. He idly fingered the Grand Cross of Bath on his chest, his thoughts miles removed from Wendover Square.

Jeannie knew he had forgotten she was in the room, so she turned to go.

He was at her side in a moment. "It's a long story, Mrs. McVinnie," he said as he escorted her back to her room again. "But, look, I think the sun will be coming up soon, and didn't you say you had to be leaving?"

"Well, I did," she began.

"Then do not let me disturb one more moment of your slumber," he continued affably. "Good night."

"You are aggravating beyond belief," Jeannie said.

"I have four lieutenants, a surgeon, and—oh, let me see—six midshipmen and any number of rated seamen under my thumb who would agree with you entirely," he said. "I wonder why they have never told me?"

"You would probably flog them and make them walk the plank," Jeannie declared, stung to an angry retort that she knew was improper the moment it left her lips.

The captain reached down and put his finger to her lips. "Hush now! By the good Lord, you do remind me of the Jeannie McVinnie I knew."

She started to say something, but he did not remove his finger.

"That's better. You'll wake my charming sister if you continue railing at me, and that, you'll agree, would be an ugly business. Go to bed, Mrs. McVinnie. Hush now! And do try to overlook the fact that although we will miss you greatly after tomorrow, we will manage somehow."

4

THE rain was long over by the time she woke in the morning, and she felt unaccountably refreshed by the puny hours of sleep granted her. Jeannie went to the window and pulled back the draperies. Perching herself on the window seat that looked out onto Wendover Square, she opened the window, rested her elbows on the sill, and let the day happen.

Up and down the street, maids were sweeping the front walks, and pushcart men walked slowly by, selling milk, pasties, and promises that their pans would never need a tinker's mending. She watched footmen striding purposefully from their employers' mansions intent on early-morning errands and full to bursting with self-importance. Grooms walked their horses up and down in the square, waiting for their masters to fork a leg over and take a prebreakfast canter in one of the great royal parks that made this part of London so much more pleasant than the crowded, smoke-foggy rabbit warren that was the City.

Jeannie rested her chin on her hand. At home, after she had flung up the window sash, she would have taken a deep, deep breath. Here there would be no smell of the sea, no pleasant tang of heather or Scotch broom to delight the eye. But she had to own that while the air was scarcely as promising, London held a vast potential for interest that Kirkcudbright could never command.

She reminded herself that she was leaving. She would spend a few moments with the captain, apologize to him one more time for good measure, pack her bags again, and hitch them onto the next mail coach venturing up the Great North Road. Somehow, the thought was less appealing than it had been last night, when she had quaked in her boots and sewed on the captain's button.

"It is merely that you do not relish the thought of another

trip on the mail,'' she told herself. She knew she had enough funds to hire a post chaise, but Jeannie McVinnie wasn't a Scot for nothing.

The air that breezed in through the open window was still tinged with a hint of winter. She closed it and jumped back in bed, grateful for the warmth. It would be so easy to close her eyes and drift off into sleep again, if there weren't the nagging matter of making a graceful exit from this house and its less-than-amiable inmates.

Her thoughts were distracted by a scratching at the door.

"Come in, please."

"Mrs. McVinnie, will you be wanting some hot water?"

"That would be delightful. Please do come in."

The maid entered the room and set the can of hot water on the washstand. She curtsied. "I can bring you some tea, mum, if you'd like."

Jeannie was about to answer when another head peeked around the corner of the door. Clare, still dressed in her nightgown, regarded her seriously for a moment, finger in mouth, and then edged inside the room to rest against the wall. Jeannie held out her arms. Clare hesitated a moment, then hurled herself across the room and scrambled up on the bed.

The maid's eyes were wide with surprise. "Lord love us, I never saw her do that before!"

Jeannie smiled and tucked Clare in beside her. "Clare and I do not stand much on ceremony. Yes, I would like some tea, and perhaps you could bring some tea with milk for my guest."

The maid curtsied again and turned away with a smile.

Clare settled herself in, closed her eyes, and promptly returned to sleep.

"You're a little dickens," Jeannie scolded softly. "And now you sleep when the rest of us must wake. Your late-night tears are a vexation. I know I could cure them in only a few days. And then . . ."

Then what? she thought as she scooted down in the bed again and rested her head on her arm. At most, you have another hour in this house, and thank God for that. She reached out and touched Clare's curls. "Well, your hair is curly like his." Jeannie giggled. "Although there is more of it."

The maid returned with tea and Jeannie sipped hers

thoughtfully as she watched Clare struggle awake and rub her eyes. She accepted her cambric tea and drank it carefully, her brown eyes fixed on Jeannie's face.

The maid watched them both. "I don't remember when Clare has taken to someone like you before, Mrs. McVinnie. She was standing outside the door—quietlike, the way she does—when I came up here with the hot water, which, I'll wager is not getting any warmer."

"I suppose I must get up," Jeannie said ruefully. "Is anyone else about yet?"

"Oh, Lord, Mrs. McVinnie! Larinda won't wake up until afternoon, more like, and Lady Smeath never rises before noon."

"The captain?"

The maid opened her eyes wider in wonderment. "I don't think he ever sleeps. At least, not like a Christian, although the beadle warned me once that sailors are only a step removed from Satan's imps."

"My dear," Jeannie admonished lightly.

"And doesn't Pringle tell me that the captain gets up every four hours and looks around, almost like he was still on his ship."

"Old habits die hard," Jeannie reminded. She handed her cup to the maid. "But do tell me your name, and have I you to thank for the warming pan last night?"

The maid bobbed another curtsy. "Mary Bow, ma'am, and yes, I know what it feels like to come into a house and stay cold all evening, indeed I do."

"Mary Bow," Jeannie repeated. "Bow. What a singular name."

" 'Tis me own alone," Mary said. "The beadle at the workhouse said since I was found on the steps of St. Mary le Bow, that would be my name. And who's to say it's not a better name than what my real name would be? Who's to say?"

"Who, indeed? Mary, I am pleased to make your acquaintance. Now, if you and Clare will leave me, I'll try out that hot water."

Mary bobbed up and down again and held out her hand to Clare, who crawled to the end of the bed and let herself down. "You should be dressed too," Mary said to the little girl.

"Although I don't wonder that your nursemaid has other things on her mind." Mary leaned closer to the bed. "I think she sneaks out at night."

Jeannie dangled her legs over the edge of the bed. "And I would be the last to doubt you."

Mary took Clare by the hand. She looked at Mrs. McVinnie as if she wanted to say something.

"Speak away, Mary," Jeannie said.

The maid blushed. "It's a foolish thing. I've never heard anyone talk like you do. Does everyone in Scotland sound like you?"

Jeannie laughed. "No. Some sound worse. Oh, dear, I fear I will be a nine day's wonder in London." She looked down at her legs. "How fortunate for my consequence that I will not be here that long."

Mary frowned. "As to that, mum, didn't Pringle say something this morning belowstairs about replacing this bedspread and draperies with a more cheerful color?"

"You must be mistaken," Jeannie said firmly. "Unless you are expecting other company."

Mary looked doubtful. "People don't generally visit this house, Mrs. McVinnie. And didn't Pringle say something about 'orders'?"

"It is a mystery to me."

Jeannie stood up, shook down her nightgown, and the maid closed the door quietly.

Her travel dress was still sadly wrinkled. Jeannie eyed it with disfavor and put on a simple wool morning dress instead, telling herself that she could probably cajole the housekeeper into taking it belowstairs for a quick sponging and a press. There would be ample time for such a simple matter. She turned back to the mirror and debated whether to wear her knit lace collar or a locket to break up the severity of her navy-blue dress. She held one in each hand and decided on the collar.

Jeannie locked it in place quickly and took another look in the mirror. "Mrs. McVinnie," she told herself, "you have simply got to make some new dresses. You look a positive dowd."

There was no remedy for it but to sigh and turn away and settle her best lace cap on her hair. For no accountable reason, she was tired of mourning colors. With vast qualms she had parted from her black weeds only last month, but even the blues and gray seemed almost too much to bear now.

It must be because spring is coming, she reasoned. The thought did not cheer her. It meant another year of half-mourning, another season of drab clothes.

She went to the window again and leaned her forehead against it. I do not mean to be disloyal, Tom, she thought, but, oh, to wear something bright again!

When Mary returned to her room, Jeannie handed over her traveling dress and asked directions to the breakfast parlor.

She located it by the wonderful smell of coffee. Jeannie was not a coffee drinker, but the fragrance of it reminded her of Tom and Galen, who would have sat for hours in the kitchen over a cup or two if she had not stirred them into motion.

Captain Summers stood at the window, his back to her, sipping his morning cup and reading the paper. He turned around when she entered; he folded the paper under his arm and inclined his head in her direction.

"I am sure you did not sleep well, what with one thing or another." He shrugged. "I am amazed that I still listen at all odd hours of the night for the water lapping, and do you know that rigging sings when the wind is right?"

She allowed him to seat her at the table. "Then Kirkcudbright is rather more quiet than your ship, Captain, if one discounts a few sheep and neighbors who will enter into heated discussions upon the price of mutton under one's window."

He only smiled.

"And we do become used to what suits us," she added, looking at the table.

He followed her glance and then tugged on the bellpull. "I can tell that you are mystified by my ship's biscuit. Let me ring for something else."

She picked up a biscuit. "It is so hard, sir. I wonder you have a tooth in your head." She put down the biscuit and felt a fiery blush cover her face. "Oh, that was rude of me."

He inclined his head again. "I have all my teeth, Mrs. McVinnie. How else could I take great nips out of midshipmen?"

The entrance of Wapping spared her from further comment. The butler came bearing tea and toast. The captain sat down at the table and reached for another biscuit.

"Wapping, these are truly excellent," he said, indicating the biscuit in his hand. "Only think how much better they will be in six months' time when I have to bang them on the table to scare out the weevils."

Jeannie choked over her tea.

Wapping turned quite noticeably green under his London pallor, but to his credit, he did not flinch. After a moment of silent reflection and considerable exercise of restraint, he addressed the captain.

"Very good, sir. Now, is there anything else?"

"Nothing. Send Pringle to me in ten minutes."

"Very good, sir."

Captain Summers dipped his biscuit in his coffee. "I do so love to torment Wapping," he said, almost to himself. "Notice how well he holds up? A butler is the triumph of science over nature. I should like one for my own."

Jeannie laughed in spite of herself.

Captain Summers finished his biscuit and thoughtfully brushed the crumbs from his coat. He poured himself another cup of coffee, and as he did so, Jeannie took the moment to observe him.

He was as neat as wax, sitting there impeccable in his morning coat. He was not in uniform, but no one, not even the downiest slow-top, could ever have mistaken Captain Summers for other than a military man. There was an air of pride about him, a superiority that reminded Jeannie forcefully of Tom, even as she told herself that they looked nothing alike. She would have continued her scrutiny and her idle speculation on what was the certain something that gave a man such an air of command, but he was looking at her now with his own intensity.

Jeannie waited for him to speak, but he only watched her. She did not think to be upset by his acute observation. She had only just that moment given up watching him, so could scarcely cry foul. There was nothing insolent in his manner. He regarded her carefully, as he would have an opponent.

Finally Summers leaned back slightly. He sipped his coffee and eyed her over the rim of the cup. "Pringle tells me your husband was with the Fifteenth Dumfries Rifles."

"He was, and so was my father-in-law."

"I remember the lads. Didn't the Rifles make up the rear-guard in the retreat to La Corūna?"

"They did. That was where my husband sustained his fatal injuries."

Captain Summers nodded. There was nothing in his face of sympathy; there was something better. Jeannie saw an understanding of the harshness of war, a matter-of-factness that was bracing but infinitely superior to sensibility, no matter how well-meaning.

"We did everything we could from the sea," he said simply. "I threw so much lead at the Spaniards behind them that I am surprised the land did not sink." He looked down at his hands. "Swear to God my ears rang for days."

There was a brief pause while Captain Summers took another sip of his coffee and then set the cup down. "General Moore commended the Dumfries before he died," he said. "We came in as close as we dared, and took off as many soldiers as we could. I remember the Dumfries pipers on the headland, when every other man was running and dodging. God, I shall never forget the sound."

"It is a regiment well-known for bravery," she whispered, and the thought stung her. She turned away so he would not see the desolation in her eyes.

He pushed himself away from the table and stalked to the window, as if the memory was too big for the breakfast parlor.

Jeannie drank her tea in silence, curiously warmed by his words. Galen McVinnie had never told her anything of the beach at La Coruña. Probably he remembered nothing of it himself. The whole terror came into focus for the first time as she sat at a breakfast table in Mayfair, and she discovered that she could look at it with equanimity. Thank you, Captain Summers, she thought suddenly.

He turned back to her. "And now, Mrs. McVinnie, can I persuade you to change your mind and remain here in our house?"

Jeannie blinked and gulped the tea in her mouth.

"You cannot be serious, not after the deception I practiced."

"Are you not Jeannie McVinnie?" he asked in vast surprise.

"Oh, you know what I mean," she said with asperity. "I am the wrong Jeannie McVinnie, as you *well* know, and I will not do."

"Granted you are much too young, scarcely more than a baby."

"Sir, I am twenty-four," she declared, stung to admission by his observation.

"Good God, Mrs. McVinnie, on the day you were born I was probably climbing a rigging in a high wind."

She stared at him and opened and closed her mouth.

The captain knelt by her chair. "Silly girl, I ran away to sea when I was twelve. And, by God, you do have brown eyes." He stood up and began to pace the room, his hands behind his back.

Jeannie watched him, fascinated, forgetting to be offended by his curious manners.

"We have already granted that you are too young, and you know nothing of London, but by God, if you don't have that McVinnie spirit!" He rubbed his hands together with an expression close to glee on his face.

"The answer is still no," Jeannie said as she rose from the chair. "And now I should see if Mary has returned with my traveling dress. I must be off, Captain Summers. It remains only for me to apologize again for my foolishness and return to Scotland."

"But I need you here," the captain insisted. "And I have already said that you will do."

Jeannie looked him straight in the eye. "Captain, I was looking all of you over last night myself. This is a most unhappy household and I refuse to be part of it."

"All the more reason you should stay, Mrs. McVinnie," Captain Summers said. The note of command was creeping into his voice.

The door to the breakfast parlor opened and the captain turned away in disgust, muttering something about "damned intrusions." Jeannie hoped that her face was not as red as she feared. She would have turned away, too, but it was Edward who stood before her, dressed neatly for the day and bearing a large, leather-bound red book with the title *A Young Gentleman's Guide to London* stamped on the cover in gilt letters.

"Edward, this is a surprise," Jeannie said. "I was just preparing to go upstairs."

Edward looked doubtfully at his uncle, who glared at him and then sat down at the table again.

"You and I need to have a talk," the captain said, his voice all business.

Edward paled noticeably and Jeannie found herself moving closer to him, standing slightly in front of him. She stared back at the captain and then turned her attention to the boy.

She could see in the daylight that he bore a slight resemblance to his uncle, although he was thin where Summers was not. His arms dangled out of the ends of his sleeves, and Jeannie knew that, although he was small now, he would be as tall as Captain Summers someday. There was a sweetness of expression about him that owed nothing to his relative, she decided. The sweetness ended before his eyes, which regarded her with disconcerting desperation.

"May I sit down?" he asked.

Captain Summers nodded and poured himself another cup of coffee.

Jeannie sat down next to him. Without a word, he opened the book and placed it before her on the table. The guide was open to the Grand Cascade. Jeannie leaned closer. Edward had written in the margin, "Truly a magnificent display. I shall remember it forever," and then initialed and dated it.

` "And I will, too, Mrs. McVinnie," he said quietly as she looked at him.

Captain Summers cleared his throat.

Jeannie pointedly turned her shoulder toward him and looked on as Edward riffled through the pages and spread out the section on the Tower of London.

"I would like most of all to go there," he said, "but Aunt says there are too many stairs to climb, and rude crowds, and the fog from the river." He frowned down at the book and then appealed to Jeannie. "But I could do it. I know I could! I didn't used to think so, but I feel different this morning." His tone was earnest. "Mrs. McVinnie, we could see it together."

"I think it is a capital notion," Captain Summers said, throwing in his mite. "You could tour the whole of London and drag along that silly widgeon of a niece of mine."

Edward looked at her hopefully.

Jeannie avoided his gaze and closed the book. "I'm sorry, Edward, but I must go, and soon, too!"

Without a word, he repossessed the guidebook and went to the door without a backward glance at her.

"Edward, I—"

The door flung open again and Captain Summers groaned and slapped his forehead. "There was a time when a man could have a cup of coffee in peace," he shouted. "I remember it distinctly."

Clare entered the room on a gallop, ran behind the open door, and flattened herself against the wall. When the captain shouted, she clapped her hands over her ears and burst into tears.

"Belay that," he roared in his best quarterdeck voice.

Before he could say anything more, the nursemaid threw herself into the room, bobbed a quick curtsy at the captain, and reached behind the door for Clare, who sobbed louder.

"Oh, no, please," Jeannie said.

The nursemaid ignored her and grabbed for Clare, who darted away and crawled under the breakfast table.

Jeannie leapt to her feet, eyes blazing, and stood in front of the table. "No," was all Jeannie said as she pulled herself up as tall as she could and raised her chin. Her voice was quiet, calm even, but the nursemaid backed away.

"I have my orders, ma'am," she said when she had recovered sufficiently.

"I am sure that your orders do not include frightening a child. Go now. I will take Clare upstairs when she has calmed down."

The nursemaid looked at the captain. Jeannie could not see him from where she stood, but the sudden draining of color from the nursemaid's face gave her every suspicion that Captain Summers was not suffering this fool gladly. She backed out of the room and vanished.

Jeannie knelt down and pulled back the tablecloth. "Come on, Clare."

The child crawled out from under the table. Jeannie picked her up and set her on her lap. She wiped her face with a napkin and then commanded her to blow her nose. Clare did as she said and then turned her face against Jeannie so she would not have to look at the captain, who still glowered.

Jeannie rested her chin on the top of Clare's head. "Sit down, Captain," she said in that same, still voice. "You're frightening her."

He sat down again. In another moment, the anger was gone from his face. "I do need you here, Mrs. McVinnie. You can see that."

"Then you are doomed to disappointment," Jeannie replied

quietly as she stroked Clare's hair. "We would never suit."

If he was disappointed, he did not show it. Summers watched her in silence for a moment more. "Very well," he said finally.

She held out her hand and he shook it. "As soon as I return home, I will reimburse you for your coach fare," she said.

"Not necessary," said the captain. "Merely the fortunes of war, ma'am."

Jeannie could afford to be generous. "Then I will donate the money to the widows' and orphans' fund, sir."

He rose to his feet and bowed. "As you wish, Mrs. McVinnie, but I stand behind my original estimation that a Jeannie McVinnie—any Jeannie McVinnie—is the only person who can bring a little order to this household." He rubbed his head. "Although I must admit that all we have succeeded with so far is turmoil and chaos."

Jeannie set Clare on her feet and took her by the hand. "Truly, sir, we could not have made this work. I would only get your back up. And I am not sure I could ever do your bidding, if I didn't happen to agree with your methods. And I do not. You cannot compel me, sir."

He made no comment, but only regarded her until she began to feel distinctly uncomfortable. Her agitation increased when she realized that he was deep in thought and scarcely minding her presence at all.

"Sir?" she ventured.

Her word recalled him to the present. He bowed again, and when he rose to look her in the eye again, she saw that he was smiling.

"Very well, Mrs. McVinnie. Wapping will engage a hackney to return you to the Bull and Hind. Your servant."

He left the room with the dignity of an admiral quitting the deck of his flagship, but as she followed him into the hall a few moments later, she heard someone taking the stairs two at a time and shouting for Pringle in a voice that demanded instant obedience. Jeannie shook her head and tightened her grip on Clare. Such a curious man. Such a strange household.

Her dress, brushed and pressed, was lying across her bed. Both bags were packed again. Clare looked from her to the bags and back again and went out of the room without a sound.

"Oh, dear," Jeannie said. She peered into the hall and

watched as Clare slowly walked to her own room, her feet dragging, her shoulders drooping. "Well, it would never have worked," Jeannie said to the mirror as she reached around to unbutton her dress. "And you know it, Jeannie McVinnie."

As she struggled with the buttons, she heard the sound of footsteps outside the door. "Oh, Edward," she sighed under her breath, "I cannot go with you to the Tower of London."

If it was Edward, he made no move to knock. Jeannie heard the sound of heels clicking together. Mystified, she tiptoed to the door and put her ear to it.

The shrill blast of a boatswain's pipe made her leap back in fright. She put her hands to her ears, but the piercing sound continued, enlarging upon the simple call with toots and flourishes. Jeannie opened the door and peered into the hall.

Pringle stood by her door, whistle in his mouth. She stared at him, her eyes wide, her lips parted in surprise. He was dressed in uniform, in the white canvas pants and blue coat of the Royal Navy.

Another door opened and Edward came into the hall.

Jeannie motioned to him and he soon stood beside her. "What is going on?" she whispered. "Why is he in uniform?"

Edward shook his head in disbelief. "If he does not stop soon, Larinda and my aunt will be awake." He took another step until he was right next to Jeannie. "I would never dare!"

Another blast of the whistle sent Clare tumbling out of her room and scrambling to Jeannie's side, Pringle clicked his heels together, turned smartly, and marched down the hall until he was directly opposite Lady Smeath's closed door.

Edward sucked in his breath. "That is as much as my life is worth." He tugged on Jeannie's sleeve. "Can he have taken leave of his senses?"

"I think not, Edward," she replied.

Pringle clicked his heels together again, raised the whistle to his lips again, and began to blow.

Jeannie recognized the longs and shorts he had blasted outside her door. She nudged Edward. "What is he playing?"

The boy concentrated on the tune, his brows together, his tongue between his teeth. "I believe it is . . . it couldn't be," he ventured, "but I think it is 'To quarters.' "

"Whatever is that, Edward? Do you know?"

"It is what they blow when the captain wishes to assemble

all hands on deck in their assigned posts. Before battle, you know.'' He looked up at Jeannie and she heard the edge of pride in his voice. ''You see, Pringle has been teaching me. I am sure that is it. Oh, look out now,'' he whispered suddenly.

Lady Smeath hurled herself from her room, her face as white as the robe she had cast about her shoulders. Her nightcap was twisted around her face until it looked like a horse's feedbag.

Jeannie picked up Clare and pressed her face into the child's curls. ''Dear me,'' she said weakly as Edward choked and sputtererd and his aunt glared at him.

Pringle marched a few paces beyond Lady Smeath's door and took another deep breath. The ear-splitting urgency of ''To quarters'' trilled outside Larinda's door, which opened slowly. Larinda blinked several times, drew herself up, and stamped her foot.

Eyes straight ahead, Pringle ignored her. With another flourish and much clicking of heels and marching worthy of the guards in front of the Admiralty House, he took himself to the head of the stairs. He bowed. ''My ladies, Edward, Mrs. McVinnie,'' he said, ''you are wanted belowdecks.''

Everyone stared at him.

''In the blue saloon.''

No one moved.

By now Aunt Agatha had managed to swing her nightcap up until it covered one ear. ''Have you taken total and complete leave of your senses?''

Pringle regarded her impassively. ''I am following my orders, my lady,'' he said, and raised the whistle to his mouth again.

''No! No,'' insisted Lady Smeath. ''I will go. Come, Larinda, give me your arm or I shall faint.'' She stormed past Pringle, who stood at rigid attention, pipe to his mouth. ''And you will wish you had never been born,'' she hissed over her shoulder. ''And neither will that wretched brother of mine.''

Pringle made no comment, but lowered his pipe, eyes forward. When the two women had descended the stairs, he looked at Edward and Jeannie, who stood close together, shoulders touching.

''I think we had better do as he says,'' Edward suggested.

Still carrying Clare, Jeannie followed Edward down the stairs and into the blue saloon. Her heart pounded as she contemplated a bolt up the stairs again. She could have her bags in hand and be out the door before anyone had time to react. She would sacrifice the traveling dress that still lay spread across the bed. She had never liked it above half, anyway. She could snatch up her cloak on the way out and hail a hackney herself.

But Pringle stood by the doorway at the front of the stairs now. She abandoned her escape plans and meekly followed Edward into the saloon, noting as she did so that all the servants were gathering in the hallway, some at least pretending to have some business there and others just gaping, eyes wide, mouths open.

Lady Smeath smoldered on the sofa, Larinda beside her, speechless with rage. Edward perched on the edge of an armchair, looking absurdly small. Jeannie sat down, Clare on her lap.

Lady Smeath noticed her presence for the first time. "You!" she rose to her feet, swaying slightly and gripping her niece's shoulder. "I had thought you long gone. Can you imagine the trouble you have caused me with the most sought-after modiste in London? If I am the laughingstock of London—and mark my words, Madame Coutant will talk—I have only to lay it at your door."

Jeannie regarded her in silence a moment until the woman sat down again. "Madam, you cannot wish me gone from this house any more than I wish myself elsewhere."

Lady Smeath opened and closed her mouth several times, and then subsided into a cold fury that was almost palpable. The silence was stupendous. Pringle continued to stand at rigid attention. In another moment he raised the pipe to his lips again.

It was a different tune this time. Jeannie directed an inquiring look at Edward, who only shrugged. When Pringle finished, he snapped a salute and held it, eyes ahead.

Captain Summers stood in the doorway, dressed in the uniform Jeannie remembered from last night, complete with medals, his star, and red ribbon. His coat was without a wrinkle anywhere, his white pants and stockings were of a whiteness that ordinary mortals could only dream of. The gleam of the gold buckles on his shoes was matched and amplified by the gold and lace of his entire uniform. From the epaulettes that weighted his shoulders to the sword at his side. Captain Sir William Summers was a marvel to behold.

His cocked hat sat upon his head and he seemed to fill the doorway. Jeannie wrinkled her nose and sniffed at the odor of tar about him. Then she noticed the tarred pouch he had tucked under one arm.

He entered the room and returned Pringle's salute.

"Very well, Pringle, my compliments," he said, and his voice held not a twitch of amiability. "You may stand down."

Pringle placed his hands behind his back.

Captain Summers walked into the middle of the room and placed the black bag on the table.

His sister rose in fury. "Get that disgusting thing off my table," she shrieked.

He said nothing, but merely stared her down, his green eyes harder than emeralds, his face immobile.

Larinda stirred uneasily and tugged at her aunt's sleeve.

"Agatha, these are the orders that you used so cleverly to command my appearance here," he said.

"And what of it?" she snapped. "Get that nasty bag off my table."

"Sit down, Agatha," he commanded.

She sat.

Captain Summers removed his gloves and reached into the bag and pulled out a piece of paper, closely written. Pellets of shot tumbled out of the pouch and dropped onto the floor.

Jeannie turned to Edward. "What is that for?" she whispered.

Captain Summers turned toward her and bowed. "In the event of capture, Mrs. McVinnie, this pouch can be tossed into the sea." He swung around to look at his sister again. "Although I cannot imagine the effect these orders would have had upon the frogs." He swept his hat off and placed it on the table.

He looked about him with an air of feigned surprise. "And are you all assembled?" he asked. "God help us."

"William, I warn you," said his sister in an awful voice.

"I don't recommend that," he returned in a voice equally frosty, for all that it was flat, toneless, and held no hint of life behind it.

As Jeannie observed him, she wondered for a moment what it would feel like to be dressed down on a heaving quarterdeck by this man. The thought sent prickles of fear traipsing down her spine.

They all watched him with varying expressions of dread, animosity, and curiosity.

Captain Summers looked down at the paper in his hand. He addressed his remarks to Agatha Smeath, who sat on the edge of the sofa, her face a wooden mask, save for the steady tic in her cheek.

"These are the orders that brought me to this duty," he said. "Your orders, I might add. We will overlook for now that they have likely made me the laughingstock of the entire channel fleet, I am sure. In the press of events pursuant to my arrival last week in this household, I find myself guilty of improper naval conduct. I did not read myself in. I will repair that oversight now."

"Really, William, I hardly think that this Cheltenham re-enactment is necessary," his sister snapped.

He bowed to her. "Since you are the one who has chosen this route of summoning me home with proper navy orders, issued by your dear brother-in-law, whom I must obey, I believe I can safely say that I am only following your wishes in this matter. Do enlighten me if I am wrong, Agatha dear."

She said nothing, but the tic in her cheek grew more pronounced.

"Ah, very well, then." Captain Summers turned smartly to Pringle. "Are all hands assembled?"

"Aye, aye, sir," barked Pringle, betraying not with the slightest expression that this read-in was different than any other.

"Excellent. We will proceed." Summers looked at Lady Taneystone. "You are Agatha Smeath, relict of the late Lord Cloris Smeath and sister of the late George Foster Summers, fourth Marquess Taneystone? And you are companion to Lady Larinda Summers and Edward, fifth Marquess Taneystone?"

"For God's sake, William, you know I am!"

"Madam, I remind you that I am following the procedure you have ordained, for whatever reason."

Summers stood next to Edward, who instinctively scooted closer to Jeannie. The movement did not go unnoticed, but he made no remark upon it.

"You sir, by your leave. You are Edward William Summers, fifth Marquess Taneystone?"

"Yes," Edward said. He caught Summers' eye, threw back his thin shoulders, and sat up straighter. "I mean, aye, aye, sir!"

Summers allowed a brief smile to flicker across his face.

How hard his eyes are, Jeannie thought. I wonder that he gets much pleasure out of life.

"Very good, sir."

Summers opened up the paper in his hands and then glanced at his captive audience again. "My name is Captain Sir William Summers, Knight of the Grand Cross of Bath. I am Summers of His Majesty's *Venture,* third-rate, seventy-four, of the Channel Fleet. I have orders from Admiral the Right Honorable Earl Jarvington, Lord Charles Smeath, Lord of the Admiralty, Knight of Bath. Oh, thank you, Clare."

Summers bent down to receive the shot pellets that Clare had collected from underneath the chair and gathered in her dress. He put them in the pouch, patted her head, and pointed her back to Jeannie.

"The orders are, to wit: 'You are hereby requested and required to repair immediately to Taneystone House of Three Wendover Square, Mayfair, and take command *pro tempore* of said house for the duration of the come-out of Larinda Summers, only daughter and heiress of the late Marquess Taneystone." He looked up from the paper. "I have now officially read myself in and have assumed total command of this household. You are all witnesses."

Pringle stepped forward into the ensuing silence, clicked his heels together smartly, and saluted again. "Welcome aboard, Captain."

Summers acknowledged the salute. He turned to Edward, a slight smile on his face. "You there, what say you? You are bouncing about on that chair and wrinkling Mrs. McVinnie's dress."

"As to that, I am sorry, Mrs. McVinnie. But, Captain, may I still call you Uncle Summers?"

Summers bowed. "As you wish, my boy."

Jeannie cleared her throat. "And now, sir, may I take my leave? If I can locate a jarvey with some skill in traffic, I might make the next mail coach heading up the Great North Road." She rose to go, setting Clare in the chair.

"Mrs. McVinnie, please be seated."

He said it quietly enough, but there was a bite to Captain Summers' words that made Jeannie McVinnie look up quickly, a slight frown on her face. Summers' eyes stared at her like emeralds with the fire in them banked. She sat, scarcely daring to breathe.

"I have not entirely finished the reading of my orders, Mrs. McVinnie. Lord Smeath saw fit to add a rider. I suspect he was in his cups and sought to provide a laugh to his companions. But it is an order, and he has signed it."

"Yes, sir," she whispered, her eyes on his.

" 'You will take upon yourself, by the authority of these orders, the command of all officers, seamen, and royal marines. By virtue of the powers entrusted in me by the lords commissioners of the Admiralty, you are to proceed with all diligence in the execution of these orders.' Here is the part that might interest you, Jeannie McVinnie," he interjected. " 'You are reminded that in these times of war and desperate emergency you have the power and privilege of impressment. You may make use of these powers in any fashion you see fit, as far as naval discipline and the Articles of War allow.' "

He frowned down at the orders for several long moments and then slowly folded them, replacing them in the pouch. When he finally allowed himself to look Jeannie in the eye, she was not sure what emotion stared back at her. It was an expression she had never seen on a man's face before, a disturbing combination of resignation, bare pleading, and iron will that mystified her, even as she began to feel the blood drain from her face. Her hands went cold.

"No," she said, her voice soft.

If he heard her, the word had no meaning to him. Summers walked slowly and deliberately around the table until he stood directly in front of her. He gave no orders, but Jeannie found herself rising to her feet as if there were strings attached to her shoulders.

"Mrs. Jeannie McVinnie, you are hereby impressed into the service of Captain William Summers, acting under the powers and privileges granted by his commission in the Royal Navy of His Majesty King George."

5

BUT, sir, you cannot—"

"I believe I can," Summers interrupted. "Lord Smeath appears to have granted me these powers and privileges in relation to this house, or at least, that is my interpretation of these orders. Would you care to dispute them with the Admiralty? I would not."

"But . . ." Jeannie looked about her helplessly. No one met her eyes.

The captain continued inexorably. "The period of impressment is two years."

"Two years," she gasped. "You cannot be serious." Jeannie sat down with a thump.

"Two years," he went on, scarcely noticing her outburst. "By choosing service, at least according to the Articles of War, my dear, you can avoid the gallows, transportation, or jail." He smiled then. "And never fear Australia. I hear the climate is salubrious in the southern reaches."

Pringle choked and began to cough.

"And I will not hold you to two years, Mrs. Jeannie McVinnie," continued the captain, his serenity undisturbed. "A month or two of Larinda's come-out will suffice."

Jeannie leapt to her feet again, her prized Scottish phlegm knocked out of the water. "You are determined that I will fill in for Jeannie McVinnie. Sir, I will not be bullied."

Captain Summers reached out and took her by the chin. "I don't want to remind you that you got yourself into this bumble broth."

She shook his hand off. "Yes, I did," she snapped. "But that was before—"

He grabbed her again. "Look at me, Jeannie," he ordered.

"That was before you looked us over and found us wanting! Well, it's too late."

She opened her mouth to speak and closed it again. There was too much truth in what he said. When she said nothing, the captain released her, whispering, "Jeannie McVinnie, I need you."

She turned away, and there was Clare and more shot pellets in her dress. The child smiled up at Jeannie and held them out to her.

Jeannie knelt beside her. "You are a tidy housekeeper. We will give these to Captain Summers. Perhaps he will choke on them."

To her intense appreciation, Pringle struggled within himself and then found something that commanded his attention at the outer reaches of the large room.

Summers was waiting for her answer. Jeannie touched Clare's curls and looked beyond her to Edward. He gazed back at her with such barely concealed excitement that she smiled in spite of herself. Dear boy, you would certainly look less pale if you were allowed out in the sun more often, she thought. I wonder that your aunt cannot see that.

She glanced at Larinda next and read only mutiny on her face. And you, my dear, want a firm hand, such as I am sure Jeannie McVinnie would have provided, from what Galen has told me of her. Perhaps what you really need is a friend.

The captain had begun to pace back and forth in front of the fireplace, walking slowly and carefully, as if, even on that level floor, he was trying to maintain his balance on a bucking deck. And you, sir, are a sad man, she thought. I don't know what I can do about that.

That she could still refuse, she had no doubt. He had no power to impress her, and she knew it. But Jeannie reminded herself that she had nowhere to go for the remainder of the spring. For only three months she could surely shepherd Larinda to parties, see to the organization of her wardrobe, and help out in whatever capacity Captain Summers dictated. And if none of the Summers was particularly appealing, well, she would learn to like them. She had discovered last year that life was not always to one's liking.

Jeannie took the shot from Clare and stuffed it in the pouch. Captain Summers stopped his pacing to watch her.

"Sir, I believe that I will submit to this impressment," she said in her clear voice. "I have not the constitution for jail, I have no burning desire to see Botany Bay, and one meets such wretched company hanging about the gallows."

He bowed to her. "My dear Mrs. McVinnie, you will not regret this."

"On the contrary, Captain, I am sure that I shall," she retorted. "But as you so clearly spelled out, I have made my bed and now must only lie upon it."

He bowed again, a smile in his eyes this time.

She put up her hand. "I have a condition of my own, sir, and I insist upon it."

"Insist?" he asked, raising his eyebrows.

"Insist," she replied firmly. "You will, from this time, cease taking the name of the Lord in vain. I cannot abide such trampling underfoot of diety, even if you are a sailor, and merciful heaven knows what they are!"

"Oh, and what are they, Mrs. McVinnie?" the captain asked without a whisper of good humor in his voice.

"Rogues and blackguards," she replied without hesitation. "And Thomas told me never, under any circumstances, to have anything to do with the men of the Royal Navy."

It was as though everyone in the room took a deep breath and held it. Jeannie looked about her in perfect equanimity, her hands clasped in front of her. She would have wished that Captain Summers would not stand so close, particularly as his face was so red and he appeared to be within a whisker of explosion. She looked him in the eye and did not waver.

"Of course, he was an army man, and reason tells me that there might be some prejudice between the two services," she said. "Possibly you are not as bad as all that. Prove it to me, Captain Summers."

She waited for the explosion that never came. As she watched him, the captain set his lips tight together, breathed deeply a few times, and then sighed.

"Very well, madam, as you wish. I shall refrain from calling upon God in moments of crisis."

"I never said . . ." she began. "Oh, you are aggravating. A prayer is different."

"I never found that prayer was efficacious while waiting to receive a broadside, madam. Have patience with me." He rubbed his hands together and turned to Lady Agatha. "And now, my dear sister—"

Larinda jumped to her feet, clutching her robe about her. "I cannot see why I must submit to any of this," she exclaimed as her voice began to climb to an unpleasant pitch. "I refuse to be tagged about by a Scottish nanny with an accent so thick that no one can understand. And she is a perfect quiz."

Captain Summers leveled his quarterdeck stare at his niece. She grew white about the lips, but she held her tongue.

"That was unworthy of a Summers," he said after a long painful moment. "But by G—Godfrey, niece, you will dance to my tune or I will put you and your aunt on a post chaise home to Suffolk."

With a sob, Larinda whirled about and threw herself at her aunt's side. "Can he do that? Oh, I do not understand."

Lady Smeath sighed, but the look she shot the captain was anything but resigned. "I did not tell you, my dear, but he is joined with me in the custody of you and Edward."

"Oh, pray do not stop there, Agatha," the captain said as he handed the pouch to Pringle and made for the door. "Larinda, I also have the last word on any suitor you drag up the front steps and drop at my feet."

Larinda gasped and looked at her aunt, who only nodded. "I cannot imagine what George was thinking when he made that infamous will," Lady Agatha said.

Larinda burst into noisy tears. "Oh, do hush," said her aunt, pushing her away. "How can one think with that racket?"

"Quite right," agreed the captain, pulling on his gloves. "I am off to the Admiralty, where, I believe, your brother-in-law Lord Smeath is awaiting me. We have some issues to discuss. Yes, Edward, do quit bouncing about! What is it you wish to say?"

Edward sprang to his feet and put his hands behind his back. "Sir, I was wondering. Could I come?"

"And run the risk of a tumble in the water? I should say not, Edward," his aunt said.

"Oh, but—"

"I won't hear of it!"

"And neither will I, my young chub," said Captain Summers. "We would bore you to death. Besides that, I will then go to Bond Street and see if my tailor is still alive and on speaking

terms with me. Larinda need not have two quizzes on .
I would never for the world, ah, scotch her chances at a
He glanced sideways at Jeannie, who still stood with her h.. .s
on Clare's curls. "But I believe the Tower of London lies in
wait, eh, Mrs. McVinnie?"

"William, I protest! Think of the dirty crowds and the fog
and miasma from the river!"

"None of which will do him a particle of harm, Agatha,"
Captain Summers said. "The Tower it is, Mrs. McVinnie. You
are condemned to it. That is my first order to you."

Jeannie smiled. "You, sir, are going to be a great lot of
trouble to me, I can tell."

"More than you know," he murmured. "And speaking of
trouble, dry your eyes, Larinda. Tonight Mrs. McVinnie and
I will accompany you to Almack's."

"Over my corpse," she flung back.

The captain stood at the door. "That will make you a most
reluctant dancing partner, I fear. How fortunate we are that the
Season is young and Almack's will likely be thin of company.
Perhaps no one will notice any *rigor mortis*."

"Quite right," Jeannie agreed. "Larinda, do you know that
your face gets splotchy when you cry like that? I hope that it
will be gone by this evening."

Larinda ran to the mirror, turning her face this way and that.
She looked at her aunt in anguish. Lady Smeath threw up her
hands and left the room, muttering something about having "no
more say over my dear dead brother's children than a hali-
but."

"I would recommend cucumbers on your eyes," Jeannie said.
"Shall I send for some?"

Larinda pointedly turned her back to Jeannie, who regarded
her a moment more in silence and then held out her hand for
Edward. "Come, lad, and let us see if Sir Walter Raleigh truly
does haunt the walk," Jeannie asked.

"And shall we see the executioner's ax?"

"I think we already have, laddie," she replied after one more
glance at Larinda's back. "Let us be off before it falls again."

They left the room together, Clare trotting along behind.

"Well, my dears, it looks as though we must submit to the
will of our captain," Jeannie said. "Edward, perhaps if you
would find your guidebook . . ."

Edward dashed ahead and soon returned with it, thumbing through it as he ran toward her.

Jeannie laughed and tried to ward him off. "Lad, you must give me time to change my dress," she protested. And time to collect my thoughts and wonder for the hundredth time since breakfast what I am doing here. Especially that.

Mary Bow was hanging up the last of her dresses when Jeannie entered the bedroom. "I heard from Larinda's abigail that you are going to Almack's tonight," Mary said, as she brushed at Jeannie's one gray silk gown. "This will do, I think," she said doubtfully.

Jeannie touched the dress and held it out. "Larinda is right. I will look a perfect quiz," she said. "Oh, Mary, I should be going to a modiste's instead of the Tower!"

Mary's eyes opened wide. "Oh, mercy me, never say that you chose jail over impressment. He is a wicked, wicked man."

Jeannie chuckled. "Yes, and Captain Summers will likely have my head in a basket on Tower Green. Mary, don't let your mind run away with you. I mean to have a pleasant stay here in London." She took another look at the gray dress; it had seemed so up-to-the-minute in Kirkcudbright. "Oh, dear. Perhaps a stay in the Tower would be preferable to an evening at Almack's, especially in the company of this dress I know so well."

"Well, it is a little simple," Mary said doubtfully.

Edward banged on the door. Jeannie released the dress into Mary's care again. "Mary, see if you can turn it into something magic by ten of the clock tonight."

She left Mary shaking her head and brushing furiously.

After considerable debate over the merits of traveling to the Tower by water or over land, Jeannie tossed a coin and hailed a hackney. With his guidebook spread across his knees, Edward directed her attention to the marvels of London and the City, pointing out buildings that she had heard of all her life and never seen until this time, in the company of a fourteen-year-old boy who knew scarcely more than she. She closed her ears to the screams of anguish coming from the jehu on the box, who cursed every cart that impeded his progress. I will enjoy this afternoon, she thought as she clung to the dusty strap in the hack and smiled at Edward, who sat with his nose pressed to the window.

They waited for some time in front of St. Paul's Cathedral as porters and carters hauled away the results of a collision between an egg cart and a fish wagon. All about them, tradesmen shouted and urchins screamed back.

Jeannie's head began to ache. It was throbbing with a life of its own by the time they paid off the driver and stood before the Tower of London. She settled her cloak about her and sniffed the air. It was a dizzying combination of fragrance from the chocolate-colored Thames that flowed past, and unrecognizable odors from Billinsgate Market, where the fishmongers hawked their wares and spit after anyone who would not buy.

As Edward took her hand and led her into the Tower, Jeannie realized the source of her discomfort. This was the first time in her life that she had ever gone anywhere unescorted. Her daily walks about Kirkcudbright, where she knew everyone, did not count. This was different. I am on my own, she thought suddenly, and Captain Summers trusts me enough to give Edward into my care.

"Mrs. McVinnie! This is no time to hang back. Think of all we have to see." Edward tugged at her hand.

Jeannie brought herself back to the moment and gave his hand a squeeze. "Lead on, laddie."

Hand in hand, they wandered through the Tower, following a group of walkers in the wake of a yeoman warder, or striking off on their own when fancy dictated. Hand in hand, they shuddered over the fate of the young princes, smothered in their bedclothes. They sighed to see "Jane" scratched on the wall of Beauchamp Tower, where Lady Jane had pined for her young husband and watched him march to his fate on Tower Green.

And there was the Bell Tower, where Princess Elizabeth was sent by her sister Mary, and then Bloody Tower, the home of Walter Raleigh for twelve long years.

And I am begrudging a couple of months at 3 Wendover Square, Jeannie thought was she listened to the yeoman warder speak of Sir Walter and his devotion to a jealous queen. She could only sigh and hurry along as Edward dragged her to another tower, and another, reading aloud from his guidebook to the amusement of fellow tourists.

The Tower was shrouded in the shadows of late afternoon when she stopped and held up her hands. "Surely there cannot be one more tower. I defy you to produce one more.''

Edward closed the book. "I think we have seen them all, Mrs. McVinnie, but look here, I have saved the best for the last."

Jeannie sniffed and was reminded forcefully of the worst-tended crofter's yard. "Edward, what is this place?"

"It is the menagerie, Mrs. McVinnie." He opened his guide-book again. "Look here, it says that King Henry the Third in 1240 decreed the creation of a menagerie."

"That explains it," she said. "I do not think anyone has mucked out the straw in all these years."

He regarded her tolerantly with the look that the young reserve for the infirm and feeble. "Can you imagine a greater treat?"

I can imagine a cup of tea and a cushion to prop my feet upon, she thought as she followed Edward into the only corner of the Tower they had not already explored from cellar to ceiling.

A gentleman lounged beside the open door that led into the menageries. He was dressed in a coat of Bath superfine and wore pantaloons of an exquisite biscuit hue. Jeannie tried not to stare, but she could not help noticing that his neckcloth was arranged into an ornate style that would have taken Tom the better part of a day to achieve. His hair was cut, brushed, and pomaded into a style that was as careless as it was calculating. The strong perfume about his person contrasted oddly with his odoriferous surroundings.

As they watched, he flicked upon an enamel snuffbox, put a pinch on the back of his hand with one practiced motion, and inhaled.

"Do you think he is a dandy?" Edward whispered. "I have heard of them."

Jeannie tore her eyes from the elegance before her. "I am sure you must be right. I wouldn't have thought this to be the haunt of men of fashion and distinction."

"And see how he looks about," Edward whispered back. "Do you think he is a spy, Mrs. McVinnie?" He clapped his hands. "That would be almost too much to hope for!"

They entered the menagerie. Jeannie covered her nose with her handkerchief. "Goodness, Edward," she gasped as her eyes watered from the fumes rising off the molding straw underfoot. "We could have foregone this treat."

Edward was tugging her forward when suddenly, immediately, her attention was captured.

Another young man, dressed similarly to the one who stood sentry by the door, was clambering over the rail that led into the elephant pit. As Jeannie and Edward stared, eyes wide, he dropped down and stood looking up at the elephant, which was looking back at him. They eyed each other in perfect accord, until one of the other sprigs of fashion at the rail leaned forward and carefully lowered a bucket of paint into the pit.

With a smile and a bow, the man in the pit caught the paintbrush that someone else tossed him, and dipped the brush in the paint. Humming to himself, he painted the elephant's ears as high up as he could reach.

"What on earth . . ." Jeannie began. She stared as the young man motioned for another bucket and painted the other ear, all the while humming to himself. Every now and then he would step back, brush in hand, and contemplate the artistry of his effort. The animal, chained to a stout post, swayed back and forth.

The light was fading fast. Edward leaned over the railing to get a better view, and before Jeannie could even open her mouth to tell him to back away, he overbalanced himself and dropped into the pit below.

"Edward," she shrieked, covering her eyes with her hands.

There was silence in the pit. The painter stopped humming. Jeannie forced herself to peer over the edge of the pit.

Edward lay below her on a pile of rotting hay. As she watched, her hands to her mouth, he put his hands behind his head and grinned up at her.

The man in the pit set down his brush. Without a word, he picked up Edward and heaved him onto the elephant's back.

Jeannie gasped and clutched the handrail. The man below smiled up at her as Edward clung to the reeking folds of the elephant's skin and found his seat.

"It seemed such a pity to waste a perfectly good elephant," he said matter-of-factly, as if he were discussing the virtue of one boot-blacking over another. "Wouldn't you agree, madam?"

Jeannie found her voice and pounded on the railing. "I would not, you foolish piker! Edward, get off that beast at once!"

The man laughed and Jeannie felt the tears gather in her eyes. She brushed them away angrily, as she heard another voice behind her.

"Allow me, madam. Really, Sir Peter."

A tall man also dressed in superfine walked toward her. His progess was almost stately, even in that noisome zoo. She noticed that, as he came toward her, the others parted to allow him passage, almost as though he were royalty. He flicked out his handkerchief and wiped it carefully over the rail before he placed his kid-gloved hand on it.

"One can never be too careful." He motioned toward Edward, whose whole attention was devoted to maintaining his balance on the elephant. "Sir Peter Winthrop would wager that he could paint an elephant's ear blue. And who is to dispute him? They will have their fun, you know."

"I never heard a more totty-headed particle of reasoning," Jeannie snapped, not taking her eyes from Edward. "Surely you could find something useful with which to occupy your time."

The man leaned over the railing. "Hold out your arms, that's a lad."

Sir Peter in the pit prodded the elephant closer to the rail as Edward struggled to his feet, wavered precariously, and held up his arms. With a quick motion the man pulled Edward up and out of the pit. He took his handkerchief again and dusted off his exquisite coat.

"The trouble of it is, madam, we can find nothing more useful."

"Dowdy women and dingy boys are such a bore," Sir Peter said. He motioned to one of the others. "There's a good fellow, a little more blue paint."

Quicker than quick, Jeannie picked up the bucket and dumped it over the railing. The sounds of anguish that rose from the pit startled the elephant, which did as all startled animals do, to the groans and laughter of the dandies far out of reach.

The elegant gentleman peered over the edge. "It appears that you are a tifle indisposed, Sir Peter," he said serenely.

The oaths from the pit made Jeannie gasp. She grabbed Edward and started to the door. "I am all right, Mrs. McVinnie," Edward protested as she tightened her grip on him.

She could not have explained to Edward why she held him so tight. Despite her shame at such an impulsive gesture, she was in the grip of anger so startling that she could scarcely breathe. She could only think of Thomas McVinnie, lying in his own blood on the beach at La Coruña, dying so fops could carry out stupid pranks in London. The thought was illogical and she knew it even as she struggled against the pain.

The man who had rescued Edward studied her face. "We did not mean anything by it, madam," he said. "It was a harmless wager, and nothing more." His lips twitched. "I will advise Sir Peter to stay out of menageries in future." She could not bring herself to say anything. The man came closer. "We have caused you some pain, I fear. Do forgive us," he said, and his eyes were kind.

He came closer, and Jeannie knew he intended to say more, but the lounger in the doorway—he must have been the watch—sprang from carefully composed lethargy into action. "The yeoman warder comes," he hissed.

One of the company gave a hand up to Sir Peter in the pit. The blue paint had sloshed over the back of his coat and the elephant had completed the ignominy on his trousers. He clenched his fist and started toward Jeannie and Edward, but the elegant man stepped in front of them.

"Temper, temper, Sir Peter. Consider that you have earned, truly earned, that prime seat by the window at White's. None will dispute you." He looked about him at the others. "Lord Billings? Lord Blankenship? I thought not."

"It is not enough," Sir Peter said, his eyes blazing.

Jeannie backed up, clutching Edward to her.

The elegant man sighed, shook his head, and stepped closer to Sir Peter. He raised a quizzing glass to his eye and looked the lord up and down.

The others were silent during the scrutiny, and Jeannie could not understand their expressions. It is almost as if they are afraid of him, she thought as she dusted the chaff from Edward and wrinkled her nose at the strong smell of ill-used elephant.

After another moment's perusal, the man removed the quizzing glass from his eye and sighed. "Sir Peter, it is well that you are near and dear to me. I would probably not tolerate such rag manners in a mere acquaintance, say, like my fat friend."

The others looked at one another; some of them laughed.

Sir Peter's complexion resumed its normal color, but the look in his eyes had not changed. "You had better hope our paths never cross," he snarled at Jeannie, and brushed past them all to the side door.

The elegant man clapped his hands together. "And now, if we do not wish to inhabit dungeons better left untenanted here, I recommend that door over there that Sir Peter had shown us. We need merely follow the, ah, the trail of blue paint. Madam, if you please?"

Jeannie shook her head and set her lips in a tight line as Edward moved forward with the others.

"Come on, Mrs. McVinnie," he whispered. "What would Uncle Summers say if he had to redeem us from Bow Street? I think he might frown on another expedition."

It was a masterpiece of understatement that Jeannie could only say aye to. "Oh, very well," she grumbled, and followed him down the narrow dark steps that led, after much winding about and false starts and stops, to another little door close by the chapel of St. Peter ad Vincula.

The others had wasted no time in distancing themselves from the blue elephant. The tulip who had served as watchdog and Lord Billings already mingled with a crowd of visitors staring up at the window where Mary of Scotland had paced back and forth on the last night of her life. The other dandies were moving with stately grace, and some speed toward the gate. Sir Peter was a blue blur in the distance.

"And so we should go, too, Edward," Jeannie said. "Lady Taneystone will be so worried if we are late."

The man was still at her elbow. "Lady Taneystone?" he murmured. "It is possible that we share acquaintance."

"I doubt it, sir," Jeannie replied. "The people I know, and care to know, have rather more on their minds than painting elephants."

"A fair hit, madam," he said, sweeping his high-crowned beaver hat off his head and placing it over his heart. He gazed about him innocently. "I know what you mean. I don't believe I ever met anyone before who dumped blue paint on a dandy."

Jeannie had the good grace to blush. "Oh, I am sorry for that. It was a momentary lapse. I only wish it were not too late to apologize to Sir Peter." She returned to her familiar litany. "You must own that you could use your time more profitably."

He replaced his hat upon his head, settling it precisely so, "Madam, I protest! I spend my waking hours—or, at least, most of them—weeding out mushrooms and pricking balloons. I assure you it is a laudable occupation." He took her hand and kissed it before she could draw away. "And I say that we shall meet again. Perhaps under more favorable circumstances?"

"It is not a wish of mine," Jeannie stated frankly.

"Oh, we shall see. Your servant, ma'am."

Another bow, and he was gone. Jeannie watched him as he crossed Tower Green, his hat tilted to one side, his cane tucked under his arm, not a hair or thread out of place. Her speculation turned to surprise as she noticed several of the crowd about the chopping block pointing after him and murmuring among themselves.

Jeannie brushed off Edward's nankeen trousers and jacket, remonstrating all the while. "And now, we had better step lively," she said as she turned him around for another brushing. "I do not know when your aunt sits down to her dinner, but I do not think she wants a young man about who smells . . . My goodness, how can we describe it?"

"Rather like Noah's ark?" Edward offered helpfully.

Jeannie laughed. "I only hope that we can sneak you past Wapping and not have to describe it!"

The ride back to 3 Wendover Square was accomplished in spanking good time. Edward was silent for most of the trip, poring over his guidebook. He looked up only once to declare that his next stop must surely be Hampton Court Palace.

"Provided we are allowed another expedition," Jeannie said. She regarded him, her eyes thoughtful. "Edward," she began slowly, "do you think—"

He smiled back at her in the same way, and Jeannie nearly laughed. "No, Mrs. McVinnie, I do not think we should say anything about the elephant in the Tower." He brushed at the straw that still whisped about his suit. "Aunt Agatha would go distracted, wondering what dread disease I would contract, and Larinda would sniff and ignore me even more, if that is possible."

"And the captain?" Jeannie teased.

"He would give me that chilling stare of his." He shuddered. "I would rather be confined to my room than have him fix that

stare upon me." He enlarged upon his theme. "Besides all that,
Mrs. McVinnie, we might have to explain that gentleman you
deckled with blue paint."

"Don't remind me," Jeannie declared. "I hope we never see
him again. That piece of work could only come back to haunt
me."

Their wish for an anonymous return was not to be realized.
Captain Summers was standing on the steps, paying off his own
hackney when they drove up.

"Great guns," muttered Edward. "Now we are in the
basket."

"Then we must go forward, anyway," Jeannie said, hoping
that she sounded more confident than she felt. "My Tom always
used to say that the true heart of a man is decided under the
guns." She smiled at Edward and patted his knee. "We shall
see what we are made of, laddie."

That her knees were made of pudding, she had no doubt, but
it would only do to smile and go forward.

Chin up, eyes ahead, Edward walked at her side.

6

THE captain watched them as they came closer. He bowed.
"I trust you had an educational afternoon?"

"Yes, indeed, sir," Edward said, rather too eagerly.

But Captain Summers was sniffing now. A frown appeared
between his eyes. "Hold on a moment, Edward. What is that
foul odor about you?" He motioned Edward back to the walk
and circled him about. "I do not think you have been near a
slaver's ship, but that is what you smell like. And what is this?
Blue paint? Edward, has your afternoon's education extended
to a too-close study of our early British ancestors?" He fixed

Jeannie with his chilling stare. "I had thought you to be in excellent company."

"There was an elephant, Captain," she said calmly, even as her knees smote together. "In the Tower."

"Of course there was," the captain replied.

He took another leisurely tour around his nephew. "And I suppose you rode it? Painted it blue?"

Edward looked at Jeannie for help.

She raised her chin and threw back her shoulders. "Sir, we prefer not to discuss it."

"I shouldn't wonder." The captain ceased his circumnavigation of Edward. He looked from one to the other, and a ghost of a smile played about his lips. "But you would like my services in disposing of Wapping in the hallway, would you not?"

The captain read the relief in Edward's eyes and touched the boy on the shoulder. "Wait here," he ordered as he went up the steps. "And be ready to march lively." He went inside and shut the door.

"I didn't think he would be so helpful," Edward said.

"I'm sure I don't know what I thought," Jeannie echoed.

The door opened and the captain motioned them forward. "Be quick, Edward," he said. "I sent Wapping on a fool's errand and he will be back in a flea's leap. Lively now, lad, lively."

With one backward glance of gratitude, Edward scurried up the stairs.

Captain Summers removed his hat and tucked it under his arm. "You, Mrs. McVinnie, will not escape so easily."

She was saved from immediate comment by the return of Wapping to the hall. The butler had a vague air of puzzlement about him. "Sir William," he began, "I cannot imagine—"

What he could not imagine never came to light. Captain Summers interrupted, and his words were like knife edges. "I have already told you that I prefer to be called Captain Summers rather than Sir William," he barked. "The lowest-rated seaman can remember. Is it too much for you?"

Wapping stared in confusion. "No, Sir Wil—I mean, Captain Summers, and should I say, Aye, aye?"

"No, you should not," said the captain severely. He turned away from Wapping, and in a moment the butler sidled from the hall, whatever pretension he possessed now dangling around his ankles.

"Oh, that was neatly done," said Jeannie. "I know a strategical diversion when I hear one. He has completely forgotten to ask you about the fool's errand."

Captain Summers was the picture of innocence, except that his lips quivered. "Oh, G—goodness, how I enjoy butlers," he said. "Who would have imagined them to be such sport?"

"You are entirely unkind," Jeannie said, belying her words with a twinkle in her eyes. "And before you remonstrate with me, sir, let me tell you that we did encounter an elephant in the Tower and Edward found himself on its back."

"Jeannie McVinnie, are you telling me that under your totally composed demeanor there is a bit of a scamp?" he asked.

"I protest! Through no fault of ours—"

The captain held up his hand. "And do you know that when you protest, there is such fire in your eyes?" His own eyes were kind. "But I will not ask any more questions, although G— gracious me, I am sure I should."

"It was, for the most part, an improving afternoon," she assured him as they went up the stairs together. "We contemplated executioner's axes, jewelry too gaudy by half, and heard any number of fanciful stories about Englishmen that I think cannot be true."

"Madam, are there no Englishmen that measure up to your expectations?"

She thought about the dandies in the menagerie and shook her head. "So far, Captain Summers, I have been sadly disappointed."

He bowed and left her at the door to her room.

Jeannie went in her room and admitted to a moment of disappointment that Captain Summers had not risen to the bait at her last comment. She knew nothing of him, but after only one day in the house of Wendover Square, she knew that he possessed a ready wit. Could it be, she thought as she removed her cloak, could it be that I have been missing a quick tongue?

It was only a thought, and she resolved to consider it some other time when she did not have to dress so quickly for dinner.

Mary Bow came out of the dressing room, practically jumping up and down in her excitement.

"Mrs. McVinnie! You cannot imagine what arrived only twenty minutes ago."

"Unless it was the Second Coming, you are correct," Jeannie

said, and then she saw the dress on the bed. "Oh, my dear, are we dreaming?"

She had never seen a more beautiful dress. It was a high-waisted, long-sleeved dress of sarcenet of that peculiar blue and gray color of the sky over Solway Firth after a squall. Jeannie touched the dress, hardly daring to breathe. "Mary, it is so fine. Like cobwebs."

She took an overdue breath and held up the dress. It hung in soft folds to the tops of her shoes, each little pleat precise and neatly sewn in. Jeannie smoothed the material over her breast. "You don't think it will be too low?" she asked.

Mary shook her head. "For some as don't have anything to hold it up, Mrs. McV, it might be. But you'll do fine."

"Oh, and I even have a pearl necklace to wear with it. Oh, Mary, this dress is worth more than my entire wardrobe. Where on earth did it come from?"

Mary darted into the dressing room. "As to that, I cannot say, but see here, there is a note." She held it out to Jeannie. "I never was learned to read."

"Then I shall read it out loud," Jeannie said with a smile, "and the two of us can puzzle over it."

" 'My dear Jeannie McVinnie,' " she read, " 'we dare not give Larinda the satisfaction of telling her friends we are perfect dowds. This dress ought to eliminate any possibility of a set-down. My consequence could not tolerate it, and your kindness does not deserve Turkish treatment.' "

"Captain Summers," they said together.

Jeannie sat down on the bed and read the note again, turning over the little scrap as if to find out more.

"Mary, how on earth did he come by this dress?"

Mary shrugged.

Jeannie stood up and draped the dress carefully over the bed again. "It will kill me if I do not find out," she said, more to herself than to the maid.

After another touch of the dress and a deep breath, she went into the hall and to the captain's door. Pringle was just going in, bearing a handful of freshly ironed neckcloths. His expression held all the tension of a man facing real peril.

"Pringle, surely you are not headed for Boney's guillotine," she teased, eyeing the neckcloths.

He shuddered. "You see, lassie, I hired on years ago as a

gunner. We are neither of us trained to the task before us.''

She smiled. ''If he is not busy yet, please tell him I would like a word.''

''Very well, Mrs. McV.''

She had only a moment to wait. Captain Summers came into the hall, wearing a dressing gown of the most incredible tapestry design. She could only stare.

The captain raised his eyebrows. ''I am not the Grand Turk, but when in Constantinople, we have been known to frequent the same tailor. Yes? I hope you have not come to scold me for extravagance.''

''No, I am not so rag-mannered,'' she replied. ''I merely wish to say thank you from the bottom of my heart.'' She regarded him. ''And my Scots curiosity compels me to ask: how on earth did you procure a dress like that in such a short time? I would not have thought it possible.''

He shut the door and leaned against it. ''My dear, when a captain requests, even a modiste jumps.''

She rolled her eyes. ''Did you bully a poor seamstress? How wicked!''

The affronted look on his face was severely undermined by the little glint in his eyes that she was coming to appreciate. ''She seemed only too eager to do my bidding. I cannot fathom it either, but there it is.''

''And how did you get the size so accurately?'' Jeannie asked.

''It was a simple matter of telling her in plain round tones that you were only as tall as the first rim on a frigate's wheel, and no bigger around than my two hands. Pringle was there to interpret.'' He reached out suddenly and encircled her waist with his hands. ''Ha,'' he declared in triumph. ''So I *was* right!''

''Sir!''

He removed his hands quickly, but there was nothing penitent in his expression. ''And I wanted a shade somewhere between blue and gray that would look especially fine with red hair.'' He smiled down at her. ''Something that might tempt a lady a little tired of mourning weeds.''

She stepped back, wondering why it was that he always seemed to stand too close. ''You have succeeded beyond your wildest expectations.'' She hesitated. ''But, sir, I do have a small independence of my own and a pension from Tom. Surely I can buy my own—''

"Nonsense," he interrupted, looking vastly annoyed. "I know it states somewhere that all impressed seamen are to be dressed by the 'kind offices of the crown.' I know that is the phrase."

"Oh, Captain, you are being nonsensical," she declared, hardly knowing whether she was more irritated with him or embarrassed at herself.

He leveled his quarterdeck scowl at her and she scowled back, not giving an inch.

He broke first, looking away and then bowing to her. "Very well, Admiral Lord McVinnie. But I warn you that I may get the urge every now and then to put something upon your back. Now, do not look at me like that," he growled, even though his eyes were kind. "I have some small notion of the expense of a London Season. G—goodness knows I have been paying Larinda's bills. They would send you into spasms!"

"All the more reason you should not be saddled with mine," she said quietly.

He shook his head. "It is nothing, and I can afford it. But I wanted you to be a credit to yourself, my dear Mrs. McVinnie." He bowed, took her hand and kissed it. "You are already a credit to me."

Jeannie smiled at him, knowing that her face was fiery red and not a little surprised to see that his was, too. "I do thank you. This dress may give me the courage to face Larinda."

"That is all I wanted." He looked like a man about to say more, but there was Pringle standing patiently by with the neckcloths. "And now, my dear Mrs. McVinnie, if you will excuse me . . ."

"Certainly, Captain." She bobbed a little curtsy and twinkled her eyes at him. "We Christians must prepare for the lions."

His face became instantly serious. "Or the guns of La Coruña or the coming-about at Trafalgar. We do what we must, sometimes, no matter how distasteful. Your servant."

She put the dress on thoughtfully, hardly aware for the moment that Clare had crept into her room and was standing in the shadows again.

Mary saw her first and sighed in exasperation. "Little miss, have you escaped from your keeper?" she said softly as she buttoned up Jeannie's dress. "Mrs. McV, should I return her?"

Jeannie put out her hand. "No. Clare, you funny-stick, sit on my bed."

Obediently, Clare climbed up and flopped herself down on the pillows, flinging her arms out and snuggling into the softness. Jeannie smiled at her.

"I promised you a story, didn't I? That will do, Mary. I can arrange my own hair."

Jeannie sat down on the bed and clasped her pearls, a wedding gift from Tom, around her neck. Clare rose up on her knees and touched the necklace, running her fingers over the pearls.

"Pretty," she said.

Jeannie hugged her. "And that is the first thing you have said to me! Come, sit on my lap. I have such a story for you."

"Don't forget the time," Mary said from the doorway. "Lady Smeath may not look like a notable trencherwoman, but she'll give you a regular scold if you're late." She rolled her eyes. "And I needn't tell you about the captain."

"I am sure he is never late to anything," Jeannie said. "I'll only be a moment."

It was a tale of blue elephants and crown jewels and swimming watery moats. Jeannie sat on the bed, her arms around Clare, until the child relaxed against her and slept. Quietly she got up, covered Clare with a blanket, and left the room.

She was late to dinner. Everyone waited for her in the foyer of the dining room. Lady Smeath sighed deeply several times and fanned herself vigorously, even though the room was cool. Captain Summers snapped open his pocket watch and spent a long moment staring down at it, divining its depths. Larinda looked at her and then looked away, a tight little smile on her face.

Edward, copiously well-scrubbed, glanced from relative to relative, swallowed several times and then walked deliberately to Jeannie's side. He bowed, a jerky, untrained motion that brought a smile to her lips, in spite of her embarrassment.

"Well done, Edward," she whispered.

He extended his arm and asked in a clear voice, "Will you partner me to dinner?"

She laid her hand upon his arm, noting how it trembled. I am not sure I would have had the courage to defy such a passel of Friday-faced elders, she thought as she smiled at Edward and inclined her head. The others followed them in to dinner.

"I washed everything I could think of," Edward whispered to her as he pulled out her chair.

"Excellent," she whispered back.

"But Captain Summers would come around me and sniff a bit," he declared as the others took their seats. "Do you think he was funning?"

"How does one know?" Jeannie murmured.

There was little conversation at the table, other than several mundane exchanges between Larinda and her aunt concerning the approaching evening at Almack's.

"And remember, my dear, that you are not to accept a waltz with anyone. This is but your first assembly at Almack's and it will not do."

"Aunt Agatha, you have told me," Larinda said. "And I am to drink only orgeat, and never sit in a chair that a gentleman has just vacated, and remember not to laugh too loud, and, above all, do nothing to disgust the patronesses." She touched her napkin to her lips and sighed.

There was something in that sigh that reminded Jeannie of her first dance. She leaned toward Larinda. "It is never as frightening as you think it will be," she said softly. "I am certain you will acquit yourself admirably."

Larinda gazed back, and for the smallest moment there was something in her eyes besides contempt. Anticipation and fear mingled there and then vanished. She tucked the napkin under the edge of her plate. "I trust that I have sufficient consequence," she said pointedly.

Jeannie's face burned with embarrassment, and again Edward leapt into action.

"You were never short of that, Larry," he declared. "Remember what Papa used to call you?"

"Hush, you little beast," Larinda burst out. She appealed to her uncle. "If there ever was a more plaguey brother, I do not know of it. And don't call me that awful name."

Brother and sister glared at each other across the table. Lady Smeath cleared her throat and rested her hand gently, delicately, on her forehead. Larinda broke off her angry stare and looked at her aunt in consternation. Lady Smeath only shook her head sadly.

"Remember what happens when I am distressed," was all she said, and Larinda stared down at her plate.

Captain Summers watched the whole tableau with his lips pressed tight together. He opened his mouth to speak, but thought better of it.

"Larinda does remind me, brother dear," Lady Smeath began. "How is it that we can get Mrs. McVinnie past the patronesses? I am certain she does not have a voucher, and considering—well, let us not pull hairs—considering her anonymity in our circle, I do not see how she can possibly procure a voucher. They do have rules, William dear, and they do keep out the scaff and raff." Lady Smeath looked at Jeannie, her eyes wide. "Of course, I am not referring to you, Mrs. McVinnie."

"Of course you are not, Lady Taneystone."

Summers took another bite of his sirloin roast and smiled back at his sister and Larinda in turn. In her own acute embarrassment, Jeannie couldn't help but observe that predatory look in his eyes.

"I was a busy sailor boy today," he said, to neither of them in particular. "Do you know that Lord Smeath was only too happy to promise that he would approach Lady Jersey this very afternoon and procure the voucher we need? I need only ask for it when we arrive in the assembly rooms."

"My brother-in-law did that?" Lady Taneystone asked, her voice rising in surprise. "Why, he would not even do that for me!"

Captain Summers spent a long moment studying the plate of meat in front of him. He speared another slice and transferred it to his plate. "G—gracious, but this is excellent after a year of salt beef from a keg. Yes, my dear Agatha, your very brother-in-law. How kind he was to me, his *deus ex machina.*" He glanced at Larinda, who was frowning. "Don't strain yourself, niece," he said blandly. "I am his god from the machine, his savior upon Mount Zion, his Isaac on the altar."

Agatha stared at her brother. "William! I never knew any of our family to allude to Scripture. How droll!"

He nodded in her direction, only the slightest quiver of his lips betraying any emotion to Jeannie. "Dear sister, I give a sermon from the quarterdeck every Sunday morning. As it is always followed by a recitation of the Articles of War, I do try to make it improving. Sacrifice is invariably my theme."

Jeannie coughed into her napkin and studied the oil painting on the far wall while Edward's eyes darted from her to his uncle, an expression of real delight on his face.

"But as I began to say, dear sister," Summers continued after he finished eating, "there are no lengths to which your brother-in-law will not go to avoid having to abandon his rack punch and fireside for the perils of Almack's. I am his to be commanded in all things, apparently."

Even Larinda had to smile. Jeannie watched her. Such a pretty girl, she thought as she tucked in one more bite of dinner. Oh, please, let us be friends.

Lady Smeath changed her mind several times as they stood in the hall waiting for the carriage to be brought around, but she decided at the last moment to accompany her niece and brother.

"Are you sure the evening will not put any undue strain on your heart?" Captain Summers asked as Pringle swirled his boat cloak around his shoulders.

Lady Smeath smiled bravely. "Surely I owe this one evening to my niece, whom I have raised all these years, with, I might add, no help from you. It is, after all, her first visit to Almack's." Again her delicate hand just brushed against her forehead. "If I am faint, Sally Jersey will find me a couch. I feel sure of it."

They endured a silent ride to Almack's. The streets were wet and shone slick and smooth under the soft light from the streetlamps.

I wonder if it is raining in Scotland, Jeannie thought, and then sighed with the sudden sharpness of homesickness.

She sat next to Captain Summers. When she sighed, he reached out and clasped her hand firmly, twining her fingers in his and giving them the briefest squeeze before releasing her. He stared continually ahead the entire time, and Jeannie could only wonder if she had imagined the moment. She remembered Tom's warning about sailors and smiled. Have no fear, my dear, she thought, I am a surely proof against seamen.

Almack's was a glittering jewel in an unpretentious setting. Jeannie looked about her with interest. She had read in the women's magazines about the place, but had never entertained the notion that she would someday be giving over her cloak to the porter and preparing to enter the famous assembly rooms. It was something that happened to others not of her acquaintance.

Larinda stood beside her, biting her lips and figeting with her dress. Jeannie turned to her, touching a curl in Larinda's hair and then another, and then giving a final pat to her necklace.

"My dear, you will do very well," she said. "Primrose becomes you."

Larinda turned anxious eyes on her. "Oh, are you sure? I so want . . ." And then she remembered herself. "You're only saying that."

The words were hateful, and Jeannie flinched in spite of herself. An uncertain look wavered in Larinda's eyes. If it was momentary shame, Jeannie did not know or care. Her own anger rose and fell as quickly as it had come.

"Larinda, I never say what is not true," she said, low-voiced and even. "I do not deal in Spanish coin." She turned on her heel and followed Captain Summers into the assembly room.

Lord Smeath had been true to his word. The vouchers were there, and in the hands of Lady Jersey herself, who restlessly fanned herself with them and then smiled up at Captain Summers. She extended her other hand and he bowed over it.

"La, Sir William, how seldom we see you men of the blockade in our assembly rooms. One would think that you prefer it that way, I own."

He kissed her hand, but did not release it. Jeannie smiled and knew that Lady Jersey would be his first victim that evening.

"My dear Lady Jersey," he was saying, "it is the will of king and country, but not of the heart. How grateful I am to be here this evening. Let me make you known to my niece, Larinda Summers. And I am sure you are already acquainted with my sister, Lady Smeath."

He released her hand after another bow, and Lady Jersey held out both hands to Larinda and Lady Smeath. "Agatha, it has been too, too long since you have been to our London," she scolded, her voice soft and breathless, the words hanging like little stars in the overheated air.

"And let me introduce another of our party," continued the captain. "Mrs. Jeannie McVinnie, who has come all the way from Scotland as a companion to Larinda."

Lady Jersey smiled and nodded. Her eyes flitted over Jeannie's face in a restless motion. "Captain, what can you and your sister have been thinking? Mrs. McVinnie is but a babe herself. My dear, such a lovely dress! Your taste is exquisite." She tapped Jeannie's hand with her fan. "There is one coming later tonight, provided the naughty boy is not shut out at eleven, who will be happy to admire that precise tone of blue."

"Thank you, Lady Jersey," Jeannie said.

"And you will make redheads the rage this Season, I vow," the partroness continued, even as her eyes began to rove the room and she returned the vouchers to Summers. With a wave of the hand, she was gone.

"An odd creature," Jeannie murmured.

"But so important to our consequences, or so Agatha will tell me. We will see any number of odd creatures this evening, I daresay," said the captain under his breath. "Come, ladies, and allow me to do my duty. It has been a prodigious while since I have danced. Sister?"

Lady Smeath gathered up her train and let Captain Summers lead her onto the dancing floor. Larinda immediately left Jeannie's side and joined a small group of young people her own age. Jeannie looked about her, found a chair, and sat in it, folding her hands in her lap.

That Captain Summers was an able dancer should have surprised her, but it did not. Gracefully he worked his way down the set of the country dance with all the agility of a man accustomed to the dancing floor. Jeannie laughed to herself. And he does not count out loud, she thought, as Tom used to do. There is not that look of a sheep at the knackerman's knife, and he does not clutch at his collar and declare himself wonderfully ill-used if he must be compelled to dance again. Tom, I would happily sit out any number of country dances if you were only here again.

The tears were ready to fall, and she was mortified. Quickly Jeannie rose to her feet and found a door partly open beside a tall window. It opened onto a small balcony. Gratefully she clasped the railing and took several deep breaths, willing herself not to think of Tom.

The dance had finished when she returned to the assembly room. Larinda stood once again with her friends. As Jeannie watched, Larinda looked her way and then turned back to her friends again. Their heads came together and there was laughter, and other glances darted her way.

And now I am being made a fool, she thought.

"Mrs. McVinnie, you look as though you have discovered your well is full of water and you are drifting upon a lee shore."

Captain Summers stood beside her again. For the smallest moment she wished he would take her hand again and hold it. She shook away the thought and did not speak until she had command of her voice.

"I would wager a plum, Captain Summers, that Larinda is telling her friends about her Scottish nanny who speaks so funny and is a perfect quiz."

"You are no quiz," he said immediately. "And I have noticed any number of young tulips giving you the rake-down."

"Absurd," she declared. "You were dancing. How could you tell?"

"I, madam, have eyes in the back of my head," he replied. "It comes from years of impressing felons and pretending they are seamen. Close observation, ma'am, close observation, is the key to survival on the water." He looked about him and shook his head. "And perhaps in the ballroom."

"I still say you are wrong," Jeannie persisted. "This is not my come-out. Why should anyone stare at me?"

"Perhaps because you are a damned pretty woman," he said frankly.

Before Jeannie could think of anything rallying in reply, the captain put his hands behind his back and scrutinized his niece. "My, she has a wagging tongue! And she is probably animadverting on her uncle, who feeds her weevily biscuit and has her flogged around the fleet for the slightest infraction. Oh, Lord." He nudged her. "Were you ever seventeen, Mrs. McVinnie?"

She twinkled her eyes at him. " I distinctly remember it. Although, truth to tell, I would never want to be seventeen again. Once was enough."

"I was never seventeen," he said, his eyes on his niece as she tittered and giggled behind her hands and looked his way and then laughed some more.

At Jeannie's look of interest, he motioned to a sofa and sat her down, ranging himself beside her. "When I was seventeen

I was laid up in Kingston with as bad a case of ship's fever as you could dream of. I did not care whether I lived or died.'' He shook his head at the memory, an odd smile playing around his lips. "But it was better than eighteen, when I was a prisoner of the Spanish. No, Mrs. McVinnie, I was never seventeen.''

She looked at him curiously. There was nothing in his voice of self-pity. "Are all men like you so hard?" she asked, without even thinking how rude the question.

If he thought her question strange, out of place in a ballroom, he did not betray it. "We are, madam. It is what keeps us alive on the blockade.''

She touched his arm impulsively, but said nothing, only wondered why she felt so close to tears again. It was foolish to think that a man like Captain Sir William Summers wanted her sympathy.

The captain laughed softly. "We are not precisely given to small talk, are we, Mrs. McVinnie? Did no one ever teach either of us proper ballroom manners? Shouldn't we laugh and joke and say things we don't mean?'' He held out his hand to her. "Dance with me now, Mrs. McVinnie.''

She shook her head. "No, indeed, sir,'' she declared, determined to lighten the curious mood that had settled on them. "What kind of a chaperone would I be, then?''

He looked down at her feet. "The kind who cannot keep from tapping out a rhythm.''

She followed his gaze and tucked her shoes under her ballgown. "No, I will not,'' she said again. "But I think that you should invite Larinda to dance.''

He sighed and rose to his feet. "You are right, of course. I can shoulder my way over there and observe at close range the fribbles and fortune-hunters who have surrounded her. And if I use my very best quarterdeck scowl, I can certainly put some to flight.'' He rubbed his hands together. "This promises to be more fun than butlers.''

Jeannie laughed and looked away, and the smile froze on her face.

A small group of men stood at the assembly-room entrance, laughing and talking with one another and scanning the ballroom. One raised a quizzing glass to his eye; another languidly consulted a pocket watch tethered to an enormous gold chain. A third man tugged at his flamboyant waistcoat, a coat of many colors that should have cast Joseph himself into the shadow.

She gulped. It was Sir Peter Winthrop, minus his blue paint.

The fourth man wore no lace or waistcoat of biblical splendor. He was dressed soberly in black, broken only by the almost startling white of his shirtfront and the single gold watch chain that stretched across his chest. He was a crow among peacocks, and she could not tear her eyes from him. He was understated, underdressed, and elegant, from his brilliantly polished shoes to his carefully arranged hair. He was the man she had raked down so thoroughly in the menagerie only that afternoon.

The man was the picture of perfection. Jeannie looked about her in amazement. Everyone was watching him, even the couples who had already begun the waltz. If the musicians scraped and twiddled at their instruments, she did not hear it. Jeannie McVinnie watched the elegant man in silence and she began to be afraid.

Without even seeming to turn his head, the man looked about the room and raised his hand to one of the group surrounding Larinda. He started in that direction and then stopped and looked at Jeannie, bowing and smiling.

Without taking her eyes from him, Jeannie tugged at Captain Summers' sleeve. "Captain, who is that man over there, the one, oh, you know, that one?"

Amused, Summers looked where she nodded. "I cannot say for sure, considering that I have been at sea for too long, but bless me, Jeannie McVinnie, you must mean the Beau. No one else is as beautiful. Not even me."

Jeannie managed a slight smile at his joke. The blood drained from her face as she noticed that the man in the doorway was watching her. "Who . . . who?"

"Beau Brummell, you owl," said the captain. "Yes, I am sure that is who you mean." He gently lifted Jeannie's hand from his arm, where she was digging into the gold swirls on his sleeve. "People say he is the most elegant thing in London, and a great friend of the Prince Regent." The captain motioned to his sister, who stood with her friends nearby, also mesmerized by the man in the doorway. "Agatha, come sit you down with us and tell us—is that Beau Brummell?"

Lady Smeath accepted the proffered seat. "Dear me, yes, William," she said, her voice so full of reverence that Jeannie could only stare. She tapped Jeannie playfully with the fan. "And let me warn you, Mrs. McVinnie. That man has the power to ruin a woman's chances at a come-out with only a word or a glance."

Lady Smeath directed her gaze back to the Beau and peered closer. "I wonder why he is looking at us. What could it possibly signify?" She shrugged. "I must do what I can to attract his attention to Larinda. Only think what his notice could mean to her."

"Yes, Agatha, think of it. Call Larinda's attention to him immediately," the captain ordered. "The sooner Larinda is shot off, the sooner I am back at sea."

Jeannie felt a cold wave rush across her body. She clasped her hands together to stop their trembling. "Do you mean . . . Oh, Lady Smeath, surely he cannot determine someone's fate during a London Season?"

Lady Smeath nodded. "I mean exactly that. I have seen it happen. He stared at a young lady once—I believe she was only laughing overloud—and looked her up and down through his quizzing glass." Lady Smeath shook her head. "And do you know, no one who was anyone sent her cards or invitations after that night? All the poor thing could do was leave town."

"Leave town?" Jeannie repeated. Good heavens, she thought, what have I done to Larinda's chances? She clutched the captain's arm again. He looked down at her in surprise. "Surely no one has that kind of power," Jeannie said.

"The Beau does," Lady Taneystone replied. "Oh, and look, is he coming this way?" She cast a quick glance behind her. "I wonder, is there someone standing behind us that he knows?"

Jeannie leapt to her feet and dragged the captain up with her. "Captain Summers," she said, entreating him with her eyes, "I would like of all things to dance this waltz with you. Right now!"

7

CAPTAIN Summers did not betray his surprise by even one flicker of an eye. "I would be charmed, Mrs. McVinnie," he said as he led her onto the floor. He clasped her firmly in his arms and whirled her into the dance pattern.

White and stricken to silence, Jeannie could only be grateful that her partner was such an excellent leader and that he was taking her farther and farther away from Beau Brummell. The Beau stood watching the dancers, standing compact and alone and utterly distinguished. Jeannie dragged her eyes away from him and resolved to dance and dance until the musicians put away their instruments, the servants put the chairs on the tables, and the porter locked the door.

They danced in silence until Captain Summers pulled her closer and whispered in her ear. "Mrs. McVinnie, I know that my charms are well-nigh overpowering and that few women alive are able to resist a uniform, especially a naval uniform, but please tell me what the hell is going on."

Jeannie shuddered and he gathered her closer.

"Mrs. McVinnie," he began, his lips practically on her ear, "have you seen a ghost?"

"It is worse," she managed, after a few more turns in the ballroom, which was growing hotter by the moment. "That man, that Beau Brummell . . . Oh, Captain Summers, he was there in the Tower this afternoon. That other man with him— oh, all of them—it was a wager. They were painting an elephant blue."

The captain tightened his grip on her waist. "Come, come, Mrs. McVinnie. Take a deep breath and begin again."

She glared at him. "You're holding me rather too tight for that!"

He obligingly loosened his grip. "There now."

His light tone heartened her. She gripped his hand tighter. "Captain, I gave Beau Brummell such a dressing-down!" Her eyes closed at the memory of it. "The things I said! Something about foolish fops with nothing better to do and what a blot they were on the English character."

"My God, Mrs. McVinnie," said the captain, and for once, she did not correct him. He gathered her close again, and the gesture was oddly protective.

"Oh, it's dreadful, I know," she said, "but I was so upset. There was Edward grabbed and thrown on top of that great beast, and all I could think about was Tom."

"Tom?" he asked, his face devoid of all expression, except for the rogue twinkle in his green eyes. "Come now. I know Spain is a strange place, but I saw no elephants at La Coruña."

Jeannie laughed in spite of herself. "I told you it was silly. But there were these perfectly able-bodied, indolent men doing something so totty-headed, and when I think that Tom died for people like that, well, it made me angry."

"And well it might," the captain agreed. "I haven't yet told you about the earl that I belted on my last shore leave, have I? And do forgive that pun."

"Forgiven," she said. "Whatever did he do?"

"He made a rude remark about gunners who could not hit the broad side of France, and I happen to know we are much better than that. I was also a little to let at the time, luffing like a topgallant."

"Well, I was not!"

"Of course you were not." He whirled her around, his attention caught by the man whispering to Larinda and then to the Beau.

"And that sprig of fashion?" the captain asked, whirling Jeannie about for a better view. "Was he there, too? I declare Larinda looks on the verge of apoplexy. I wonder what he is telling her?"

It was Sir Peter Winthrop, and he was darting angry glances at her and gesturing in an animated way to Larinda, who stood open-mouthed.

Jeannie swallowed again and the captain looked down at her in alarm.

"My G—goodness, Mrs. McVinnie. Your face is quite green!"

"At least it is not blue," she said mournfully. "That is the man who teased Edward. I—oh, you won't like this—I dumped blue paint all over him, and the elephant—oh, gracious, what the elephant did."

The captain appeared hard put to restrain himself. "I think I can guess. Jeannie, you are a scamp and a rascal! Had I been given any inkling—"

"You would not have impressed me?"

He threw back his head and laughed as he pulled her closer. "By G—gracious, you are a prime item, Mrs. McVinnie."

She only sighed. "I don't understand. I am fine in Scotland."

The captain only laughed again.

Jeannie stopped, but he pulled her along. "You do not appreciate the seriousness of this!"

He was looking over her shoulder. "Oh, I should not have called attention to us. Have a care now. The Beau approaches on our starboard bow."

She closed her eyes as they whirled past Brummell, down the hall, and into the card room. The cardplayers within looked up in surprise and some indignation, except for a lady so old that her face appeared to have sunk inside itself like a dried apple.

With a chortle of triumph and an arch look at her partner, an equally elderly gentleman dressed in the mode of the last century, she thumped the seat next to her. "Sit down, dearie, do," she commanded in the overloud voice of the hard-of-hearing. "I was only just saying to Lord Hammersmith over there—wake up, you old fool!—what do you have to do around here to get good whist players, and here you are. I call that good fortune." She thumped the chair again.

With a fleeting glance at Captain Summers, Jeannie sat down.

The old lady peered close at her. "You don't look like one of those schoolroom chits, and thank God for that. I don't think a modern miss could play a rubber or two without falling on the floor in a dead faint from the mental exertion. No, I don't want a schoolroom lass."

"I assure you that I am a long time from the schoolroom," Jeannie replied.

"Oh, centuries and aeons," Captain Summers added. "Jeannie, will you insist on speaking drivel forever?"

Jeannie politely overlooked the informality of his address, and was rewarded with a wink.

"And from the sound of you, dearie, you're a long way from your hearth, too."

"That I am, madam," she replied. "A very long way."

"And this husband of yours—"

"He's not—I'm not—we're not—" Jeannie stammered, not daring to look at the captain.

The old lady fumbled in her reticule and dragged out a pair of spectacles, which she perched on the end of her nose. "I only wear them when I want to see something," she confided to Jeannie. "I fear they make me look old." She turned her attention to the captain and looked him up and down. She nodded and grunted. "My mother used to warn me about sailors, too," she said, and patted Jeannie's hand.

Only by the exercise of the most rigid discipline could Jeannie maintain her countenance. "Very wise of your mother," she murmured serenely.

Captain Summers glowered at her. He opened his mouth to rebut when the door was thrown open and Lady Jersey stormed into the room. The captain started visibly and opened his mouth to speak, but Lady Jersey was in no mood to listen. She marched directly up to the captain.

"It is too bad, Sir William," she declared. "Too bad!"

Jeannie felt her face go red and then white. Had Beau Brummell already announced to the assembly that Jeannie McVinnie was not fit *ton* company?

"Lady Jersey, I can explain," she began.

Lady Jersey did not take her eyes from Captain Summer's face. "Sir, have you been on the blockade so long that you cannot recall the smallest rules here at Almack's?"

Jeannie held her breath and closed her eyes.

"How dare you ask a lady for her first waltz without consulting me? Or Countess Lieven? She is here tonight, too. I would not have thought you so rag-mannered."

"Lady Jersey, if you please, that was my—" Jeannie tried again.

Captain Summers grasped the back of his chair and shook

his head. "How careless of me," he exclaimed, his eyes full of contrition.

"It was more than careless," Lady Jersey replied, just warming to her subject. "The ballroom is buzzing!"

Again Captain Summers gave her that frank look and sighed, a sound so full of meaning that it seemed to come from below his feet.

Jeannie stared at him and fought down the sudden urge to smile.

He sighed again and made a helpless gesture with his hand. "Lady Jersey, you cannot imagine how many nights and days I have stood watch and watch about from the foretop roost, my eyes glued to the French coast, wondering how much longer before I would summon the drummer to beat 'To quarters' and we went into action." Again that gesture. "I would think about dancing, sometimes, and some nights it was the only thing that kept me warm." Again that sigh.

Jeannie could only look away.

"It's cold in the foretop roost, Lady Jersey, and when the sleet runs down inside your greatcoat, why, there's no chill quite like it." He put his hand over his heart. "The memory of Almack's sustained me." He took Jeannie by the hand. "And here was this lovely lady, and that waltz! It is a particular favorite of mine. I've whistled it when the guns were run out and the men were ramming home their charges, just to give the lads heart."

Jeannie cast down her eyes, took a deep breath, and held it. If I don't look at him, we might brush through this, she thought. But surely Lady Jersey is not swallowing this Banbury tale. She peeked a look at Almack's formidable patroness.

Lady Jersey stood perfectly still, her large dark eyes filled with tears. "I had no idea, Captain Summers," she managed to say finally.

The captain shook his head as a pitiful smile flickered across his face. "And the lads at the guns took such pleasure in a simple tune." He bowed his head. "For some, that little waltz was their last reminder of home."

Lady Jersey sobbed out loud and fumbled for a handkerchief she had tucked in her bosom. She dabbed at her eyes and held her hand to her mouth until she was completely in control again.

"Captain Summers, you are forgiven a thousand times," she

said, her voice scarcely a whisper. "How easy it is to forget the war when we are safe and sheltered here."

The captain shook off his air of melancholy and squared his shoulders. He bowed to Lady Jersey and kissed her hand. "You are all kindness," he said in a husky voice. "Thank God there is an England."

Jeannie had to sit down and cover her face with her hands.

The captain laid a heavy hand on her shoulder. "These are trying times," he said simply. "Surely you understand."

And it will shortly become even more trying if you do not shoo that woman out of here, Jeannie thought.

The captain clapped his hands together. "And so, my dear Lady Jersey, if I may?" He bowed again and held out a hand to her. "I ask you, Lady Jersey, to forgive me."

Lady Jersey dried her eyes and said, "You are forgiven."

"You are all kindness, madam," he managed to say.

Lady Jersey smiled tremulously. She reached up and patted Captain Summers' cheek. "Dear, dear boy," she whispered. "How proud your mother would be if she could only see you now." With those words, she turned and glided out of the room, her hands clasped in front of her as if she had just come from the communion rail.

Captain Summers stood by the door. "My mother would give me such a raking scold that the chandelier would rattle," he said as he quietly closed the door. He reconsidered. "No, she would have looked at me mournfully and patted her heart like this. It's no wonder that Agatha is the way she is." He shook his head and laughed.

"Many nights in a foretop roost, indeed," Jeannie said indignantly. "Since when?"

"Since twenty years ago, when I was a God-help-us midshipman and puked on the captain from the lookout. G—gracious, he was so surprised."

Jeannie sank into the chair again. "And whistling a waltz as you went into battle! Captain Summers, you must be guilty of the basest kind of perjury."

"Profoundly so, madam," he assured her, "particularly as we sail into battle. That is generally when I invoke the Lord's blessing upon the French." He took out his watch. "I suggest that we do not brave the ballroom again until much later. What say we join this delightful couple in a rubber or two?"

The old lady jabbed her finger at the chair opposite Jeannie and prodded Lord Hammersmith under the table. The old gentleman sat up and looked about him, as if trying to remember what century it was.

"Lady Hammersmith, is it?" Captain Summers asked. "Will you deal? I will partner Mrs. McVinnie, if she has decided that I am not past redemption."

"You are," she declared, "but I am more afraid to attempt the ballroom again."

"It takes a rogue to know a rogue," he said as he unbuttoned his uniform coat and loosened his neckcloth slightly.

Jeannie gave him a speaking look and refused to rise to the bait. She calmly took up the hand dealt her.

That Captain Summers was an excellent whist player was soon borne out to her during the first rubber. By paying careful attention to his discards and correctly interpreting the meaningful looks he cast her way from time to time, she was just able to keep up with his skill. Each new trick laid down in front of her caused Lady Hammersmith to gasp and sputter and turn an unhealthy shade of red that clashed with the purple of her gown. They played for shillings at first and then half-crowns, the captain sliding money across the table to her without a word and ignoring her when she protested.

The candles were guttering lower when Lady Hammersmith announced the stakes at five shillings a trick. The captain did not blink an eye, even though Jeannie McVinnie's Scots soul experienced the acutest sort of agony at such a waste of money.

Shillings, crowns, and pounds changed hands from rubber to rubber. For all that he appeared asleep or at least remarkably dithered, Lord Hammersmith put up a stiff competition. Lady Hammersmith talked to herself, carrying on a fascinating conversation that would have sent Jeannie into whoops if she had not been dealing in shillings and pounds and therefore taking herself quite seriously.

And then the game was over. A trail of tricks stretched in front of Captain Summers, and Lady Hammersmith threw down her remaining cards in disgust. "Lord Hammersmith," she exclaimed to her husband, "you ought to order me to give up cards."

Lord Hammersmith muttered something and closed his eyes again.

Captain Summers swept up the money in front of him and divided it in two, shoving half across the table toward Jeannie. "My dear, I think I will abandon the sea and start a gaming hell with you. Think of the fortune we will reap."

She shoved the money back at him. "We will do no such thing. Why, how could I sleep nights?"

"Very comfortably, and probably upon satin sheets," he said frankly. "You certainly have an instinct for whist, at any rate. Please, half of the earnings are yours."

When she still looked mulish, he stared back at her and lowered his voice. "Or I will drop the coins one at a time down the front of your dress."

"You wouldn't dare," she said, but gathered up her share of the money, her eyes on him.

"Well, you never know what a sailor will do," he told her, and leaned back in his chair, patting his stomach. "I wish we had a big platter of currant duff and some jam to spread all over it. And a tot of rum. My gracious, that would be a fitting conclusion to this evening!"

She smiled at him. "Currant duff?" Her smile grew larger. "Tom used to beg me for hard bread. 'Just like the quartermaster gets,' he would say. 'And mind, Jeannie, butter so thick that it leaves a mustache when I bite into it.' "

Captain Summers raised his eyes to hers. "A good memory?" he asked, and his voice was gentle.

"A very good one, sir," she said.

He nodded, rose to his feet, and stretched. He opened the door and went into the hall, and was back in a moment. He motioned to her. "It appears that the Beau has retired from the lists, at least for the moment. And bless me, here is my sister, ready to give us a scold. Agatha dear," he said.

Agatha snapped her fan open and plied it vigorously. "A fine pair of chaperones you two turned out to be," she declared, biting off each word. "And there was no one but me to watch over Larinda!"

"How fortunate, then, that you decided to come to Almack's after all," was the captain's bland reply.

Lady Smeath eyed him suspiciously, but obviously thought better of a reply. Her lips trembled. "I am tired," she said, her voice small again. "I will find Larinda."

The captain watched her go. "That is probably more exertion

than she had expended on Larinda's behalf since my niece had chickenpox at six," he said, more to himself than to Jeannie.

"Captain, you are unjust," she said.

He only smiled.

They reentered the ballroom, which was still thick with company despite the late hour. The air was murky with the odor of mingled perfume, pomade, and candlewax.

The captain sniffed the air and cast a glance in her direction. "Correct me if I'm wrong, Mrs. McVinnie, but does your expression tell me that you wish you were breathing in a draft of North Irish Sea air?"

"While you long for the breeze around Ushant?" she asked, her eyes twinkling back at him.

He shook his head. "No, ma'am, not that. It smacks of the blockade. I would settle for some of that Irish Sea, too, provided there was currant duff, and—"

"And a tot of rum," she finished for him, and they laughed together.

Larinda hurried toward them, her eyes bright, her cheeks red from dancing. She took her uncle by the hand. "Uncle dear," she said, the wheedling tone unmistakable, "do tell me that we are engaged for the theater tomorrow night? Did you not mention the Theatre Royal yesterday? I am sure that you did."

"I believe that was the course," he agreed, "but I do not recall that you considered the matter entirely to your liking."

"Oh, Uncle, how you carry on. Only think! Beau Brummell himself expressly wanted to make sure that we would be there." She looked at Jeannie for the first time. "And he was quite insistent that you be there, Mrs. McVinnie. Imagine that?"

"Imagine that," Jeannie said. She looked carefully at Larinda and the girl stared back, a smile of triumph in her eyes. "Of course you told him yes?"

"Of course, Mrs. McVinnie. I know what the Beau can mean to the success of a young girl's come-out."

So Jeannie's great set-down would likely come at the play, probably during intermission, when the patrons mingled together in the boxes. There would be sufficient audience and then some, for a long appraisal through his quizzing glass and a sharp turn on the heel. Jeannie patted her heavy reticule and raised her shoulders. It would be best to take her whist money and engage a seat on the next mail coach north.

Jeannie observed Larinda's proud profile during the silent ride back to Wendover Square. At least it appears you are in league with the Beau and that dreadful Sir Peter, she thought, and my misfortune will not touch upon your own career. If you were to become their target, I would have a worse regret.

"My dear, let us remain at home in the morning," said Lady Smeath as they drew up outside 3 Wendover Square and the coachman spoke to his horses.

"Aunt, how tedious," Larinda said as she yawned.

Lady Smeath patted her hand. "My Larinda, there is every likelihood that you will have morning callers. Don't be such a slow-top." She glanced at Jeannie. "Perhaps we can send Mrs. McVinnie on our errands."

"That is what I am here for," Jeannie replied. At least, for now, she thought.

"I have spoken for several articles of clothing at Amalie's in Bond Street."

"Very well, madam," Jeannie said, and then settled herself into a silence that lasted until she was inside the house and up the stairs, the captain quiet behind her.

Edward's door was closed. On impulse, Jeannie slipped out of her dancing shoes and tiptoed into his room, holding her candle high. He was sound asleep in his bed, the guidebook open on his chest. Jeannie picked up the book. "Look, Captain," she said, for he had followed her into the room. "Should I worry? He has opened it to the Admiralty House on Whitehall."

The captain peered over her shoulder. "No, my dear, I should worry. I am certain he has an expedition planned for me. He will likely renew his plea that he be allowed to follow my trade and take to the water as a midshipman." He closed the book in her hand and set it on the night table. He stood a moment longer, looking down at Edward. Without a word, he pulled up the sheet higher around his nephew's neck and touched his cheek. "Dreadful child," he whispered. "No end of trouble."

Jeannie smiled in the dark, bent down, and kissed Edward. She wrinkled her nose. "He still smells a little like elephant," she whispered back to the captain, who laughed softly, put a hand on her elbow, and steered her from the room.

Lady Smeath and Larinda had already gone to their rooms. "Well, Jeannie McVinnie," the captain said, "I thank you for a most entertaining evening." He touched his pocket. "I never thought in my wildest imaginings to make a profit at Almack's, but then, I never had such an accomplished partner before."

Jeannie blushed and then stood still, listening.

Clare was crying. Without a word to her escort, Jeannie hurried down the hall. She could hear no one within except Clare.

The captain joined her at the door.

She turned to him, her anger rising. "Captain," she began, her voice brusque. "It is a wonder that you tolerate such mismanagement."

She went inside. The nursemaid nodded in front of the fireplace, her head leaning far forward and bobbing up and down as she snored.

"If this isn't beyond enough," Jeannie declared in round tones as she set down the candle in her hand and went in the next room. Without a word, she picked up Clare from the bed and sat down with her in a chair close to the window. Still in silence, Jeannie pulled Clare's head down until she rested against her. Jeannie wrapped her arms around the child and held her close.

A log dropped on the fireplace in the other room. Through the open door, Jeannie watched as the nursemaid leapt to her feet, squeaking in surprise at the sight of Captain Summers seated in the chair opposite and staring at her.

"I wondered when you would wake," he said, cutting the air with his words. "It would seem that you are singularly useless as a tender of children."

Clare stared and then burrowed deeper in Jeannie's arms when she heard the woman's voice in reply, arguing that she only followed Lady Smeath's orders.

"Sh, little one," Jeannie whispered as Clare began to whimper. "My dear, I think you have come to the end of your lonely nights."

Clare watched Jeannie's face several long moments. She must have finally been satisfied with what she saw, because she closed her eyes and was soon asleep. Jeannie remained where she was, holding the sleeping child close to her.

The voices were much lower in the next room, the captain doing much of the talking. When he was done, there was another spell of silence and then the door closed. Jeannie smiled in satisfaction to hear the quick footsteps of the nursemaid receding down the hall. She waited another minute and then the captain entered the nursery.

Jeannie put her finger to her lips. The captain scooped the sleeping child from her arms and put her back in bed. Clare cried out, and the captain knelt beside her, his hand gentle on her back, until she closed her eyes again, and her breathing became regular. When he was sure she slept, he covered Clare with a blanket and left the room, motioning Jeannie to follow.

He closed the door behind them and added another log to the fireplace in the nursery sitting room. Without a word to her, he stayed by the fire, holding his hands out to the warmth that grew as the log caught.

"I have dismissed her, that miserable excuse of a nurse," he said finally. "She will cry and object to Agatha, and I expect there will be a mighty scene in the morning, but she will not stay." He still did not turn around. "I am only sorry that I did not do it sooner, Jeannie—Mrs. McVinnie."

Now that the woman was gone, Jeannie could feel some generosity. "I am sure that you did not realize how things were for your daughter, Captain," she said. "And now that you know—"

"She is not my daughter," he interrupted, and sat down beside her.

"But I thought . . . Didn't Pringle say—"

"I am sure many think that may be the case," he interrupted, and made a dismissing gesture with his hand. "At one time, I thought it to be so, too, or else she would not be here." He noted the question in Jeannie's eyes and spread out his hands. "I suppose I should explain."

Jeannie had left her shoes outside the door to Edward's room, and her feet were cold. She tucked her legs under herself, not taking her eyes from Captain Summers' face. He looked no less harsh in the half-shadow of the nursery sitting room, but she could not see the color of his eyes in the gloom, nor the rest-lessness in them that was becoming so familiar to her, even in the short space she had known him.

He rose again and stood with his back to the fireplace, his hands clasped behind him. "Do you know what it feels like to be lonely?"

His abrupt question startled her, and she made a small sound of protest. Good God, she thought, do *I* know what lonely feels like? How dare he? She noted again the starkness of his face and swallowed the angry words that rose to her lips. She nodded. "I have some small idea," she said, unable to keep all the bitterness from her voice.

"You are lonely now," he said, watching her face closely. "But you have not always been lonely, and you will not be lonely for long, I fancy."

"I suppose it is so," she replied, remembering her thoughts, half in jest, at Abbey Head as she considered the possibility of remarriage. She wondered at the sorrow of his words and quite forgot her own irritation.

"I have always been lonely, Jeannie McVinnie," he said softly. "And by some rare and stupid failure of character— which, I must add, is entirely pleasing to me most of the time—I have bound myself to the loneliest position in a solitary profession."

The fire was growing hotter; he moved away from the hearth, but came no closer to her, sitting down in a chair opposite. Jeannie watched him, a little smile darting about her lips. *In a moment now, he will spring up and pace about. I do not think I have ever seen him decorate a chair for more than five minutes at a stretch.*

He rose to his feet even before the thought left her mind, and he leaned one hand against the mantel. "Blockading is dirty business, Mrs. McVinnie, dirty business. It's month in and month out, tacking and wearing off a hostile coast, watching, all the time watching, for a ship to bolt the harbor or another to seek entry. It means fanning out over an empty ocean in all weathers, watching for . . . what? Watching all sides, maintaining a vigilance so compelling that after a while you cannot sleep."

It was almost the same speech that he had made to Lady Jersey, but there was bite in back of it this time, and a war weariness that reminded her so much of Tom and Gelan McVinnie that she felt the familiar prickles down her spine.

She nodded. "I know what it is not to sleep, Captain," she said, her voice low and scarcely to be heard above the crackle of the logs in the fireplace.

He did not seem to hear her. "And then, when you cannot take one more night of it, the flagship signals you in, and you make for a port and meat that doesn't crawl off the plate and water that isn't green and as thick as porridge.'' He turned back to the fireplace, unable to meet her steady gaze. "And other pleasures, the kind that let you sleep. Ah, God.''

He leaned both hands against the mantel and stared down into the flames. "She was the wife of a Portuguese merchant in Oporto.'' He shook his head and managed a small laugh. "While he was busy cheating my first lieutenant in the harbor, I was in bed with his wife. I supposed there was some justice in that, Jeannie. One seldom gets something for nothing.''

He looked at her then, as if wondering about the effect of his words on her.

"One never gets something for nothing, Captain,'' she responded, keeping her voice light, so he would continue. "At least, that is how things are in Scotland.''

He nodded and backed up to the fire again. "And so it was. She told me she was with child before I left the port. Told me she loved me. No one ever told me that before. Not even my own mother.'' He sighed and clapped his hands together in that familiar gesture of impatience. "And then it was back to the blockade for another year. Do you know how slowly time can pass?''

Oh, I do, Captain, she thought. Each hour is a year long, and the clock wears out with being stared at. Time hangs so heavy that it almost becomes an effort to breathe. "I have some notion,'' she said.

"Letters would come for the others, but never for me. I did not know that she could even write.'' His voice turned musing with the memory. "We didn't spend overmuch time in her husband's library.''

"And then?'' she prompted when he fell silent.

"Then it was to Oporto, finally, a year later.'' With a visible effort, he continued. "The quarter where she lived was practically leveled.''

Jeannie's eyes grew wide. "Napolean?'' she asked.

He shook his head. "No, not there. Not then. It was an earthquake. The coast is prone to them, regrettably. The servants told me that she was dead but that the child was alive and in a convent.''

He sat down then, but that lasted no longer than a few breaths and then he was on his feet, this time to pace the room in that slow, deliberate stride that she could imagine on his own quarterdeck. "I learned all this from servants, who directed me to the convent. I took the child, named her Clare after a favorite aunt, and saw to it that she was sent to England and Lady Smeath." He looked at her. "What else could I have done?"

"Nothing, Captain. But didn't you say—"

"That she wasn't my daughter?" He laughed, and the prickles traveled her spine again. "The merchant got his due, Mrs. McVinnie. And here I thought he was so stupid! A few months after Clare was in Suffolk at the family estate, I received a letter from my Oporto lady love, stating that she was very much alive and demanding a king's ransom to hush up the whole affair."

He shook his head, unable to meet the expression in her eyes. "I had been gulled like my lowest-rated seaman. No telling how many times she had played that game on unsuspecting, randy captains." He rubbed his chin and Jeannie could almost see the gleam that she knew was in his eyes, only this time the mockery was turned inward. "I suppose she and her bandy-legged little goat of a husband had played that trick on other captains with sirs in their names, captains with wives high in the instep, hopeful children, and honor to worry about." He chuckled. "I had none of those things, so what did it matter? She had the wrong man this time."

"Except that you thought she loved you." Jeannie spoke into the early-morning quiet.

"So I did," he agreed. "What a fool I was."

"What did you do?" she asked, and went to the fire herself to warm her hands.

"I wrote back to say I wouldn't pay a farthing, no matter who she told." He rubbed his hands together and turned to the fire, too. "Her last letter came last year after La Coruña to inform me that my mother's ancestry was questionable and that I was a pernicious captain with less honor than a slaver. And by the way, the child living in such comfort in Suffolk was only a waif from the streets, orphaned by the earthquake, and what did I think of that?"

The chill went to Jeannie's heart. "How can people be so cruel?" she asked out loud.

"I suppose that sailors have been duped like that since the first Carthaginians got out of sight of land." He sighed and leaned his shoulder against the mantel. "No, the real cruelty lies in what I did then to Clare. I made a dreadful mistake."

She couldn't even bring herself to ask, because she already had a terrible inkling.

The captain was watching her face, and he spoke slowly, weighing out his words like tea by the ounce. "You've guessed it, haven't you? I made the mistake of confiding in a letter to Agatha that Clare really wasn't my daughter, after all."

He went to the door of the nursery then and opened it, peering in at the sleeping child. "That damnable letter was the end of any exertion Agatha ever made on Clare's behalf. And you see the consequence before you. Clare seldom speaks and glides around hugging the walls, her eyes too big for her head. Poor waif. She is being raised as I was raised, with no one to love her."

Jeannie reached out and touched the captain's arm. "No one, Captain?" she asked softly. "Not anyone in your whole life?"

He shrugged. "My mother was quite taken with George, because he was the first son, even though a bigger block I never met." He smiled at the expression on her face. "God knows I was not a lovable little chap—all ears and elbows if you will but look at that portrait in the long gallery back in Suffolk. And I was endless trouble. You may ask anyone on the estate. Always restless, always running away."

And why ever not? she thought.

He strode to the window and pulled back the draperies. "Look now, the night is going fast." He let the curtain fall. "There was one who loved me, and bless us both, it was Jeannie McVinnie. How curious this whole thing is becoming."

Jeannie stared. "I truly do not understand, Captain Summers," she said finally. "Galen McVinnie tells me that his aunt Jeannie wrote of you in her letters. I believe he said that the kindest thing she ever called you was a 'hell-born babe.' "

He smiled. "You have hit upon it. But I knew she loved me, especially that day when she let me out of the cellar where I had been locked for some infraction or other, gave me her quarterly earnings, a push out the door, and told me to run off to sea."

"She didn't!"

"She did! Oh, I was brought back soon enough, but she was gone by then, dismissed without character. And then it was only a matter of time before Papa finally stirred himself enough to get me a midshipman's berth. I was twelve."

"Good God," she said.

"Now, Mrs. McVinnie, mind your tongue," he chided.

"And that was why she was dismissed," Jeannie said, wonder in her voice. "Galen did have his questions. I believe the whole family did." She put her hand to her mouth to hide the smile, and laughed in spite of herself.

"It was sound, Scots advice. See how successful I am. I am a posted captain, and rather higher on the ratings lists, a Knight of the Grand Cross of Bath for some tom-fool thing I did that I never would have done had I allowed discretion to rule over valor. And I am a wealthy man from prize money. I am a sea captain of no uncommon skill and ability." He turned back to the window again and watched the pink dawn sneaking in under the cover of darkness. "I only wish . . . Well, I don't know what I wish, and see here, Mrs. McVinnie, I have kept you up all night with this idle chat."

Jeannie came away from the fireplace, glad enough with the thought of her own bed. She took a last look at Clare, sleeping with her hands tucked under her cheek. To her way of thinking, she did look like the captain. But I was looking for that, she thought, and I found it—or thought I did.

She opened the door into the hall and then turned back to Captain Summers, who stood by the window, watching her. "You can still change this, you know." She dropped her eyes, nonplussed by the intensity of his gaze. "I only wish I could be here to help."

He sighed. "And I can only regret that you got on the bad side of the Beau. Well, I could have used your assistance this London Season." He raised his hand in a half-humorous salute. "But I don't wonder that, given the circumstances, I would have said the same things to him. Good night, Mrs. McVinnie. It seems we are always saying good night, and soon good-bye."

"It does seem that way," she agreed. "So good night to you. And I did have a fine time at Almack's. It is something I will remember."

Dawn was still far enough away to consider at least a few hours in bed. Jeannie undressed and pulled on her nightgown. The bed looked so soft and the pillow so inviting, but she went to the window seat instead and made herself comfortable. I shall think on this matter for the captain, she told herself.

In another moment, she slept.

8

JEANNIE woke as she always did, as though someone had been calling her name and had only just left off. She could feel the warmth on the other side of her eyelids, but she had no curiosity about it, so she wriggled onto her side and kept her eyes closed.

Sleep was out of the question. She was awake, her mind already busily traveling down the road it had veered onto last night when it was so rudely interrupted by sleep. Is it possible, she thought, that no one has ever loved Captain Summers?

Jeannie tucked her hand under her cheek and scrunched herself lower. Consider the situation, she told herself. He went to sea at twelve, Lord love us, and we have been at war ever so long, and he has been on the blockade, well, long enough. When would a man like that have a chance to love anyone, outside of that dreadful woman in Oporto?

There was nothing wrong with the way he looked, she decided, if one discounted the thin-lipped, provoking stare of his, which she suspected was there for the purpose of reducing the marrow to jelly in the interest of duty. He was tall and there was enough of him to hang on to, if one should choose to do so. Jeannie smiled to herself, remembering how Tom would growl and tickle her when she said something about so much of him to love.

True, the captain's hair was thinning in front, but it was curly and a trifle at odds with the excruciating correctness of his carriage and uniform. She thought he possibly had a dimple, but she couldn't be sure. He didn't smile enough for her to recall offhand. His eyes were a marvelous, deep-sea green and quite his best feature.

There is no reason why you should remain unloved and alone, Captain Summers, Jeannie decided. If he was a posted captain, he had adequate income, and he had mentioned something last night about prize money. There was likely his share of income from the Summers estate, too, and where on earth would a man on the blockade have an opportunity to spend it? He was a good whist player, surely the best she had ever partnered. He wasn't the kind of man to be susceptible to indiscretion in play and pay.

True, he had an unfortunate air of command about him. Captain Summers was not used to disagreement. She considered that aspect of his character a moment. He needs merely to find a cozy little lady who likes to be bullied a bit, and he will be happy enough, Jeannie thought. I must admonish him to dance a little more at Almack's the next time he escorts Larinda there, and stay out of the whist room, where his only companions would be octogenarians and dowdy widows. She smiled at last night's memory and filed it away. If Lady Smeath can be compelled to exert herself, surely she could bring to his notice some female of her acquaintance. Of course, this paragon would have to be an independent lady who does not mind solitude for great stretches, someone who wouldn't worry overmuch if a letter does not come regularly.

Oh, but then, that would not be love, she told herself crossly, and found that her thoughts had neatly circled about again and were running down the same useless track: Is it possible that no one has even loved Captain Summers?

I must mention to Captain Summers that he should take advantage of this London Season, she thought. Think of all the lovely young ladies at Almack's last night. They cannot all be brainless and vapid. Nothing would bring out the bully more in Captain Summers than a totty-headed female; it would make him retreat even farther from Parson's Mousetrap. I will see what I can do.

Oh, mercy, tonight is the theater. Why am I worried about Captain Summers?

The thought of facing Mr. Brummell produced an agitation that would find relief only in movement. Jeannie hurled herself over onto her other side and nearly rolled out of the windowseat. Someone giggled, and she opened her eyes, startled.

Mary, her face filled with laughter, stood close by, holding a can of hot water. "Begging your pardon ever so much, Mrs. McVinnie," she asked, the laughter barely suppressed in her voice, "but does no one in this house sleep in a natural way?"

"I cannot answer for the other inmates of this peculiar establishment, but I was merely trying to think last night in the window seat," Jeannie said with dignity as she hugged the blanket around her. "Did you cover me with this? How kind you are."

Mary's eyes still danced. "Did you do a lot of thinking, Mrs. McV?"

"Scamp," declared Jeannie. She sat up, tried to stretch, and winced. "I am too old for window seats."

"I looked in on Edward last night early, before you returned, and there he was with his precious guidebook draped over him," said Mary as she set down the water and tidied about the wash stand. "This morning Clare had one of the captain's gloves clutched to her face. Heaven knows where she got it." Mary leaned closer. "And between you and me, I don't think that the captain ever sleeps. He must be a dreadful trial to his midshipmen."

"Is he about already?" Jeannie asked as she stood up and stretched out her arms to the midmorning sun, which was streaming in the open window.

Mary poured the water in the basin and tested it with her finger. "Up and gone, like a hound on a hare. And do you know what? He took Clare with him."

"Did he?" Jeannie exclaimed.

Mary handed her a towel. "He did. The two of them sat together in the breakfast parlor, Clare sitting on that stack of books and the captain deep in his morning paper. Such a comical sight. Clare would peek around the paper until he had to fold it and put it away, but he was smiling."

Jeannie hugged herself and then whirled about. Good for you, Captain, she thought as she laughed at the expression on Mary's face.

"And do you know, he helped her finish her baked egg, wiped her mouth, and then asked her quite solemnly if she would like to take the morning air with him. And then off they rode, as proper as you please and looking as fine as five pence in the late master's barouche." Mary looked about her with a conspiratory expression. "I begin to think that Captain Summers really is a fine figure of a man, especially when he wears his uniform and sits up so straight."

"I wonder where they can have gone?"

"I heard the captain say something to Pringle about an errand that wouldn't wait and then a morning call on Lady Jersey."

"Lady Jersey?" Jeannie wondered out loud. "Whatever can he be up to?"

"I am sure I would never have the nerve to ask. Will you be needing my help, Mrs. McVinnie?" Mary asked as she backed toward the door.

Jeannie shook her head, but then she put up her hand to stop the maid. "One moment. Is Pringle about?"

"Ma'am?"

Jeannie hurried to her desk and scribbled a note. "Give this to him, please. And Edward?"

Mary stopped at the door again. "That reminds me. The captain told Edward most specifically that he was to be your dog-robber today." Mary's eyes were full of questions. "I wonder what he can mean. And there is a list for you on the breakfast table. I believe it is from Lady Smeath."

That will be my errand list, Jeannie thought as she locked the door behind Mary and gave herself a quick wash. She hurried because the room was cold. Even the hot water in the basin could not compete with the chill, and she soon had a towel draped about her shoulders.

She stood still then, suddenly oblivious to the cold and she realized that this was the first morning in many more mornings beyond a year that Tom had not occupied her first thoughts. She wrapped the towel tighter about her and sat on the bed, leaning against the bedpost.

"It is this way, Tom," she said out loud. "Clare and the captain really do occupy my mind at this moment."

Jeannie dressed herself thoughtfully, looking again at the dress she had worn to Almack's last night, which Mary had hung up carefully in the dressing room. She had left the beautiful garment in a tangle about her feet when she stepped out of it last night. "I have become quite dissipated with all this rare living, Tom," she excused herself as she dressed.

Her collection of dresses was truly meager and looked especially sparse hanging in the generous dressing room. She contemplated the evening to come at the theater and looked about her for something appropriate.

"What does one wear to a character assassination?" she asked herself as she fingered one dress and then another. "I dare not wear the captain's silk again, at least not so soon. There is always my gray silk." She held it out. "We are such friends, but no one here knows that."

Jeannie traced her finger over the plain neckline. Perhaps a new collar and a little gathering of flowers at the neck would make all the difference. But that would only declare her to be a complete dowd. She had noticed no one at Almack's last night wore anything remotely resembling a collar, lace or otherwise. It was all décolletage and diamonds. Jeannie looked down at her own décolletage and sighed. "Hopeless, hopeless."

She let go of her gray dress and leaned against the door. "It is a lowering thought, Tom," she whispered. "Why did I ever say such things to Beau Brummell?"

Jeannie gave her head a toss. Such reflection was only slipping her deeper into melancholy, and she was grateful when a knock at the door interrupted her unprofitable thoughts.

"Mrs. McVinnie, I say, Mrs. McVinnie." It was Edward. "Are you about yet? Uncle Summers has given me a commission."

Jeannie patted her hair into place and opened the door. Edward stood before her, dressed in nankeen breeches and coat, his guidebook tucked under his arm, his hair still wet from a good combing. She pulled him into the room. "No elephants, I trust?"

Edward peered at her and permitted himself a smile. "Not a bit of it," he declared. "I am to direct you to Amalie's on Bond Street to pick up some foo-fra for Larinda." He jingled some coins in his pocket. "Uncle Summers says we are to take a hansom cab."

"That is by far too expensive," Jeannie said as she settled her chipstraw bonnet on her curls and tied the bow under one ear. "We will go by hackney."

Edward shook his head. "I dare not, Mrs. McVinnie. The captain told me that if you were to say that, I was to ignore you."

She laughed and fluffed out the bow. "Very well, Edward, if he insists that we go in style, we can only be grateful it is his money."

Edward allowed her only the briefest stop in the breakfast room for tea and toast and then led her into the bright blue of a March morning. He hailed a hansom cab and gave directions.

Jeannie settled herself among the cushions. "That was well done, Edward," she said.

"I used to be afraid of them," he confided, and then blushed.

She patted his knee and cast her eyes upon the morning scene. A sedan chair, borne by two servants, swayed gently on its long poles, while a querulous voice from within demanded to know where they had learned to drive. Jeannie smiled. Her attention was drawn to a grinder man with a hunched back, who had set up shop on the street corner and brandished his knives at the urchins who capered about him, trying to touch his hump for luck.

And there was a pie man, talking to himself as he walked along under the smell of hot mincemeat and rum. Edward watched him too, leaning out of the carriage.

"Don't you do it, Edward," she admonished as they passed right by the pie man and the fragrant temptation balanced on his head.

Edward only grinned at her and ducked back inside. "I would have liked some mincemeat," he said, his tone suddenly wistful. "But Aunt Agatha swears it is troublesome for my digestion."

"Your digestion," Jeannie declared. "I think there is not a subject less troublesome to young boys."

Edward nodded. "So I told Aunt Agatha once, but she reminded me that I am delicate."

Jeannie shook her head. "No one who rides an elephant is delicate, Edward."

He looked doubtful. "But Aunt says—"

"Perhaps your aunt is wrong," Jeannie said quietly. "And she could be wrong about your headaches, too."

His eyes brightened. "Do you know, Jeannie? I have not had a headache since you came, I do believe." He put his hand to his mouth. "I should have called you Mrs. McVinnie."

She touched his knee again. "I think you should call me Jeannie. No headaches, eh? I am good luck to you, laddie, if to no one else."

The hansom cab deposited them on Bond Street in front of Amalie's, a plain storefront with the name in discreet gilt letters over the door.

"I do not think we could afford such a place, Tom," Jeannie said softly as she eyed the cool gray stone exterior.

"Beg pardon," Edward asked.

She touched his shoulder. "It is nothing, laddie. I talk to myself."

They went inside to the gentle tinkling of a bell that summoned a well-dressed woman from an inner room. The woman—it could only have been the modiste—was dressed all in black, with a white lace cap set upon black hair and a lace fichu about her shoulders. She looked Jeannie up and down seemingly without moving her eyes.

"Yes?" she inquired in cultured tones, and that one word seemed to ask volumes about Jeannie's ancestry, aspirations, and the relative value of the clothes she stood in.

Jeannie twined her fingers in her plaid cloak. "I am here to collect a package for Lady Agatha Smeath, aunt and guardian of Larinda Summers."

"And you are?"

"Jeannie McVinnie," she said, wishing for the second time in as many days that she did not sound so Scottish, so "dratted plaid," as Tom joked to her once.

In a blink of her eyes, the guarded look left the woman's face. She did not go so far as to smile, but her expression ameliorated to a marked degree. She clapped her hands, and Jeannie stared. Other women came silently out from behind a curtain, seamstresses and a linen draper with a bolt of clothes in his gloved hands. Without a word, they regarded her and then vanished as quickly as they had appeared.

Jeannie stared after them. "Edward, what on earth?" she whispered.

The boy only shrugged, his eyes as big as hers.

Without a word, the woman disappeared behind the curtain and then returned with a small package. She gave it to Jeannie and patted her hand. "Did it fit?" she asked.

"Did what . . ." Jeannie began, and then she understood. This must be the modiste that Captain Summers had bullied so relentlessly yesterday. She nodded. "Very well, thank you. I have never had a lovelier dress."

The modiste inclined her head in a grand gesture worthy of Lady Jersey herself. "Captain Sir William Summers was most particular about that shade of blue. We will do better next time, Mrs. McVinnie," she assured Jeannie.

"Oh, I am sure that is not necessary," Jeannie said,

floundering about in a conversation she did not entirely comprehend.

"But it is, madam, and now that I have seen you, I understand," insisted the modiste. "I would never do anything less than my best for someone who risks life and limb, defending our shores from the machinations of that European tyrant."

The woman dabbed at her brimming eyes, and Jeannie sighed. The captain had most definitely been here, spreading his bewildering charm before him. The man has no scruples at all, she thought as she smiled and fled the shop, Edward close upon her heels.

So this is Bond Street, she thought as she looked about her, tucked her arm through Edward's, and joined the other shoppers and strollers, each one more exquisite than the one before. Dandies on the strut, their eyes on one another, comparing seals and fobs, neckcloths and boot blacking, moved in stately progress along the busy sidewalk, stopping here and there and gazing in a window, seeking no more than their precious reflection. Young women were abroad, too, followed closely by footmen and maids. They minced along the broad walkway, eyes straight ahead or primly cast down, performing miracles of flirtation with the toss of a head, a flick of the parasol.

Jeannie's fingers strayed to the ribbon of the bonnet she had considered so stylish only that morning, wondering, in the midst of all this finery, why she had thought herself well-turned-out when she left Wendover Square. I have nothing to recommend me except my impudence, she thought.

"Come, Edward, let us hurry," she whispered to her companion.

But Edward was staring about him, even as she. He gaped after a tulip so encumbered by his high neckcloth that he could not turn his head, and goggled at another spring of fashion in pantaloons so tight that Jeannie could only blush and look away.

Edward tugged at her sleeve. "Jeannie, if I must look like that when I am older, I will definitely run away to sea and wear canvas trousers like Uncle Summers."

Jeannie smiled. "I am sure when you are old enough, all this will not seem silly."

He looked doubtful of this wisdom. Edward stopped and leaned against a wall as he opened his guidebook. He studied it a few minutes, turning the pages, until his eyes brightened. "Did you not wish to do some shopping?" he asked.

Jeannie looked about her at the shops, each as elegant as the one they had lately quitted. "Yes, I do," she said slowly, "but I do not think Bond Street will be kind to my pocketbook."

He jabbed his finger at the guidebook and Jeannie peered over his shoulder. " 'The Pantheon Bazaar,' " she quoted, following his finger, " 'where all of London shops. No prices cheaper in any part of the realm.' Lead on, Edward."

"Although I cannot imagine it could be cheaper than India," Jeannie mused as they shook the dust of Bond Street off their shoes and walked toward the bazaar on Oxford Street.

"India?" Edward asked, his eyes wide, his tone reverential. "Were you actually there?"

"Goodness, laddie, London is the farthest south I have ever ventured," she stated in firm tones, "and I don't mean to change that. No, I have two brothers there who are great letter-writers. One is an official in the East India Company and the other is a major in the army."

"I truly do want to run off to sea," Edward confided. "Aunt Agatha doesn't like to talk about it, but Papa said once that Uncle Summers did just that. I would like to."

She smiled. "It is a hard life, laddie."

"I know. But still, I would like it above anything."

Jeannie made no reply, but touched his shoulder as they hurried along. He took her hand and they walked in amiable companionship to the Pantheon Bazaar, which was, as the guidebook pointed out helpfully, impossible to miss. Shoppers, many of them women, all of them intent and purposeful, streamed into the massive building. As near as Jeannie could tell, no one came out.

"Goodness," she said, "I had no idea."

They came closer, and were soon swept into the building by the swarm behind them. Jeannie clung to Edward's hand, determined that neither of them would disappear, never to be heard from again. She thought briefly of Galen's housekeeper in Kirkcudbright and knew that the enormity, nay, the responsibility, of shopping here would reduce even Mrs. MacDonald to silence.

"Do you know what you are after?" Edward shouted so he could be heard above the buzz of ladies about him.

"Merely a shawl to wear with my gray dress," she shouted back. "Oh, do hang on, Edward!"

She found the shawl, a rose-colored bit of finery at a ridiculously cheap price, even by Kirkcudbright standards. She also found a pair of silk stockings, a bottle of rosewater for Larinda, and a tortoiseshell comb for Lady Smeath. I will make them all farewell gifts, she thought. A foray deeper into the building produced a length of toweling that Edward frowned over when she pounced upon it.

" 'Tis for a towel doll," she explained. "Something for Clare. I don't know a Scottish child without one."

"She doesn't have a doll," Edward said.

"I know, laddie, I know."

She was st anding still then, trying to think what to get the captain, when Edward jostled her arm.

"Jeannie, do you know those ladies?" he asked. "They have been staring at you this last minute and more. And then they giggle. I don't think that is at all the thing."

She looked where he gestured with his hand, and felt a small tug at her heart. The two young ladies had formed part of the group about Larinda last night at Almack's. When they realized she was watching them, they put their heads together, laughed, and then drifted into the crowd.

Larinda has obviously been busy, Jeannie thought, and so, I am sure, has Beau Brummell. Does everyone in this dreadful town plan to attend the theater tonight?

Jeannie gave a small shake to her shoulders and turned back to the matter at hand. "I could get him a hairbrush," she said to Edward.

"He has hairbrushes, and besides, Jeannie, I am not sure he wants to be reminded about his hair."

She laughed in spite of her discomfort. "How true! Some bay rum, then?"

Edward shook his head again. "He already has quarts and quarts of the stuff."

"What, then? Oh, look, Edward!"

She led him to a table piled high with scarves, and began rummaging through them for the scarf that was precisely the right shade of green.

"I don't know about that," Edward said doubtfully.

"It must be cold on the blockade, I think. Ah!" Jeannie pulled out a cashmere scarf of deep green and rubbed it against her cheek. "This will do." She dug a little deeper and extracted another one, this a bluish gray. "This will be yours, Edward, when you are someday on the service of his majesty aboard a ship of the line in the Baltic."

Edward shook his head. "Aunt Agatha would never permit it."

"Well, then, at Oxford or Cambridge. And don't shake your head over that!"

They were headed for the exit, clutching Jeannie's treasures, when Edward stopped before a counter of gloves. He considered the situation at length, stalking about the pile, while Jeannie stood by in silent amusement. He found a pair of pearl-gray gloves.

"I thought maybe something for Larinda," he said, his voice gruff, as if he expected her to laugh at him. "I don't know that I like her much lately, but she is my sister and she used to be a bit of fun in Suffolk before she started wearing her skirts long and pinning up her hair. It could be that there is hope for her," he concluded generously as he counted out the money and paid the shop girl.

"I think it quite admirable," Jeannie agreed.

Her good humor deserted her outside the Pantheon. There, sniffing delicately among the fresh flowers and setting aside rose after rose, was Beau Brummell. He was dressed impeccably in blue Bath superfine and buff trousers without a crease, his neckcloth of an impossible white. His hair was as carefully curled as last night and he smelled better than the roses. He smiled when he saw her, and tipped his hat, his glance taking in Edward, who stared back, fascinated. The ladies seated in the barouche behind him looked her up and down and then glanced at each other.

"Advise me, Mrs. McVinnie," he said as he looked from rose to rose. "Which will it be?" When she hesitated, he came closer. "I await your decision," he said, "or will you declare this too frivolous? I have been here these ten minutes and more, trying to decide."

The laughter in his eyes surprised her at first, because it seemed to be directed at himself. His tone was self-deprecating, even as his eyes twinkled. She had to smile in return, despite her misgivings. She thought for a fleeting second of the grasshopper fiddling away in Aesop's tale, and picked a red rose without any hesitation. She took a deep breath, broke off the stem, and carefully placed it in his lapel.

"That will do, sir," she said when she stepped back.

He looked down at the rose. "Everyone in London, my dear, who is anyone in London, would have chosen the white. That is my color."

"Perhaps it is time you tried something new, Mr. Brummell," she replied, and the ladies gasped. "Ha' ye nae head of Bobby Burns, sir?" she asked in her deepest brogue. "Bobby and his red, red rose?"

He nodded and smiled. "And that is what I get for asking a Scot to select my rose? Even if all of London would take issue with you?"

"Even so, sir," she declared. I have gone too far to back down now, she thought, raising her chin and narrowing her eyes in that expression that used to put Tom in a quake. "And as for everyone in London, I do not care."

Brummell regarded her in silence for a moment. She watched as his hand went to the quizzing glass that dangled on its ribbon. And now he will stare me out of contenance in front of all these people. Well, get it over with, man, and let me go home to Kirkcudbrightshire. She looked him right in the eye.

Brummell fingered the ribbon and then twirled it around his finger. "Can we look for you at the theater this evening, Mrs. McVinnie?"

She let out the breath she had been holding and her evil genius spurred her on. "So many have taken such an interest in my entertainment habits, sir, but, yes, you may depend upon it. You see, I have never been to a play before and I mean to enjoy myself tonight."

He clucked his tongue. "Never to a play, Mrs. McVinnie?"

Her eyes laughed back at him, daring him. "Never, sir! Can you imagine a more provincial dowd?" She looked around for Edward, who clutched Larinda's gloves and stared at her. "Come, Edward, we have other things to do, and we should not intrude upon this man's valuable time. Please excuse us, sir, but we have to find ourselves a hackney."

"A hackney, Mrs. McVinnie?" The ribbon spun faster.

"Yes, Mr. Brummell. It is a wonderful economy. Good day, sir."

With another nod in his general direction, Jeannie turned on her heel and took Edward by the arm. I will not look back, she told herself, else I turn into a pillar of salt. She knew without seeing them that many pairs of eyes bored into her back, but she resisted the urge to gather up her skirts and run. Damn him, she thought suddenly. I gave that dreadful man every opportunity to hand me a set-down right here. He must be reserving it for the theater.

Edward hurried to keep up with her. She stopped when they turned the corner and he caught up. "Jeannie, was that Beau Brummell?" he asked, out of breath. "The Beau Brummell? The man at the menagerie?"

She nodded to all his questions and allowed misery to wash over her. "Yes, Edward, the very man I scolded so roundly in the menagerie. Dear me!"

She gathered her packages close to her again and started walking. Her mind raced ahead a hundred miles an hour, rehearsing and rehearsing all the things she should have said, and could have said, but didn't. I must be the most foolish woman who ever drew breath, she scolded herself. When I am home again before my peat fire, I will resolve never to attempt a joke again, practical or otherwise. I will be sensible and astute beyond my years and never again will I venture any farther south than York. No, Carlyle.

Perfect in her misery, Jeannie scarcely felt the slight tug upon her wrist. She pulled herself out of her deep revery in time to watch a ragged boy running away from her, dodging through the crowds on the sidewalk.

She whirled around to Edward, but he dropped his guidebook and took out after the thief, waving his arms and shouting to attract attention. Jeannie stared down at her wrist. The thief had neatly cut her reticule handle, which dangled like an overlarge bracelet on her wrist.

She ran after Edward, stopping to pick up the guidebook and the gloves he had dropped in his precipitate pursuit. "Edward?" she called. "Edward? Do have a care, laddie!" But Edward had vanished down one of the narrow side streets and the crowd had closed behind him.

Jeannie thought of Captain Summers and shuddered. He had been so nice about the elephant yesterday. Whatever would he say when she told him that the fifth Marquess of Taneystone had been set upon in a dark alley by a cornered cutpurse, and was probably lying there even now, a knife up under his ribs? She ran faster, fighting the desire to fling aside her parcels and really tear out.

The alley she turned into was narrow and overhung with the upper stories of ancient buildings that appeared to be standing only by the grace of God and the fact that a strong wind had not passed that way since the Great Fire, at least. And there were other folk in the alley, slim, shrinking figures who hugged the shadows and eyed her parcels, talking among themselves. Grimly she clung to the purchases and refused to be cowed.

When she despaired that this was the right side street, she saw Edward and the young cutpurse. Edward sat on top of the thief, who lay facedown in the dirt of the alley, saying dreadful things for one so young.

"Enough's enough, laddie," she said, and hurried forward.

Edward looked up at her and grinned. His nankeen breeches were torn at both knees and his coat was ripped under the arm, but that was nothing to the black eye that sprouted, even as she watched, horrified. Edward held up her reticule and gave it a triumphant shake.

"Thank the Lord," she said. "Edward, your eye!"

"It'll be a great shiner," he said. He tried to keep his voice matter-of-fact, but the excitement took over. "Jeannie, I have never had a black eye before. And, Jeannie, I have wanted one, truly I have!"

The boy pinned underneath Edward muttered something unintelligible.

Jeannie knelt beside him. "If Edward gets off you, will you go away?" she asked.

The thief stared at her. "You mean you won't sic the watch on me?"

Jeannie shook her head. "No," she said simply. "I expect ye are just hungry. Now, do ye promise? I'm asking in all sincerity, laddie."

The boy nodded, not taking his eyes from her face.

Jeannie stood up. "Very well, Edward. You may let him up." She took her torn reticule from Edward and put a handful of small coins on the ground beside the cutpurse. "We'll thank you not to trouble us further," she siad. "Come, Edward."

They started for the alley entrance, picking their way more

carefully this time through what looked and smelled like a century's accumulation of trash.

"Oh, laddie, this is not our neighborhood," Jeannie said. "And so close it is to Oxford Street and the bazaar? Do ye think fine folk like the Beau have ever been in such a place as this, I'm wondering?"

Edward shook his head and put out his hand to stop Jeannie. "I think we might be in more trouble," he said, his voice so low she had to incline her head to hear him. "Look there."

The entrance to the alley was blocked by a crowd of people, each as ragged at the cutpurse. Edward stopped moving, but Jeannie prodded him forward.

"Come on, Edward," she said. "We can only go forward under the guns."

No one yielded as they approached. Behind her, Jeannie heard the sounds of coins clinking together as if someone rolled them over and over in his hand. She sighed. "Oh, dear."

Before she could say anything more, the cutpurse shouldered past them and into the knot of hard-eyed men. "Give way, you blighters," he shouted as he shoved past. "Come on, give way for the gentry mort and cove. They haven't all day to lallygag with the likes of you."

Her heart in her mouth, Jeannie followed the thief and held tight to Edward, who had no difficulty keeping up with her. The crowd closed in behind them and she took a firmer grasp on her reticule.

And then they were in the street again. The cutpurse tipped his filthy hat to her. "Any other gentry mort would have screamed and I'd be on me way to VanDieman's Land." He turned to Edward. "Put a piece of beefsteak on it, governor, if ye have any," he said, and then blended back into the alley.

"Well, I never . . ." Jeannie began. "Edward, let us find a hackney before our luck runs out entirely."

Edward was silent for the better part of the return, resting his chin on his hand and gazing out the window. "Jeannie, I think Aunt Agatha will be disturbed by this."

It was a masterpiece of understatement, and if she had not been feeling the pangs of guilt, Jeannie would have laughed.

"And the captain," she said.

The thought reduced both of them to silence again.

Before either of them wished it, the hackney set them down

in Wendover Square. By the judicious application of spit to Jeannie's handkerchief, Edward had managed to remove some of the worst grime from his hands, but there was nothing that could be done about his torn breeches or his eye, which was, by now, swollen entirely shut.

"I don't remember when I ever saw a more impressive black eye," Jeannie said, unable to keep the awe out of her voice as he helped her down from the hackney and paid the driver.

Edward held the guidebook close to his chest and watched the coach drive away. "I did want to go to Astley's Amphitheater tomorrow," he said, speaking mostly to himself. "They have wild animals there, I am told."

Jeannie barely repressed a shudder. "And you would be eaten alive, and then where would we be? Come, laddie, and let us dance to the piper."

He took her hand. "Do you think Uncle Summers will fly into the boughs?"

She nodded. "I think that is a fair assumption, laddie."

Edward patted his guidebook. "Do you know, Wendover Square was so stuffy and dull before you came, Jeannie?"

Jeannie groaned, took a deep breath, and knocked on the door.

Wapping opened the door, and was bereft of speech. He stood ramrod-straight in the open doorway, opening and closing his mouth like one of Galen McVinnie's Highland trout, his eyes wide and staring.

His amazement lasted only a moment. He closed his mouth with an almost audible snap, cleared his throat a few times to remind himself that it was still there, and announced in booming tones to the hallway behind him, "Captain Sir William, the lost are found."

Edward sidled in closer to Jeannie and tightened his grip.

"It's about time," Summers said as he and Larinda came quickly into the entrance hall, closing the door to the sitting room behind him. He drew up short at the sight of Edward, and Larinda bumped into him.

Jeannie winced at the expression in his eyes. Any moment now he will yell, she thought, and I will disgrace myself forever by bursting into tears. She waited.

Worse than outrage was the total silence that reigned in the hall. The captain executed a remarkable recovery and walked around Edward, stopping in front of him, his hands clasped behind his back. "At least you are not blue," he said, his voice, to the untrained ear, almost affable. "And you do not smell like an elephant."

He permitted his gaze to fall upon Jeannie. "Ah, Mrs. McVinnie! How glad I am that we did not send Edward out this morning unattended and without any guidance." His tone had a decided edge to it. His eyes opened wider. "If it is not too, too much, may I ask, what has happened to the tidy fellow who left with you this morning?"

"There was a cutpurse, Uncle Summers," Edward explained, stepping forward. "And I gave chase."

"You never did," Larinda declared.

Edward squarred his shoulders. "Don't be hen-witted, Larry," he scolded. "I tackled him and sat upon him and twisted his leg until he gave back Jeannie's reticule." He looked at Jeannie for confirmation. "Didn't I?"

She placed her hands on his shoulders. "Indeed you did. Without your help, I would have lost all my earnings from whist last night."

Larinda rolled her eyes and clutched at her throat in remarkable imitation of her aunt, while Captain Summers set his lips in a tight line. "No need for die-away airs, Larinda," he said. "Would to God that you could play whist."

The familiar dancing light was back in his eyes as he shook his head. "Jeannie McVinnie, what are we going to do with the two of you?" he asked the wall beyond her shoulder.

"Actaully, sir, the cutpurse recommended some beefsteak," Edward offered helpfully.

"Did he?" asked the captain.

Edward nodded. "And he was most helpful in getting us through that rather seedy crowd that had gathered in the alley."

"The alley?"

"And probably because Jeannie was kind to him and gave him a handful of coins."

The captain stared at her. "You gave money to a thief? Why didn't you summon the watch?"

"I think he was only hungry," Jeannie said. She raised her chin and narrowed her eyes. "Captain, I know it was not to your liking—"

"Good God, woman! You could even now be bound for the Barbary Coast in a slave ship!"

Edward clapped his hands. "Now that would have been an adventure, Jeannie!"

"Edward," said the captain in an awful voice, "you will surrender that damned guidebook to me. At once!" he roared when Edward hesitated.

He grabbed the book and shook it under Jeannie's nose, speechless with some emotion that Jeannie couldn't understand.

But she wouldn't let it be. There was something about his fury that lit a spark in her own mind. "That's what comes from impressing seamen," she said quietly. "You can't bend everyone to your will, Captain."

"Edward, upstairs," he roared. "I'll deal with you later."

Jeannie stamped her foot. "Over my dead body!"

"Don't tempt me!"

"Oh," shouted Jeannie. "Don't you dare carry on like Lord Nelson! We are not much the worse for wear, and Edward is proud of that black eye."

"How dare you talk to me like that!" the captain raged.

"I'll talk to you any way I like, sir!" she shouted back.

Larinda gasped and hurried Edward toward the stairs.

"We didn't plan the things that happened!" Jeannie doubled up her hand into a fist and started toward the captain.

Captain Summers grabbed her wrist. He held her in a tight grip until he was breathing regularly again and the color had come back into his face. In another moment, he could command his voice.

"I suppose next you will be telling me what a fine time you had."

"Well, Edward did," Jeannie said calmly. She worked her wrist out of his grip. She wished he would not stand so close to her. She found herself resisting a curious urge to cast herself upon his chest and sob her heart out.

And that would never do. Don't be a fool, Jeannie, she told herself as she looked up at him. You only have to get through this evening and then you will be home.

The door to the sitting room opened. "I say, Sir William, what is going on?"

Grateful for an excuse to move away from the captain, Jeannie looked toward the sitting room door. The voice was familiar and sounded of moors and lochs. Tears started in her eyes. "Oh, never tell me . . ." she began, and then looked at Captain Summers. "Captain, who—"

"Larinda and I have been entertaining your company this hour and more, Mrs. McVinnie," the captain said, his voice calm again, the flash in his green eyes restored. He managed a small chuckle. "We can only make out one word in ten, but the fellow—and doesn't he look fine?—claims to be a close friend of your late husband's, and who am I to dispute him? Captain, I apologize for the disturbance."

" 'Tis nothing," came the cheerful voice again. Jeannie put her hand to her mouth, her eyes wide. "I'm used to Jeannie McVinnie and her crotchety ways."

Jeannie shoved her packages at the captain and ran to the sitting-room entrance, just as a soldier in the Dumfries Rifles uniform filled the doorway. "Bartley!" she exclaimed, and hurled herself into his open arms.

He grabbed her and whirled her about. "The verra same, ye bonnie lassie," he said when he set her down again. He cupped her chin in his big hands and put his face close to hers. "I'd have known that scolding tone anywhere. Thank the Lord ye nae hae changed!"

"God help us," said Captain Summers.

9

CAPTAIN Summers looked from one to the other. He walked to the window and stared out, as if seeking inspiration from the newly budding trees and afternoon sun. Jeannie watched him and felt instantly sorry for her outburst. Poor man, you walk back and forth from window to door as if you are still on your quarterdeck. Poor man. She sighed.

Bartley MacGregor, Captain Bartley MacGregor of the Dumfries Rifles, drew himself up to his full height. "I trust that little Jean has not been sae troublesome as I remember," he asked, his tone brotherly, his eyes twinkling.

"Probably much worse," said the captain slowly. "I believe I will retire and extract my gray hairs in the peace and quiet of my room."

"It's all in knowing how to handle her," Bartley explained patiently, as if he were speaking of a quarrelsome child. "I hae known the lassie since, Lord love us, Jeannie my pet, has it been since I sat behind ye in dame's school?"

She nodded. "And you cut off one of my braids!"

Larinda spoke from the doorway. "Oh, surely not!"

MacGregor looked around at her, his blue eyes large and innocent. " 'Twas a dare, lassie."

"No more than she deserved, I am sure," murmured Captain Summers.

Jeannie decided to be charitable and overlook the querulous tone of his voice. "And there I sat, with one pigtail," she said. "Have you no pity, sir?"

"None whatsoever," he replied, but the lurk of good humor was coming back into his voice. "Most of the men I command—even those impressed, my dear—have only one pigtail. It is more than sufficient."

With what she considered remarkable forbearance, Jeannie held her tongue. She turned back to Bartley MacGregor. "Bart, what brings you here? I cannot flatter myself to imagine that you would come all this way to London just to see me."

"Nae, lassie, even though I appreciate your regard, however fleeting. I shall speak the truth and shame the devil. We of the Sixteen and Seventeenth are only just back from Canada, and I thought to stop in Kirkcudbright." He stared at her with that wide-eyed look that brought back memories, and was making Larinda giggle. "And what should I find but the knocker quite vanished from Galen McVinnie's door and the house entirely shut up. My heart fain to breaking, I inquired at the greengrocers', and he told me that Galen was flaunting himself in Dumfries with the other lads of the Rifles."

Jeannie laughed out loud. "And probably planning his trout campaign, I have no doubt."

"Nae doubt at all, Jeannie, my light," said Bartley agreeably. "He told me you had gone to London to help out."

Captain Summers muttered something that no one chose to examine closely, and stalked back to the window.

"And we are on our way to Spain—this time all of us—so I thought I would hurry ahead. I am staying at Burton's in Oxford Street, where all good officers go, I am told." Bartley took Jeannie's hand in his and raised it to his lips. Larinda sighed and Jeannie barely repressed a smile as Captain MacGregor kissed her fingers. "And there I shall remain, for the space of only a day or two, until we embark for Spain again." He looked over at Captain Summers, his voice oddly stern after the light banter. "And by God, sir, we will go in the front door this time!"

Summers raised his hand, as if giving an imaginary toast. "Victorious war," he quoted, a smile of his own playing about his lips. " 'Ocean's of gore.' "

Bartely nodded and grinned. " 'Prizes galore. Beauty ashore.' I'll drink to that any day. I hope to see ye comfortably in the harbor of Lisbon and Oporto again, sir. Unlike some of my stamp, I like to know the navy is hanging about."

"Good of you, sir."

Jeannie smiled. "You already know how well I wish you."

Bartley's voice turned serious again. "We Dumfries lads have never taken to piping ourselves off a beach, Jean. I only wish that Tom were with us yet."

"So do I, Bart," she replied, and busied herself with a minute examination of the cuff of her sleeve.

The conversation flagged at that point, until Captain Summers picked it up in one deft swoop. "Now that you are here, you must take dinner with us tomorrow night," he said, smoothly stepping into the awkward space. "Unfortunately we are otherwise engaged tonight. We will see you tomorrow?"

"You will, Sir William," Bartley said.

"I'm sure Lady Smeath will echo my—"

The only echo from Lady Smeath was a shriek from upstairs.

* * *

Captain Summers set his lips in a tight line again. "I think that my dear sister has chanced upon Edward, her wandering nephew."

"It would seem that way," Bartley said. He flashed a grin at Jeannie. "A braw and bonnie lad, is young Edward. No skellum, he. We could find a place for him in the Rifles, Captain, if he gets an itchy foot."

Captain Summers was already across the room. He paused in the doorway, as if to speak, but shook his head and hurried up the stairs.

"Oh, dear, I am in such trouble," Jeannie said with a frown on her face.

"Jeannie! Surely the captain will overlook one small boy's adventures."

Jeannie unconsciously assumed the captain's quarterdeck pose and traveled to and from the window. "It is more that that, much more. And I owe it all to my own extravagant tongue, and . . ."

She stopped. Larinda was eyeing her from the doorway with an expression of ill-concealed satisfaction. Her smirk deepened into a smile, which she bestowed in equal proportions upon Jeannie and Captain MacGregor. Bartley grinned back at her, tucked his cocked hat firmly under his arm, and made for the door himself. He held out his hand to Larinda and bowed over it.

"Your servant, Miss Summers," he said, and swept his hat over his heart. He winked at Jeannie. "I'll see you tomorrow. Do try to stay out of daunting splore, Jeannie McVinnie, joy of my life," he said, and then he was gone. They listened to him whistling his way down the front steps.

Larinda waited until the front door closed behind him. "I wonder that anyone can understand him," she said, just loud enough for Jeannie to hear.

"It's not so hard, Larinda," Jeannie said in a voice equally quiet. "It only wants a bit of effort to understand someone else. That is all."

Larinda was silent. Jeannie went to the packages that the captain had dropped on the sofa. She found the bottle of rosewater and handed it to Larinda. "A going-away present from me," she said, her voice clear and her head high.

"I do not understand, Mrs. McVinnie," Larinda said, her eyes wide with surprise, that little half-smile lurking around her mouth.

"Let us not waste each other's time," Jeannie said. "I know full well that you have been actively campaigning among your friends for my removal, and I can only anticipate the treat in store for me this evening at the theater."

The hard light left Larinda's eyes for a moment, but only a moment. She came closer to Larinda. "Aunt Agatha and I—we had such great plans—and then Uncle Summers brings up this, this absurd idea of a Scottish nanny for me. How could I preserve any consequence at all, with a nobody—for that is what you are—a nobody trailing me about."

Jeannie took it without flinching. "Perhaps your uncle cares enough about you to see that you have a little badly needed guidance."

"My uncle cares nothing for anyone," she flung back at Jeannie.

"You are wrong, but I shall not convince you," Jeannie said, not raising her voice. "You must see this for yourself someday."

"Larinda, go to your room at once," said Captain Summers from the doorway. His voice was deadly quiet and his eyes gleamed like emerald chips.

Larinda faltered and started for the door. She stopped short when she heard footsteps on the stairs.

"I told you not to interfere, Agatha," said the captain without raising his voice or looking over his shoulder.

"I will spring to the defense of my niece," said Lady Smeath, who stormed into the room. "A fine lot of help you have been in the raising of these orphaned children."

"Be fair, Agatha, for once. Thanks to Napolean, when has my life been my own?" said the captain, following her into the room and shutting the door behind him with a decisive click. "Let's have it out, here and now."

Jeannie sat down in the chair he indicated. Her heart was in her mouth and she wanted nothing more than to leave the room, but she folded her hands together and was silent.

Lady Smeath took several agitated turns about the room and then she flung up her hands. "For years and years I have been planning Larinda's come-out—with George's entire approval, I might add, brother," she said, directing a look of venom at the captain. "It is a large enterprise to find a husband."

The captain went to stand beside Jeannie's chair, resting his hand along the back of it. "And did you not think that Mrs. McVinnie might have some skills along those lines that could be of some help?" he asked. "I realize that my original Miss McVinnie would have fallen short there, but what a happy chance that Mrs. McVinnie came along. I think she could advise Larinda in the getting of a husband." He smiled at her. "She seems to have done tolerably well, if reports serve."

Lady Smeath's face turned an ugly shade of red. "You cannot compare the situation, William, surely you cannot!" Her hands flailed about in the intensity of her agitation. "A Scottish nobody married to a captain in a provincial regiment? How dare you compare our circumstances?"

Captain Summers gripped both of his hands on the chair until the wood protested. "Cheeky of me, isn't it?" he agreed, the affability in his voice causing prickles to traverse Jeannie's spine. "I had thought men and women to be much alike when they fall in love, no matter what their station. But I bow to your better knowledge, Agatha." He shrugged. "To anyone's better knowledge, for that matter."

"A nobody and a nobody," Larinda said, joining her aunt in battle. "Uncle, you are absurd."

Jeannie felt her face go white. "He wasn't a nobody," she protested. "Don't say that. Pray don't wound me that way."

"Go to your room at once, Larinda," the captain snapped, his face a study in cold fury. "I won't have you speaking such impertinence of the dead."

Larinda burst into tears of rage. "And I won't have this woman tagging me about. You speak of impertinence. She is already the laugh of London for speaking so unwisely to Mr. Brummell. Would you have her ruin me, too?"

"I don't think she could, Larinda. Go, now, or I shall happily forget that I have a piece of paper telling me that I am both an officer and a gentleman."

Larinda sobbed and marched to the door. Jeannie rose quickly from her chair and picked up the package and the gloves Edward had purchased for her. She held them out to Larinda, who snatched them from her.

"Here is the parcel from Amalie's and these gloves are a gift from Edward. I suspect he is a trifle indisposed, or he would give them to you himself."

"Edward?" asked Larinda. "What on earth for?"

Jeannie opened the door for her. "I cannot imagine really, except that he holds you in regard, as a brother should." She tried to touch Larinda's shoulder, but the girl moved away. "It may not be the high kick of fashion to show fondness for someone as insignificant as a brother, but quite frankly, he can be such an asset in learning how to get along with opposite sex." She managed a crooked smile. "Thanks to my brothers, I could regard with equanimity hairs in the washing basin and boots to trip over in the dark." She reached out and grabbed hold of Larinda's sleeve for a touch. "No matter how large the enterprise, how grand the design, my dear, love does become a bit mundane, eventually, for nobodies and for the great of our society. Indeed, I suspect that is part of its charm."

It seemed to Jeannie that Larinda's expression softened for just a moment. She hesitated in the doorway, and then the moment passed and she was gone, running up the stairs, sobbing.

Captain Summers looked at her with an expression bordering on pride. "An admirable bit of plain-speaking, Jeannie my light," he said, "if I may quote the estimable Captain MacGregor?"

She said nothing.

Captain Summers stood by the door, a look on his face halfway between amusement and irritation. "Ah, now, quick steps on the floor above, and then bang goes the door. I begin to understand my niece, Mrs. McVinnie. Wretched child. It will be a wonder that anybody marries her." He turned to his sister. "We may have to up the ante and increase her marriage portion. A desperate measure, but what can one do?"

"Hush, Captain," Jeannie said. "These are trying times. Now if you will excuse me—"

"Not yet," Lady Smeath declared in round tones. "I have

only just come from my poor nephew's bed of pain, Mrs. McVinnie. It wrenches my heart to see him lying there, so still and white.''

"He will be recovered admirably by morning, Lady Smeath," Jeannie assured her. "And then, if I know anything about little boys, he will strut about and contend that it was forty thieves that set upon him in the dark alley."

Lady Smeath raised her lace handkerchief to her eyes. "You are perfectly heartless to tease me with this."

"Agatha," said Captain Summers in a threatening voice.

She ignored him and sobbed into her handkerchief. "And his heart is so feeble."

"There is nothing wrong with his heart," Jeannie said calmly. "Or his digestion. He is neither consumptive, nor feverish, nor given to choler. He is brave and forthright, and a valuable friend of mine already. If he is allowed to have his way, he will likely join the navy and serve His Majesty with distinction and verve, possibly like his uncle."

"My blushes, Mrs. McVinnie," said the uncle.

"Before I leave this house tomorrow, Lady Smeath, Edward and I will probably take ourselves one more lark, provided the captain will return the guidebook."

"Only if I am allowed to accompany this expedition."

"Very well, sir, if that is the condition," she replied, her chin up. "And now if you two will excuse me."

She went to the door and remembered the packages. She found the comb for Lady Smeath and handed it to her. "I wanted to give you some little something as a parting gift." She gave the green scarf to the captain. He accepted it with a smile.

"This is for those cold nights on the blockade, sir, when you are sitting in the foretop roost and humming your little waltzes from Almack's," she explained, her face, all but her lively eyes, absolutely serious.

"I will wear it next to my heart," he said, glancing at his sister. "I do have one, Agatha, despite popular rumor in this household."

She took the remaining packages and walked slowly upstairs. She paused at the door of her room, changed her mind, and went to Edward's room, knocking softly.

Pringle opened it. He motioned her in and Jeannie came on

tiptoe. Edward was sleeping soundly, a damp cloth over his eye.

"Poor laddie," she said. "Pringle, you should have seen him take out after that cutpurse."

"I can well imagine, Mrs. McVinnie. He reminds me more and more of his uncle."

Jeannie nodded. "I have the feeling that you have refurbished other black eyes."

"Among other things. It's all part of my job," he allowed. "A cold cloth does wonders, although we would be better served to wring it out with saltwater. But one cannot have everything in London."

"One cannot," Jeannie replied, her tone as serious as Pringle's.

After another moment of looking down at Edward, she went to the door, which Pringle held open for her. "As to the other matter, madam, it has been carried out—not without, I might add, the stiff objections of Lady Smeath's French cook. He does not understand, but then, what are we to expect of the French?"

"What, indeed?" Jeannie murmured.

In thoughtful silence she went to her room, kicked off her shoes, and spread out the toweling she had purchased for Clare. She found the little sewing kit she always carried with her, reminding herself that she should repack everything as soon as possible. She hung up the shawl she had purchased at the Pantheon Bazaar, noting as she did so that Mary must have sponged and pressed her gray dress. Oh, dear, she thought, this dress will do nothing but announce to the world that I am everything Larinda claims, a dowdy Scottish nursemaid who can only be understood one word in ten.

"And how could anyone say such things about you, Tom?" she asked herself out loud. "She never even knew you. Poor child."

But time was passing. She gave the dress a pat. "And I would gladly trip over your boots in the dark again, Tom," she said, and then closed the dressing-room door.

A few swift slips of her scissors turned the toweling into strips. Several neat rows of hand over hand stitches transformed the strips into a doll with arms and legs. Jeannie held it against cheek. It would be a softer treasure than the captain's glove.

She had not thought to purchase buttons. Jeannie went to the dressing room again and took two buttons off a dark-blue morning dress she had no plans to wear between now and her certain departure in the morning. The buttons were blue, and quite the right size for eyes. Humming to herself, Jeannie sewed them on firmly and snipped the thread.

A proper doll should have a bit of plaid about her, Jeannie thought. She had none except her cloak, and that was too dear to cut. Except . . . this was for Clare.

Jeannie went into the dressing room again and took a good look at the cloak, deciding after some thought that a little strip of plaid facing near the bottom of the hem would not be missed. In a moment she was hemming it carefully, and then draping it over the shoulder and under the arm of the towel dolly. She had no gold button to serve as a brooch, so she secured it at the shoulder with a pin. "Well, she is a doll a long way from home, and a pin will do in this foreign territory," Jeannie said under her breath.

She went quickly into the hall, hoping that no one was about, wishing to speak to no one. The upstairs maid dusting the painting by the stairs paid her no mind. She went to Clare's room and quietly opened the door.

Mary Bow sat by the fire, holding her hands out to it. She looked around when Jeannie came in and bobbed to her feet, remembering in time to put a finger to her lips.

"She's fair worn out, the little one is, Mrs. McVinnie," Mary whispered. "However that is, the captain said she was as good as gold at Lady Jersey's."

After a peek at the sleeping Clare, Mary closed the door to the nursery. "I was going to drink some tea," she said, indicating the pot by the fireplace. "Will you join me, Mrs. McVinnie?"

"With pleasure," Jeannie looked about her. "And has that dreadful nursery maid been turned off?"

"Oh, indeed," said Mary, her eyes widening. "And do you know, Captain Summers has put me in her place. I never dreamed of such a good thing, but there it is."

"An excellent choice," Jeannie said as she took the cup from Mary. "And the other one is gone."

Mary sat down next to Jeannie. "She thought to fuss a bit, but the captain just looked at her. You may have seen that stare."

"I have," Jeannie said, taking a slow, careful sip. "Mary, you will be such an improvement."

"I will strive in earnest," Mary said seriously, but her eyes twinkled. "Clare and I have an understanding already. And do you know, she said my name?"

"Bravo," Jeannie said. She touched Mary's arm. "How nice to know she will be left in good hands."

Mary searched her face, frowning. "You're not going anywhere, are you?" she asked.

Jeannie took another sip and then cradled the cup in her hands, enjoying the warmth. "Well, let us say I will likely be returning to Scotland quite soon."

"Homesickness," Mary asked.

"Oh, something like that," Jeannie replied. She hated to be evasive with Mary, but there was no point in letting the servants know of Larinda's malicious tongue and her own foolishness.

Mary nodded. "I have never had to worry about being homesick," she confided. "When you come from a workhouse, you don't long to be back in it."

Jeannie smiled and finished her tea in silence, watching the flames licking at the logs and grateful for the warmth. The afternoon had turned chilly. *Or perhaps I am feeling less sanguine than usual. And here I was so relieved at the thought of going back to Kirkcudbright.*

She set down the cup and picked up the towel doll. "Just a little something for Clare. I noticed that she did not have a doll, Mary, and every little girl should have one, I think."

"I never had a doll," Mary said, and there was something wistful in her voice that gave Jeannie's heart a twist. "But I did want one."

Jeannie went into the room. Clare still slept, her hair tangled about her face. *How long her lashes are,* Jeannie thought as she bent over the little bed, the doll in her hand. *No, I suppose she does not look like the captain.* She kissed Clare's cheek, and the little one stirred but did not waken. Close to tears, Jeannie tucked the doll in the crook of Clare's arm, arranging the little plaid and pushing in the pin firmly.

She straightened up and watched Clare another moment. "I wish," she said quietly. "Oh, I wish . . ."

Her thoughts were unprofitable, and she dismissed them. Galen would say that little in the world is served by dwelling upon it, she thought. It only leads to megrims of the worst sort.

"And I have had enough of those for a regiment," she said out loud.

Mary was unpacking her few belongings when she came into the sitting room again. Jeannie whispered good day and hurried out the door, mindful only of getting back to her own room. She was still absurdly close to tears and she didn't really know why.

The upstairs maid was coming out of her room. She closed the door behind her and came to Jeannie, barely able to contain her excitement.

"Mrs. McVinnie! Mrs. McVinnie! It is beautiful! Oh, it just came."

"Whatever are you talking about?" Jeannie said as she opened the door to her room and gasped out loud.

Lying on the bed was another dress, a dress for the theater, a dress of deepest emerald, cut scandalously low across the bodice. On legs that felt rubbery, she came closer and touched the beautiful garment, admiring the long, tight sleeves, the deep flounce, and the almost sinful softness of the velvet. She ran her hand along the grain of the fabric, knowing in her heart of hearts that even if there were other dresses like this in her life, there would never be one this magnificent.

There was nothing ostentatious about it, nothing showy that would embarrass her. It was a dress of impeccable quality, and something more. She sat down beside it on the bed. The woman wearing this dress would know without any doubt that she was loved.

Jeannie blinked. Never before had such an odd notion flitted through her practical brain. She waved her hand in front of her eyes, as if to brush away some silliness. She giggled and closed her eyes, covered her face with her hands, and counted slowly to ten. She opened one eye and then the other and laughed out loud. The dress was still there. Next you will pinch yourself, she thought.

As she sat there, scarcely daring to breathe, a second thought washed over her like a wave over a figurehead. I can't possibly accept this dress. I daren't. She looked through the open door and into the dressing room, where her gray dress hung and suffered dreadfully by comparison. Jeannie sighed and fingered the green velvet again. In this dress, she thought, I would have a little more heart tonight. She put her hand to her mouth to smother a laugh. My goodness, my heart will be bared for everyone to see in this dress.

But it would never do, and she knew it. "I must find the captain," she told herself in the mirror, wondering for only a moment at her heightened color and the unmistakable sparkle in her eyes. He will simply have to understand that I couldn't possibly accept this. Oh, dear, I hope he doesn't give me that stare.

She went into the hall after one last look back at the dress. She tiptoed down the hall, wondering, as she did so, why she did so, and tapped on the captain's door. He opened it, and she burst into tears.

"Good God, Jeannie, whatever is the matter?"

Her face red and humiliated, she could only shake her head, stand in front of him, and sob. Without a word, he wrapped his arms around her tight and just held her. She cried and cried and he did not flinch or try to draw away or do anything but rub her back and then press her face gently into his shirtfront, which was rapidly becoming quite damp. She cried until there was not a tear left in her entire body, and then she rested her head quietly against his chest and listened to the steadiness of his heartbeat.

When she was silent finally, except for hiccups, he took her by the shoulders and held her away from him.

"What, doesn't it fit?" he asked.

She stared at him and then managed a watery chuckle. She sniffed and he gave over his handkerchief. She blew her nose obligingly and wiped her tears.

"I'm sorry," she said. "That was silly of me."

"I suppose you've come to tell me that you can't possibly accept such a dress."

She nodded. "Something very like that."

Without a word, he took her by the hand and walked her to

the stairs, where he sat down and patted the tread beside him. She sat, not daring to look at him.

But the captain wasn't look at her, but down at his hands. "Do you know, Jeannie, I have something of a reputation in the Channel Fleet. It's a chuckle-headed thing, I suppose, but there you are."

Mystified, she tilted her head toward him. There was nothing but kindness in his eyes—no quarterdeck scowl, no look of a man counting to ten and still angry. She relaxed and leaned against the railing.

"I've been known—when there's time, of course—to put on my best uniform before sailing into a fight. There's something so insolent about dressing out in silk stockings and white breeches, my best sword just so, my Knight of the Bath star polished to a fare-thee-well." He smiled down at his hands. "I supose it makes me feel brave, Jeannie, for I am not a brave man."

"But, Captain," she protested, "such a dress!"

"Made completely to my specifications, I might add, and don't I have excellent taste! Who would have thought it? Not I, surely." He took her hand in his, kissed it, and placed it back on her knee. " 'I want something totally remarkable for a redheaded lady,' I told them at Amalie's. 'Something so beyond the ordinary that everyone in the theater will notice.' "

Jeannie smiled and dabbed at her eyes again. "It is so kind of you."

He looked about him in all directions and put his finger to her lips. "Don't spread the word about, Jeannie," he whispered. "I have a reputation to maintain."

She laughed out loud. "Very well, sir. I will wear that 'totally remarkable' dress into battle tonight and pile my hair up high and look like Boadicea at the head of her charioteers."

"At least that. After all, I am certain Daniel did not set foot into the lions' den wrapped in a Turkish towel. Which reminds me, somehow. Don't move."

He got up and hurried to his room, coming back in a moment with a small canvas bag, which he dropped in her lap. She pulled apart the leather ties and drew out a necklace unlike any other she had ever imagined, green and square-cut, with a startling flaw like a wound, running through it. Her eyes widened and she sucked in her breath.

"Will," she breathed, not taking her eye from the single stone that blazed back at her. "What is it?"

He didn't answer. She looked at him, impatient for a reply, and saw a peculiar light in his eyes. "What is it?" she prompted him again.

"You called me Will," he said simply.

"Oh, dear," she replied. "That was vastly impertinent. Do forgive me. I suppose I was carried away by this pretty thing."

"No. No. I like it." He was looking at her then, but also beyond, at a time past or future she could not tell. "No one has ever given me a nickname, and I like it. Please call me Will from now on."

She considered the matter, a frown creasing her forehead. "William is too formal, and Willy too childish. Will has a certain resolution about it." She rolled her eyes. "Oh, dear, such a dreadful pun. I should be ashamed."

"Yes, you should," he agreed affably. "And I will call you Jeannie, which I have been doing anyway and which you have been so polite as to overlook. Are all Scottish lassies so well-mannered?"

"I am hardly a lassie anymore," she corrected him. "But, yes, of course we are all well-mannered."

"You are very much a lassie," he insisted, and then he just looked at her, the slight smile on his face breaking up the hard lines around his mouth and nose. "Even though you feel a century and more old."

She glanced at him quickly. "Yes, I do. How did you know?"

"Oh, I know." The smile was gone then. "Ask anyone who has been to war. Ah, well."

Jeannie waited, and then she waved the necklace in front of him. "What is it, please?"

He leaned close to her in conspiratorial fashion. "Treasure from the Spanish Main," he confided. "Truly, Jeannie," he said. "Don't look at me like my wits have gone wandering. It was from my very first prize ship, a Spanish merchantman

bound for the dons of Cádiz, God bless them. I was just a
midshipman then. I think I was fifteen. And didn't everyone
laugh when I insisted that I wanted that stone. But I did. It was
the most beautiful thing I had ever seen.''

He took it from her and held it up so it caught a little light
from the stairwell window. He ran his finger over the flaw that
cracked across its surface like a lightning bolt. ''A magnificent
stone. And do you know, the emerald is the only stone I know
that is enhanced by a flaw.''

The captain put it back in her open palm and curled her fingers
around it. ''I wore it in a little bag about my neck. I suppose
it became rather a good-luck piece for me. I hung on to it
through two years of Spanish captivity.'' Again his expression
deepened. ''Oh, God, I could have traded it for a crust of bread
on some days.'' The moment passed. ''When I was paroled
and commissioned lieutenant, I had the stone placed in that
setting.''

He leaned back and rested his elbow on the landing. ''George
and Agatha both teased me to have it valued and then shoved
into the family vault at Critchlow and Doubt's, but that seemed
a sad fate for something so extraordinary.''

Jeannie traced her finger around the square-cut stone. ''I
wonder that you did not make a present of it to the lady in
Oporto,'' she said, almost to herself.

He did not appear surprised at her words. ''I did consider
it, Jeannie, but . . . I don't know. It didn't seem right, for some
reason.''

''Someday, if you marry, you can give it to your wife,'' she
said.

''I expect I will. Someday. But tonight, it's yours,'' he said.
''If it hits you too low, I can take out a link or two. Nothing
simpler.'' The captain got to his feet and pulled her up to him.
''Of course, to do it justice, you must hold your head very
high.''

''I'll do that. Thank you, Captain.''

He raised his eyebrows.

''Will,'' she corrected, ''but only when we are alone. It still
seems so impertinent.''

''Much better. And now, my lady Jean, I recommend that
it is time to dress for dinner. I intend to look quite splendid

myself tonight, and as I am older than you and wanting in your high looks, it takes me a bit of time.'' He laughed. ''It takes time to arrange every lock to make it appear that I have more hair than I do.''

She waved him down the hall, but stood where she was a moment longer, gazing down at the magnificence that sparkled in her hand. She closed her fingers around it finally, a smile playing about her lips.

No matter what happens tonight, no matter how dreadful the set-down, I will have this to remember always. I will tell Galen about it later, when we will have it to warm ourselves this coming fall. And perhaps he will think me brave.

She dressed slowly, thoughtfully, giving herself a good wash first, wishing that she could once and for all scrub off the little light-brown freckles that dotted her shoulders and chest. She pulled on her silk stockings, appreciating the way her legs felt. ''This could become a sinfully extravagant habit,'' she said. ''How grateful I am there is no Pantheon Bazaar in Kirkcudbright.''

Mary and Clare knocked on the door and she ushered them in, sitting Clare, towel doll clutched tight, on her bed to watch, and to drape the emerald around the doll's neck, while Mary arranged her hair.

But it wasn't right. Even Mary could feel it. ''I don't know,'' she said doubtfully. ''You looked finer than sunrise with your hair up last night, but I don't know.''

Then Jeannie laughed softly to herself and took out all the pins. Swiftly she brushed her red hair until it crackled, and plaited one long braid down her back. She talked Clare's doll out of the necklace and secured it around her neck, and then stepped back for Mary's appraisal.

Mary observed her and then a smile came to her lips. ''I don't know why that looks perfectly right, but it does,'' she said slowly. ''You will be a true original tonight.'' She stepped back, too. ''And this dress is a perfect fit,'' she said as a puzzled look came into her eyes. ''Almost as if you were standing right next to the captain when he gave his orders.''

''Now that is food for thought,'' Jeannie declared. ''Oh, Mary, am I late for dinner again?''

''Not if you hurry. Come on, Clare.''

They descended the stairs, Mary clattering ahead with Clare, and the little girl looking back at Jeannie, her eyes bright with appreciation.

Jeannie looked down at herself and blushed. Goodness, Mrs. McVinnie, she scolded herself, only Tom has seen this much of you before. Goodness, she said again, I must remember not to bend over for any reason, and heaven help me if I should bob about! What can the captain have been thinking?

She descended the stairs and came face to face with a bouquet of red roses that filled the small table by the dining-room door. The others stood about, Larinda lovely in pink, but her eyes stormy, Lady Smeath dressed in fading beige that precisely matched her complexion, the captain entirely awe-inspiring. Only Edward was missing, and this did not surprise her.

But there was the bouquet. No one said anything as she moved slowly toward the table. There must have been fifty roses in the bowl, each one red and still flecked with droplets of water. The scent was almost overpowering.

And there, in the front of the arrangement, was a single white rose. Jeannie reached for the white card propped against the china bowl. With cold fingers, she picked it up.

" 'As fair art thou, my bonnie lass,' " she read out loud.

She turned the card over. There was nothing more. No signature, no indication of any kind where the flowers had come from.

But she knew.

Jeannie crumpled the card in her hand. The Beau was going to such lengths to ensure that this would be a memorable evening. How dare he?

She would have turned away, but the dining-room door opened and Wapping stepped out.

"Dinner is served, Lady Smeath, Sir William," he said.

10

DINNER began in silence so extraordinary that even Wapping permitted himself the luxury of surprise. The only inmate of the dining room who seemed at peace was the captain. After a long, slow wink at Jeannie, which sent the color rushing back into her cheeks, he addressed his attention to the soup.

The soup was removed in silence and replaced by the fish, and then Lady Smeath could stand it no longer.

"Those roses, Mrs. McVinnie," she ventured, her voice at the same time casual and remarkably contrived. "I wonder where they could have come from."

Jeannie smiled at Wapping, who set the fish in front of her. She held her silence until butler and footman left the room. "They are from Beau Brummell, I believe," she said calmly as she picked up her fork.

In the act of raising her glass to her lips, Lady Smeath sloshed wine on the tablecloth. Larinda choked and put her napkin to her lips.

"Bless me," said the captain. "I never imagined François to leave a bone in the sole, Larinda. Let me only speak to him and he will never dare again."

In a masterful moment, which Jeannie could only regard with awe and some admiration, Lady Smeath regained control of herself. "I wonder why he can have done such a thing."

"Indeed, yes," said the captain. "Bones in fish are discouraging to one's digestion."

Lady Smeath's fork grated on the plate. "Brother, you are driving me beyond distraction. You know I was referring to the Beau."

"And not the bone?" the captain inquired.

Jeannie fixed the captain with a stare that could melt rocks, and set down her fork. "I can only credit Mr. Brummell's behavior to two notions, my lady, neither of them palatable."

"Like the fish," Summers inserted.

With the greatest effort, Jeannie ignored him. "Either Mr. Brummell is playing a huge joke on someone in this room, likely me, or he plans to make wild, mad love to me at some later date."

Captain Summers grinned and reached for his wineglass. He raised it high and said, " 'Beauty ashore.' "

Jeannie smiled back and Lady Smeath cast down her napkin. "Brother, if I hear another shabby navy toast at this table . . ." she threatened.

"Not even 'Jollity and Mirth'?" he asked. "Larinda could use a dollop of jollity and mirth, my dear Agatha." He peered closer at his niece. "My dear, the bloom is quite gone from your cheeks. A dismal prospect, and the Season only just beginning."

"Captain," Jeannie reprimanded.

He grinned at Larinda and picked up his fork again.

Course followed dreary course. The food tasted worse than wood shavings to Jeannie, but she held her head high, ate what she could, and artfully rearranged the rest of it on her plate. The dining-room door was open, and she could smell the spicy scent of roses from the hall.

When the maid and footman removed the final course, Lady Smeath cleared her throat and tossed out another ball of conversation.

"I say, William, what are we seeing tonight at the theater?" she asked.

"I daresay, precisely what you want to," he said, and pushed his chair back a little. He put his hand to his forehead, and Jeannie was forcefully reminded of his tableau with Lady Jersey the night before. "Oh, but you are referring to the play, are you not? Silly of me. I believe it is *The Merchant of Venice.* By Shakespeare, Larinda."

"I know that, Uncle," she replied, her voice testy. Jeannie could scarcely blame her.

"I am relieved to hear it," he murmured, and took another sip of wine.

This man would drive the devil to an unnatural act, Jeannie

thought as she watched Captain Summers. No wonder Galen's Aunt Jeannie McVinnie had written such anguished letters home. The thought of Will Summers as a young boy made her close her eyes and bow her head in silent mirth.

She opened her eyes to see the captain watching her, a look of inquiry in his eyes. When she said nothing, he leaned toward her slightly. "You realize, I need hardly tell you, that it is the height of rudeness not to share a joke at table," he said.

She twinkled her eyes at him. "I will never tell, sir."

"Never?"

"Possibly at a later date," she amended. "Much later."

"When I am in my dotage?" he asked helpfully.

She laughed out loud, and was spared the daggers from Lady Smeath's eyes by the arrival of the sweet.

François himself bore it to the table. Lady Smeath started in surprised. He gazed back at the dowager with an expression of infinite sorrow, mingled with the acutest sort of shame that Jeannie had ever seen on a man's face. Jeannie looked closer. Were those tears standing on his lashes? Surely not.

He set the covered dish in front of Captain Summers. With a sigh he slowly removed the lid, averting his eyes as he did so, as if the sight was more than he could bear.

The captain gazed down at the uncovered, steaming mound before him with an expression on his face only just short of ecstatic. He looked around at Jeannie and blew her a kiss.

The footman approached and François leaned upon the fellow as if unable to sustain himself any longer. The footman experienced a momentary difficulty with a cough deep in his throat as he placed a silver dish beside the steaming pudding.

"I did not know if you liked strawberry jam, but it's a particular favorite of mine," Jeannie said.

"G—Godfrey, I've been known to eat strawberry jam from the jar with my fingers," he said, his tone reverential.

The footman, still struggling within himself, placed several plates beside the pudding. He handed Captain Summers a large spoon, stepped back until he was out of Lady Smeath's line of vision, and allowed an enormous grin to stretch from ear to ear.

Captain Summers cut into the pudding and sighed. He plopped a generous serving on the plate and looked at Lady Smeath. "This, my dear Agatha, is currant duff, the food of the gods, created by Lord Neptune himself. Please be the first. Of course, you must slather it with jam. Agatha?''

Summer's sister looked everywhere but at the plate he proffered her. "I wouldn't dream of putting that disgusting concoction on a fork, much less in my mouth," she declared. "And strawberry jam? At *dinner*?" She shuddered.

"Larinda?" he asked.

Larinda didn't even bother to reply. An angry flush was rising from her neck. She stared in fury at the opposite wall.

"Jeannie, surely you will join me," he asked.

"I will, sir, but only half that much, please."

He set the plate in front of him and spooned out a smaller slice, covering it with jam before setting it in front of her. Summers poured the remainder of the dish of jam onto his helping of currant duff as Lady Smeath looked on in wide-eyed horror and Larinda made helpless sounds in her throat. Summers turned around to François, who was listing heavily on the footman's shoulder.

"Magnificent, François. You are to be commended," he said. "I would kiss you on both cheeks, but then your face would be sticky. Please accept my undying gratitude. If you remove the remainder and keep it covered, it's just as good for breakfast. Cold."

François lurched back in dismay. With shaking hands, he covered the duff and whisked it off the table. He left the room, head down, shoulders bowed, a broken man.

"If he gives me notice tomorrow, brother, you will regret that you were ever born," said Lady Smeath.

Captain Summers appeared not to hear her. He ate his way steadily through the pudding, pausing only to scrape the last bit of jam from the dish. When he finished, he leaned back in satisfaction and ran his finger around the waistband of his breeches.

"That's quite the nicest thing anyone ever did for me," he said. "Did you put Pringle up to it?"

"I did." Jeannie pushed away her plate. "It's so filling, Captain."

He eyed the remainder on her plate, regarding it seriously for a moment, and then shook his head. "I daren't, do I?"

"Your credit is not that good at table presently," she said.

He nodded, sat a moment more in complacent introspection, and then tugged out his watch.

"Agatha, the curtain rises in less than one hour. I suggest that we adjourn to the theater."

Without a word, Agatha swept from the room, followed by Larinda. The captain watched them go and turned to Jeannie, the mocking glint gone from his eyes. He tipped a touch more wine in his glass, reached over, and did the same to Jeannie's. He rose to his feet and held up the glass. Jeannie did likewise.

"Victorious war," he said, and drank.

Jeannie followed suit.

"So much for my shabby navy toast," he said, his good humor unruffled. "How kind of them to leave the room so I could take this opportunity to tell you you look as fine as five pence."

"So do you, Captain."

He nodded.

'Will," she amended.

"Much better." He held out his arm to her. "Are we ready to brave the lion's den?"

She hesitated. "Sir, Will, I believe this concerns only me. I don't want to involve you in this silliness with Brummell."

He took her by the arm. "Jeannie, the first duty of a captain is to his ship and his men, even his impressed crew, I find myself . . ." He paused, as if wondering how to word it, "Vastly involved."

"I cannot imagine why," she said.

"Perhaps I'll tell you later, when you're in your dotage," he said inexplicably, and then tugged at her braid. "Very nice. Different, but nice. I think Bartley MacGregor would approve."

"Quite likely," Jeannie agreed as they walked slowly to the dining-room door. "I depend on him to propose at least once or twice in these next two weeks."

Captain Summers stopped in his tracks. "My G—gracious, Jeannie, you take that calmly!"

She nodded and repressed a little laugh. "It is only that he has done since we were both eighteen, Will. He proposed once a week, without fail, and once a week I turned him down."

"And Tom?"

Jeannie gazed thoughtfully at the opposite wall. "He only proposed once."

The captain was silent then. In the hallway he helped her with her cloak and then swung his own about his shoulders. Lady Smeath and Larinda had already adjourned to the carriage. Captain Summers tucked Jeannie's arm in his and walked her down the steps.

Jeannie hung back and for the smallest moment she leaned against the captain's shoulder. "Do you suppose this is how Marie Antoinette felt in the tumbril?" she asked, her voice an anxious whisper.

"I think not," he whispered back. "Jeannie, I will stand by you."

She looked up at him gratefully. "Do you know, sir, I do not understand why I was so afraid of you at first. You're quite the kindest man I ever met."

He put his finger to her lips. "Don't let it get about, Jeannie. I could never send a foretopman out on the yards if there were some suspicion that I was human."

The Theatre Royal on Catherine Street was ablaze with flambeaux as the Summers' carriage deposited them on the steps. A cold wind blew from the north and Jeannie clutched her cloak around her. She touched the captain's emerald necklace to reassure herself that it was still there, and traced her finger over the flaw. The stone was warm from her skin. Then how is it that my hands feel so cold? she thought.

She stood behind the captain, watching him as he helped Lady Taneystone and Larinda from the carriage. Wearing his hat and outlined against the lights from the theater, he looked enormously tall and remarkably capable. Jeannie sighed. A person wouldn't have to travel alone on the mail coach and afraid of everyone with someone like this close by. She gave herself a mental shake and patted the emerald one last time. And how odd it is, that a boy of fifteen should want such a gem and hang on to it through such desperate years. How tenacious you are, Will.

She found herself walking beside Larinda, who only glanced at her once but said nothing. They went up the steps in silence and into the light of many candles. So many people stood about in the lobby, some of them in naval dress like the captain. Others wore the elaborately frogged uniform of the Life Guards, and others the dashing short capes of the hussar regiments. Jeannie looked again at the captain, who was nodding and speaking to several of his brother naval officers.

She admired the dignity of navy-blue and white. Almost as elegant as Brummell, she thought, and then winced. Oh, why did I have to think of him? As she hung back from the Summers' party, she remembered again the red roses that mocked her from the dining-room entry hall. Why would he do such a thing? Men are so strange.

And then Captain Summers had her by the arm and was gently pulling her forward. She was introduced to Commodore Sir This, and Captain Lord That, and then the crowd parted and a large, red-faced man with elaborately powdered hair of the last century grasped her hand in both of his.

"Mrs. McVinnie," the captain was saying, "let me introduce to you Admiral Lord Charles Smeath, First Lord of the Admiralty, and . . . well, my lord, are we any actual relation? I am never sure of these connections."

Smeath rumbled out a laugh that sounded like a foghorn. Jeannie regarded him in fascination. "Damn me, William, your brother George used to say all the time that you might have been a ditch-delivered foundling, for all the attention you ever paid to family connections."

Summers flashed an angry red as the muscles in his cheek twitched.

"My, but that is a rude thing to say, my lord," Jeannie burst out. Her eyes grew wide and she slapped her hand over her mouth.

Captain Summers stared at her, his eyes as wide as hers. To her vast amazement—and the amazement of his fellow officers grouped around in shocked silence—he threw back his head and laughed. To her further amazement, he grabbed her head in both hands and planted a kiss on her forehead before he went off into another gust of laughter.

Lord Smeath stared. " 'Pon my soul," he said finally, "I believe this is a first." He looked around him at the other naval officers. "I say, has anyone else ever heard Summers laugh before?"

The other officers looked at one another and chuckled among themselves, but to Jeannie's ears it was a relieved sort of laughter. Lord Smeath joined in and then took Jeannie by the hand again.

Her face flaming red, Jeannie curtsied deeply and raised her eyes to his. "Forgive me, my lord," she said. "I have an imprudent tongue."

"Apology accepted," said Lord Smeath. He patted her cheek with his meaty hand. "I daresay, Sir William, that you never impressed a prettier one."

The captain had resumed control of himself again. "There is no question about that," he agreed, "even if she will spring to my defense like a lioness."

Lord Smeath fastened his eyes on her again, looking her over, staring at Summer's emerald and the cleavage of her dress. "And is she dependable, too?" he asked.

"Without question. I'd trust her with everything except a guidebook."

Lord Smeath looked at him in surprise and shook his head. "An excellent thing, then sir, an excellent thing. We may need you more on the water than in the theater, and soon. Come 'round to the Admiralty tomorrow."

"My lord?"

"It may be that you will put out to sea again sooner than any of us supposed. What, cat got your tongue, boy? I seem to recall in the not-so-distant past a fiery letter from the HMS *Venture*, asking me what in bloody hell I was doing sending you to London."

"My lord, I would never be so heedless of your station," Captain Summers protested.

It was Lord Charles' turn to laugh. "Belay it, my boy, and well away somewhere! I never read a letter so full of unspoken irritation, let us say. And who can blame you?" He leaned forward and whispered, "We know what Agatha Smeath is, do we not, and I would rather face a broadside than escort my sister-in-law to more than one party a year."

He patted Jeannie's hand and released it finally. "How lucky for me that Captain Summers was not stationed in the West Indies for Larinda's come-out, or the Baltic, God spare us! And now, sir, I bid you good evening. It is time to find my box and fall asleep."

With a nod to William Summers and another pat of Jeannie's cheek, Lord Charles turned and was gone, making his ponderous passage through the crowd which parted before him like the waters of the Red Sea under Moses' advice.

Lady Smeath waited for them by the stairs, her face full of

irritation. She waved a playbill at her brother-in-law. "It is too bad, William," she exclaimed, thrusting the paper under his nose. "Only look there. Some nobody from the provinces is playing Shylock. Look, brother. Edmund Kean! Whoever is he?"

"I am sure I do not know," said the captain. "Where is that dratted niece of mine, now? Ah, yes, Larinda, be so good as to join us."

Larinda left her circle of friends, who clustered about the stairway, their heads together, arms about one another's waists. Jeannie ignored them resolutely and fingered the captain's necklace.

Larinda hurried to her aunt's side and took the lady by the arm in her excitement. "You cannot imagine, Aunt Agatha," she said, her voice soft. "Everyone is buzzing with it. The Beau has arrived at the theater." She paused for dramatic effect. "And do you know what?"

"I feel endlessly confident that you will tell us," said the captain.

"Do you know, he is wearing a red rose in his lapel." She looked about her in triumph. "I wonder what it can mean. Don't you wonder, Mrs. McVinnie?"

Jeannie gritted her teeth and forced herself to smile back. "I cannot think of a topic that interests me so little as the color of a rose in a gentleman's lapel, Larinda. Surely everyone is not so deeply involved as you might think."

"Oh, but they are," Larinda contradicted. "Everyone is aching to discover what the Beau is up to."

The captain took Lady Smeath upon one arm and offered the other arm to Larinda. "Then perhaps, dear niece, it is a good thing that the unknown Edmund Kean is performing Skylock tonight. Obviously no one will be watching."

"I am convinced you are right," Lady Smeath said seriously as she made her stately way up the stairs. "This strange turn of events will occupy everyone's attention tonight."

Jeannie could only hold her tongue and walk in Lady Smeath's wake, eyes ahead, head high. The captain looked back at her once and winked. It's easy for you to be amused, she thought. You're not headed for social ruin. You weren't so unwise to criticize the entire dandy set to Beau Brummell's face.

She was acutely aware that she was being examined up and

down, even though no one stared at her. There were darting glances from behind fans and the casual perusal of men in high, starched collars who took her measure without appearing to go beyond a languid glance about at nothing in particular.

Well, sirs, let me give you something to look at. Jeannie removed her cloak and draped it over her arm. She gave the necklace one final pat and raised her chin up, secure in the knowledge that if Captain Summers thought she looked as fine as five pence, then she must. She did not look down at herself; such an expanse of bosom would only cause her to quake and blush, and be grateful that the Reverend McDougal of her Kirkcudbright parish church was not there to huff and puff and tell her, for the Lord's sake, to put some clothes on.

Her thoughts very much centered upon the things of the world, Jeannie followed the others into the dress circle, down the highly polished corridor, with the chandeliers winking and turning slightly from the motion of the strollers passing by, each candle a tiny star in a constellation. The paneled walls were dark w ith age and lined with pictures. Playwrights, poets, and players, Jeannie thought as she moved along.

The usher bowed them into the Marquess of Taneystone's box and left them to their own devices. Larinda went immediately to the front of the box, preening herself in studied unconcern where all could see her. Lady Smeath joined her there, nodding and bowing to her friends in other boxes, pointing out acquaintances of merit to Larinda.

"That gentleman there, Larinda," she said, and gestured with her chin, as she smiled at another. "Twenty thousand a year."

"But, Aunt Agatha, he is ancient," protested Larinda.

"Only thirty-four, if memory serves me," Agatha said as Captain Summers growled from the back of the box and slung off his cape.

Lady Smeath continued her perusal of the brightly lit theater. "And do you see that young man in those ridiculous biscuit-colored pantaloons?"

"He is so handsome," Larinda said.

"He is also heavily in debt. Avoid him as you would the plague."

Jeannie listened in silence, thinking of Tom, with no fortune to recommend him, army pay, and a small house in Kirkcudbright. It was always sufficient, wasn't it, Tom? she thought.

Lady Summers concluded her inspection of the evening's prospects finally and motioned to Jeannie to come forward. "Mrs. McVinnie, such a magnificent sight," she exclaimed, her mood expansive. "I cannot imagine its equal anywhere."

Jeannie approached the front of the box and looked across the other boxes, her heart captured by the winking diamonds in tiaras and necklaces, the shimmering dresses, the waistcoats of various patterns, crisscrossed by heavy gold fobs, seals, dangling monocles. The air was heavy with the odor of candle-wax. She looked down. Standing below in front of the orchestra were others, women in dresses that appeared molded to their legs, and men who jostled them and laughed, their eyes looking up to the tiers above, as if searching for a way out.

"The scaff and raff," Lady Summers said, following her glance. She made an impatient gesture with her hands. "I do not know why they are allowed in the theater. They can have no interest in the play."

And you do? Jeannie thought.

Larinda clutched her mother's arm. "Look there! To the royal box. Is that not the Prince himself? And there beside him, Brummell?"

Others had noticed the arrival of the Prince Regent and Mr. Brummell. For a moment, the audience hushed its chatter. There were ragged cheers from the pit and then the hubbub recommenced.

Jeannie looked where Larinda had gestured, in time to see Beau Brummell raise his quizzing glass to his eye and train it upon her. Her first instinct was to step back out of his range of vision, but she did not. Instead, she dropped a slight curtsy in the Beau's direction, and was immediately torn between amusement and exasperation at herself.

"Look, he sees me," Larinda declared. "Oh, and he does have a red rose in his lapel. How incredibly droll." She executed a deep curtsy and continued to look about. "Over there, do you see? Lord Wassom has removed his white rose from his coat. And Sir Peter Winthrop also!" She clasped her hands together. "I would almost be willing to wager that during the first intermission, they will bolt the theater in search of a red rose."

"They'll never find one," Captain Summers said from the

back of the box. He chuckled. "I vow that London's entire arsenal of red roses resides at Wendover Square now."

Jeannie scarcely heard him. She gazed at Prince George, marveling that a man of such immensity could stand there so precisely and look so perfectly at home. And why ever not? she thought. No one would dare snub this man, surely

Almost against her will, Jeannie directed another glance at Beau Brummell and discovered he still stood where she had last seen him, his glass trained upon her person. As she held her breath in amazement, the Beau removed his red rose from his lapel, kissed it, and replaced it. Other eyes turned toward the Taneystone box, and the conversation ebbed and flowed like waves on a beach. The Beau, unmindful of the chatter about him, nodded again in her direction and then turned his attention to some comment from the Prince Regent beside him.

Larinda darted to the door of the box and let herself out as Lady Smeath watched fondly.

"Surely she should not be out there by herself," Jeannie said.

Lady Smeath only smiled. "Larinda is a high-spirited girl." She snapped open her fan. "I am sure you cannot imagine such a thing, Mrs. McVinnie."

Jeannie leveled a stare of her own. "Madam, I have not always been a widow."

"Bravo," came the captain's voice from the shadows in the back of the box.

Lady Smeath ignored him, even though a high flush spread across her neck. She slammed the fan shut and sat down.

In another moment, just before the great chandeliers were slowly raised and the lights dimmed, Larinda swept back into the box. She sat down next to her aunt. "You cannot imagine it, Aunt," she said, her eyes dancing, "but on the curb below is Sir Peter Winthrop, rummaging through a poor flower girl's basket, tossing flowers right and left, searching in vain for a red rose. The man is practically in tears. And the flower girl is crying and tugging at his sleeve and calling upon any number of Hibernian saints to stop him."

"How sad," Jeannie murmured as she sat down.

Captain Summers came forward and dropped onto the settee beside her. "Sir Peter or the flower girl?" he asked.

"Oh, both," Jeannie said. She scooted herself forward to the edge of the settee and looked across at the royal box again. To her ever-enlarging surprise, Beau Brummell caught her eye again and blew her a kiss.

The captain watched the graceful gesture, humor evident in his eyes. "I wonder what he can be plotting."

"We will likely find out soon enough," Jeannie replied, her voice quiet. She leaned back then, focusing her attention on the stage, where the curtain was slowly pulling back. As Venice slowly revealed itself before her eyes, her uncertainty lessened. She thought again of the Beau and his red nose, and she began, unaccountably, to hope.

11

IN a shimmer of light and sound that reverberated like the tinkle of tiny bells, the chandelier rose higher and higher until the audience was in semidarkness. A young man, clad in the rich stuff of a Renaissance merchant, strolled down to the brightly burning footlights.

" 'In sooth, I know not why I am so sad,' " he said, and gestured toward his friend.

Jeannie sighed. Then you must be the veriest slow-top, she thought as she unconsciously edged closer to the captain.

" ' . . . and such a want-wit sadness makes me,
That I have much ado to know myself.' "

I thought I knew myself, Jeannie considered. I used to be sensible and modest, carefully planning out everything, mothering my father-in-law like an old-maid aunt. She glanced down at her bare expanse of bosom. Good Lord, I used to wear more than this to bed, she thought, even when I was married! She forced her attention back to the stage as Salarino took his turn.

" 'Your mind is tossing on the ocean . . . ' "

The captain sighed. With a quick look at his sharp profile,

Jeannie shoved aside her own dismals. She raised herself up and whispered in his ear. "Did you ever see two mopers worse than we?" she asked. "I sigh, and then you sigh, as we wish ourselves elsewhere."

He did not take his eyes from the stage as he reached for her hand and raised it to his lips. "Guilty as charged, madam," he said finally, "and yet . . ." He left the thought incomplete and then he released her hand. "Oh, I do not know about that."

Jeannie dragged her eyes toward the stage again. Likely this time tomorrow evening she would be on the mail coach again, headed north. Galen had pocketed the key to the house on McDermott Street, but he had left a spare with the Reverand McDougal. The reverend would protest and argue about her being alone, but he would let her in. And he would insist that she write to Galen, whose sense of honor would compel him to abandon trout streams far to the north and come to her rescue. *I cannot do that to so kind a man*, she thought. *Galen has as much need to forget as I.*

She would go instead to Edinburgh and drop herself on her sister's doorstep. Agnes would invite her to stay, of course, and all her nieces and nephews would be glad to see her, at least until the one whose bed she had appropriated began to chafe at sleeping on a pallet, or until Jeannie found herself standing by the window and wishing herself elsewhere. *But where would that be?* she asked herself as she stirred restlessly.

She knew the captain was looking at her. *He is probably examining me as he would a fretful child*, she thought. She sneaked a glance at his face. It was indistinct in the darkness, but she felt his breath on her cheek.

He said nothing, and she directed her gaze to the stage again. *I shall return to Scotland and set about the business of finding another husband*, she thought seriously. *I cannot continue to be a drain on Galen, no matter what Tom made him promise as he lay dying. And I cannot trespass on the good nature of my sister. She has enough to deal with. I cannot precisely recall how one goes about finding a husband, though, and even if I did, could I possibly get lucky twice in one lifetime?*

The captain nudged her out of her reverie. He leaned close and his gold epaulet tickled her shoulder. "You must tell me what you are thinking, my dear Mrs. McVinnie," he whispered.

"Your face is so set and your mouth all screwed to one side. It would appear that you are contemplating Dr. Guillotine's famous remedy for head lice."

She stifled a laugh and looked at Lady Smeath, who was engaged in a deep discussion with Larinda and paying no attention. "Very well, sir, since you asked. I was merely thinking that when I return to Scotland, I should seriously get down to business on this task of finding another husband."

The captain laughed out loud, and the man in the next box hissed at him to be silent.

He put his arm about her shoulder and drew her closer. "This is such an onerous task?"

"Well, yes, it is," she considered. His epaulet was tickling her collarbone now, and she wished he would back away a bit. "Not everyone wants a widow, even one who is—or at least has been thought—amiable. Now, if I had a fortune, Will, someone might be tempted. But as it is . . ." She was silent.

He patted her shoulder, and she thought he would relinquish his grip on her, but he did not. He whispered in her ear, his breath on her ear sending little shivers down her spine. "It shouldn't be so difficult, Jeannie," he said. "Do you know, one of the nicest things about you is that you always look as though you were possessed of a handy fortune." He was so close that she felt, rather than heard, his chuckle. "I suppose it is the way you hold your head, or maybe it is the look in your eyes. No, you shouldn't anticipate any trouble in Scotland, unless the men there are from another galaxy, and somehow, I doubt that."

He did release his hold on her then and she edged carefully away from him and sat on the edge of the settee, her arm resting on the railing. As she centered her attention on the stage once more, she could still feel his eyes boring into her back. She turned to him. "See here, Will, we had better enjoy this play. Only think how much you spent on tickets."

He threw back his head, stared at the ceiling above, and laughed. Lady Smeath glared at him and slapped his knee with her fan. "Brother, this is beyond enough," she hissed.

"I would be better," he whispered back, "but Mrs. McVinnie insists on being such a nonsensical wit-cracker."

"I am no such thing," she declared indignantly, and then

covered her mouth with her hand as the much put-upon man in the next box shook his fist. "Dear me," she said. "I am merely prudent, merely—"

"Scottish," the captain concluded.

Jeannie set her face resolutely toward the stage again, determined to enjoy herself. It would be scandalous to spend so much on tickets and then not enjoy anything. The ax will fall soon enough, she reminded herself grimly. Might as well kick up my heels while I can.

And then Scene Three began, and suddenly, in the space of only a few scant minutes, Jeannie knew that Captain Summers had been amply repaid for the price of admission. She watched, her mouth open, her eyes riveted to the stage below, as the unknown Mr. Kean from the provinces sidled and insinuated his way toward the footlights in his black gabardine robe and skullcap, and grasped an audience in his hands.

He spoke only a few lines before the audience finally became silent. There was a brief rustle of playbills as everyone took a glance to see who had become Shylock before their eyes, and then the audience was still, all discussion of fashion hushed, all ambitions and schemes thrust aside for the moment. When the curtain came down to signify the interval and the chandeliers were slowly lowered again, no one moved. No one spoke. There was only silence for a long space and then a wave of rhythmic applause, and more applause.

"Magnificent," the captain murmured. "I must confess that that display was almost worth my change of address to Wendover Square."

The applause roared on. People were standing now.

"Do you know, Jeannie, I am reminded of Trafalgar."

"What?" she asked, surprised out of her single-minded contemplation of the closed curtains.

"I was only a fourth lieutenant then, God bless me, and commanding on a lower gun deck, but something told me— God knows what—that we were into something very big. And so it was. So it is tonight." He leaned forward confidentially. "I do not think the unknown Mr. Kean will be unknown anymore, do you?"

She shook her head and looked across to the royal box, which swarmed with visitors. Captain Summers followed the direction of her gaze.

"I think that the Beau is too busy to enjoy a stroll around the dress circle right now."

"Just as well," Jeannie replied as she stood up. "I'm too busy to entertain him right now. Excuse me, please."

He stood and looked at her, a quizzical gleam in his green eyes. She offered him no explanation, and he asked for none.

"I'll be right back."

"I never doubted it," the captain replied. "You, madam, are made of stern stuff."

The stairway was crowded with playgoers buzzing about Mr. Kean, or else heatedly discussing the meaning of the red rose in Brummell's lapel. Her quick descent to the street level was unnoticed. Fools, Jeannie thought as she hurried across the wide lobby and onto Catherine Street.

The air was cool and a stiff wind blew from the river. Jeannie sniffed the fog-laden air and wrinkled her nose. Better not to speculate on the source of the odors that drifted about London like the eleventh plague of Egypt. As she looked about her, Jeannie thought briefly of Kirkcudbright, with its spanking breezes and crisp air.

She shook her head in dismay. The scene was much as Larinda had described it. A flower girl scrabbled about in the roadway, still gathering her flowers that Sir Peter Winthrop and his cronies had strewn about in their search for red roses.

Jeannie watched in surprise, wondering why it had taken her so long to collect such a few flowers. As she looked on, the flower girl patted the stones in front of her, and Jeannie realized she could not see.

Without a word, she crossed the flagstones to the gutter, crouched by the flower girl, and collected all the flowers that appeared to have any life in them. The girl stopped her restless search when she heard Jeannie, and then her face filled with fear. Jeannie touched her hand.

"No harm intended, my dear. It appears to me that you could use some help."

After a moment's consideration, the flower girl nodded and continued her blind search for her wares.

Jeannie quickly plucked up the flowers and replaced them in the basket. She got to her feet and brushed off her gown. "There, now. That should make it a little better," Jeannie said. She helped the flower girl to her feet and shook out her dress.

"Might this help, too?"

Jeannie looked up in surprise. Captain Summers stood on the curb with Larinda. He pressed a crown in the flower girl's palm.

The child felt the coin all over as wonderment grew on her face. "Mary and every saint bless you, sir," she said.

"I have need of it," the captain said quietly. He offered Jeannie his arm, and she took it. "We must return now, my very dear Mrs. McVinnie. Larinda here was anxious after you and wanted to assure herself that you had not bolted the theater. And here we came outside, to find that was precisely the case."

"Don't," said Larinda. Her expression was unreadable, remote. She started to say something else, but closed her mouth, turned about on the steps, and hurried inside the theater again. Captain Summers watched her go and then tucked Jeannie's arm tighter in his.

"Dare we hope—is it too much to ask—but did I just spy the slightest glimmer of uncertainty in fair Larinda's eyes?"

"Don't tease her, Will," Jeannie said. "No one ever declared that growing up was easy."

He turned to face her, both hands grasping her elbows. "And yet you will defend her, after she has been so rude."

"Of course." She raised her eyes to meet his. "Had you ever been seventeen, you might understand."

He said nothing for a moment, until she shivered in the cool air. "Ah, mercy," he exclaimed finally, the exasperation alive in his voice. "Children are wretched and should be drowned at birth, every last one! How grateful I am that, to my knowledge, I have none."

"There is Clare."

His frown only deepened. "So there is. But she is not my child."

Jeannie said nothing. The captain released his grip on her as his frown lifted, and he gave a self-conscious laugh. "Mrs. McVinnie, you are a wonder."

"No," she said baldly. "I am bossy and inclined to pick fights and say what I should not. I shall have to owe you that crown until tomorrow."

The captain shrugged. "Your credit is unimpeachable." He patted her hand, his good humor restored. "Besides, I happen to know that because you are Scot, you surely have not spent all of our whist earnings. There, now, that is what I was searching for.''

Jeannie couldn't help but smile at him. She turned back for another look at the flower girl, who was carefully wiping off each flower with the hem of her dress. ''Do you think she can find her way home?''

The captain nodded. ''I am sure of it, my dear. Come along and let us finally ring the curtain down on our own adventure. I weary of waiting for battle. The tubs are full now and the guns run out.'' He laughed. ''It remains only for the fuse to be lit.''

Larinda was already seated in the Taneystone box when they returned. She sat in the shadows this time, her face averted from the stage, engaged in an inward contemplation that the captain was kind enough to overlook as he walked past her to the front of the box.

The now-familiar grind of rope on pulley signified the raising of the chandeliers as the next act commenced and then the next. Friends came to the box during each interval, and with every knock on the door, Jeannie's heart thumped. She watched Beau Brummell as he still sat in the royal box with the Prince Regent, wondering if he enjoyed toying with her like a cat with a mouse. Only one interval remained now.

But then Portia was before them in her lawyer's robes. ''The quality of mercy is not strained,'' she began, her voice clear and striking the back walls of the Theatre Royal like daggers thudding into a target. Portia pled with the judges of Venice while Larinda sat in the rear of the box and sniffled.

''I definitely sense a change of heart coming on,'' the captain whispered as Portia cautioned Shylock to extract his pound of flesh and shed no blood in so doing. He took out his handkerchief and handed it behind him to Larinda.

Jeannie rested her elbows on the railing, hardly aware of him. She heard Larinda blow her nose vigorously and asked herself, Why is it that we are so often too late to be of any use?

It was the wrong thought. It was the same thought that teased her and pulled her back to last year and the dreadful knowledge that she would always be too late for Thomas McVinnie, even as Larinda's wisdom had come too late to spare Jeannie. Tears spilled down her cheeks, and she was grateful for the darkness.

The captain placed another handkerchief in her lap. ''I seldom travel without two,'' he whispered. He looked closer. ''But you do not cry for Bassanio and Portia, do you?''

Jeannie wiped her eyes and shook her head. Don't ask me, please. Then it would be too much.

He said nothing more, only grasped her hand and did not relinquish his hold on her until the chandelier lowered again and the interval was upon them.

Jeannie dabbed at her eyes one last time, smiling faintly to herself as she looked about the audience and observed the numbers of ladies clutching handkerchiefs. She brushed at the dress again where she had knelt in Catherine Street, took a deep breath, and turned to Larinda.

''My dear, shall we stroll about the dress circle? I know it is what you wish and I shan't be the guilty party in depriving you of your pleasure.''

Larinda started and then shook her head. ''No, Mrs. McVinnie, let us not.''

''But we must, Larinda,'' Jeannie reminded her gently. ''When one chooses to set something in motion, there is often no turning back.'' She smiled in a recollection. ''Indeed, my dear, I chose to play a little prank on Jeannie McVinnie's name, and you chose to ruin me. Let us play out our hand.''

Lady Smeath was the first out the door, her face a mask of worry where first there had been only triumph. Larinda, after a fleeting look at her uncle's face, followed her aunt.

Captain Summers offered Jeannie his arm again.

She shook her head. ''No. I should not involve you at all in this. I wouldn't wish to ruin your credit.''

He took her hand and placed in on her arm. ''Don't you know by now that I have no credit to ruin, and I don't give a tinker's damn anyway?''

''Why are you doing this?'' she asked simply.

''Because you are crew,'' he replied as promptly. ''I never run from a fight.''

They left the box and entered the dress circle. Despite all the people grouped about, eyeing the paintings and one another with a studied air of unconcern, the dress circle was amazingly silent. Jeannie's heart thudded in her bosom and she gripped the captain's sleeve.

He touched her hand. ''Gently on the gold leaf, my dear,''

he said. "Let us tack and wear about like normal folk. Moving targets are always harder to hit."

She smiled because he expected it of her.

"We could discuss the weather, Mrs. McVinnie," he said, his tone conversational, "but I prefer to consider tomorrow's final excursion, which you have promised Edward. I recommend a trip to the Deptford Yards. It is not as aesthetic as the Tower, but I am homesick for the smell of hemp and tar, and general naval blasphemy. Edward will find it vastly educational."

Jeannie laughed outright and then tightened her grip again, gold leaf and all.

Beau Brummell walked toward them, nodding and smiling to the other patrons of the arts who had accumulated in the dress circle by the thousands, or so it seemed to Jeannie. Sir Peter Winthrop, who had found a red rose, peacocked about in the Beau's wake, a smile of triumph upon his face.

Jeannie thought of the flower girl searching the stones for her wares, and the smile left her face. She glanced at Larinda and noticed that her face, too, was pale. Larinda looked at Sir Peter and shook her head, but he merely broadened his smile and bowed to her.

"For what we are about to receive, may the Lord make us truly thankful," the captain muttered.

Jeannie stared at him, momentarily diverted, as the Beau bore down on them. "Sir, what do you mean?"

"That is the seaman's prayer as he is about to receive a broadside. And look here, if you will, and observe that I am in my finest uniform, and you, my dear, are still as fine as five pence. Chin up."

The Beau was in no hurry. He made his stately progress from friend to friend, admiring this one's gown, clucking over that one's waistcoat, flicking specks of imaginary dust off another's coat, and casting about the pearls of his conversation.

The captain rubbed his chin. "Dash it, Jeannie, but he reminds me of Jesus on Palm Sunday, except that I feel there is some humility lacking." He considered the Beau again. "And I defy our Lord and Savior to tie His neckcloth with such divine precision."

"Captain," Jeannie exclaimed, "is there nothing you will not say?"

He looked down at her, an arrested expression on his face. "Oh, there is. Believe me, Jeannie, there is."

She had not the time to ask him more, for the Beau stood before them in all his quiet splendor. He rested his weight delicately on one hip, assuming an air of vast unconcern over the remarkable figure that was his alone. No extravagant waistcoat for him, no superabundance of fobs and seals. He stood before her utterly elegant, and she held her breath and waited for him to raise his quizzing glass, rake her from stem to stern, and administer his patented set-down.

No one in the dress circle made any more attempts to appear uninvolved.

Good heavens, Jeannie thought wildly, is everyone breathing together? I shall grow distracted.

The Beau fingered his quizzing glass. After a moment that stretched into the next century and beyond, he suddenly turned to Larinda.

"Larinda, my dear," he began, "is this lady not your Scottish nanny? Pray introduce us."

Larinda's face turned a remarkable shade of putty. "No, please," she whispered.

The Beau opened his eyes wide in disbelief. "My dear, I insist," he said. "You and Sir Peter have been telling me such interesting things about her, and I am desirous of acquaintance."

"Sir, I am Jeannie McVinnie," Jeannie said as she pried her fingers from the captain's uniform and stepped forward. "I met you in the menagerie several days ago, when I had no idea who you were."

"Mrs. McVinnie, everyone knows who the Beau is," Sir Peter stated in round tones. He glanced around him for confirmation of this fact and smirked when there was a general chuckle throughout the dress circle.

"Not everyone, Sir Peter," Jeannie replied. Her fingers strayed to the emerald necklace and she clung to it like a lifeline. "Some of us manage to struggle well into maturity without this knowledge."

"Bravo," the captain said behind her in a low voice. "A hit below the waterline."

She nearly turned around in surprise. He must have come up quietly behind her. And I told him not to get involved, she thought. For someone so smart, he is remarkably ignorant.

But the Beau was smiling at her. Even in her terror, Jeannie sensed that the smile was genuine, unlike Sir Peter's shark grin. She loosened her death's grip on the necklace and let her breath out slowly.

Brummell swung his quizzing glass back and forth like a pendulum. Jeannie forced herself to look away from the hypnotic motion. "Mrs. McVinnie," the Beau began after a moment's careful thought, "now that you have become better acquainted with our frippery society, what have you to say about it? I am all ears." He cast a sidelong look at Larinda, who made an inarticulate sound deep in her throat, and raised his eyes.

Jeannie considered the question. If I must fall into the pit through this conversation, oh, let it be an easy fall, she thought. "This is indeed a city where there is much to do and much to see," she said evasively.

The Beau shook his head at her reply. "Too easy, too easy by half, Mrs. McVinnie. It has been expressed to me—by you, bless my soul—that we are a singularly foolish lot, fit for a midden. I may have been wrong, of course, my hearing is not acute."

Jeannie could hardly believe her own hearing. Beau Brummell, the master of the set-down, was giving her an out of sorts. She could titter, and blush, and declare that she had never said such a thing, and perhaps, just perhaps, the Beau would brush it under the rug. She could retire from the dress circle with her dignity at least intact.

As she contemplated her reply, looking from the Beau's calm assurance to Sir Peter's smirk of victory impending, Jeannie McVinnie knew right down to her shoes that she could not give Beau that satisfaction.

She released the necklace and took a deep breath. "You were not wrong, sir," she replied, "and I have seen nothing to change my opinion." She warmed to her subject and only regretted that her voice shook a bit from the intensity of it. "I have seen people tonight all of a twitter over red roses and white ones. Such silliness is not worthy of you, sir."

Sir Peter gasped, fluttered his hands about his lapel, and then laughed at her.

Enraged, Jeannie wrenched the red rose out of his lapel and

shook it under his nose. "You wretched man," she hissed.
"You wouldn't rest until you had strewn that poor girl's flowers
all over the road. Don't you realize that is her livelihood?"

Sir Peter's eyes narrowed. "She is nothing. And I hardly
consider my actions your business."

"No?" Jeannie asked. She moved closer to him and he backed
away in an undignified scramble. "I made them my business
when you left that little blind girl to grope about for her flowers.
How dare you?"

Sir Peter raised his hand and Captain Summers leapt forward
and grasped his wrist. "Only touch her and I will call you out,"
he snapped, his voice full of command and hard as steel.

The dress circle was utterly quiet as Beau Brummell strolled
leisurely forward, still swinging his quizzing glass. Jeannie
sucked in her breath and her eyes filled with tears as he slowly
raised it to his eye.

But he was looking at Sir Peter Winthrop. "Peter, really,"
he said gently. "Since you could not hit your valet with a sponge
at five paces, I recommend that you resist the challenge from
this, er, this officer who, I think, could kill you with his eyes
alone."

The captain released his hold on Sir Peter and stood back a
pace. He carefully placed both hands behind his back, but he
was still breathing heavily.

Sir Peter had gone remarkably pale. He turned to Brummell
and grew more milky yet as the Beau slowly looked him up
and down, not once, but twice, his eye magnified by the quizzing
glass, his face calm.

"Peter, you must agree that was not worthy of you,"
Brummell said gently, as if he would admonish a child. "But
do breathe, sir, in and out, in and out again. Ah, that's more
like it." He turned to his audience. "Sometimes a little reminder
works miracles."

Someone smothered a laugh, and someone else went into a
prolonged coughing spasm. Sir Peter looked about him, his face
dead white, as if he wore powder. Brummell peered closer at
his face and shook his head.

"Sir Peter, I wonder that you are well! Such an unhealthy
pallor does nothing to forward the claims of your rather
presumptuous waistcoat. Perhaps a repairing rustication to your
Derbyshire estates would be just the thing. The Duchess of

Rutland is forever telling me that country air puts a bloom in one's cheeks. Only observe Mrs. McVinnie.''

Brummell allowed that bit of intelligence to sink in as he removed his quizzing glass and pocketed it. He turned to Jeannie. ''My dear Mrs. McVinnie . . . Good God, madam, how attractive your hair is that way! In truth, I have been meaning this little while to ask you whether you truly prefer red roses to white, but there was such a distraction from the stage. Lord, there is nothing like raw talent to ruin an evening of quiet chatter in one's box.''

Jeannie laughed. ''You are a very amusing man, Mr. Brummell, for all your frippery ways.''

The Beau turned to the others collected about them. ''I adore the way she rolls her rrs!'' He took her hand and bowed over it. ''Lovely, lovely Jeannie, will you honor me with a turn about Hyde Park tomorrow afternoon? I will listen to you say 'Brummell' and 'frippery fellow' in that inimitable way, and consider myself the better for it.'' He sighed. ''It is early in the Season, but I will do my duty and peacock about.''

He glanced beyond Jeannie then and noticed Larinda. ''My dear, if you will behave yourself and mind your Scottish nanny, we will likely find space in the carriage for you. And you, too, Captain,'' he added, ''although I suspect we would be slow company. There will be no one to throttle.''

The captain merely bowed and kept his own counsel. A bell tinkled; the interval was over.

The Beau kissed Jeannie's hand and released it with such a sigh of reluctance that she chuckled. ''My dear, would you favor me with your company for the remainder of the play? I am sure the Prince Regent will be delighted to make your acquaintance.''

Jeannie shook her head. ''Your offer is so kind sir, but no, I will not.''

The Beau waggled his finger. ''My dear, you are the first to refuse such an offer.'' He leaned closer and whispered in her ear. ''Has no one told you I am immensely important?''

She twinkled her eyes back at him and was gratified by the gleam of self-deprecating humor in his own. ''I am well, well aware, sir, but look you here, I want to see this play through, and something tells me that we would only talk in the royal box, and I would miss my treat.'' She touched his sleeve. ''And didn't I tell you only this day that this is my first play?''

He bowed. "You did, and I shall not insist. Until tomorrow, then?"

"Until tomorrow."

He bowed again, including Captain Summers in the gesture this time. He strolled over to Larinda, who stood on the brink of tears, and touched her under the chin. "Remember, my dear Larinda, that beauty may be skin-deep, but meanness cuts right to the marrow."

She nodded and blinked back her tears. The Beau continued his progress around the circle, chatting and pausing here and there, as if nothing had happened. The patrons of the arts closed in behind him, and the bell rang one more time.

The first person to approach them was Lord Charles Smeath, who shook his head at Captain Summers. "Really, Captain, you were safer in the blockade." His voice was serious for only a moment, and then a laugh rumbled out of him like thunder from distant guns. He rubbed his hands together. "I thought for a moment that Sir Peter would make water before our eyes."

Summers smiled. "Like any number of midshipmen you could name, my lord?"

"Aye, sir, aye, beginning with one young sprite aboard the— oh, let me see—the *Temeraire*?"

"No, my lord, it was the *Barfleur*." Summers laughed. "And here I was, hoping no one remembered that."

"Enough of these salty stories, my lords."

Lord Smeath looked about. "Lady Jersey approaches on a larboard beam," he said, and extended a meaty hand, which swallowed up both of Lady Jersey's hands.

She nodded to Captain Summers, but addressed herself to Jeannie. "Mrs. McVinnie, excellent! I daresay that we will see much of you in the best circles this Season, and I, for one, can only count that a pleasure already."

Jeannie bowed her acknowledgment, but her expression was puzzled. "I do not understand, my lady."

"It means, my dear, that you have a highly effective champion now. I predict that invitations to every event in London will come your way now."

"Oh, surely not," Jeannie declared.

Lady Jersey nodded. "The postman's back will break with them. He will come with a wheelbarrow."

The bell rang for the third and final time. Lady Jersey kissed her hand to Lord Charles. ''I would not miss this final act, although I fear that since Shylock has already had his final scene, it will fall sadly flat.'' She inclined her head toward Jeannie. ''Mr. Kean is another one who will find his postbox crowded with invitations.''

She was gone with a wave of her hand.

Jeannie turned to the captain. ''What were you doing at Lady Jersey's today?'' she asked.

''Oh, Clare and I sat in her saloon and ate any number of cream cakes—at least, Clare did—and chatted about this and that,'' the captain said innocently.

''And would I be surprised to discover that Lady Jersey is a particular friend of Mr. Brummell's?'' Jeannie asked.

''Possibly. But look here, I think we must come to the rescue of my esteemed sister. Agatha appears to have gone aground.''

Jeannie regarded the captain as he hurried forward to assist Lady Smeath, who was draped in a chair, moaning softly as Larinda waved smelling salts under her nose. Sir, you have been paving my way and choose not to discuss it.

She touched the necklace again. How deep must I go in your debt? I wonder.

And why?

12

LARINDA'S bracing administration of spirits of ammonia had pulled Lady Smeath's eyes back into their proper orbit. The woman looked about her wildly and saw only the backs of the theatergoers scurrying to their seats. Her eyes filled with tears and she began to sob out loud.

"Larinda, you are ruined," she cried. "See how everyone deserts us!"

"Mama, it is the beginning of Act Five," Larinda declared prosaically, and then looked around at Captain Summers. "Uncle, I fear we must take Aunt Agatha home."

"Yes," Lady Smeath said, and sobbed even harder. "Home to Suffolk, ruined forever."

"Belay it, Agatha," said the captain. "With the possible exception of Sir Peter Winthrop, no one's ruined."

The mention of Sir Peter's name caused Lady Smeath's eyes to roll back in her head again. Grimly Larinda applied the vinaigrette again, with the same results.

"He is ruined?" she sobbed. "And I had such high hopes for him, Larinda. Ten thousand a year. I feel certain he would have made an offer for you."

"And I would just as quickly have sent him to the rightabout," said the captain. "Well, Jeannie, I fear we must abandon this place."

"No," interrupted Larinda with a hand on his arm, "if you will summon the carriage and help me with Aunt Agatha, I will go home with her." She raised her eyes to Jeannie's for the smallest moment. "I think Mrs. McVinnie would like to stay for the play."

"I would, Larinda, above all things, but can you manage?" Jeannie asked quietly.

A slight smile crossed her face briefly. "I have managed her before, back in Suffolk." Her eyes clouded with embarrassment. "And I have a dreadful headache. Uncle?"

"Handsome of you, Larinda. And thank you."

The captain lifted Lady Smeath to her feet and put his arm about her waist. "Come, come, Agatha, let us go below. My dear Mrs. McVinnie, I will return. If you hurry back to the box, there is time to hear Portia and Bassanio carry on."

Jeannie nodded to them and returned to the box, closing the door behind her and leaning against it for a moment. If she could have, she would have propped a chair against the door handle to keep the world out. She was grateful for the chance to be alone and consider the startling events of the evening.

There was no question in her careful Scot's mind that Beau Brummell considered her a pleasant diversion for this year's London Season. "I think, Mr. Brummell, that you have seen one too many Seasons and are becoming a trifle jaded,'' she said out loud. ''Very well, then, sir, I will divert you, but only for Larinda's sake.''

With a sigh of relief, she stretched out her legs in a manner decidedly unladylike and leaned back in the settee. To her surprise, tears streamed down her cheeks again. She enjoyed the luxury of a hearty bout of tears that drained all pent-up emotions from her and left her feeling infinitely better.

She blew her nose and wiped her eyes. Alas, Jeannie McV, she thought, as she straightened up, you will have to postpone the matter of looking for another husband, at least until this Season is over and you have returned home.

As she watched Portia and Bassanio declaring their continuing affection for each other, she had another thought, one that made her smile in the dark. She would help Captain Summers find a wife. It was certainly high time that he married, and there must be somebody in London who would take kindly to a military man. Heaven knows I would never marry into any service again, especially the navy, that most suicidal of professions, but there must be somebody who would. Of course, Will is a bit forbidding upon first acquaintance, but that soon passes. Perhaps Lady Jersey can recommend someone to me, and I can forward the captain's cause.

She was still smiling when Captain Summers returned to the box. He regarded her with no small amusement. ''My dear, you look as smug as a foretopman with prize money.''

She nodded. ''I am plotting to do you a bit of no good, Captain Summers.''

He sat down next to her and gave her a nudge when she said nothing more. ''Well, do I get a hint so I may run for cover, or must I be surprised?''

''I have decided to find you a wife.''

The captain gave out a crack of laughter, and the weary man in the next box growled something about an upstart generation with no appreciation for the Bard of Avon.

''Do hush, Captain, or they will throw us out of the theater, and not even Brummell could salvage my reputation,'' she scolded. ''I propose to find you a suitable wife. Larinda will not claim all my time, Clare is in excellent hands, Edward has his guidebook—''

''Do not remind me,'' the captain groaned.

"So there is time, don't you see? I foresee few difficulties. You look remarkably well in that uniform, you have a noble bearing, a sizable fortune, or so I would assume."

"Sizable, my dear," he agreed. "If the war should end tomorrow, *deo volente,* and I were cast at half-pay upon the shore, I would not need a begging bowl."

Jeannie stifled a chuckle at the thought of the impeccable Captain Summers in tatters and begging for his bread.

"You're a trifle stern upon first acquaintance, but—"

"But not now, eh, Mrs. McVinnie?" he asked, and rested his arm along the back of the settee, not exactly touching her shoulders, but close enough.

She leaned forward, "No, not now," she said after considering the matter. "I find you excellent company. Of course, the blasphemy and swearing must stop."

"God's b—bones, Mrs. McVinnie, now you go too far," he teased.

"Oh, do be serious! You must only apply yourself a very little to find a wife. I cannot be convinced that it would be a difficult matter. You merely have not been ashore long enough to pursue the matter before."

He grew serious then. "Suppose I were to tell you that I have specifically avoided the shore because I did not wish to become entangled in some woman's net?"

Jeannie teased in turn. "Are you afraid, Will?"

"I am."

He yawned and relaxed then, as she had done before his return to the box. He turned his attention to the stage and said no more until the play was over and the chandelier lowered for the last time. They rose, along with the rest of the audience, and remained standing until the Prince Regent took his ponderous way from the royal box. Beau Brummell paused only long enough to search out the Summers' box and blow a kiss in her general direction.

She watched him in some amusement. "I can only be grateful to him for saving me from my own folly," she said, "and must credit it entirely to the fact that Mr. Brummell must be dreadfully bored."

The captain turned to her in surprise. "You think yourself boring? God's bal—ballast, madam, we have not had a dull day since you dropped yourself upon our doorstep. I wonder that the Beau will have the stamina for one hour in your company, let alone an entire Season!''

"Then you have led a dull life indeed," she replied tartly. "And I know that not to be the case."

He shook his head in agreement. "No, ma'am, no, indeed. Aboard the *Venture*, we waver between total tedium and stark terror." He shook his head. "It does wonders for the digestion."

They left the dress circle and took their leisurely way down the grand staircase, letting the crowds swirl around them. Jeannie listened to the captain with half an ear as she watched the crowds, noting this time that though people stared at her, the look was different. I hope you like what you see, she thought as she held her head higher. I will strut about only for Larinda's sake.

They had sent the carriage on ahead with Lady Smeath. Jeannie sighed as the captain shouldered his way through the crowd of theatergoers outside, remembering her experience only days ago in hailing a hackney to take her to Wendover Square. Goodness, she thought, was that only a few days ago? I feel I have been here forever, or at least that I have known Captain Summers forever. How odd.

As she watched, he stepped off the curb and exerted himself no more than to raise a finger when two hackneys stopped. She opened her eyes wider. How did he do that?

Jeannie allowed him to hand her into the coach. She leaned forward as he shut the door and they started off. "How, sir, do you command such obedience from hackneys? I stood an age in the pouring rain only the other night, trying to get one to stop for me!"

He removed his hat and placed it upon the seat beside him. "Oh, it helps to wear a tall hat and look like someone who eats cabbies for tea." He flicked a curl of hers that had come loose from its moorings and dangled by her ear. "Besides, my dear, they probably didn't even see you. I say, do you stand on a box to hail cabs in Scotland?''

She made a face at him. "Not as a rule. I daresay I never had to hail a hackney before."

He tucked the loose curl behind her ear. "When you get tired of going it alone, my very dear Mrs. McVinnie, will you remarry?''

She considered his question and thought about scolding him for impertinence, but could not. "I suppose so, Will," she replied thoughtfully, her finger straying to the curl. "But I do not think I will let that be my only consideration for marrying again."

When he merely angled his head to one side and continued looking at her, she wrinkled her forehead and then held her hands out in front of her. "Am I a fool, Captain Summers? I suspect I am, for I have this foolish wish." She let out her breath in an impatient rush. "Oh, bother it all, Captain, but I would like to fall in love again. Isn't that absurd? I mean, everyone knows that you love only once. But still, the thought is appealing."

When the captain said nothing, Jeannie was grateful that the darkness hid her red face. She bundled herself deeper in her cloak and rested her chin in its folds. "I suppose it is foolish."

"It's not foolish, Jeannie, not at all," the captain replied softly, his voice so gentle that she looked up in surprise and then stared down again at her cloak.

"You must have really loved Thomas McVinnie," the captain said after another moment's pause, his voice strangely intense. There was none of the hard edge to it that she had come to accept as a matter of course.

"I did," Jeannie said in a small voice, and then rushed on before her courage failed her. "And I would wish to love someone like that again." When the silence from the other side of the carriage continued, she managed a small laugh. "I suppose it is because I am such a Scot, sir, that I hate to waste all that love." Jeannie curled up into the shadows on her side of the hackney, embarrassed and uncomfortable with herself. "Sir, I have never discussed such a topic with anyone, and surely not a man."

"Oh, and you think a man would not be properly sympathetic?" the captain asked, the slight edge back in his voice again.

Jeannie burrowed deeper in her cloak, thoroughly out of sorts with herself. "Nothing of the kind, sir," she protested. "It is just not a subject that . . . Well, it is a matter of some trifling delicacy."

"And you think that I have never known what it is to want someone? Want someone so much that it becomes physical pain? You err, child, you err."

"I didn't mean to be impertinent, sir, truly I did not."

"And you are not impertinent. Merely more honest than most of us. Jeannie, you have my complete confidentiality," he said, and tugged on her cloak until she sat upright again. "Don't pull into your shell like a turtle. Twenty-four is a little too young to leap into an open grave and pull the earth over you." He tugged on her cloak again and reached for her hand. "Perhaps you're the one who ought to look for a mate during this London Season. You seem to have more ambition than I."

Jeannie shook her head. "I will wait for a Scotsman, sir."

"Captain Bartley MacGregor?"

She made a thoughtful face. "Perhaps it does bear consideration, and after all, he will likely continue to propose on a regular basis." She sat in contemplation for a moment and then smiled. "I could certainly like him a great deal. That would not be difficult. But botheration, sir, I have vowed a mighty vow never to marry a military man again." She leaned forward. "You, sir, are evading the issue. I am determined to find you a wife." The captain shuddered elaborately and Jeannie laughed out loud. "Sir, you must do your family duty!"

"I refuse to be impressed into matrimony," he declared in firm tones. "Do I not do enough duty for George Number Three? My dearest Mrs. McVinnie, be fair. Weevily bread, salt-water showers, *mal de mer,* and a wife? You jest."

They had pulled up into one street and the hackney slowed down.

"Which one, sir?" asked the jehu.

"Let us out here; we will walk the rest of the way," the captain said. "Come, come, Mrs. McVinnie. A walk will do us good."

She took his hand as he helped her from the carriage. He did not relinquish his hold on her, even after he paid the coachman and set off at a spanking pace down the middle of the deserted street. She hurried along beside him, tugging at his hand until he slowed down.

"See here," she said breathlessly, "I will not tease you further, Will. But mark my words, sir, someday you will fall in love and then . . . Well, you'll see," she concluded vaguely.

"My, aren't we articulate this evening," he said, and tucked her arm in his. "Here we are, flushed from your incredible triumph at the theater, a triumph, I might add, that surely must rival Mr. Kean's, and all you can do is worry about me. I suggest that you devote some thought to the bargefull of invitations that will be borne your way on this morning's tide.''

"I can't imagine such a thing," she said as he paused at the front door for the key. ''The Beau will have forgotten the entire incident by now, surely.''

The door swung open as the captain fished about in his pocket for the key. Wapping stood before them in all his magnificence. ''Sir William, we never lock the door before all the inmates are inside,'' he said in an injured voice.

"I can assure you that the inmates are now accounted for, Wapping," the captain said. "I recommend that you go to bed."

"But, sir, who is to see you upstairs? I cannot imagine where Pringle has taken himself off.''

"He's in his hammock, you old silly," the captain said. "I told him not to wait up for me. Now, good night."

His jowls quivering with indignation, Wapping locked the door behind them with a decisive click, bowed, and left without another word.

"I had a cat like that on my last ship," was Captain Summers' comment as Wapping left in furious dignity.

Jeannie turned on the captain. "You are amazingly rude, sir."

"Yes, aren't I?" the captain agreed. "Madam, consider the results. I do not wish people to hover about me. I deplore being loomed over, if you will. Now, will you require any support in taking yourself upstairs? If so, I will summon Wapping again.''

Jeannie giggled. "You know I do not require such assistance.''

"I know all too well," Summers murmured.

I wonder what he can mean, thought Jeannie as she extended her hand, suddenly shy again. "Thank you. Thank you for being such a friend tonight, Will."

He took her hand and bowed over it. "I already told you that I stand behind my crew. Pleasant dreams, Mrs. McVinnie.''

She started up the stairs and then turned around. "Captain, I should return your necklace.''

He stood in the half-light at the foot of the stairs, candle in his hand, looking up at her, his expression oddly familiar. For the briefest second, he reminded her of Tom, his face wreathed in shadows and taken up with his own thoughts. She had the peculiar desire to hold out her hand to the captain, knowing somewhere deep inside her body that he would take it and follow her upstairs.

You are being utterly ridiculous, Jeannie McVinnie, she scolded herself. Captain Summers would do nothing of the kind. Her hand went instead to her neck.

"Your necklace, sir?" she said again, wishing her voice did not sound so breathless.

He shook his head. "No, not now. I expect you might have occasion to wear that dress again. It can wait, and besides, it looks better on you."

"Good night, then, sir," she said softly.

He kissed his fingers to her and remained at the foot of the stairs.

Jeannie padded silently down the hall, peeking in first at Clare, who slept with the towel doll tight in her arm. Edward slept, too, a beatific expression on his face. Jeannie glanced at the guidebook beside his bed, open to the page on the Admiralty House. So that will be tomorrow's expedition, my dear, she thought. I hope I am equal to it.

She let herself into her room, sighing with relief as she kicked off her shoes and threw herself across the bed. She put the emerald up to her cheek, enjoying the warm weight of it against her face. In another moment, she held it up to the moonlight that came from the window, turning it this way and that, but it was too dark to catch even a glimmer. Her mind went blissfully blank of any thought save the need for sleep and the urge to loosen her dress.

She was tugging at her belt when someone knocked on the door. Jeannie rose reluctantly and went to the door, her ear against the wood.

"Please, Mrs. McVinnie."

It was Larinda. Without a word, Jeannie opened the door. Larinda, dressed in nightgown and robe, came into the room. She shut the door behind her quietly and sat on Jeannie's bed.

Mystified, Jeannie watched her a moment and then sat down beside her. Silently, Larinda laid her head in Jeannie's lap and closed her eyes.

Jeannie started in surprise and then sat very still. When

Larinda said nothing, Jeannie tentatively pulled back the girl's hair from her face and rested the back of her hand against her cheek.

Still Larinda said nothing, only rested her head in Jeannie's lap like a tired child. Jeannie began to stroke her hair and then to hum softly.

Gradually Larinda relaxed. She did not open her eyes as Jeannie patted her shoulder.

"I am so sorry," she said at last, and Jeannie had to lean closer to hear. "Please forgive me, forgive us."

"There is nothing to forgive," Jeannie replied, her voice soft.

Larinda sat up then, but she would not look Jeannie in the eyes. "I fear I am as vulgar as my aunt," she said, with a catch in her voice that went straight to Jeannie's heart.

"Oh, my dear," said Jeannie. "She only wanted what she thought best for you."

Once begun, Larinda did not try to stop. "And here I was, so afraid that you would ruin my credit. So afraid that the Beau would scoff and make fun of me because of you, and it was the other way 'round, wasn't it?"

Jeannie held Larinda's face in her hands. "As far as I can see, my dear, the matter is closed. If I choose not to remember it, you cannot make me."

Larinda cried then, and Jeannie hugged her close, speaking softly. "After all, dear, I practiced my own deception on this family by coming here, didn't I? I knew full well that I was certainly not the Jeannie McVinnie the captain expected."

Larinda pulled herself away from Jeannie then and met her glance finally. "I am glad you did come. Please overlook my folly, if you can."

Jeannie drew Larinda close again for another hug. "I have already told you it is forgotten. Now, if you do not get to bed soon, you will have dreadful bags under your eyes and you will look a hagged twenty-four instead of a mere seventeen. Go along now."

After another hug, Jeannie walked Larinda to the door. Larinda gave her another glance that said more than words could, and closed the door quietly behind her.

Jeannie took off her dress, and as it settled around her, she just stood there in the middle of it. I am convinced that I have not the strength for children of my own, she thought. Imagine if Clare were to wake up and scream now, or if Edward were to throw out spots. She stepped out of the dress and draped it carefully over a chair, hoping that Mary would feel charitable in the morning and brush it out properly. She took the necklace off and placed it on the table by the bed.

There was another knock at the door. Jeannie sighed, but did not budge from the bed where she sat.

"Oh, who is it?" she finally said in a loud whisper.

"Captain Summers, demanding your presence, and lively now, lively."

The gooseflesh rose on her arms. How foolish I am to sit half-bare like this in a draft, she thought as she rubbed her arms and wondered where the breeze was coming from, since the windows were closed.

"Not now, Captain," she said.

"This is not a suggestion, madam," said the voice with the familiar hard edge. "It is more in the way of a friendly command."

"Sir, I—"

"Surely you have a robe, Jeannie," he said, anticipating her objection. "Find it and move about handsomely now."

"I know when I am being coerced," she said pointedly.

"Excellent, Jeannie. Step along lively now."

"Aye, aye, sir," she said at last, torn between amusement and exasperation. "Could this not wait until morning?" she tried again as she pulled on her robe and buttoned it high up the front.

"It *is* morning, madam," he said. "According to my watch."

The captain stood in the hallway in his stocking feet. He had removed his uniform coat and he carried a dusty bottle in one hand, and two glasses.

Jeannie eyed him with some suspicion, but if he even noticed, he did not call attention to it.

"I daresay I never saw a more proper-looking robe," he commented.

"I daresay you never did," she agreed, resisting the urge to either laugh or box him about the ears. "And it is flannel, too."

"I do not doubt it, madam. Follow me, please. There is a trifling ritual we must perform."

"I must be crazy to do this," she muttered as she followed him down the dark stairway.

"Madam, you were crazy to leave Scotland on such a hare-brained whim," he said over his shoulder.

Jeannie could think of no proper answer as she trailed him into the breakfast parlor. A small lamp winked on the table, which had already been laid out for breakfast.

"Sit down."

She sat, curiosity winning out over exasperation. Jeannie watched as he popped the cork and little puffs of dust settled on the china place settings. Jeannie laughed as he wiped the neck of the bottle on the tablecloth, and wondered at Wapping's distress in the morning.

"Who would have suspected my late, dim-witted, under-lamented brother to have possessed such a treasure in his cellar?"

The captain poured a small libation into one cup and tasted it, rolling the liquor around in his mouth for a moment before swallowing. "Good Godfrey, there is nothing closer to heaven than smuggler's brandy."

Jeannie regarded the glass with some trepidation as he filled it much too full. "Oh, really, now, Captain, I am not a drinker of brandy."

He filled his own glass and held it high. "Raise your glass, Jeannie McVinnie," he ordered.

She did as he said.

"Brandy is for heroes, my dear, or didn't Thomas ever tell you that?"

She shook her head.

"Consider this part of your nautical education, then," he said briskly. "To Jeannie McVinnie, who does not want for courage. Come, come, my dear, it is a toast."

Jeannie took a sip and coughed as the fumes filled her nose and the liquor burned a path down her throat. "This ought to be against the law," she croaked.

"Actually, it is," the captain agreed. He tipped his head back and drained the glass. "At least, smuggler's brandy is." He poured himself another glass. "I am in the custom of celebrating a victory after a battle, as soon as we are able. It does wonders for the men to knock back an unexpected tot of rum. You may ask my lieutenants."

Jeannie took another cautious sip. The brandy traveled down more pleasantly now, creating a warm spot in her stomach that reminded her of a parlor fire after a cold day. Two more sips and the glass was empty.

"It must be an acquired taste," she said as she watched him refill her glass, not thinking to object.

"I certainly acquired it," he agreed, sitting down and pushing his chair back so he could prop his feet on the table.

Jeannie moved the china out of the way and then sat back in her chair, sipping thoughtfully and wondering why the room was taking on a soft glow and Captain Summers sounded so mellow and far away.

The captain drank deeply and tipped more brandy in her glass. "Many is the evening we have sat around the wardroom table." He touched her glass with his. "To Jeannie McVinnie, who cares about flower girls and ungrateful heiresses."

Jeannie drank the brandy without a murmur this time. "Do you know, Will, Larinda apologized to me tonight? Just before you knocked." She held the glass out for more. "I don't know when I have been more surprised." She swirled the contents of the glass, creating a miniature whirlpool. "Although, truth to tell, I don't know that anything should surprise me anymore." She suddenly clinked his glass with hers. "Here's to blue elephants, Wapta—Captain Will Summers, and here's to red roses." She hiccupped and peered more closely at the glass. "Dear me! It appears there is a hole in this glass. Do let us trade."

The captain filled his glass again and obligingly handed it to her.

"I suppose this whole evening points to the sad fact that I will be called upon to accompany you and Larinda to balls and routs, and more plays than even Lope de Vega wrote."

"It does, indeed, William," Jeannie declared, and then winced and pressed her hands to her ears. "I don't mean to shout."

"You're not shouting, Jeannie. I can barely hear you." The captain belched. "Hell's bells, I seem to have no manners."

Jeannie rested her arms on the table and started to giggle. "Did you see the cook's face when he presented you with that dum pluff—I mean, lum tuff?"

"You mean that pum luff," said the captain helpfully.

Jeannie nodded. "That's it. Dear me, I thought I would disgrace myself for all time when he set that before you." She stared down into the little glass. "Come to think of it, what am I doing here?"

"Merely celebrating a little victory," the captain replied after some moments of contemplation. His voice was serious. "Indeed, I have discovered through hard experience that there are not many victories in life, and one should properly salute those that come along."

"True enough, sir," she said, but did not hold out her glass again. "But, Will, I fear that I am starting to list a bit."

"Not noticeably," he replied at once, and took another sip. "For a female, you have remarkably good bottom."

"Thank you, sir!" Jeannie rose to her feet with the air of one unfamiliar with her body. "I say, sir, was this room built upon a slant? How devilish difficult it must be to keep things on the table."

The captain laughed. At least she saw that his mouth was open, but she heard not a sound. There is something wrong with my ears, she thought, and shook her head. The slight motion sent her tumbling back to her seat. She giggled again, hoping that the captain would not notice how foolish she was becoming.

But Captain Summers had tipped the bottle up to his eye and was peering into it. "I wonder where it has all gone," he was saying to himself. "Trust George to buy a bottle only half-full."

Jeannie laughed again. "No Scot he," she attempted to say, but the words didn't sound right. She shook her head again to clear it and decided not to pursue the matter.

The captain was on his feet then. Jeannie rubbed her eyes. He seemed even taller than usual, his head far away from his neck. And then he held out a long, long hand to her. After a moment's consideration, she took it.

They supported each other into the hallway and Jeannie gazed in disbelief at the stairs, each tread two feet high and stretching into an infinity of darkness at the top. "I really don't think I can do it," she said, and sank down on the bottom stair. "Just leave me here," she said, and waved him on. "Save yourself." She giggled.

The captain picked her up and started up the stairs. With a

sigh, she closed her eyes and rested her head against his chest. She wanted to tell him that his heart was pounding much too loud, and he would wake Wapping's inmates, but she couldn't think of enough words.

The captain slammed open her door with a bang loud enough to wake the dead, and then she was sinking into her mattress. Someone undid the braid in her hair, running long fingers through the plaits to straighten them out. He tugged the covers up around her shoulders and rested his hand on her arm.

The captain must have been tired, too, because he knelt by the bed and leaned his lips on her cheek for a long, long moment. Jeannie sighed again and pursed her lips. The captain laughed and got to his feet.

"Good night, Jeannie," his voice boomed from the doorway. "I trust you'll be none the worse for wear."

She was asleep.

Morning came with a velocity that would have astounded her, had she felt more like thinking about it. Jeannie's head drummed against the pillow as she struggled to open her eyes. Something was screeching and carrying on by the window, the racket more troubling than the noise of one hundred Billingsgate fishwives. She clapped her hand over her ears and tried to press herself into the pillow.

"Mrs. McVinnie, 'tis only wrens," said a familiar voice.

It required vast strength of purpose, but Jeannie managed to open one eye. Mary stood before her, holding out a battered tin cup.

"The captain says you are to drink this."

The captain? Merciful heavens, what did I do last night? Jeannie closed her eye and twitched the covers up higher upon her shoulders.

"Go away, Mary. Cannot you see that I am dying? I would prefer to go about the business alone."

Mary slammed the cup down on the table and Jeannie winced. "Gently now," she admonished, and then raised herself up on one elbow to peer into the cup. It was a vile brew, deep black in color. Jeannie shook her head. "I wouldn't drink that without vast coercion."

Mary clucked her tongue. "Well, then, I suppose that will follow."

The door opened and in a moment Clare bounced onto the bed. Jeannie groaned at the sudden motion and then closed her eyes again as Clare snuggled next to her, cuddling close in her arms. Jeannie wrapped her arms about the child, resting her cheek upon the curls that flew about every which way.

The door opened again. I do not understand why my room must suddenly fill up like an auctioneer's hall, Jeannie thought. She groaned again as someone sat on the bed and scooted Clare over.

"Come, come, Jeannie, handsomely now. There's a good girl."

The captain's voice grated upon her ears like fingers on slate. She shuddered and reached for Clare again. "Go away," she muttered. "I am dying and I'd rather not have an audience, if you please."

Captain Summers laughed and she tried to push him off the bed. She opened her eyes at the same time finally and stared at him until he swam into focus before her eyes.

He smelled divinely of bay rum, and he was shaved and trim and tidy, and she wanted to throttle him. Instead, she pressed both hands tight against her temples. "Did I really drink all that brandy last night?" she asked.

He nodded. "Aye, and I really should apologize."

"Heaven's protection, sir, what was in that brandy?"

"Brandy, I do believe," he said helpfully, and held out the brew to her again.

"I wouldn't put anything in my mouth again that you recommended, sir," she said in what she thought were round tones, but which only sounded pitiful to her ears. She tried to turn over and face the wall. Clare bounced out of her way obligingly, and Jeannie wailed as the bed rocked.

Captain Summers set down the cup and pressed against her shoulder until she was facing him again. "Now, my dear, I do recommend this brew," he said, and waved it under her nose again. "I fear that Mary did not present it in the proper light."

Wearily Jeannie dragged herself up on one elbow and looked into the depths of the cup he held out to her. "Tom warned me," she began.

"God knows you should have listened to him. This will help, believe me."

She raised her eyes slowly to his. "I suppose this is an old family recipe, handed down from mizzled sire to castaway son?"

His lips twitched, but he preserved his countenance in a remarkable manner. "Rather, I think . . ." He paused and looked about him to Clare, who had tucked herself in beside Jeannie again and regarded him with wide eyes. "Actually, I think it came out of a whorehouse in Lisbon," he whispered. "But my dear, rest assured—"

"Oh, hand it here," she said, reaching for the cup.

Rather than trust it to her, the captain put his hand against her back and raised the cup to her lips. "If you block off the back of your throat, then you can't smell it," he advised. "That's how we drink four-month-old water. Ah, very good very good. I guarantee that you will feel more the thing in a short while."

Jeannie glared at him. "You really are unscrupulous."

He only smiled and raised his eyebrows in an inquiring fashion. Avoiding his glance, Jeannie carefully sat upright in bed. She tugged the blankets up discreetly, folded her hands in her lap, and waited for death to overtake her.

It did not. In a moment, her stomach had ceased to pitch and yaw, and the wrens outside the window became wrens again. When Edward hurtled into her room, she could almost regard him with equanimity.

He stared at her, his eyes wide, and then cast his attention upon his uncle. "Uncle Summers, doesn't she know she is to accompany us to the Admiralty House?"

"Hush, you vile young chub," said the uncle with considerable spirit but no rancor. "I have only just now rescued her from an untimely death, or at least a deep decline, and you are raving on about an expedition? Give the woman a decent interval to get her pins under her again."

Edward devoted his attention to Jeannie, looking her up and down. "Uncle Summers told me you were luffing a bit, but I think that is all a hum. You look—"

"—as fine as five pence," the captain concluded.

Jeannie glanced from nephew to uncle. "I will not budge from this house today," she declared.

"Oh, you must," Edward protested. He started to say more, but cast a glance at his uncle, swallowed, and then continued. "Believe me, Uncle, I do not complain about your company, sir, but have you noticed how everything seems more fun when Mrs. McVinnie is along?"

The captain nodded and took the cup from Jeannie's hand. "I have noticed that, too."

Jeannie ignored them both and toyed instead with Clare's curls.

Edward tried again. "Mrs. McVinnie, Clare told me that she wanted to come along. We need you."

It was Jeannie's turn to stare. "Clare told you?"

Edward nodded. "Didn't you, Clare?" he asked.

"Yes, I did," Clare said emphatically.

The captain and Jeannie stared at each other. Jeannie cuddled Clare closer. "Well, then, of course I will accompany this expedition," she replied. "Only give me a moment to find my land legs again."

"That won't be necessary, Mrs. McVinnie," the captain said as he stood up and clapped his hands together. She winced and he grimaced. "My apologies. We will go by the waterman's route to the Almiralty House. It is the only way, really, and Edward expects it of me, even if I do get a touch of queasiness in very small boats." He looked from Edward to Jeannie. "Promise me that nothing will go wrong."

"We promise," they said together. Clare chiming in as the echo.

"Why is it that I do not believe you?" the captain asked.

There was no need of reply. Larinda stood in the doorway, holding out the front of her dress. As everyone watched, she pranced to the bed and dumped the contents onto Jeannie's lap.

Envelopes with seals on them and cards of invitation rained down. Jeannie gasped.

"Tell me . . . Oh, surely it is not all for me."

Larinda, her eyes shining, rifled through the pile of mail and then laughed at the expression on Jeannie's face. "This is only the morning post," she exclaimed, holding up one envelope after another. "Lord and Lady Fotheringham wish the pleasure of your presence at their masked ball Tuesday next. Sir Edwin and Lady Lucas beg your attendance at an evening at Marchmont.

Mr. and Mrs. The Honorable Gervaise Willing-Jarvis request your person at a small champagne supper this evening.'' She held the note for Jeannie to read. ''Nothing elaborate, only our closest friends.''

''A regiment,'' stated the captain, ''complete with camp followers, sutlers, and cutpurses.''

Larinda plumped herself down on the bed and Jeannie clutched at her stomach. ''And this is only the half of it! Mrs.McVinnie, our best sitting room is full of red roses, and there are any number of modistes in the second saloon, all of them straining to measure you for gowns and hats.'' She rolled her eyes. ''Wapping is convinced they will come to blows at any moment.''

''I do not understand,'' said Jeannie. ''What can they possibly want with me?''

Larinda began to gather up the invitations. ''Don't you see? I have only heard of such things from others, but Aunt Agatha declares that modistes will practically kill for the honor of dressing you.''

''I cannot afford such fal lals,'' Jeannie protested.

''But you can! That is the beauty of it! All they require is that you wear their clothes, and when someone begs to know who made your dress, you merely drop the name. The next day, that modiste will have more business than she can stare at.''

''I couldn't possibly do that,'' Jeannie said.

''Why ever not?'' asked the captain, tossing in his morsel. ''I would have thought such economizing measures to have a great natural appeal to one of your—shall we say it?—shrewd background?''

Jeannie could only stare. ''Larinda, next you will tell me that Beau Brummell himself waits below.''

Larinda clapped her hand to her mouth. ''I forgot!'' She shook her head at Jeannie's alarm. ''No, no, it is not the Beau, but that Scottish captain. You know, the one with the marvelous shoulders who is so hard to understand? He waits below.''

''Not any longer,'' said the captain. ''Well, well, Captain MacGregor, join the menagerie.''

Bartley MacGregor filled the doorway, taking in the clutch of humanity sitting on Jeannie's bed. He was resplendent in full regimentals, his kilt pleated to a nicety, his plaid draped just so over his shoulder and secured there with a massive brooch that would have weighed down an average fellow. Larinda sighed and scooped more invitations toward her as she gazed at all that Celtic splendor.

"Jeannie?" MacGregor said, the uncertainty in his voice at odds with his total magnificence.

"The very same, Bart."

"Wapping told me ye were indisposed, fancy that."

"It's hardly any wonder, is it," said Summers, "considering the glut of flesh in here. I only hope no one carries typhoid fever."

Bartley MacGregor strode forward. The glint in his eyes set off clanging bells in Jeannie's already overtaxed brain.

"No, Bart, not here,"she warned, but he waved her to silence.

"Jeannie, light of my life," he voice boomed out, "won't you let me take you away from all this? I would like to marry you."

Larinda sighed again. Edward shook his head in utter disgust. Captain Summers tugged at his chin. Jeannie put her hand to her temple and then slowly sank down in the bed.

"Bart, ye meikle kail! Not again!"

13

CAPTAIN MacGregor blinked, looked from one member of the household to another, and managed a small laugh, even as a fiery blush spread across his face and into his blond hair, where it showed through like a bad sunburn.

"I did not mean to declare myself with such suddenness," he said finally. He came closer to Jeannie's bed. "It has been over three years since I have proposed, Jeannie, light of my life, and I fear I am dreadfully out of practice.''

"Not discernibly,'' the captain murmured.

Jeannie glanced his way in surprise, wondering at the slight note of petulance in his voice.

Captain MacGregor bowed to no one in particular. "As a rule, I do not generally propose in crowds. Egad, it was startled right out of me.''

Jeannie patted the only empty spot left on the bed. "You might as well join us,'' she said, "and my answer is still no, you marvelous man.''

He shook his head at her offer and remained on his feet. "Not ever, Jeannie?'' he asked softly.

"Oh, Bart!'' She hesitated. "If you were to sell out, perhaps.''

"I won't do that, Jeannie me light,'' he replied, his voice no louder, but with a conviction in it that carried his words throughout the room. "Not while Boney strides about the continent and we fight the world alone.''

"Hear, hear,'' the captain murmured. "How well I understand you, Captain MacGregor.''

Bartley looked around in surprise, as if he had forgotten there was anyone else in the room but Jeannie. "It becomes a personal matter, eh, Captain Summers?''

"As you well know.'' Captain Summers started to clap his hands together again, but a look at Jeannie's white face stopped him. "Sir, let us go below and leave this lady to button herself up. We have an expedition planned to the Admiralty House and Deptford Hard.'' He rose and patted Jeannie in a gesture that did not offend her in the least, to her later amazement. "You are welcome to accompany us, Captain MacGregor.''

Bartley shook his head. "As a rule, I avoid the water, sir.''

"Wise of you.''

"But I wish to go to sea,'' said Edward.

Bartley looked down at him in his lazy, indulgent fashion. "Laddie, you're daft.''

"So I tell him,'' Captain Summers agreed, "and tell him again. What will it take, I wonder, to convince him otherwise?''

"I am not sure you can do it,'' Larinda said. She rested her head upon Edward's shoulder with a gentle gesture, and he looked at her in real surprise. "Papa used to say so.'' She raised her eyes to her uncle's and did not waver. "In fact, he once told me he thought Edward would come to no good because he was as stubborn as you, Uncle."

Jeannie held her breath, waiting for an explosion of monumental proportions, but the captain only stood there, his face expressionless.

"Then there is no hope for the lad, Larinda." He touched Edward, too, and went to the window. "I think we will include Greenwich in our expedition, Mrs. McVinnie. If that does not do it . . . ." His voice trailed off. He stood at the window, hands behind his back, and no one spoke or looked at anyone else.

He turned around finally. "Niece," he said, "let us escort this wounded lover to the breakfast parlor, where there is all manner of bacon, ham and eggs. Excuse me, Jeannie, but some of us are hungry." He winked at her. "I believe there is even dum pluff."

Jeannie laughed in spite of her discomfort and pressed her hand to her forehead.

"Ah, and here is Mary, looking for her lost lamb. Lively now, Clare, lively."

"All this room lacks is my aunt," said Larinda as she steered Edward toward the door.

Captain Summers rolled his eyes. "Agatha is indisposed," he said. He twinkled his eyes at Jeannie. "Although, if she is put in charge of all those modistes waiting below, she may recover. Dare I, Jeannie?"

"Certainly," she replied promply. "But she lacks my measurements."

"I can supply them," said the captain with a perfectly straight face while Bartley blinked his eyes again and the red flush rose from his shirt collar a second time. "Mrs. McVinnie, I squirrel away all manner of statistics. Madame Amalie was kind enough to furnish them yesterday when I picked up the dress, and who knows when one might require such information?"

"Who, indeed?" asked Jeannie. I wonder, she thought, if ever a time will come when this man will not surprise me. Life with him would never be dull.

"Come, Clare," said the captain to Clare, who had scrunched herself down in the bed. "If you do not, you will be left to languish on the dock."

He plucked Clare from under the covers and handed her to

Mary, who curtsied and flashed a grin at Jeannie as she bore her charge away.

The door closed behind them all and the room was mercifully quiet but strangely empty. Jeannie scooted to the edge of the bed and dangled her bare legs over the edge. Captain Summers' brew had settled her stomach, but her head still floated a foot off her neck. For someone who attended all of Dr. Wyslip's temperance lectures in Dumfries last year, you are remarkably profligate, she told herself. Demon rum, indeed. No one had ever warned her about brandy.

Or about Captain Will Summers, either, she thought as she gingerly balanced on her feet and waited for her head to reach her neck again. Devil take the man, was there ever such an odd collection of honest compassion and imperial decree? I wonder that anyone tolerates him, she thought as she carefully trod a straight line to the windowseat and sat down.

"Mrs. McVinnie?"

It was Captain Summers again. "Come in," she said, and tucked her feet under her nightgown.

He merely stuck his head in the door. "Agatha has fallen all over herself to order the modistes about. I hope you do not mind, but I am discovering that when she is occupied, Larinda's life is smoother." He came into the room and leaned against the door, shutting it. "Her taste may not equal yours, my dear, but for the Lord's sake, she will be occupied."

"You are kind to think of it, Will," Jeannie said simply.

"Don't let it get about," he said, and the hard edge crept into his voice again.

"And if I do?" she asked.

He had no answer for her, but merely regarded her in silent contemplation from the other side of the room.

As she watched him, she saw another light creep into his eyes, one she had not seen in a man's face in well over a year. Jeannie did not even think he was aware that his expression had changed. She had seen the same light in Tom's eyes many times before he blew out the candle and came to bed.

She was wise enough not to be offended. It was a man's totally instinctual compliment to her womanhood. As sure as she sat there with a vast headache, she knew that if she held her hand out to him, he would be at her side. It was an intensely powerful feeling, and one not at all unpleasant. Quite the contrary.

She made no move, and he came no closer.

"I'll save you some tea and toast," he said finally, and his voice sounded rusty.

"Very good, sir," she replied. "And you'll promise to have me back here by five of the clock?"

And then the little flame in his eyes was gone. "I had forgotten," he said. "You are promised to Brummell, then, are you not?"

"So it would seem."

With a cursory nod, he left the room. Jeannie gathered herself together in the window seat and rested her chin upon her knees until her head cleared. As she slowly dressed herself, a glance in the mirror told her that her face was destined to be fashionably pale this morning. A pity it is not a prettier face, she thought as she turned her head from side to side, even if Tom did declare it the most beautiful visage he had ever seen. Tears started in her eyes and she wished fervently that she was home, where it was safe.

How missish I am becoming, she thought as she piled her hair on her head and attacked it with hairpins. I have not felt so giddy since, oh Lord, since I fell in love with Tom. This will never do.

She glanced around the room before she left it, and noticed the emerald necklace on the bedside table. She picked it up and put it back in the leather pouch, then almost stuffed it in a drawer, but changed her mind and tucked it under her pillow.

Jeannie could smell the roses as she came slowly down the stairs, yesterday's roses from Brummell by the dining-room door and the bouquets in the best sitting room. She peeked in the room and clasped her hands together in delight. The room, sunny with the morning's light, seemed to breathe out the peppery fragrance of roses in full bloom, and roses with petals furled and waiting. As she took in the scene, her headache finally disappeared.

This is better than your nasty brew, Captain, she thought as she walked from bouquet to bouquet, reading the names on the cards, names that meant nothing to her, but everything to Larinda and her hopes of a Season.

Jeannie heard laughter from the breakfast room and she smiled to herself, remembering the shouts and anguish of her first night in Wendover Square. How could I have been so afraid of that man? she asked herself.

There was one last bouquet in the corner of the room on top of the harpsichord. It caught her eye because of all the bouquets, it was not roses. It was only a little nosegay of violets with a note attached. She held the note up to the light. "To a Genuine Article. Until this afternoon. Brummell."

"And what role do you perform in this peculiar drama, sir?" she said out loud as she twirled the little bouquet between her fingers and then sniffed it. "I am never clever nor witty, and I trust you will tire of me soon."

By averting her eyes from the cold plum duff that the captain was knocking back like a starving man, and by focusing her whole heart and brain on dry toast and scalding tea, Jeannie accomplished breakfast. Lady Smeath fluttered around her, animosity forgotten, nattering on about sprig muslin and half-dresses and a domino—"Oh, Lord yes! Every woman needs one!"—until Jeannie felt her headache returning.

The captain grunted with pleasure as the last bit of plum duff disappeared, and he leaned back in his chair, at one with the world. "Really, Captain . . . Oh, hang it, man, may I call you Bartley?"

"Certainly, sir," replied Bartley with a grin and a last swipe of toast around the egg on his plate.

"Well, then, Bartley, I would be honored if you would join us on the trip to Whitehall." The good humor left his voice. "It will be educational in the extreme."

Bartley shook his head and glanced sideways at Larinda. "Miss Summers has made me a better offer. We are to adjourn to the bookroom and sort through these invitations."

"Pick the juiciest one for tonight," Jeannie teased.

Larinda opened her eyes wide. "Mrs. McVinnie, are you faint of heart? I shall choose at least three! We can strategize and grace three events at least."

"It is a simple matter," agreed Lady Smeath with all the aplomb of Wellington. "I'll have Cook prepare us a little restorative before you start out that will keep you moving along."

"I had something like that once in Barbados," Captain Summers commented. "I moved for a week."

Bartley exploded with a crack of laughter and Edward grinned.

"Brother, you do try me," Lady Smeath said, and her voice shook.

Jeannie rose hastily, marveling at the way her stomach heaved about. She knocked over the rest of her tea. "Dear me, Lady Summers, how clumsy. I'll just dab this up, and, Captain, shouldn't we be off then?"

"A diversion worthy of Collingwood, Jeannie," the captain said under his breath. "One would think you paced the *Royal Sovereign* at Trafalgar."

"I'm going to crack you over the head if you don't stop tormenting your sister," she replied under her breath.

Captain Summers reeled back in mock horror. "I'm all a-quiver."

Edward grinned and took Clare by the hand. "Come, come, missy, lively lively," he said, in remarkable imitation of his uncle.

Lady Smeath followed them into the hall. "If someone should chance to come calling this morning, Larinda will attend." She giggled behind her hand. "I have already received a note this morning from Lady Catherine Ryecart." She clasped her hands to her bosom. "Edwin Ryecart is a trifle short and heaven knows his title isn't as old as ours, but, Larinda, only think: ten thousand a year in funds."

Captain Summers opened his mouth to comment when Jeannie grabbed him by the arm and tugged him toward the front door.

"You're a forward baggage," he whispered in her ear as he allowed himself to be hurried along.

Jeannie pressed her lips together. "And you're not safe in mixed company," she declared.

"On the blockade I am seldom in mixed company. I forget."

"On land *or* sea, rag manners are rag manners," she stated, and he laughed, but softly, so as not to discommode her tender head.

"Wait, Jeannie," said Bartley behind them. He came toward her quickly and drew her to one side. "I am sorry for making a fool of myself upstairs," he said. "I didna mean to do that, but ye know me, Jeannie gal, better than anyone, I vow."

"That I do, Bartley," she agreed, wishing that the captain would not linger, but move ahead like a polite man would.

"Actually, I have something else to tell you, and it may be less pleasant than a proposal."

Jeannie felt the familiar cold augur drill a hole into her middle. She put her hand to her stomach. "Can it keep, Bartley?" she asked.

He shook his head. "Not long, Jeannie. Word has got about the regiment, and I don't like what I hear. I want you to set me straight."

She felt herself go whiter still. And now it has come to this, she thought. I knew it would, somehow. They are such a close-knit band of brothers. Jeannie gazed steadily into Bartley's eyes. "Come back tomorrow and we will talk."

He nodded, grasped her hand, and kissed it. "I don't believe it, of course." He flashed a grin to Clare, who stood admiring his bare knees, and strode back down the hall to Larinda, who stood with her arms full of invitations.

"Believe it, Bartley, dear," she said, and did not realize she spoke out loud. "Believe it."

The captain came closer and put his hand under his elbow. "Do you need to find a sofa, Jeannie?" he asked, his voice half-serious, his eyes full of questions.

She shook her head and then raised her chin. "Nothing like that, Will."

When she would say nothing more, he shrugged and picked up Clare, bobbing her down the front steps until she squealed. Jeannie stood where she was another moment, flogging herself with unquiet thoughts, before she hurried after them.

The barouche waited for them in front of the house, the horses sedate, much to Edward's dismay. "I like the hackney better, Uncle," he said over his shoulder as he clambered in and made himself comfortable. "Mama's coachman is an old grandmother."

The captain lifted in Clare. "Nephew, let us consider Mrs. McVinnie's delicate state."

Jeannie looked at him suddenly. How odd you should use that expression just now, she thought. How odd. She stood where she was. Jeannie McVinnie, your ravens have come home to roost, and you thought to outfly them?

The captain was holding out his hand to her. "Jeannie?" he was asking, "are you there?"

She smiled automatically and reached for his hand, grasping

it much too tight. He frowned at her in real consternation. When she said nothing, he handed her up into the barouche and returned the pressure.

"I trust you will remember that I am still very much your friend," was all he said before turning his attention to Edward, who was poring over his guidebook.

"Nay, you lump of shark chum, close that infernal book," he roared in his best quarterdeck fashion. "I don't need a guide to Whitehall. Clare, sit you down before you wrinkle Mrs. McVinnie."

They drove at a sedate pace to Whitehall and the Admiralty House, squeezing through the narrow gate and rolling to a stop before the wide columns. As the coachman jumped down to lower the steps, the porter, a one-legged man with a pigtail, limped out of the entrance hall, his hand already raised to a salute.

"Captain Sir William Summers," he shouted, and clicked his shoe against his peg so smartly that Jeannie thought he would topple over. "Sir!"

The captain straightened his cocked hat and winked at Edward. "They don't do that when you're a lieutenant, my boy. And when you're a midshipman? Lad, even the dogs lift their legs on you. But I'm number 130 now on a jealous list of 614 at last reckoning. Ain't it a grand business?"

Edward smiled and nodded, and Jeannie was chilled to the bone, grateful deep in her heart that Edward didn't recognize such shivering sarcasm. She raised startled eyes to the captain's face and saw only the martinet who had ordered her into his room less than a week ago to sew on a button, and handsomely now, lively. She turned away, wondering what he was doing.

She followed thoughtfully up the steps with Clare, who skipped along beside her. The captain captured her other hand, and the child settled into a more seemly pace.

The marble hall was empty, except for the man in livery who stood up from his desk and crossed off a name. "Sir, may I show you into the board room? His lordship will find you there."

Unsmiling, his eyes the hardest green Jeannie could imagine, the captain nodded. The attendant bowed them into the board room and the captain clapped his hand on Edward's shoulder and walked him directly to the tall windows that gave out upon the Thames. Jeannie watched him a moment. He said nothing to the boy, only looked out over the water. His hand went to Edward's head and rested there.

Clare had skipped off to a row of cylinders on the oak wall. She climbed onto a chair and pulled at the closed one with its tassel dangling. With a squeal, she pulled one and gasped when it unrolled and snapped back up the wall.

Jeannie hurried to her and Clare turned her face into Jeannie's skirts. "You are an inquisitive sprite," Jeannie said mildly, as she pulled down the chart and gazed upon the Baltic Sea. Such a clever arrangement of maps, she thought. She pulled down another and then another, gazing upon the oceans of the world, places foreign to her and the very blood that flowed in Will Summers' veins. Jeannie traced her finger along the sensual outline of Brazil as it tucked in toward the River Plate.

"The Portugee are a people without any scruples, madam," boomed a familiar voice. "But, by God, the women!"

Jeannie smiled at the map and then arranged her face soberly and turned to face the First Lord of the Admiralty. He looked much the same as he had last night at the theater, except that the front of his uniform was dappled with snuff and his fingers stained with ink.

He followed her gaze. "Lud, Madam, I used to be a sailor. Now I push a quill around a page and let others stalk the lee side of the quarterdeck."

Captain Summers turned from his contemplation at the window and saluted, coming forward with his hand extended. "What news, Charles?" he asked when they shook hands. "We know each other too well for much formality."

Charles did not reply, but regarded Edward a moment, and then turned to the curious clock on the wall beside the charts. "What o'clock is it, my boy? Lively now, lad. A quick answer keep the boatswain's knot off your back."

Edward gulped and almost ran to the clock. He studied it for some moments while Summers' lips twitched and Charles rumbled deep in his throat.

"I don't know, my lord," Edward admitted finally.

"What?" roared the First Lord so loud that even Jeannie jumped and Clare's lip began to quiver.

Edward bore the blast without wilting. He cast a glance at his uncle and then squared his shoulders. "No excuse, my lord," he said, his voice reedy but firm.

Lord Smeath slapped his knee and fished two candies from his desk drawer, tossing one to Edward and the other to Clare.

"What o'clock, Summers?" he barked out.

Summers took his turn before the dial. His grin faded as he stared at the face. "Damn," he exclaimed. "And damn again."

"Exactly so, Captain. I think I will be needing you again, and soon."

The First Lord inclined his head toward Jeannie. "It is a weather vane, Mrs. McVinnie. Dash it, you are a beauty! A weather vane that turns and turns on the roof and does not lie."

"And it is an east wind, Charles," said Summers. "That means the French will try to stir themselves from Brest and work a little mischief. God, and here I am."

"Not for long, I think." The First Lord heaved himself into his high-backed chair at the end of the long, polished table. "And if you go, I must escort Agatha here and there, and jolly Larinda."

He was silent then, his face registering vast disapproval of the prospect. Edward edged himself to the charts again and took Clare by the hand.

"No orders yet, Charles?" Summers asked finally.

"No, my boy. Nothing that good. But the wind has been blowing in that quarter for a little time. You will have orders soon. Be ready when they come."

"Aye, aye, sir."

Lord Smeath nodded and popped a candy in his mouth. He sucked on it vigorously. "And he will leave you to carry on, Mrs. McVinnie?"

"I suppose, my lord."

She was standing close to the table. To her surprise, the First Lord reached up and pinched her cheek so hard that her eyes watered. He winked at Summers.

"If you were twenty years older, you could do this, my boy."

Summers shook his head. "I wouldn't dare."

"Then rip off both epaulets, William Summers, and bare your back for the cats. You're no sailor."

The captain only smiled.

Lord Smeath turned to Edward. "And what about you, lad? A life at sea for you?"

Edward nodded, his mouth open.

The First Lord glared at him. "Well, then, well, then?" he asked in that same impatient growl that had collapsed sterner men than the boy who stood before him.

"Aye, aye, sir," Edward managed, his face on fire.

Captain Summers shook his head. "No, Charles, not this one. He is the only son of my dead brother and the head of this family. He will not go to sea."

The First Lord placed his hands behind his back, paced about, and twiddled his fingers together. "I remember hearing that one. Lord bless me, 'twas my own father."

He paused in his ponderous wanderings. "Of course, I was not the head of my family." He looked down kindly enough at Edward. "It's for the best, lad."

When no one said anything, the First Lord took another glance at the weather dial and winked at Jeannie, who was hard put to maintain her sober countenance.

"That was all I had to tell you, William. I am sorry there is not more news for you, but when it comes, when Pellew of the White Fleet looks about and finds you far from sea, it will come suddenly, as you well know."

"As I well know."

"Do we see you at Lady Jersey's tonight?"

"It is likely. Thanks to Beau Brummell and whatever magic Jeannie worked on him, all the doors in London have been flung wide open. Our skids are well-greased."

The First Lord sighed with relief. "And the sooner Larinda is leg-shackled, the sooner my sister-in-law, God bless her, will retreat to Suffolk and spend her days describing her urban triumph at length to the local squire's wife and anyone else who will listen. It cannot be too soon."

They took their leave of Lord Smeath, who was deep over his papers long before they closed the door behind them.

The anteroom had filled up with officers, many of whom hailed Captain Summers and waylaid him with conversation while Jeannie gathered the children about her.

At last the captain rejoined them. He put his arm about Edward again. "You should have seen this hall on the day of Lord Nelson's funeral. More gold and lace I have never seen." He looked out toward the Thames again. "And you should see it when it is crammed with half-pay officers practically lighting

candles to hurry the misfortunes of those above them in rank."
His voice took on a harder edge. "Lop goes the arm or leg,
my boy, up goes the officer beneath him. Hurrah for death."

Edward directed a puzzled look at his uncle while Jeannie
rested her hand on Captain Summers' arm. The pressure of her
fingers recalled him to the moment. "Too much, Jeannie?" he
asked softly, so Edward could not hear. "I know not how else
to discourage the lad. That is all I am about."

They walked out of the building and came to the famous
Whitehall Steps. Jeannie tightened her grip on Clare, who
danced about and clapped her hands at the sight of the slowly
moving Thames. Wherries and sculls clustered about the steps
like goldfish awaiting a feeding, each waterman calling out his
price. Captain Summers raised his hand and pointed, and one
boat maneuvered closer. Summers lifted Edward on board and
the boy stumbled forward, his face alive with pleasure.

Despite her delight with the water, Clare came less eagerly.
"Careful there," the captain said. "The tide is going out, Clare,
and the steps are slippery."

When Clare had been deposited in the boat, Captain Summers
helped Jeannie, keeping his hand firmly tucked inside the waistband of her dress. He seated her carefully in the thwarts and
sat beside her, not relinquishing his hold until she reminded him.

"Deptford," the captain said.

"Aye, aye, sir," the waterman replied as he and his mate
began to row.

The tide was racing down to the sea far away, and the boat
shot along, a water bug among closely packed trout. Clare sat
on Jeannie's lap, clutching her towel doll, turning her face into
Jeannie's bosom. Captain Summers touched her curls and tried
to get her to look around, but she only shook her head and
burrowed into Jeannie.

He smiled. "Little one, are you not descended from that
conniving race that sent out sea captains beyond the edge of
the world? What say you, Edward?"

Edward said nothing, only looked away and kept his death's
grip on the gunwales as they flew along.

They smelled Billingsgate almost before they saw it. Captain
Summers wrinkled his nose. "I never did care above half for
fish," he said to no one in particular.

Without any warning, Edward leaned over the gunwales and vomited into the river. The oarsman laughed until Jeannie froze him with a long look. Oblivious, Edward paid no mind and did not turn around from his contemplation of London by water.

Captain Summers nudged Jeannie and pointed. "My dear Jeannie, the Tower of London. I wonder. Do you suppose that unfortunate pachyderm is still blue?"

"Don't remind me," Jeannie exclaimed.

They were all silent then, watching as the oarsmen navigated the river and dodged here and there among the larger craft that plied the river in both directions. Several times Jeannie, her eyes scrunched shut, wanted to press her face into Captain Summers' chest, just as Clare was doing to her, but she only gulped and prayed that the watermen had consumed less spirits than she had the night before.

Another sharp bend, and Deptford Hard stretched before them, the great naval yard. His seasickness forgotten, Edward looked this way and that. He turned around to his uncle and grinned, his freckles standing out clearly in his white face. He could scarcely keep his seat when his uncle pointed out a fifth rater, the largest ship in the yard.

"Is it as fine as the *Venture*?" Edward asked, his voice breathless.

"No, lad, nothing's as fine as the *Venture*." Summers loooked closer. "Ah! It is the *Calliope*." Without a word he stood and, carefully balancing himself, raised his hand in a smart salute as the wherry shot past. He sat down only when the ship was far astern. "The *Calliope*," he murmured, and then leaned forward toward Edward. "A gallant ship, my boy, and bound for the West Indies soon enough. I spent many a summer's day running up and down her riggings. I wonder, does Captain Russell Jones still command here?"

"Where now, sir?" asked the waterman.

"The hospital. You may wait for us there."

"The hospital?" Jeannie asked as the little boat threaded its way among the fighting ships and frigates of the Royal Navy and the barges victualing them.

"From the gold lace of Whitehall to the hospital, Jeannie. One cannonball can put you there."

The hospital rose before them, another graceful contribution from Christopher Wren to the English countryside. The wherry-man angled them expertly to the wharf and cast a line to secure the boat.

Captain Summers pried Clare from Jeannie and carried her up the steps to land. "You are such a lubber," he said softly, and pressed her head against his chest. "Silly girl. Come, Edward. There is someone here I especially want you to meet."

Wren had not stinted in the design of the hospital. The main hall was lofty and busy with the comings and goings of attendants and sailors on crutches or peg legs. Other men lay on cots, waiting for the morning sun with its healing rays to reach them.

The smell of the sickroom was all about them. Jeannie groped about in her reticule and raised a handkerchief to her nose. Under the strong disinfectant was the smell of festering wounds and the odor of men in fever. It reminded her forefully of Galen McVinnie, and the long, long months she had nursed him in Kirkcudbright, listening to him weep for his son and hiding her own double anguish.

"Let me wait outside," she said to Summers.

The captain did not answer her. He stopped a sister hurrying by, whispered some words to her, and handed Clare into her keeping. The child clutched at her towel doll, but did not cry.

"Captain, please!"

"Come with us, Jeannie. Here's my hand," said the captain.

She grabbed it like a drowning sailor and clung to him as they mounted the broad staircase that was also littered with convalescents.

Close to tears, Jeannie watched Edward out of blurred eyes. His back was straight, and even though his face was pale, it was composed. The muscles worked in his jaw, and he swallowed too often, but he uttered no protest as they passed the wounded and the dying.

Up another flight of stairs, this one narrower now, and across a catwalk that led them around the great main hall, and then Captain Summers stopped outside an open door. He put both hands on Edward's shoulders. "Do you know why I have brought you here, my boy?" he asked finally.

"I think so, sir," Edward replied, and then managed a crooked smile. "You want to frighten me?"

"I thought I did, lad, but now I just want you to meet someone dear to me. Come, Jeannie. Chin up."

They entered the long ward, which was well-lit by the sun and growing warm. Nuns glided about, bringing in the noon meal. The odor of bean soup tickled Jeannie's nostrils and mingled with the smell of wounds and musty old men.

There was not a whole man in the entire ward. There were parts of men, men with no arms, no legs, no eyes, and others with combinations fantastic and grotesque. It was a giant workshop of unfinished bodies, as though the toymaster had done so much and then walked away, out of caprice or boredom.

The captain stood still before a cot where a white-haired man sat, his eyelids closed over sunken cavities. A fly rested on his chest. He flicked it off with the stump of one arm that ended at his elbow. Jeannie looked down and swallowed. He had only one leg.

Summers said nothing. Jeannie was too shocked to bring herself to look about at Edward. To take her mind off the broken man before her, she studied the captain's profile. He stood so quietly, hat in hand, his lips drooping down as they did when he was not alert. He dropped his hat on the bed.

"Captain Summers?" asked the man, raising his face as though he could see William Summers. "I thought I recognized your stride."

"The very same."

"You're not thumping along on a peg? Thought you would be, from what I heard of Cabo San Lucar." He let out a crack of laughter. "I heard someone carried you below, and you swearing all the way!"

Summers grinned and sat down beside the curious lump of a man. "Who told you that faradiddle?"

The seaman raised his shoulder in a shrug. "One of the lads who only came here to stay a short while. He's out back now, filling a hole."

"As we all will, Matthews."

The seaman laughed again. "Not me, sir. I have your promise in writing." He pointed his chin down at the leather bag about his neck. "And don't you know I have it memorized? 'Caleb Matthews, sailing master, is to be taken out to the Channel and dropped in the water.' A proper, decent burial for me, sir."

He looked about him. "But you're not alone, sir, are you, and one of them's a lady." He sniffed the air. "They smell different, sir, even the worst of them."

"Thank the Lord for that, Matthew. That is Mrs. Jeannie McVinnie. Touch his shoulder, Jeannie."

She reached out and patted him, resting her hand on his shoulder and praying that she would not shame him by trembling.

He tucked his whiskered chin on her hand for a moment and smiled. "A proper lady, Captain. Smooth hands."

"A very proper lady, Matthews. And here is Edward, my nephew. He thinks he will go to sea. Nephew?"

Edward, even paler than before, inched forward and sat himself gingerly on the cot. His hand was shaking as he reached out to touch Caleb Matthews, as Jeannie had done. He sucked in his breath as the seaman suddenly raised his stump of an arm along Edward's face, quickly and lightly, and then down his back.

"He's not got much meat on him, sir," said Matthews.

"No, but then neither had Nelson, if you will recall." Will Summers grinned. "And he will likely hang on to all his hair and not run to fat, as I am doing right now."

The stump reached out again and felt of Summers' middle. Matthews laughed. "Buttons stretched a little tight, sir? Get you back to sea, sir, and be right smart about it!" Matthews looked around at Edward again, as though there were sight somewhere behind his closed lids. "And take this one with ye. He'll do."

Captain Summers rose to his feet and held out his hand for Edward. "We must be off." He lingered, his eyes tender. "Does the sister read to you every night?"

Matthews nodded, and a grin split his face from ear to ear. "Every night from the *Naval Chronicles,* and the others what can, they gather 'round, too. I know more about what is going on in the fleets than the First Laddie of the Admiralty, I vow. And she reads me your letters as many times as I like."

"You're warm enough?"

"Yes, sir, thankee."

There was nothing more to say. Will laid his hand against the old man's neck, leaned forward, and kissed his cheek. Tears started in his eyes, and Jeannie had to look away. He turned back as Edward raised his hand and rested it on the old man's neck, while he laid his cheek alongside the weather-beaten face.

Jeannie took her turn and kissed his cheek.

"When he was a little bitty midshipman, I was his sailing master," Matthew said simply as he rested his chin on her hand. "I flogged him once for giving me a saucy answer, and he cried."

"I never talked back to you again," said the captain.

"Aye, sir, but you have cried since then, I vow."

"Not often, Matthews. Maybe not enough. Good day, now. I'll be by again. You have my word on it."

Matthews chuckled to himself. "Don't the other lads envy me! Every two or three years, I have a visitor."

Jeannie turned her face away, but there was nowhere to look except into other eyes. She stumbled toward the door. Edward took her by the arm and they waited in the passageway until Captain Summers joined them.

He said nothing as they retraced their steps, retrieved Clare, and left the building. White-faced, Edward hurried ahead and vomited again, leaning over the railing by the wharf.

"Did you have to do that?" Jeannie asked, her voice no more than a breath.

"Yes. I wish to God someone had done this to me when I was twelve and full of it."

"But it wouldn't have stopped you," she burst out.

He looked at her in surprise. "No, of course not. But at least I would have been warned." He looked at his nephew, who was on his knees now, resting against the railing, exhausted. "And that counts for something."

Captain Summers helped Edward to his feet, wiping his face and straightening his coat.

"It is a hard, hard service, nephew." He sighed and looked back at the hospital. "Sometimes the lucky ones die. Well, Edward?"

"I will go to sea, Uncle. I will."

"Perhaps you will," Summers said. His voice grew hard again. "And if you do and I find out that you have let your men rot in hospitals, I'll let the cat out of the bag myself and flog you around the fleet."

"Yes, sir," said Edward seriously. "But it won't happen. Not now."

Jeannie looked from one to the other, her gaze resting on the captain. I love you, Will Summers, she thought suddenly. Her stomach seemed to drop down to her shoes and then bob up again to her throat. How could I have done such a stupid thing?

14

THE watermen deposited them on Whitehall Steps as the early-afternoon sky puckered up with clouds and rain threatened. Clare lost her footing on the slimy steps and tipped herself into the water. Jeannie started after her, but the captain grabbed the back of her dress again.

"Edward will do it," he said, as the boy waded off the lowest step and into the evil brew that passed for the Thames at low tide. He scooped up Clare and grabbed her towel doll before it drifted downstream. Captain Summers took off his uniform coat and wrapped Clare in it and Jeannie helped Edward up the steps.

"Edward, you are a hero," the captain said.

Edward, squeezing off some of the mud from his jacket, looked up in surprise and grinned for the first time since they had left the hospital in Greenwich. He laughed self-consciously and made a face as he held out the bedraggled doll to Jeannie. "I'd feel more like a hero if you took this doll, Mrs. McVinnie," was all he said. He sloshed beside Jeannie toward the Admiralty House.

The captain watched them and shook his head. "I don't know that it is possible to accomplish an expedition in safety with all of you," he said. "Edward, what is that sticking out of your pocket?"

With thumb and forefinger, Edward pulled out the muddy guidebook.

"Hand it here," the captain ordered.

He set Clare down and ruffled through the soggy pages, his eyes boring into the pages as though he searched for some great wisdom that had so far eluded him. Edward looked at Jeannie, a question in his eyes, but she merely put a finger to her lips and kept him quiet.

Captain Summers stared a minute more at the book without seeing it, equally oblivious to the stares and smiles of brother officers, their hats cocked forward against the little breeze, who moved toward the steps, coveted orders in hand.

Finally Will looked up from his perusal of the guidebook and spoke to none of them in particular. "Children are a plaguey lot," he said. "I wonder that anyone sets out to have them."

Jeannie hid her smile behind her hand, even as the Captain fingered Clare's wet curls and picked her up again. Guidebook in hand, he started for the street and then stopped suddenly, set Clare down again, turned around, and threw the book in a wide arc that took it far out into the Thames. The officers at the top of the steps looked back at him in amazement and whispered among themselves. Edward could only stare, his face long, his mouth half-open.

After another moment spent in contemplation of the deed, Summers clasped his hands behind his back in that familiar gesture and walked slowly toward Edward.

"Nephew, your guidebook days have ended. I have other reading in mind for you. Come, you wretched children. If I remain here any longer, I will lose all credibility and even Lord Smeath will have no choice but to put me in command of a garbage scow. Lively now."

He hurried them along the walkway to the street, where he stopped a hackney and lifted in the children. He was helping Jeannie up when he paused, her hand in his, and looked back at the Admiralty roof, where the weather vane turned slightly in the light breeze. It moved this way and that, but it always bore toward the east.

Jeannie watched his face, noting how the corners of his mouth turned down and his eyes hardened. He took a deep breath and let it out slowly. He looked down at Jeannie and tightened his grip on her hand.

"I have a good first lieutenant. Not brilliant, mind you, but good." His eyes went back to the weather vane. "I hope he is good enough."

Clare's teeth were chattering by the time they arrived at Wendover Square. Captain Summers held her close, his chin resting on her head. Edward squirmed in his soggy clothes. Once or twice during the silent ride home he had opened his mouth to address his uncle, but Jeannie trod upon his foot and he remained silent.

Despite their stealth in entering the house, they had the misfortune to encounter Lady Smeath in the hall. She shrieked, threw up her hands, and ran to Edward, not touching him, but fluttering about like a cabbage moth. She darted angry glances at the captain and Jeannie and muttered, "Outside of enough," over and over until Jeannie wanted to box her ears.

As Edward dripped on the floor, Lady Smeath whirled about to excoriate her brother. "William, such carelessness speaks of an unsound mind." She passed her hand in front of her eyes. "One would think you were determined to wrest his title and fortune from him by a tumble in the Thames."

"Unworthy of you, Agatha," Summers said, his lips set in that thin line that Jeannie dreaded.

Lady Smeath's demon spurred her on. "One has to wonder," she said, and dabbed at her eyes. "Poor, fatherless child, and him practically an invalid! Now I suppose you will tell me that he rescued that little Portuguese by-blow, and I should be happy."

The captain reeled back as though she had struck him. Without a word, he picked up Clare and walked slowly up the stairs, calling for Mary.

"I'm sure I don't know what he is so exercised about," Lady Smeath sniffed.

Jeannie stared. No, you probably do not, she thought as she watched Lady Smeath take Edward gingerly by the sleeve and head him up the stairs, calling out for the butler and the upstairs maid.

Jeannie followed slowly. She glanced at the clock as she mounted the steps. It wanted less than an hour to five o'clock, when she would be on her way to Hyde Park with Beau

Brummell. The prospect filled her with dread. I suppose I must be witty and sparkling, she thought. I would still rather throw all my clothes in a bag and sneak off to Scotland.

Lady Smeath had gone in search of the butler, leaving Edward to stand dripping in the hall. The captain came out of Clare's room and saw him there.

"When you are clean again, come to my room," he said, and looked about him with an air of studied disinterest. "Now that your guidebook rests in Neptune's back pocket, I will suggest some different activity. To while away the tedium of the hours, I think it is time for Pringle to instruct you in navigation. Here now, lad, steady as you go!"

Edward had leapt forward to grab his uncle. He laughed instead and lowered his muddy arms.

"You may use my sextant. It is in my room. Pringle knows where."

"Sir!" was all Edward could manage. "Sir," he said again, and all rational thought fled his brain. Tears came to his eyes and he tried to brush them away, leaving a streak of Thames mud across his face. "This is the best day of my life," he wailed.

The captain nodded. "You must be very careful with the sextant. I lost mine at Trafalgar. This one was a gift to me from Caleb Matthews, who had no need to raise a sextant to blind eyes after Trafalgar."

Edward's face was serious again. "I will be so careful, sir," he said.

"See that you are, lad. I have no greater prize, really." He smiled beyond Edward's head to Jeannie. "Not even my emerald."

They heard Lady Smeath's footsteps on the stairs again. The captain opened the door to his room. "Not a word to my sister yet, my boy. We may have to wear her around to this idea."

"She will never agree," Edward said quietly.

Without a word, Jeannie went into her room and shut the door. She sat down on the bed and stared at the wall, grateful for the moment to be alone with her thoughts, which were disquieting in the extreme.

She could not possibly be in love with William Summers. Even the idea of it was so totty-headed and irrational that she smiled in spite of herself. Jeannie remembered her thoughts on the interminable ride from Kirkcudbright to London, when she had calmly rehearsed in her mind the prospects of marriage.

She laughed softly and began to unbutton her dress. She had decided then that her next husband would have to be just like Tom, with a tall, slim build, blue eyes, of course, nice dark and wavy hair. She sighed. The kind of hair to run her fingers through and not worry that she would pull it out. And above all, any husband of hers would have to be even-tempered like Tom, someone she could be comfortable with, and not a bully with a sharp tongue and a wit that could slash like a cutlass.

Oh, do be fair, she thought as she went to the dressing room in hopes of finding something interesting to wear. Will Summers is tall, certainly, and I've never seen anyone so breathtaking in uniform. But that's not necessarily so much Will as it is the uniform, she rationalized. Lord help us, navy men are elegant. I wonder that such distracting elegance is not against the law. It must be the color of the coat. Or perhaps it is those hats?

She hauled a walking dress off the peg and shook it. Strange that he still looks so good, even when he is not in uniform. He's even a bit shabby, because, truth to tell, all his civilian clothes must be at least five years out of style. Somehow, it doesn't matter.

With a laugh, Jeannie acknowledged the sheer idiocy of a proposal from Will Summers and felt unaccountably better. She put the dress on the bed and sat at her dressing table to brush out her hair, her comfort restored. The point is moot, you silly nod, she told herself, which will make the cure easy. Will Summers, Sir William Summers, was the younger son of a marquess. He would never marry the daughter of a country doctor. Never.

Well, possibly he would if she were wealthy, and beautiful into the bargain. Jeannie grinned at her image as she brushed her hair. Tom thought she was beautiful, but Tom loved her. And wealthy? She rolled her eyes. By careful economy, she could just manage on her widow's stipend and the little money her father had left her, if she didn't indulge in too many wild extravagances, like this impulsive trip to London and the purchase of too many clothes.

She considered the clothes and blushed. The only new clothes had so far been purchased for her by Captain Summers, and with the cock-and-bull story about "wanting my crew to look good." Lord, and I let him. What a silly I am. And now, if Lady Smeath was correct, she would have a wardrobe merely on the good name of Beau Brummell.

Beau Brummell. Jeannie frowned into the mirror and began to brush her hair faster. She glanced at her watch on the table. He will be here in fifteen minutes and I am sitting in my chemise. She jumped up from the dressing table and pulled the dress over her head, wondering how she would manage the buttons in the back and wishing that Mary were around. She buttoned all that she could reach from each direction and sank onto the bed again. None of these careful conclusions, beyond the obvious fact that he would never ask her, approached the real reason that she would never consider marrying Will Summers: he would never be around, just as Tom was never around.

"Jeannie McVinnie, you have spent all the solitary Christmases, birthdays, Easters, and anniversaries that you wish," she said out loud as she pulled her hair back from her face and secured it with a barrette. "You are tired of talking out loud to yourself. You wish someone to answer back. William Summers will never do for that, not in a million years."

Where would he be when I truly needed him? she asked. Where was Tom? She bowed her head. And where was I when Tom needed me?

The thought chilled her to the bone. She closed her eyes against it, even as she remembered Galen McVinnie, and those long days and longer nights when she sat up with him and he looked at her in that questioning way, as if measuring the courage of her soul. She opened her eyes. And having measured her, he had found her sadly wanting. And now there is Bartley, who has questions, too.

Her hands were cold, and she clasped them together. The stares in Kirkcudbright were not so hard to bear, and truth to tell, people have a way of forgetting about the dead who were never in their midst much anyway. But there was the regiment, and Galen, devoted to her because he had promised Tom, and loving her as a daughter-in-law because it was expected of him. Only when he was tired and his leg pained him did he allow that speculative look to settle in his eyes. Someday he will ask me to tell him the truth, she thought, and then what will I do?

Why was it that none of her questions had any answers to them? Jeannie reached around for the last few buttons. Drat.

Jeannie opened the door and stuck her head out into the hall, where there was not a servant in sight. She edged along the wall toward Clare's room. Surely Mary was within.

She heard someone on the stairs and froze, crossing her fingers and hoping it was Mary to do up her buttons.

Bartley whistled his way into the hall. He smiled at Jeannie and raised his hand in greeting.

"Bartley, what are you doing here?" she asked, her back against the wall.

"Oh, I don't know," he replied cheerfully. "After Larinda— Miss Summers—and I finished sorting out the invitations, she needed an escort to Hookham's to return a book, and then one thing led to another and here I am still. Lady Smeath came stomping down the stairs a moment back and said that you were up here." He stopped and looked at her face. "Jeannie, are you all right?"

"I'm fine," she said, "only I must hold up this wall until I find someone to button up the back of my dress. Is Larinda below?"

He laughed. "Turn around, Jeannie," he said.

She shook her head. "It's much too improper."

He looked around elaborately at the empty hall and then raised up one corner of the runner on the floor and peered under it. Jeannie giggled and turned around.

"I would close my eyes, Jeannie dear, but then I would be fumbling about. Hold still. How can I perform this maneuver if you are laughing?"

He did up her buttons and she turned about again and curtsied playfully. He took her by the hand. "Jeannie, do you have a moment to spare?" he asked, and all the fun went out of his eyes.

Her smiled vanished. She looked up at Bartley MacGregor's dear, honest face. It was an expression totally without guile. Tom had remarked to her once that Bart would probably be fleeced by every double-dealer he came across. "You'd have to hit him over the head with a caber, Jean, to get through to him that everyone's not as honest as he," Tom had said.

Jeannie held tight to Bartley's hand. She could make an excuse and avoid him for another day, but there must come an end to it. It was time to put a ghost to rest, even if it meant . . . whatever it would mean to one so devoted to her.

"I have a moment, but only that," she said, her voice low.

She thought for a moment to take him into her room, but she went instead to the nursery and opened the door. A small fire burned in the hearth of the little sitting room, but all else was quiet. Mary must have taken Clare down the hall to the bathing room. Jeannie motioned for Bartley to follow her and she closed the door behind him.

He sat down on the sofa, tucking his kilt about him, but rose almost immediately and went to the fireplace, where he rested his arm along the mantel. He didn't say anything for the longest time, so Jeannie cleared her throat.

"You have been hearing rumors about me?" she prodded, her voice scarcely above a whisper.

He nodded, but still did not speak. He shook his head at the floor and then looked her in the eye.

"Jeannie, you couldn't have done what I'm hearing." He came closer and took hold of her hands. "It's too unlike you to be believed, but . . . ." his voice trailed off and he couldn't look her in the eyes.

"But everyone believes it?" she asked.

He nodded. "When we got back to Dumfries from Canada, we joined the remnant of boys who had been on the beach at La Coruña. All the women were whispering and whispering that, that . . . Ah, Jeannie, that you never came to Portsmouth, not in those whole three weeks when Tom was dying and Galen so close to it that the doctor had to use a mirror more than once to see if he still breathed."

Jeannie was silent.

Bartley let go of her hands and backed himself up to the fireplace as if he had taken a sudden chill. "I mean, the other women came. All your lady friends. It was hard day and night traveling, but they came and stood by their men as the women of the Dumfries Rifles have always done. But you weren't there."

She shook her head. "It's true, Bartley," she managed.

"Oh, Jeannie," he burst out, "how could ye do such a thing? Colonel Mackey's wife said she sat up with Tom and all he could do was call for you and stare at the door each time it opened, with such a light in his eyes!"

"Please don't," Jeannie said, and sat down on the sofa because her legs wouldn't hold her.

Bartley couldn't stop now that he had begun. "Then just before Tom died—my best friend, Jeannie, never mind that he was your husband, too—he told Lady Mackey that you would come. Kept insisting, even as his eyes sank in his head."

Jeannie covered her face with her hands.

Bartley sighed and sat down heavily beside her on the sofa. "And that's the story Lady Mackey tells. How Tom started up at the last moment with such a look in his eyes when he realized that he was all alone." He shook his head. " 'Ach, such a mask of terror to wear through the eternities,' is how Lady Mackey describes it." He touched Jeannie then, pulling her hands away from her face and clasping them firmly. "That's the story she puts about the regiment."

Jeannie looked into Bartley's eyes, Bartley she had known since they were both children. She saw looking back at her that same wary look that stared out from Galen's eyes when he thought she wasn't aware.

"Jeannie McVinnie, how could ye be such a coward?" Bartley asked in amazement. "I never would have thought it possible." He ran his fingers over her knuckles and then put her hand to his lips. "Tell me there is something more to the story, please. I have to know."

With a great effort, Jeannie rose and took her place in front of the fireplace. She was colder than she could ever remember before, but there was no warmth from the flames. For a moment she considered telling him what he wanted to hear, but only for a moment.

"There is nothing more to the story, Bartley, nothing more," she said.

He stared at her, and gradually the wary look gave way to contempt and then resignation. "Then it is all true what Lady Mackey tells?"

"You have said it," Jeannie whispered.

"Jeannie!" Bartley leapt to his feet. "And we all thought ye such a braw, bonnie lass! How could ye?"

He went to the door and wrenched it open, looked back at her once and tried to speak, and then left the room. In another moment, she heard him pounding down the stairs, probably out of her life. For a year she had anticipated the wretched scene that had just played itself out, but in all her anxiety she had erred in one respect: it was much, much worse than she could ever have imagined.

She turned to the fire, wishing for some warmth from the flames that glowed with all the heat of a papier-mâché imitation. As her head finally cleared and the roaring in her ears receded, she heard the unbelievable sound of clapping.

"Bravo, Jeannie, bravo," said the captain from the inside door to Clare's room. "I never heard a more touching story, or one less true."

She gasped, whirled about, and clapped her hands over her ears. "Stop it!"

He stopped clapping, leaned against the doorframe, and stuck his hands in his pockets. "One should never eavesdrop, of course, but you two didn't give me the opportunity to announce myself. I thought you were Mary returning with Clare from the bathing room."

Jeannie edged toward the door. "It's not a thing I'm proud of," she said when she was able, "and I'll thank you not to spread the word about."

The captain shook his head. "Jeannie, I just told you I don't believe a word of it."

"Bartley does," she said. "You heard him. And Galen does." She tried to smile, but it died on her lips. "And Tom did. And each of them knows me better than you."

"I'm not so sure about that," he said. "You cannot fool me." He came closer and held out his hand to her. When she only backed closer to the door, he let it drop. "I've seen you face lions in the theater, and all for my silly niece, who only wanted to do you mischief. You would no more abandon the man you loved than fly to the moon. God, how I envy Tom!" He came closer, but did not reach for her. "Something happened, and you're shielding someone. I wish I knew who and why."

She said nothing in her defense, but she stopped her movement toward the door.

"And there you stood, such a little lady, Bartley railing at you, begging you to tell him if it was true, and all you could say was, 'You have said it,' and play Jesus to Pontius Pilate."

He came forward quickly, before she could dart out the door, and cupped her face in his hands. "But look here, lady, I am not railing at you." He kissed her nose. "I will do my utmost

to make you comfortable around me." He kissed her forehead.
"I have no winning ways because I never needed any before,
but, my dear, if you need a friend, I am here."

He released her and she bolted to the door. "I have to go
downstairs," she managed to say. "Beau Brummell is below
by now, I am sure of it."

He caught at her hand before she could dart away. "Then
Mrs. McVinnie, I recommend that you put on some shoes. Even
the Beau couldn't bring bare feet into fashion, I fear."

She fled to her room, leaning against the door until she
regained some semblance of command over herself, and then
hurried into her shoes. Jeannie knew without looking in a glass
that her face was white and anxious. She rushed to the mirror
anyway and pinched her cheeks until she drove some color into
them. With fingers that trembled, she straightened her skirts
and forced herself to take several deep breaths.

Bartley was gone. She had driven off her dearest friend, next
to Tom. "And Tom, you are dead," she said out loud. "I must
remind myself."

There was a knock at the door, and Jeannie's fingers tightened
on her skirt. She prayed that it was not the captain, for she knew
she would tell him everything, and her disclosure would serve
no useful purpose.

"Yes?" she asked.

"Mrs. McVinnie?"

"Yes?"

"I'm sorry, but it didn't sound like you," said the upstairs
maid through the door. "If you please, Mr. Brummell is
below."

"Very well," she replied. After another look at herself, a
quick scrutiny that took in her person from shoe tops to collar,
but did not include a glance into her own eyes, she left the
room.

Brummell was not alone. Lady Smeath, bereft of words for
once, sat and smiled at him, while Larinda, awed by the
personage before her, attempted conversation. She glanced
around in relief at Jeannie's entrance.

The Beau rose at once, magnificent in a coat of Bath superfine
that did not admit a wrinkle anywhere, a neckcloth of both
mathematical genius and discreet symmetric proportions, and
trousers that stretched from waist to ankle without the obscenity

of a single crease. Jeannie could only stare in frank delight, forgetting her misery for the moment.

"Sir, how do you manage to look so fine all the time?" she asked as she extended her hand.

He bowed over her hand and smiled up into her face. "My dear, it is the result of arduous labor and sacrifice of untold numbers of neckcloths upon the high altar of fashion." He sighed. "Style is a vigorous taskmaster, Mrs. McVinnie. I wonder that I have the strength for it."

As they watched in fascination, he took an exquisite enameled snuffbox from his pocket and flicked it open with his thumb in one practiced gesture, expertly extracting a pinch and placing it upon the back of his other hand, where he sniffed once, twice.

He gazed back at them in modest satisfaction. "I would imagine that I devoted more time to learning to do that than you spent learning your catechism, Mrs. McVinnie."

"I do not doubt it, sir," she agreed, a twinkle back in her eyes, "although I am not sure that the 'Whole Duty of Man' is to sneeze."

The Beau rolled his eyes and touched his forehead. "Touché, madam! Why is it that I am continually undone by your Scottish plain-speaking?"

"I am sure Mrs. McVinnie does not mean it," Lady Smeath interjected quickly.

"Of course she does," said the Beau severely, but lightened his accusation with another airy wave of a bow, in itself a work of nature. "But we are dawdling, m'dear! How are we ever to find a husband for Larinda—or you, for that matter—if we discuss my snuff?"

"I am sure you do not need to find me a husband," Jeannie said.

"Oh?" asked the Beau in surprise. "Have you already accomplished such a feat?" He looked about him elaborately. "I trust you have not cast yourself upon Captain Sir William Summers." He shuddered. "Why the Admiralty suffers them to return from the sea at all, I cannot fathom. Army officers are gallant—I know because I was one—but sea captains? Merely grim, madam. I contend that a steady diet of biscuit and salt beef makes no man capable of intelligent decisions." He chuckled. "Only consider our noble Duke of Clarence and see if I am correct."

"You are severe, Mr. Brummell," Jeannie said.

"I am," he agreed amicably. "So long as Boney keeps the captains upon the waves, we will run along tolerably well. But madam, you can imagine the threat to our amiable society when all those morose little gods in uniform are cast upon the shore? It doesn't bear thinking upon." He paused a moment in melancholy reflection and then brightened. "But, my dears, this gloomy cast gets Larinda no closer to a husband. Lady Smeath, your servant. Come, ladies."

He offered an arm to each young woman and led them outside, where the groom stood at the head of his horses. The Beau helped Larinda into the back seat of the phaeton and handed Jeannie up beside him. He took the whip from its socket and nodded to the groom. "I cannot abide the high-perch phaeton, Mrs. McVinnie. Such altitude gives me the nosebleed."

Brummell's progress to Hyde Park was remarkable for its snail's pace. He was constantly bowing and nodding to pedestrians. More than once he stopped the phaeton in the middle of the roadway to allow a conversation between carriages.

"I wonder, sir," Jeannie said after he had nodded to a clutch of ladies waiting to cross Regent Street who curtsied deep as he passed. "Do you know everyone in London, or does it only seem that way? "

He feathered his careful way around a carter rumbling by before answering. "Yes, I know everyone in London," he agreed. "Whether I choose to acknowledge them often hinges on the weighty matter of how their neckcloth is arranged, or whether"—he smiled sideways at Jeannie—"or whether they wear red or white roses. It is a matter of some concern."

Jeannie glanced behind her at Larinda, who was contemplating the crowds on Piccadilly, her chin resting in her hand. "Sir Peter Winthrop?" she asked, her voice low.

The Beau shook his head. "Alas, a sad case. He saw the need for a little rustication. 'Twill do him wonders." He sighed. "Some people haven't the stamina for a London Season."

In another block, they entered Hyde Park and joined the other carriages passing in review down Rotten Row. Brummell looked over his shoulder at Larinda. "Pay close attention, my dear. We should espy any number of choice spirits with which you could form an eligible connection."

Larinda only smiled, but her air of quiet reflection returned as soon as the Beau addressed himself to his horses again.

"We might stroll about after we have traversed the length of the row," Brummell explained. "One should reconnoiter the terrain before attempting an advance on foot, especially so early in the Season. Ah ha!"

He reined in slightly and pointed with his whip to a gathering of several young gentlemen. "Larinda, look you over there. I espy a covey of eligibles. Not a man in the group worth less than ten thousand a year." He looked closer. "Most of them appear to possess their own teeth, and Lord Spaulding over there has been known to utter at least one witticism before in his life."

Jeannie laughed out loud and the Beau nodded approvingly.

"Hurrah for you, madam. I was beginning to think that something was deviling you." He leaned closer and touched her shoulder with his. "Madam, I could find you a husband with less difficulty than you would imagine."

She shook her head again. "No one on this road is hanging out for a pensioned widow."

"Then we will find a nabob who does not care about the size of your purse, m'dear. Oh, look, Larinda! Twenty thousand a year on the starboard beam, if I may quote the estimable Captain Summers. His breath is bad, but he breathes."

And so it went, down the row and back again. Jeannie nodded and smiled, noting with amusement the young ladies, with their fashionable close-cropped hair, who had attempted to braid their hair in imitation of her own style at the theater last night. There were red roses everywhere. The men who had scrutinized her so archly at Almack's and the women who had stared outside the Pantheon Bazaar were all amiability as they approached Beau Brummell's phaeton as though it were the Fisherman's Throne in St. Peter's Basilica.

Such dissembling, she thought, and then the smile left her face. It is no worse than the deception I have practiced upon myself. In sudden shame of the acutest sort, Jeannie lowered her eyes and spent a moment in serious examination of the stitching in her kid gloves. I would disdain these foolish fashionmongers, and I am no wiser than they.

The unfairness of her situation washed over her like a full bucket, suddenly thrown. While she raised laughing eyes to Mr. Brummell and uttered witty profundities that she could not recall

the moment they left her mouth, she wanted to leap off the
phaeton, pick up her skirts, and run and run until she reached
Kirkcudbright. She smiled and flirted, even as she longed to
throw herself on her knees and sob out the whole business at
Galen McVinnie's foot.

But she could not; she dared not. She had promised she would
not.

Another traverse of the row took them to Hyde Park Gate
again. By this time, Jeannie's lap was full of more invitations
to luncheons al fresco, masked balls, routs, theater parties, and
quiet evenings *en famille*. Larinda appeared slightly more
cheerful, and the Beau was positively shaking his own hands.
He drove with a flourish and high good humor back to
Wendover Square, where he led them to the door. He kissed
Larinda's hand and then bowed for a longer time over Jeannie's.

"My dears, you are fairly launched," he decreed as he finally
released his hold upon her and stepped back. "In future, I
promise a dance to each of you at any gathering we find
ourselves gracing, should you so desire. I shall sport a red rose
for the remainder of this Season." He paused in momentary
thought, as if wondering how this could be any better. A light
came into his eyes. "And for you, Mrs. McVinnie, I will paint
a miniature of myself." He took her hand again. "Something
to tweak any bashful suitors and bring them up to the mark."

"You are all condescension," Jeannie said with a smile.

"Indeed I am," he agreed, and released her hand once more.
He walked to the phaeton and tipped his hat. "And much too
exalted for my own company. Do I see you tonight?"

He did, and at all three events that Larinda had selected for
the evening's enjoyment. He danced his way down a country
line with Jeannie, carrying on a playful conversation even as
his expressive eyes darted about the room. Jeannie could only
mind her steps and wonder at her dancing partner's agility.

She did not lack for partners, some seeking her out because
of their curiosity, and others wanting to know more about
Larinda. She said all that was polite, and tried not to allow her
own eyes to stray about the ballroom as she searched for Captain
Summers.

After squiring Lady Smeath about and then bounding
energetically through a mazurka with Larinda, he had abandoned

the dancing floor. He spoke to one one, and no one singled him out for attention. He stood alone, a man used to the over-powering solitude of command at sea. As she danced and flirted gently, Jeannie felt her heart go out to him. She looked at the single females who circled the ballrooms on the arms of their partners, wishing one of them would look about long enough to at least flutter her eyelashes at the lonely man who stood so erect with his hands behind his back, staring across a sea of people.

Their next remove took them to Wembley Place and the home of Lord Something or Other, who, Lady Smeath assured her, only attracted the truly exalted into his circle. There was a card room, and Captain Summers vanished into it as soon as he saw that his niece and his impressed crew were busy doing their duty.

At some point after the clock had struck innumerable times and the room was becoming muzzy with smoke from the candles, he resurfaced and asked Jeannie to dance.

She made a face at him. "Sir, you are to ask some eligible female. How are you to find someone during this Season if you fraternize with your crew?"

He only smiled and took her in his arms. "Hush," he ordered.

Everytime Jeannie stood this close to the captain she was reminded of their first meeting when she sewed on his button. Her eyes went first to the button and she tugged on it without thinking. He chuckled. She blushed and stared at his Knight of the Bath insignia, which was on her eye level.

"You may tug on that, too, if you choose," he offered.

"I will not, and you must excuse my impertinence. I am—"

"—merely a managing female of Scottish persuasion who likes to assure herself that all things are right and tight, spit-spot and proof-positive. I do remember that much about my own Jeannie McVinnie," he concluded. He stopped suddenly on the dance floor, narrowly averting a collision with a member of the Life Guards. "I'm so tired of being in overheated rooms," he said as he led her off the floor and out onto a balcony overlooking Lord Something or Other's garden.

"Much better," he said as he breathed deeply of the damp earth. "One becomes used to wind in the face." He turned toward her. "Especially on the weather side, this way. That's how I know if the ship is on course. The wind hits me right here." He turned again and rested his elbows on the balcony railing. "Damn this east wind," he said softly. "Damn it."

He was silent then until the dance finished and other couples, laughing and breathless, joined them on the balcony. Jeannie could sense him becoming more and more agitated by the chatter about him. She moved closer and put her hand over his. He started in surprise, but did not draw away. He laughed softly. "Did you know that under Article Twenty of the Articles of War, a crew member can be hanged for touching the captain?"

"I'll have to remember that," she said.

"See that you do," he said in his captain's voice, which he immediately ameliorated. "But not too soon."

Lady Smeath cried off after the second ball, pleading a sick headache. After arranging a ride home for Larinda and Jeannie with friends, she tottered toward the door, leaning heavily on her brother's arm. She was not too far gone to offer Larinda a pearl or two of unwanted advice, and to tell her to make herself available in the morning for a meeting on the subject of Larinda's own come-out ball.

"We must do it, and soon, my pet, no matter how indifferent my health." She fluttered her hand toward her heart and shook her head. "Your future is all that matters."

"Yes, Aunt," Larinda said, her voice filled only with a noticeable lack of enthusiasm.

Lady Smeath frowned and set her lips tight. "You know that is what we have been planning for," she exclaimed in rallying tones. "Didn't we plan and plan all last year in Suffolk? For years, I vow." She patted her heart. "I never had a daughter of my own. This is everything to me."

"Yes," Larinda agreed. She managed a slight smile before turning back to the baronet's son who waited like an overeager puppy for his turn to dance.

Not until the stars were winking out and the dawn making perfunctory gestures did Larinda and Jeannie return to Wendover Square. Larinda had slept against Jeannie's shoulder all the way from Vauxhall to Regent Street. Jeannie propped herself against the window and gazed out at the night. The trees, their leaves still half-grown, were waving gently in the little breeze.

"It blows from the east, Captain," she murmured out loud, her eyes ready to close. "What can it bring tomorrow?"

Wapping openerd the door for them when he heard their

footsteps on the front steps. Larinda dragged her shawl up to her shoulder again and asked Wapping if there were any messages for her. When he shook his head, she only sighed, looked as though she would ask Jeannie something, and then went to the stairs, pulling herself up them hand over hand.

Wapping cleared his throat. "Mrs. McVinnie, the captain requests that you join him in the breakfast parlor."

Jeannie shook her head. "You tell the captain that I am no hero tonight and require no brandy. Good night, Wapping."

Wapping cleared his throat again and said louder this time, "Mrs. McVinnie, I think you had better do as he says." He lowered his voice and looked about, as if wary of agents from foreign shores. "He received a missive from the Admiralty House, and he is in rare ill humor."

"Oh, no," she said, fully awake now. She ran down the hall and into the breakfast parlor.

Summers leapt to his feet when she entered the room and closed the door behind her. Without knowing why, she held her arms out to him and folded him in a strong embrace.

"My ship, Jeannie, my ship," was all he said.

15

THERE was nothing Jeannie could say. She held the captain close instead, resting her head against his chest until his agitation lessened. And even when his heart had ceased to pound so vigorously, she felt remarkably disinclined to release her grip. He was warm and comfortable and she wanted him.

That thought was sufficient to cause her to drop her arms as though he burned. Captain Summers stepped back suddenly and ran his fingers around his collar, muttering something about the trouble with overheated rooms as he looked about for the brandy bottle, which Wapping had placed upon the sideboard. He uncorked the bottle and looked at her inquiringly.

Jeannie shook her head. "And not much for yourself, sir," she said.

He nodded, not put off by her command. He sank into his chair again and stretched his feet out in front of him. He took a swallow of the brandy, mused it around in his mouth for a moment, and then pushed the letter toward her.

She read it slowly, frowning over the nautical phrases, and finally raised a questioning eye to him.

Summers took the letter back, stared at it again, and then crumpled it in his hands. "It was that damned east wind, Jeannie," he said when the silence was heavy as mist between them. "Just as I feared. What can my lieutenant have been thinking? A ship of the line came out and broadsided the *Venture.*"

He threw himself to his feet again as though the room were several sizes too small, and paced about, clapping his hands together in agitation, until Jeannie reached up when he passed her and grabbed them. He leaned his hands on her chair then and looked down at her.

"What will happen to your first lieutenant now?" she asked.

The captain resumed his pacing, his hands firmly clasped behind his back this time, even though his fingers twisted together.

"When the mast went by the boards, it took him along. And the sailing master, and eight of the crew who were bracing sail, and two marine sharpshooters in the roost. Such a butcher's bill, Jeannie. I can't even count that high."

Jeannie sprang to her feet this time. "God in heaven," she exclaimed, her hands to her face.

With a slight smile, he took her hands from her face and clasped them in front of her. "Don't swear, Jeannie," he said.

She shook her head. "Don't tease about it."

"I'm not teasing, my dear. It's the only way I can bear it."

She sat down again slowly and the captain rested his hands on her shoulders, his long fingers light but firm. His hands did not tremble this time. For the briefest moment, she rested her cheek against his hand.

"When do you leave?" she asked, her voice low.

He released his grip and sagged down into the chair beside

her. "That's the damnedest part of all, Jeannie," he said. "There's nothing in that note about my leaving. Not a damned word. Lord Smeath has no intention of losing his handy substitute during Larinda's London Season. The *Venture* can rot for all he cares."

"It will come into port, won't it?" she asked.

He shook his head. "No. There are lighters in the Channel Fleet with spare masts. They've probably already stepped another mast."

"Surely he will change his mind and release you from these ridiculous orders," Jeannie said.

"I will go to the Admiralty House first thing in the morning and wait in that damned anteroom until he sees me. If he will see me," he added, and passed his hand in front of his eyes. "I've seen him keep captains posted higher than I waiting for days."

The thought sent him bounding to his feet again. He went to the window and wrenched up the glass, leaning out into the east wind that blew across his face, a breeze that mocked as it cooled.

"I hate overheated rooms," he raged, "and floors that don't move, and how *quiet* this place is. There's no boom of the sails when they lower, and no rigging to sing." He leaned against the wall and stared at her, his hands shoved deep in his pockets. "Jeannie, have you ever been wild to be somewhere, just wild?"

It was her turn to rise and walk to the window, to breathe deep of the cool night air. It braced her as she considered the view outside for a moment, made her decision, and turned around to face the captain.

"Oh, Will, I have been wild to be somewhere," she said quietly.

The intensity of her voice startled Summers. He watched her as she came away from the window, and then held out his hand to her.

"Tell me, Jeannie," he said, the frustration and worry gone from his voice as though it had never been there.

Why am I doing this? she thought. Do I want his approbation? His pity? She looked at him, really took in the agitation in his eyes. Or do I love him so much that I want to divert his mind from his own troubles? I wish I knew.

"I should not," she began. "It is not a subject I had ever

thought to discuss with anyone, and assuredly not a man.''

"Tell me, Jeannie," he repeated, and tugged on her hand until she came away from the window and sat down next to him. He hitched his chair closer and patted her hand. "There ought to be something in the Articles of War about the duties of impressed crew to tell the captain whatever he asked, but there is not.''

She smiled, because he expected her to. "I tell you only because you will likely be going away soon, and I do not wish you to think ill of me,'' she said.

"I already do not think ill of you, dear Jeannie McVinnie,'' he replied, "and you know it.''

"Then you are alone in the world in that respect, sir,'' Jeannie said frankly. "There is an entire regiment that is convinced I deserted its beloved Thomas McVinnie. As if I ever could,'' she added more softly, her eyes far away beyond the wall of the breakfast parlor.

The steady pressure of Captain Summers' fingers on her hand recalled her to the moment and she took a deep breath.

"The news of La Coruña came when I was visiting my sister Agnes in Edinburgh,'' she said. "I started out at once, of course, and by myself. Most of the other wives left from Dumfries. I was to join them in York.'' She tightened her grip on Captain Summers' hand. "Oh, you don't want to hear this!''

"I do, above anything I have ever heard, Jeannie,'' was his quiet reply.

"None of them knew.'' She paused, took another deep breath and started again. "None of them knew I was with child. I hadn't even written to Tom yet because I was shy about it, even with Tom. I knew he would be so pleased, and Galen, too, but I didn't want them to worry about me alone in Scotland, and they so far away.''

"That's understandable,'' the captain agreed. "There is nothing more profitless than the quarterdeck frets.''

She nodded. "You understand.''

"Most certainly. Why do you think that when sailors get a packet of letters all at once, they read the last one first, just to make sure everything is right and tight at home?''

Jeannie brightened. "I do that, too! Or rather, I used to. But there I was.''

"Jeannie, how far along were you?'' the captain asked.

"Five months, and a little more," she replied, remembering again as her eyes clouded over. "Just far enough along to have established 'considerable rapport,' as Agnes, who has four of her own, would put it." She smiled at the puzzled look on his face. "Captain, the baby was moving about by then and I had someone to talk to instead of just myself. And such company he was."

"Oh." Captain Summers waited a moment more and, when she did not continue, prodded her. "And so you started out from Edinburgh?"

"I did. We got as far as Penicuik, and the carriage suffered the loss of a wheel." She frowned down at her hands, which were entwined in the captain's. "We were going quite slow, and it was the merest bump. Will, I thought nothing of it, really. They procured another carriage and we set out again."

She looked him in the eye. "How do these things happen? I was so careful. And yet, the pains began, and I suffered a miscarriage on that mail coach."

She closed her eyes against the memory of it and bowed her head as her face paled. "There were all those men on the coach, and none of us knew what to do. I could only sit there and watch the carriage floor turn red."

"Oh, Jeannie," was all the captain said. "And you had no friend beside you?"

She shook her head, but did not raise it. "They took me back to Penicuik, and the landlord's wife put me to bed. But there wasn't anything anyone could do."

The captain was silent. He put his arm around her.

"When it did not appear that I would stop bleeding, the landlord sent his son bareback on a horse to Edinburgh to the medical college, thank God for that. Dr. Cruikshank pulled me through."

Jeannie raised her head then and looked the captain in the eye for a brief moment. "I don't remember anything, really, except that I felt so cold. And empty."

She shivered at the thought, freed her fingers from the captain's hand, and wrapped her arms about her middle. The captain poured her a jolt of brandy, handed it to her, and she drank it without a murmur.

"See here, sir," she protested mildly, "you will have me a drunken sot before too many more days pass."

He only smiled and put his arm around her again. "Surely the regiment understood when you told them what had happened. No power on earth or in heaven could have got you to Portsmouth."

"Indeed, no," she replied as she set down the glass and took up her narrative. "I didn't remember anything for more than a week. After I was coherent again, I told Dr. Cruikshank my dilemma, and he addressed an immediate letter to Colonel Lord Mackey in Portsmouth, explaining the circumstances."

Jeannie shrugged off his arm about her shoulders and rose to her feet. "We waited for a reply, and the most curious letter came back. I shall never forget it, even when I have forgotten everything else about the whole dreadful time."

She walked to the end of the table and sat down there, placing her hands facedown in front of her. "I tore it into a thousand pieces, but I'll remember it until I die, Will, and probably beyond." She put her hands together. "He informed me that Tom was dead, and Galen so close to death that there was hardly a difference. He wrote that he would not breathe a word about the baby to Galen, for fear the sad news would tip him over the edge, and I was not to say anything either."

"Good God, what a monster," the captain exclaimed.

"No, no, I do not think so," Jeannie replied. "He was just more concerned about the welfare of his men than anything else. And he had this else to tell: Galen had a bad heart, and this definitely would have been his last campaign, no matter the outcome. The doctor assured him that my sad news, on top of all the rest, would not be good then, nor later. Yours sincerely," she finished as she tried to swallow the gall that rose with the memory.

"But surely the regiment," he began, and then stopped, his own face bitter. "No. He told no one, did he? He couldn't."

"You have it, sir. And his wife started those rumors about my cowardice. He said nothing to her in my defense and Galen was none the wiser."

Jeannie sighed and got restlessly to her feet again. The only sound in the room was the rustle of her dress as she walked up and down. "When I could walk again, I went home to Kirkcudbright and signed for Tom's coffin four weeks later. I buried our little bairn with him. No one knew except Agnes. My brother-in-law had been away on family business in Fort

William, and I made her promise not to tell him. He would have created a muckle row and, in truth, Galen was so sick.''

"But Jeannie, the unfairness," the captain began, and then clapped his hands together in exasperation. "Oh, damn the man!"

Jeannie walked around to the captain and rested her hands on his shoulders this time in a soothing gesture. "Nay. He was so kind," she said as her voice hardened. "Only think ye, he wrote me a letter and assured me that someone as bonnie as I would find another man and there would be other bairns." Her grip tightened on his shoulders. "But I did't want another man, and I wanted that baby! Men are heartless, Will. I wonder that women tolerate them."

Captain Summers smiled faintly, but said nothing. He covered her hands with his own, and they remained in silence until Jeannie looked up and noticed that the dawn was coming.

"Goodness, it is late," she said.

"Early, my dear, very early," the captain corrected. He removed his hands from Jeannie's and stood up. "You must tell Galen," he said. "You must write to him at once."

She shook her head. "Don't you see that I cannot?"

"I don't see it, and you wouldn't either if you thought it through. He deserves to know, and if it give his heart a jolt, well, that is the fortune of war, I suppose."

Jeannie shook her head again. "I cannot agree." She smiled up at the captain and backed away from him. "It's enough for me to know that somewhere in the world, tossing about on some pesky ocean or other, is someone who knows and, I think, cares."

"Oh, I do, most emphatically," Captain Summers agreed. "And we don't toss, we pitch. And yaw, but only occasionally." He laughed then, a self-deprecating laugh with a touch of shyness in it that Jeannie found delightful. "And do you know what? You'll think this silly beyond belief, but I had almost worked up my nerve to propose to you tonight, after that dance. You know, when I dragged you onto the balcony. And then all those damned people came."

Jeannie stared at him. "But that was before I told you all this. That was when all you had to go on was Bartley's sudden disgust of me. I don't understand."

He took her hands again. "Jeannie, you block, I told you I

didn't believe a word of that.'' He raised her hand to his lips and kissed her fingers, keeping his eyes on her face. ''I love you. Silly, isn't it?''

I love you, too, Jeannie thought, even though the entire prospect is ridiculous in the extreme, and you will shortly realize that, I am sure.

''Love isn't silly,'' she hedged.

''Mine is,'' he replied, and tugged her closer. ''I've never been in love before. I feel sillier than Larinda at her blasted Season. When I don't see your face close by, I'm miserable.'' He laughed that self-conscious laugh again. ''I went to play whist tonight to work up a bit of courage to declare myself, and lost every hand. Jeannie, I never lose at whist. It must be love.''

She laughed and touched his cheek. ''You're a bit feverish, too. I suppose you'll say that is love, too! Captain, I—''

He let go of her hands. ''I know, you're going to tell me that you're well aware of the honor I do you, but—''

She touched his lips with her fingers. ''Oh, cease your blathering, Captain! All I was going to say was that is rather sudden and I would like a little time to think about it.''

''We don't have any time, Jeannie,'' he reminded her. ''I could be out of here by this afternoon, and then it's back to that infernal blockade.''

''I know,'' she agreed, ''but it will keep long enough for me to think about it.''

She put her hands behind her back. And it will give you time to reconsider marriage to a Scottish widow with nothing to recommend her but a passable face. You can do better, Captain, and you should. The thought was vastly unsatisfactory, but it gave her the courage to move quickly to the door and open it.

He was by her side in a moment. ''I don't know that I could ever mean as much to you as Tom,'' he began doubtfully, ''but life is a risk, Jeannie, and I'm willing to take it.''

Before she could edge out the door, he took her face in his hands and kissed her.

In idle moments in the last few days, Jeannie McVinnie had contemplated such an event, even as she scolded herself for light-mindedness and refused to entertain the notion that she had considered a kiss from the captain that first night she sewed on his button. The only man who had ever kissed her before was Tom McVinnie, and to the best of her limited knowledge, he was wonderfully proficient. Bartley MacGregor had tried on several occasions, but she had always moved a little faster, dancing out of his reach, to his good-humored chagrin.

The captain's lips were warm, and he smelled slightly of brandy and metal polish. It was the easiest matter in the world to close her eyes and kiss him back. When she wasn't paying attention, her hands strayed up to his neck and she stood on tiptoe to reach him better.

For some reason or other, one kiss wasn't enough. Jeannie could only credit this excess to remarkable deprivation on the blockade. She considered it her patriotic duty to respond with some spirit when he kissed her again and again, little kisses that sent her heart leaping about like a wild animal.

The captain broke off the encounter before she was quite ready, and her eyes flew open in surprise, to find him smiling down at her. "A certain spirit of enthusiasm was noted among the crew when Captain S. issued an order," he said out loud, as if reading his words on some imaginary paper. "That's what I should put down in the log if we were at sea."

He put his hands about her waist and set her off a little from him. "So consider my impetuous offer, Jeannie," he said, his voice a little breathless. "I can think nothing finer than to spend the rest of my life kissing bonnie Jean Summers. With the idle diversion tossed in, of course," he added, and laughed when she blushed.

"You're ridiculous, Will," she protested, and then shrieked when he grabbed her again and scraped his early-morning whiskers along her cheek.

"Do be more quiet, Jeannie," he ordered, and kissed her again when she opened her mouth to remonstrate with him. "You'll wake up Wapping, and you know how I love to bait butlers."

She rolled her eyes and pushed him away, and then attempted to gather her dignity about her again. "I had no intention of doing that," she insisted. "I can't imagine what you must think of me."

"Well, I had every intention of doing that," the captain said, "and I think you are adorable. Marry me, Jeannie."

She shook her head. "It's folly, and you know it, Captain, but I promised that I would think about it, and I shall."

He folded her in his arms once again and spoke into her hair.

"Consider it well, but don't give it too much thought, dearest. I had a Scottish captain once when I was a lieutenant. He would chew through a problem so many times that he never could make a decision. Damned unfortunate in a captain. We did not miss him over much when a hurricane swept him away."

She giggled and he kissed the top of her head. "Now go upstairs, Jeannie. If you're lucky, you might crawl into bed before Clare wakes up and decides to join you."

Suddenly shy, Jeannie darted up the stairs and blew him another kiss from the safety of the landing. He waved a hand at her and went into the bookroom.

Jeannie undressed and got into bed. She longed for the luxury of lying in bed until all hours and considering the matter before her. She pillowed her head on her hands and stared at the ceiling, wondering how it was possible for her well-bred resolutions to be overthrown without a struggle.

She smiled then and put her hand upon her stomach. At least he knows, she thought. At least someone besides me and my sister know that there was a baby, and I can talk about it, if I wish. How dreadful to think I might have gone through life and no one would have known that Tom and I created a life.

With a sigh, she turned her thoughts again to the matter closest at hand. He is everything you do not want, Jeannie, and you know it, she told herself. He is a sea captain engaged in the most dangerous profession there is. And you thought Tom was gone too much? Will Summers will be forever away, and home only long enough to tease you and then leave your bed empty. And he is not fond of children. Her smile faded and she tugged the blanket up around her neck. Or is he? And you will be at the mercy of the postman's whistle once again.

The door opened and Clare padded into the room. She peered up onto the bed to see if Jeannie slept. With a triumphant chortle, she scrambled across the end of the bed and threw herself into Jeannie's open arms.

Jeannie tucked her in so close that the child seemed like an extension of her own body. "Clare, you silly, you will be cold and blue."

Clare shook her head. "I will not. You are warm."

Jeannie opened her eyes wide. "Clare, that is more than you have ever said to me before." She kissed her and then tickled

her until Clare giggled and squirmed. ''Did you just not have
something to say before?''

Clare cuddled in close again and shook her head, the subject
closed as far as she was concerned. Instead of further reply,
she held out her towel doll to Jeannie.

Jeannie turned the doll over in her hands. Other than having
suffered a sea change from white to melancholy gray after her
dip in the Thames, the doll appeared none the worse for wear.
Jeannie looked closer. Someone had sewn a gold uniform button
on the shoulder where the tartan came together. ''Captain
Summers?'' she asked.

Clare nodded, her eyes anxious. ''Will he be in trouble?''

Jeannie smiled and shook her head. ''I think not, my dear.''

Clare sighed in satisfaction and reclaimed her doll.

Jeannie hugged her close and watched as Clare's eyes grew
heavy. *And what is to become of you when Captain Summers
goes back to sea?* she thought. *And what is to become of me
when I marshal my wits about me and tell him no?*

It didn't bear thinking on, but she thought on it anyway, until
she was as limp with indecision as Clare's doll. When not
another moment of worry could force its way into her head,
she gave it up for a lost cause and went to sleep.

Jeannie woke up only an hour later, groggy and surprisingly
ill-at-ease. For the smallest moment, she hoped that she had
imagined the whole declaration in the breakfast parlor. But she
knew she had not imagined the wonderful strength of Captain
Summers' lips against hers or the peaceful feeling of protection
that had enveloped her. It was all as real as Clare sleeping beside her, and just as uncertain as the child's claims on Will
Summers.

She sat up carefully so as not to disturb Clare, and regarded
herself in the dressing-table mirror on the opposite wall. The
face that stared back was anxious and worried. What had
happened to the competent, organized, rather staid window who
had traveled south only a week ago? *I was so sure of everything
then, and now I am sure of nothing except that saying good-
bye to Captain Summers will number among the hardest duties
I have ever done.*

And say good-bye she must. He would realize the wisdom
of it soon enough and probably thank her for not taking him

seriously when he was so vulnerable. If only he were not so comfortable to lean against . . .

Jeannie, this will not do. She had seen unequal marriages before. She thought of Laird Robert Maxwell, who resided in that decrepit stone pile on the way to Brixton Head. He had courted and married a mill-owner's daughter, had used her money to restore his ancestral home, and then was too embarrassed by his wife's imagined deficiencies to exhibit her in public.

Such a thing will never happen to me, Jeannie decided. She would not give Captain Summers the power over her life to wake up one morning and look upon her with loathing because she was so far below him in station. She sighed. But just to spend one night in his arms, just one sleepless night tracing his body with her hands and pillowing his head on her long hair.

Jeannie McVinnie, you are the worst kind of a fool, she told herself severely as she got out of bed, sponged herself off with cold water from the pitcher, and hurried into her clothes. Too bad ye hae nae a hair shirt, Jeannie, or a scourge to whip yourself with, she thought, and then smiled a sour smile. "Ye can give up Captain Summers for Lent."

The thought had all the invitation of a pitcher of Highland water dribbled over her bare body, but it braced her, and she resolved firmly to nip such silliness in the bud before it got out of hand.

There was no opportunity in the breakfast parlor. Captain Summers, freshly shaven and smelling of bay rum and dressed impeccably in another uniform, stood by the window and read the *Times* while Larinda and Lady Smeath considered the day's occupation and made plans for Larinda's come-out ball.

" 'Twill be a frightful expense," Lady Smeath warned her brother's back. "We'll need new gowns, of course, and flowers, and potted plants, an orchestra, and a caterer."

Summers only grunted and turned the page. Taking this for agreement, Lady Smeath continued, "And I'm not sure that the ballroom draperies are equal to such an event as this must be."

Another grunt and rustle of paper, and Lady Summers looked in triumph and added the suggestion to her growing list.

"And a partridge in a pear tree," Larinda said suddenly, her eyes twinkling at Jeannie.

A third grunt from the captain sent Jeannie coughing into her napkin while Lady Smeath skewered Larinda with one glance and drummed her fingers on the table in a menacing fashion.

Captain Summers took out his pocket watch, studied it with great interest for a moment, and then clicked it shut. He went to the door and motioned Jeannie to follow. Before he closed the door behind him, he looked at his sister. "I'd go easy on the four calling birds and three French hens, you two. It must be the very devil to clean up."

He closed the door behind them. Jeannie tried to be severe with him, but the effect was hampered by the grin that threatened to spread across her face. "You must have been the veriest trial to poor Jeannie McVinnie twenty-five years ago," she said. "It is only a wonder that your father didn't put you to sea in a basket like Moses."

He nodded in total agreement. "He would have if he could have, I am sure." He put his arm about her waist. "I wonder, should I mention to Agatha that while I have no aesthetic objection to swans-a swimming, I cannot allow maids a-milking in the ballroom." He drew Jean closer for emphasis. "I didn't know Larinda had a sense of humor. Could she become almost human, do you think?"

"I think there is a distinct possibility, Captain Summers. Now, unhand me before the servants see us."

"Very well," he agreed amicably enough. "Stop in the bookroom a moment and see how profitably Edward spends his time, now that his guidebook is jetsam."

She allowed Captain Summers to lead her by the hand into the bookroom. Edward, with Pringle looking over his shoulder, stared at a chart in front of him. He looked up and waggled his quill pen at her.

"Mrs. McVinnie, only think! Pringle is teaching me to navigate." A light came into his eyes and he looked at his uncle.

"I told you not to entertain the notion yet," Captain Summers warned. "I have not yet mustered the courage to mention this to your aunt, who will in all likelihood flutter about and call me a rascal and a mountebank and say that I am sending you to a watery grave for my own purposes. This whole event will want no little tact, Edward, and probably all the skill of a Richelieu."

He came closer and studied Edward's work. He blinked his eyes, and then his shoulders began to shake, even as he wiped the huge smile off his face and his lips turned down in that familiar, grim stare that she was finding strangely attractive.

As she watched in amazement, he crossed himself and winked at Pringle. "Edward," he began, his voice frosty, "thank God you do not wear a hat, or you would be guilty of a serious breach of etiquette."

Edward slewed around to stare up at his uncle. "I don't understand, Uncle Summers," he said.

"According to your longitudinal reading, we are upon holy ground."

"Sir?"

The captain pointed to Edward's smudged figures and the answer he had circled. "From the looks of this, you have placed the *Venture* square in the middle of St. Peter's Basilica, probably at the high altar." He sniffed the air elaborately. "I wonder that we cannot smell the incense."

Edward laughed, frowned over his figures another moment, and then crossed out a number and wrote in something else. He held up his paper and Captain Summers nodded in approval.

"Excellent, lad, excellent. Now we are tacking along the coast of Valencia, where every good blockader longs to be," Captain Summers nodded to Pringle. "As you were."

"Aye, sir. We'll practice outside with the sextant, sir, if you think that advisable."

"I do." After another look at Edward's work, Captain Summers nodded toward a pile of letters. "See that those are posted right away, Pringle."

"Aye, sir," Pringle hesitated. "Are, are you off to the Admiralty House?"

"Aye. And I will sit there until I have an audience with His Pudginess, the First Lord of Procrastination. Jeannie, walk me to the door and let us talk."

She followed him into the hall. "I have put you in an awkward position, my dear, even setting aside my declaration, which I trust you will put your mind to."

"Yes," she agreed, her face alive with merriment.

"Oh, God, you're beautiful," he said.

"No, I am not! You have merely been at sea too long. Now,

what is it? And don't look at me like that. Suppose the servants were to happen by?"

"You are a source of continual amusement to me, dearest," he said, and kissed her hand. "I won't be here for Larinda's come-out, with any luck at all. It will fall upon your shoulders, Jeannie."

He put his arm around her waist as they strolled toward the door. "I suppose navy lads have been doing this to their women for years and years. You get to make all the arrangements and do the dirty work. It's vastly unfair, but I must confess to endless relief."

Jeannie laughed. "At least you are honest enough to admit it."

"I am. Kiss me, Jeannie. I'm off to engage the enemy at the Admiralty House."

She kissed him, standing on tiptoe. He picked her up, planted a noisy kiss on her lips that echoed in the entry hall, and set her on her feet again.

"I'll stay there until I'm done." His hand strayed to her face again and he touched her cheek. "And do think on what I have suggested, my dear."

"I shall, Will."

"Make up your mind, you Scottish grammarian! Shall or will?"

She was still smiling as she pushed him out the door and turned to face Larinda, who was struggling not to laugh out loud.

"I heard that," she said.

Jeannie put her hands to her red face. "How could you help? Oh, Larinda, I don't know what to do."

"I think my uncle knows what to do." Larinda turned to the roses that still spread their perfume about the entry hall. She twitched out the blossoms beyond full bloom and laid them on the table. "But Jeannie—oh, may I call you that?—Uncle Summers does. Jeannie, what about Bartley, Captain MacGregor?"

It was Jeannie's turn to look away. "I do not think he will be proposing to me again. We had a slight falling-out yesterday."

"I wondered." Larinda was silent a moment and then chose her words carefully, her voice offhand, casual. "Do you think he will come back at all?"

Jeannie looked at Larinda and noticed the blush that had risen to her cheek. Trimming roses must be a strenuous business, she thought. "My dear, I thought you could not understand one word in ten that he uttered."

"I am up to one in five, now," was Larinda's quiet reply. She turned around to face Jeannie then, and her eyes filled with tears. "Aunt Agatha will be so upset with me. Jeannie, all I want to do is go home to Suffolk. I want to sit in my room, look out at the ocean, and think."

Jeannie sank into a sofa. "That makes two of us, my dear." She patted the space beside her and Larinda flopped down. "I do not know two females who could have made a better botch of what promised to be a smashing London Season."

Larinda laughed out loud, even as she wiped the tears from her eyes. "Too true, Jeannie! And here is Brummell, ready to squire you anywhere, and we have more invitations than the Grand Turk's harem could possibly do justice to, and all the pretty gowns in London." She burst into tears and sobbed on Jeannie's shoulders. "And if Bartley does not return, I will go into a nunnery."

Jeannie chuckled. "Only think how well-dressed you will be, my dear." She put her arms about Larinda. "I don't mean to quiz you, but sometimes it's less wearing to laugh than to cry." She kissed Larinda's cheek. "And think what crying does to your face."

Larinda stopped at once and sniffed. "Oh, I had not thought. Suppose Bartley should come and see me like this." She leapt to her feet and looked in the mirror. "What will he think?"

Jeannie joined her in front of the mirror. "You'll discover that Bartley doesn't worry overmuch about things like that. Oh, Larinda, I hope he comes."

They were unable to convince Lady Smeath that the sole desire of their hearts was to remain *en famille* that day.

"What! You would abandon all these offers for your amusement?" Lady Smeath shrieked. "When I have worked and slaved so hard for you to get them?" She clutched at her ample bosom. "My heart is pounding like a drum."

Jeannie was kind enough not to remind Agatha Smeath why the offers had poured in. She set her lips in a firm line and tried to reason what Captain Summers would do in such a situation.

The thought brought a smile to her face. No, she would not deal with Lady Smeath that way.

Larinda clutched at her handkerchief. "But I don't want to go to the Kensington Gallery this morning with Lord Tutton." She sobbed into the soggy scrap in her hand, and Lady Smeath stared at her in openmouthed surprise.

"You have prejudice against paintings?"

Larinda sobbed harder.

Lady Smeath raised her eyes to the ceiling and patted her chest. "I think I will lie down," she said, her voice filled with deep regret. "My heart, Larinda, you know how it is."

Jeannie watched Larinda, wondering if she would rise to the bait that Lady Smeath held out, wondering if she would knuckle under at the threat of her aunt's health, and cosset her and soothe her and bend her will to her Agatha Smeath's petty tyranny.

Larinda dried her eyes. "Yes, perhaps you should do that, Aunt. I will send a little note to Lord Tutton, and I am sure he will understand. If you are indisposed, my place is surely at your side, not staring at some Rembrandts."

Check and mate, thought Jeannie as Larinda held her shoulders erect and gazed at her aunt. For the first time, Jeannie noticed something of Captain Summers' look in that level stare that Larinda directed at Lady Smeath. A daunting family resemblance, she thought as she watched the little scene before her. If Bartley MacGregor has the good sense to return today, he will find himself in capable hands.

After another moment, Lady Smeath wilted under Larinda's even gaze. She murmured something about a headache coming on and took herself upstairs.

"That was rude of me, I suppose," Larinda confessed, more to herself than to Jeannie. "But my aunt schemes and plots." She stopped and looked with some embarrassment at Jeannie. "And so did I." She managed a little laugh. "With all these newfound scruples of mine, I will likely not find a husband here in the marriage mart, but I hope I can return to Suffolk a little wiser than I left."

I wish I could have said that, thought Jeannie as she nodded to Larinda and let herself out of the breakfast parlor. I seem to be growing more foolish by the minute. When Captain

Summers returns from the Admiralty House, I will give him my answer straight.

The thought unnerved her. She darted up the stairs, grabbed a pelisse from the dressing room, and hurried out into the sunshine. She walked swiftly, her head down, not looking to the right or the left, until she came to the little park that hid itself between Jermyn and Regent streets.

With a thankful sigh, she sat down on the bench by the pond and stared into the water. There was no east wind this morning. The surface of the pond was as smooth as a mirror.

As she watched the water, thinking of home and Tom, and Captain Summers, the water began to move in ever-widening ripples. Surprised, she raised her chin off her hand and watched as a young boy, presided over by his nanny, launched his schooner onto the water. He prodded it with a long pole until it was in the middle of the pond.

The sails hung limp with no breath of wind to push them anywhere. The boy's face grew longer and longer, and Jeannie thought he would surely cry as the boat just sagged in the water, a thing of no more beauty than a fledgling bird.

As she watched, a little breeze ruffled the tops of the trees and then dipped down and made itself known to the people far below and the sailboat that drifted without bearings.

With a crackle and slap, the sails caught the breeze and the schooner heeled over, tottering upon the edge of capsizement. Shouting encouragement, the boy ran around the pond, raising his hands high as he ran, as if to inspire his sailboat. When it righted itself and came swooping toward him on the breath of the wind, he clapped his hands and capered about until Jeannie wanted to join him in his mad, glorious dance.

"All ye that go down to the sea in little boats and do business in great waters," she whispered out loud. I would like to have a son capering about on the water's edge, a son not afraid of the east wind or a lee shore. Someone who would stand firm and hold a true course when everyone else had a different opinion.

She would marry Captain Summers. If he wouldn't be home above five times in as many years, she would learn to live with it. She would have to learn to make every precious moment with Will Summers pay with interest. When other women were tired to distraction of wifely duties and boring routine, she would still be alive to the wonder of Captain Summers, who only came home to go away again, who would love her, but who would always be restless on land.

Jeannie sighed and got to her feet, circumnavigating the pond herself, which by now was a mighty sea of choppy water that bore a whole fleet of boats. A handful of lads had joined the first captain, who stood watch over his schooner, alert to the nuance of wind and wave.

She found herself in Jermyn Street again. A half-hour's brisk walk would take her to the Admiralty House, where she could quite profitably spend the day with her beloved captain. Jeannie shook her head. She did not belong in the Admiralty House. The news could wait until he returned to Wendover Square.

Jeannie walked slowly toward the Summers' house. Pringle and Edward stood beside the fence, shooting at the sun overhead with Caleb Mathew's beautiful sextant. Jeannie stopped to watch, noting that Edward's trousers were getting short and his wrists were starting to come out of his sleeves. Soon he would be as tall as his uncle.

Edward tucked the sextant under his arm and waved to her. "Mrs. McVinnie, see what I am learning," he shouted.

She waved back. "Do be careful with that sextant, my dear," she said. "When you are a great proficient, you can teach me."

He looked doubtful. "I would, but surely that it not something for a lady to know."

She laughed. "You are likely right, laddie. Just keep the *Venture* off lee shores and out of the Vatican, think ye."

He patted the sextant and turned back to Pringle for further instructions, and Jeannie entered the house. The front hall was deserted, and she was grateful. A few moment's quiet reflection in her room would be welcome indeed. As she climbed the stairs, she thought of Galen McVinnie and resolved to write him a letter. She could not bring herself to tell him of the sad events of last winter, but perhaps someday she would.

It would be hard enough to explain Captain Summers to the uninitiated. Galen would never understand why, after a year's widowhood, she was ready to caper to the altar again, and with someone as thoroughly unsuitable as a sea captain.

No more do I understand it. Perhaps if he comes to know Captain Summers . . . Ah, well. I will likely be living far away from Scotland anyway.

That unwanted thought brought tears to her eyes. It was an exile she had not considered until this moment, and, in its own way, no less wrenching than death. She leaned her forehead against the windowpane. Captain Summers, come home quickly, or my resolve will vanish altogether.

She opened her eyes and looked across the square. Bartley MacGregor was coming toward the house. She admired his familiar, marching stride and wiped her tears. As she removed her pelisse and straightened her hair, she heard light footsteps running down the stairs and the sound of the door flung open. I will wait here a minute or two, she thought. Why interrupt Larinda?

When she came down the stairs several minutes later, Bartley was seated in the parlor, Larinda beside him. He rose when she entered. There was a moment of uncertainty in his face, and then it was gone when she held out both hands to him.

"We were wondering how to spend a dull morning without company, Bart," she said.

"That's a whisker, Jeannie dear," he said. "I sorted that list of invitations yesterday, and as I came into the house, didn't I see a carter dropping off packages at the servants' entrance? Larinda—Miss Summers—tells me that you are expecting a great parcel of clothes. And bless me, but there were roses in the hands of the delivery lad who followed."

Jeannie smiled. "It's nothing of importance, I vow. Whatever brings you to visit us this morning?" she asked.

Again that uncertainty filled his face. "I wanted to apologize to you, Jeannie, first of all," he said.

"None needed," was her quiet reply. "Even if we do not completely understand each other, let us remain friends."

"So it shall be." Bartley turned back to Larinda. "And I came to tell you that we are leaving this afternoon for Portsmouth."

Larinda burst into tears just as Edward threw open the parlor door, waving the sextant about. Bartley looked from one to the other, his blue eyes filled with confusion and then a sudden joy that took Jeannie's breath away. Oh, Bartley, she thought as she watched him, you are far gone, and it is high time.

He produced a handkerchief and grasped Larinda firmly by the back of the neck. "Blow, lassie," he ordered. She did as he said, and then sobbed into the handkerchief as he looked on in amazement, his face redder than his regimentals.

Edward regarded the tempest before him with an expression of disgust. "Oh, Larry, do dry up! I want to show Captain MacGregor what I have learned this morning. Sir, do come outside for a spell, please."

By now, Larinda was sobbing in good earnest on Bartley MacGregor's shoulder and his arms were about her.

Edward tugged at Bartley's kilt. "Please, sir, that only encourages her."

Larinda wrenched herself away from Captain MacGregor and glared at her brother. "Go away, you wretched monster," she sobbed, and then buried her face in the handkerchief again.

"Nay, lassie, nay," said Bartley as he took her hand. "I would like you and Edward, and Jeannie too, to see me off this afternoon from the Couched Lion. We leave at five."

Larinda renewed her outpouring of misery and Edward stared at her in dismay. "Larry, you look like a ripe tomato." He laughed and poked her. "I don't think there are enough cucumbers in all of London to take the red out of your eyes before five o'clock a year from now."

Larinda wiped her nose and glared at her little brother, her voice low and filled with anger. "Edward, if you don't go upstairs right now and take that ugly hunk of scrap metal with you, I am going to tell Aunt Agatha, and she will pack you back to Suffolk."

The threat seemed real enough to Edward. Muttering something about sisters being the eleventh plague of Egypt, he clutched the sextant close to his chest, shook his head at Bartley for encouraging this folly, and left the room.

Larinda's tears subsided as soon as Bartley sat her down close beside him on the sofa. He looked at Jeannie helplessly, and she could only smile back, invent some little errand that demanded her immediate presence in the bookroom, and shut the doors of the sitting room behind her.

When she returned fifteen minutes later, Larinda was smiling in a misty fashion as Bartley MacGregor held her hands. They looked up when she entered, but Bartley did not rise this time.

"I have convinced Miss Summers to write to me in Portugal," he said to Jeannie.

"Every day," she added, and gazed up at him with an expression just a degree or two shy of worship.

"Nay, lassie," he protested. "Such a waste of good paper and ink."

"Not a bit of it," Jeannie exclaimed. "Only think on, Bartley. You will have more mail than the entire regiment. They will envy you and call you a devilish dog with the ladies."

Bartley considered the issue. "It is a pleasant thought," he agreed. He turned back to Larinda to say something more, but it never got out of his mouth.

The sitting-room door banged open and Edward threw himself into the room, his face white and his eyes staring out of his head. He looked from Larinda to Jeannie, and then with a wail of his own ran to Jeannie and buried his face in her skirts.

Her arms went around him. He was shaking even as he sobbed.

"Edward, what is the matter? Good heavens, laddie!"

Edward was bereft of speech. He could only shake his head and burrow deeper in her dress, as if to hide himself.

And then she knew. Jeannie grasped him by the shoulders and shook him until he stopped sobbing. "There, laddie, now," she said, her voice quiet but filled with command. "The sextant."

He opened his eyes wide. "I didn't mean to, Jeannie, I didn't!"

She sucked in her breath, her own voice unsteady. "What didn't you mean to do? Oh, Edward, speak."

He covered his face with his hands as Larinda hurried forward and knelt beside him, her face as white as his own.

He gave himself a shake and took the much-used handkerchief that his sister offered without a word. He wiped his eyes and looked at Jeannie, such desperation on his face that her heart sank into her shoes and stayed there.

"I just wanted to get a perfect reading, Jeannie, that was all. I climbed out onto the roof and . . ." He began to shake again. Jeannie took a firm grasp of his arms. "Jeannie, I dropped the sextant. It's in pieces on the walkway."

16

"EDWARD, no," she whispered, and knelt beside him, clutching his shoulders.

He stared back at her, and the terror in his eyes went straight to her heart like a bolt flung from a crossbow. There were a thousand words she could have showered upon him, each more cutting than the last, but not one of them came to mind as she hugged Edward to her and he sobbed in her arms.

"Bartley, go see," she said over her shoulder.

MacGregor turned on his heel and ran out the door. He came inside much slower, the ruins of Caleb Matthew's lovely sextant in his hands.

"I couldn't find all the mirrors," he said as he held it out to her.

Jeannie sat on the floor and cradled the sextant in her lap, looking it over, feeling the tears start in her eyes. The wreckage was complete, the instrument twisted and broken. There was nothing they could do to repair it. She touched it hesitantly, as she would a wounded animal found dying by the side of the highway.

Edward dried his eyes, but every now and then a shudder shook his frame. "Uncle Summers will kill me," he said, his voice filled with shock.

"I am sure he would like to," Larinda said frankly as she touched his shoulder. "But I do not think it will come to that. Oh, Edward, how could you!"

Edward shuddered and tore his eyes from the sextant. "I only wanted to make him proud." The word caught in his throat like a bone, and he could not continue until Jeannie took hold of his arm. "Proud of me, Larinda. Oh, Larry, I wanted him to know that I was ready to go to sea."

Larinda sighed. "We'll be fortunate indeed if he does not send all of us packing back to Suffolk."

"Don't make matters worse, Larinda," Jeannie said quietly.

After another moment, Bartley helped Jeannie to her feet. "I don't see how you can make this one right with the captain, Jeannie me light," he said in an undertone to her. He managed a crooked smile in Larinda's vicinity. "I feel a very churl to leave you all at this delicate point, but I have a post chaise to catch at five o'clock at the Couched Lion." He rested his hand for a moment on Edward's head. "You'll come through, laddie. After all, if worse comes to worst, you can take the king's shilling and sign on as a drummer boy for Spain. Think of it. You can learn a foreign language in only a couple of weeks."

Jeannie stamped her foot. "Bartley, I'll thank you to keep your precious advice to yourself," she declared, and softened her words by holding out both of her hands. "Do be careful, Bartley. I'll be thinking of you. As I always do," she added.

He smiled and kissed her cheek before she could duck away. "There, now! I've always wanted to do that. You take care of yourself." He turned to Larinda and words failed him. He could only look at her, his heart in his eyes, and then grab her, kiss her full on the lips, and run for the door.

Larinda put her fingers to her lips and stared after him, too startled to cry. She wandered to the door and watched Bartley MacGregor rush down the front steps and into the street, leaving the door swinging wide. She stood there a moment more and then came into the room again, her face white, her eyes large and filled with tears.

Jeannie regarded her for only a moment, figured that love could wait, and then devoted her attention to Edward, who was struggling with his own agony.

He took the sextant from her and made an attempt to straighten the scale back into the index arm. As he bit his lips and exerted all his strength, the drum and vernier fell onto the carpet and rolled under the sofa. With a sigh, he set down the battered instrument. "Maybe Captain MacGregor is right," he murmured. "Mrs. McVinnie, I have a sudden patriotic urge to serve our king in a foreign climate."

Jeannie hugged him to her once more. "Not a bit of it, laddie," she said, crossing her fingers and hoping that she sounded more confident than she felt. "But do go upstairs right now. I think it would be better if you let me tell him first.''

He nodded, sighed again heavily, and started for the door. He stopped and stood absolutely still, an inarticulate sound coming from his throat.

As Jeannie looked at him in surprise, she heard the carriage at the front steps, the murmur of deep voices, the door slamming hard, the heavy footsteps coming up the front walk. She closed her eyes and wished herself far away from Wendover Square as Captain Summers stalked into the sitting room, threw off his boat cloak, and dropped into a chair.

Larinda, Edward, and Jeannie stared at him, and he stared back. When no one said anything or even moved, he looked from one to the other.

''Has something happened?'' he asked at last. ''You look as though you have seen a ghost.'' He tried to smile, but the effort failed him. ''I know I am not Adonis, but I will not bite.''

He said no more when they still did not respond, but his eyes fell upon the battered sextant lying on the sofa. Edward began to edge toward the door.

''Move and you're a dead man,'' he said, and his voice held such menace that Jeannie felt her heart skip a beat. She forced herself to move toward Edward, to stand in front of him.

''And, by God, don't hide behind that woman's skirts,'' the captain continued, rising from the chair.

Edward gasped, but he moved away from Jeannie, clasped his hands behind his back, and stood in the center of the room, shaking like a leaf. He closed his eyes as the captain came toward him, and then opened them when his uncle passed him and went to the sofa instead.

He picked up the sextant and cradled it in his arm like he would a child, touching it, running his fingers down the crooked lines that used to shoot the sun. With a curious laugh that made Jeannie cringe and Edward sob out loud, he held the telescope to his eye. He laughed again, and there was just the tinge of hysteria in his voice.

Summers must have heard it too, because he took a deep breath, and when that wasn't sufficient, another one, and another. His face went from red to white, and Jeannie forgot her own fear and hurried toward him.

''Will, perhaps you had better sit down,'' she advised, and took his arm.

He shook her off and went to the chair again by himself, passing Edward as though he were not there. He sat there, resting his elbows on his knees, watching Edward, saying nothing, until Jeannie wanted to shake him. Instead, she held her head high and twisted her fingers together.

"Edward," he said at last, and Edward looked at him, the tears streaming silently down his face.

"Sir?" he said, his voice only the approximation of speech.

"I have counted to ten twenty times now, and I am still no less angry than I was when I began."

Edward hung his head and Jeannie felt her heart break.

"Look at me, Edward, and pay close attention."

Edward raised his eyes again.

"You must be callous indeed to have no regard for what that sextant means—meant—to me. Go to your room now. I'll deal with you later. I am afraid what I would do if I tried to deal with you now. Get out of my sight."

Without a word, Edward ran from the room. Larinda, her own face a mirror of her brother's, followed him. Jeannie stared at the carpet, afraid to move, but more afraid to leave Will Summers alone. After a moment more of contemplating the pattern in the carpet, she raised her eyes to Will Summers' ravaged face.

He stared back, and gradually his complexion returned to its normal color. After another moment, he leaned back in his chair and closed his eyes, as if unable to meet her gaze anymore.

Jeannie continued her perusal, wondering how it was possible for one middle-aged man to look so old. Do I look that old? she thought. Have my own troubles made me someone I wouldn't recognize if I looked in a mirror? If they have, then I may have missed the point of life.

"That was terrible of me," he said at last.

A moment ago, she would have agreed with him, but she could not now. She pulled up a chair beside him. It wasn't close enough, but he had given her no leave to sit on his lap. "No, Will, it was justifiable."

"That still doesn't excuse it."

She touched his hand, relieved when he did not draw away. "You can't be a captain all the time. It's not really a crime to be human." She took the sextant from his hands and set it beside her chair. "Your 'plaguey nephew,' if I may quote you, destroyed your most valuable possession."

He nodded and then reached for her hands. "And now my esteemed brother-in-law has taken away the rest of it, Jeannie. Ah, Jeannie."

He gripped her hands and raised them to his lips, not to kiss them but as though to stop himself from saying any more.

"Please tell me, Will, please," she said, her voice urgent. He had to speak.

He released her hands as suddenly as he had grabbed them. "He will not see me. I watched captains and lieutenants and middies come and go, and there I sat, like a lump of ambergris. He will not hear me. He would rather the *Venture* sank to the bottom of the Channel than give up my service as Larinda's escort for this damned Season. God, I loathe him."

His voice was filled with such hatred that Jeannie felt herself grow cold and hot in turn. How could I ever, for the smallest moment, have thought I had any hold on this man? she asked herself. He has no thought but for his ship and crew. And yet I love him and I will marry him.

When she could speak, she asked, "What did you do?"

Summers looked at her then for the first time since he had sat down. "I tried another tack. We captains always have another tack, Jeannie. It is our stock-in-trade, our *deus ex machina.*" He smacked one hand into the other. "I will not go quietly aground on a lee shore, Jeannie."

He slumped down again and shook his head. "Do you know what I did? I wrote a desperate note to your quixotic protector, Mr. Beau Brummell himself. Pled with him to speak to dear Freddy for me." When her expression remained blank, he continued. "The Duchess of York. I wonder that it will help, but it might." He chuckled to himself. "Of course, no man likes his balls squeezed, but, Jeannie, I have to try. Forgive that."

"Forgiven," she said promptly, her face pink. "I hope it works. You must be back at sea, and soon."

He heaved himself from the chair and walked to the window, hands behind his back. "Yes, indeed, Jeannie. I'm the very devil on land."

"I didn't mean that."

He turned around to face her. "It's true, dear, too true. I am comfortable at sea. I am entirely my own master and no one crosses me. I don't have to deal with human relationships and there are no Edwards."

"Or Jeannies," she whispered.

He started, and the truth of her words sank in. "No Jeannies," he agreed. "I'm no bargain, my dear." He closed his eyes with some finality.

She folded her hands in her lap and stayed where she was.

He opened his eyes. "You're still here? My, but you're hard to get rid of, Jeannie McVinnie," he said, his voice calmer now, his tone more familiar.

"I don't scare easily, sir," she said, a touch of humor in her own voice. "Besides all that, someone should not be alone at a time like this."

He took her hand again, but gently this time. "You were very much alone at your worst moment, or so I remember."

She nodded. "That was different, Will," she said, keeping her tone light. "You forget I am a Scot. We have reserves that you Englishmen can only dream about." She rose. "Let me ring for Wapping. I am sure he can have a bottle of brandy here in jig time."

Summers shook his head. "No, Jeannie. Ring instead for coffee. I need a clear head. If Brummell fails me—after all, we cannot all expect miracles at his hand—I must think of something else."

She returned in a few minutes with a pot of coffee and poured them each a cup. He sipped it in silence, and took a cake, which she passed to him. "I haven't had anything to eat in quite a while," he admitted after three more cakes disappeared from the plate.

"Or slept since goodness knows when," she added, and grimaced over the coffee.

"True. I am more used to that, however. While you're making faces over that coffee, Jeannie, tell me what to do."

She could think of nothing, and was spared from exposing her ignorance by a discreet tap on the door. The captain looked up in annoyance, but Jeannie touched his shoulder and went to the door.

It was Wapping. He held out a letter to her. "From the Admiralty House, I do believe."

At his words, Captain Summers was on his feet and across the room. He snatched the letter from Wapping and hurried to the window, where the afternoon light was fading fast. He read quickly, and a smile came to his face. He slapped the letter with his hand, swung Jeannie around, and kissed her soundly before he set her on her feet and thrust the letter under her eyes.

She tried to catch her breath as she scanned the lines; then she looked at the captain, who had already gathered up his boat cloak and the battered sextant. "The Duke of Clarence?" she asked.

"Can you believe my fortune? Brother Billy was visiting him when the letter arrived. Jeannie, I am off!" He threw open the door and shouted, "Wapping, find Pringle and tell that old bag of bones to stuff the needfuls in a duffel and stow the rest."

Jeannie hurried into the hall with him, grabbing for his arm and having no success. "Will! Wait a moment!"

He stopped on the stairs, impatience written on every line of his face. "Hurry with it, Jeannie. I have a packet boat in Portsmouth to catch."

She grabbed his arm and hung on. "You simply have to speak to Edward before you leave. You can't just go away without a word. It would be too cruel."

And have you a thought for me? she wondered to herself. Am I only here when you are on land, or in some desperate need, and then far, far away, even when we are in the same room?

He sighed with impatience and then embarrassment. "I was pretty hard on the lad, wasn't I?"

She nodded. And on me, too, Captain. Do you even remember that you asked me to think about marriage to you and to give you an answer? I have my answer now, as foolish as it seems to me at this moment.

He looked up the stairs, where Pringle waited. "I suppose you are right," he said reluctantly. "I will go to him. Pringle! Pack at once. I'll give you ten minutes."

"Aye, aye, sir," shouted Pringle, that same joy across his face.

Captain Summers mounted the stairs and hurried down the hall to Edward's room. Jeannie went back into the parlor and retrieved the broken pieces of the sextant from under the sofa.

She looked out the window and saw Mary and Clare walking toward the house, returning from the park.

There was a high-perch phaeton pulling up to the door. Jeannie put her hand to her forehead. Good God, it would be Lord Tutton, ready for his trip to the art gallery. She shook her head. No, that was this morning, and we cried off. A closer look identified the dandy as Sir Reginald Dewhurst, who had begged for the honor last night of accompanying Larinda and her Scottish nanny to Hyde Park.

Jeannie leaned against the door. Was it five of the clock already? Larinda is likely crying her eyes out in her room, and I have the headache. Was there ever such a dreadful start to what had held out the promise of being a glorious London Season? How could I get myself involved in this huggle-muggle?

"Jeannie!"

She raised her head.

"Jeannie, I need you. Smartly now!"

How many sides to this complex man are there? she thought as she ran into the hall, ignoring the knock at the door. The captain sounded even worse than he did before, although Jeannie was not sure how that could be possible. She started up the stairs and then stopped, her heart in her throat. Edward! She grabbed up her skirts and hurried faster, even as the captain met her in the hall, his face a mask of distress.

She ran to him and clutched his hand. When he could say nothing but point in the direction of Edward's room, she shrieked and ran down the hall past Lady Smeath, who had come out of her room and was looking about in surprise.

She flung open the door. The room was empty. The only sound was her own labored breathing. The window was wide open, and the wind blowing from the east again, blew the curtains wide. Jeannie looked down at a scrap of paper on the carpet and picked up the note that the captain must have dropped on his way out of the room.

With fingers that trembled, she smoothed it out and read it.

"I only want to shoot the sun with no obstructions and make you proud of me. I have decided to take Captain MacGregor's advice," she read, and the color drained from her face. "I love you, Captain Summers. Your nephew, Edward."

Jeannie sobbed out loud. Captain Summers was back in the

room. Without a word, he took her in his arms. "What kind of animal am I?" he asked her, his lips tickling her ear. "Dear God, put me to sea quickly, Jeannie, for I have done enough damage on land."

With enormous effort, she stopped crying and wiped her eyes on the hem of her dress, ignoring the look of amazement on Lady Smeath's face as she stared into Edward's room. His face absolutely without expression, Captain Summers handed the note to his sister, who read it and fainted.

He caught her expertly on the way down and deposited her on Edward's bed. He turned to Larinda, who had trailed her aunt into the room and who stood openmouthed at the scene before her. He handed her the troublesome note with the warning. "Don't you dare faint, Larinda. We haven't time or space for another one."

Her lips set tight together, Larinda read the note and then held out her hands to Jeannie, who hung on to her.

"I blame myself," she said quietly, "so don't drag it all upon yourself, Uncle Summers, I beg. Oh, Jeannie, I was beastly to him. You heard me."

Jeannie nodded, too miserable to speak.

"I want to know, what did Bartley tell him? I don't entirely understand this note," said the captain.

"Oh, Uncle, Bartley was only teasing, but he as much as suggested that Edward take the king's shilling and join the army," Larinda explained.

"What?" roared the captain in his quarterdeck voice.

Jeannie put her hands over her ears, and Lady Smeath opened her eyes, looked about, and closed them again with amazing finality.

Ignoring the pained expression on his lady love's face, Captain Summers set his lips in that familiar tight line. "If that isn't insult to injury, I don't know what is," he raged. "That my nephew would even think to join the goddamn army." He shuddered. "I ask you, Jeannie, is this a piece of work, or what?"

Jeannie gasped. Her lips started to twitch and she burst into laughter. Will Summers stared at her as though she had taken complete leave of her senses, muttering something about females with more hair than wit, more bounce than bottom. In a moment

Larinda was in whoops, too. She sat down on the bed on top
of her aunt, who moaned and sent Larinda bounding to her feet
in greater merriment than before.

"Belay it, you two," he snapped, his patience at an end.
"Have both of you sent your wits wandering about the countryside?"

Jeannie could only nod and grope about in her pocket for a
handkerchief, which she dabbed at her streaming eyes. When
she could speak again, she picked up the crumpled note. "Dear
me," she said, "Will, you have no idea . . .'

There was nothing in his face that even hinted that he understood, so she sobered up, even though she did not dare look
in Larinda's direction. "It was merely the way you said it. Do
hush, Larinda."

"I thought Edward was an intelligent lad," he said, his voice
filled with wonder, "but the *army*? Good God."

He spent another moment in thought. "I suppose that silly
young chub would want to get as far away as possible. Larinda,
do you suppose he would follow Bartley MacGregor to Portsmouth?"

She considered his question and nodded. "Yes. If he were
in the middle of Spain, that would get him far away from you."

"Larinda," he roared again.

"Hush, Uncle," she said quite calmly. "It can't be good for
you to have your face turn so red. Jeannie, tell him to calm
himself."

Jeannie only smiled. "He doesn't listen to me either, my
dear."

"If you were my crew," he began wrathfully.

"I am your crew," Jeannie reminded him.

"Oh, so you are," he said, "No, you are not! Oh, by God,
I am getting more confused by the minute." He clasped his
hands behind his back and paced back and forth until he had
some measure of control, and then grabbed up his cloak again.

"Jeannie, get your toothbrush and bundle up. We're off to
Portsmouth on the mail coach. It's the quickest way I know,
and there's no other place he could have gone if he's planning
to leave the country with the army. God help us."

"I'm coming, too," Larinda said.

"Indeed you are not," Summers snapped, totally out of
patience. "Someone has to cosset Agatha and you're elected."

"Wrong, indeed, Uncle. I have done that since Mama died and Aunt Agatha came to live with us," Larinda replied. Again Jeannie noticed that remarkable Summers resemblance in the way her lips came together and her eyes flashed. "I said some terrible things to Edward. He may never forgive me for them, and I don't blame him, but I shall try to make amends. If I am not allowed to come with you, I shall simply travel unescorted on the next mail coach."

He paused in the doorway, an arrested expression in his eyes as he measured his niece. She glared back at him and raised her chin higher.

Summers smiled unexpectedly and then touched her under the chin. "Larinda, it could be that you are much too good for the fops on the marriage mart this Season. Very well, if you must. After all," he concluded with a rare flash of humor, "someone has to give Jeannie McVinnie some countenance."

Jeannie stuck her tongue out at him and hurried from the room. She calmly gathered her comb, brush, toothbrush, and toothpowder into her reticule, pulled on her pelisse again, and swirled her cloak around her.

Larinda already waited in the hall, her face pale but composed. A smile lit her eyes for a moment. "For someone intent upon cutting a dash in London, I have certainly come down in the world, Jeannie," she confessed, and then the little smile was gone. "But we must find Edward before he goes for a soldier. And perhaps, perhaps he'll let me be a better sister." She looked shyly at Jeannie. "I can learn, surely."

Jeannie took her hand. "I am sure of that. You've already suffered through a hard lesson, my dear. Let us go downstairs."

Downstairs was no better. Sir Reginald Dewhurst had quitted his high-perch phaeton and was demanding to see Larinda or Jeannie McVinnie. Wapping, his eyebrows raised to the point of caricature, was barring the way most effectively while Mary tried to soothe Clare, who wailed in the sitting room and would not be comforted.

Sir Reginald's rather spotty complexion was growing more colorful by the minute when he espied Larinda. He could not turn his head because his shirt points threatened his circulation, so he swiveled his whole body to watch her descent of the stairs.

"Ah, you are here! Come, my dear, and you, Mrs. McVinnie.

I do not want to miss a minute more of the Hyde Park stroll."
He giggled. "Without my gossip, I am thoroughly unmanned."

Larinda, her mouth pulled down primly in an expression that
Jeannie was already regarding as dangerous, held out her hand
to him. "I am afraid you are doomed to disappointment, Sir
Reginald," she said. "A family emergency calls, and I am off
to Portsmouth with Mrs. McVinnie."

"Portsmouth?" he gasped as if she had named some rare
disease. He snatched his hand away, fearful of contamination.
"My dear, no one goes there but soldiers and diseased tars."

"I beg your pardon?"

Captain Summers, taller by many inches now with his hat
on his head, descended the stairs, followed by Pringle with one
sea bag. "I'd call you out for that remark, Sir Reginald," he
growled, "but I haven't time right now." He smiled his gallow's
smile, which caused even the veteran Pringle to swallow and
look away. "Do make yourself available for when I next come
off the blockade, sir."

"Yes, sir, I mean, no, sir," stammered Sir Reginald as he
retreated in complete confusion.

"Larinda, what a silly fop," Summers said.

"Yes, isn't he?" Larinda agreed as she pulled on her gloves
calmly. "Your sister tells me he is worth more than Golden
Ball. But I think he and I would not suit."

"I suppose you prefer a penniless Scotsman with nothing to
recommend him but his bare knees."

"It could be that I do."

"I can send Bartley MacGregor to the rightabout in a gypsy's
jump, Larinda," he continued, pulled on his own gloves, and
settled his hat more securely.

"You can try, Uncle Summers," she said, "you can try."

He smiled, winked at Jeannie, and then looked toward the
sitting room. "And what nonsense is going on in there, or dare
I ask?" he asked.

He gave the matter a moment's careful thought, then shrugged
his shoulders and went into the room, where Clare sobbed on
Mary's lap. When he knelt beside her in front of the sofa, she
buried her face in Mary's bosom and cried harder.

"Mary, come now, and tell me, what is the difficulty here?
As if we haven't enough to worry about at the moment."

Mary went pale at the tone of his voice, but she merely stroked

Clare's ringlets. "I am sure that she is afraid you have come to take her back to Portugal, sir."

Captain Summers' expression grew more thoughtful. He turned to Jeannie, who stood by his shoulder. "I would have, only a week ago, Jeannie," he whispered as she rested her hand on his shoulder. "In fact, I was planning on it, before you came. It seemed like the only thing to do." He was talking more to himself than to Jeannie, and she was wise enough to remain silent. "But now? What should I do, Jeannie?"

"It is your decision, Will," she replied, hoping for the best. "You have said she is not your daughter, and she has no ties in this household. I do not believe Lady Smeath has any interest in her welfare. She never speaks to her, and as a consequence, Clare is silent."

He touched Clare's hair, and then his hand went to the towel doll. He straightened the tartan that had twisted about on the little gold button. "Clare, I will not take you to Portugal, but neither will I leave you here," he said, his voice final.

Clare stopped sobbing and pulled herself upright in Mary's lap, her eyes wide and her mouth open.

"When Jeannie McVinnie returns here in a day or two, she will take you and Mary home to Scotland with her."

Mary gasped and clapped her hands. Clare rubbed the tears from her eyes and leaned against her again. Jeannie stared at the captain.

"Jeannie, you'll catch minnows," the captain said. "Now close your mouth and nod your head yes. You're still my crew, at least until I quit Wendover Square, and I expect obedience." He sighed. "God knows I don't seem to merit it from anyone else in his plaguey household." He took her by the hand. "Do this for me, Jeannie," he pleaded, "and for Clare. And I think, for you."

Jeannie returned the pressure of his hand. "Yes, we'll go back to Scotland," she said quietly, "although heaven knows what Galen McVinnie will say." She kissed Clare. "I had cleared out a space some time earlier in my room, Clare. Mary, there's a little alcove at the top of the stairs for you. It isn't much," she said doubtfully.

"You know I don't mind," Mary assured her.

After another look at Clare's face, Jeannie allowed the captain to help her to her feet. "We'll manage just fine, Captain."

He clapped his hands together in triumph and then noticed Wapping hovering anxiously in the doorway. "By the way, Wapping, when Lady Smeath comes around again, tell her she is rid of me at last, and Clare and Jeannie, too." He thought a moment. "I couldn't mention anything to her about Captain MacGregor. We'll let Larinda occupy herself for this Season, which, by the way, you silly goose, has scarce begun, trying to convince Auntie that a penniless Scot will be well-suited for a husband." He let out a crack of laughter. "By God, she'll find that amusing."

He knelt again to kiss Clare, who threw her arms around his neck and rested her cheek against his. Jeannie watched and then looked away as tears sprang into his eyes.

When she looked back, the captain was in complete control again. He went to the door and motioned to them. "Pringle has secured us a hackney. Excellent fellow!" He indicated that they should follow him. "My fondest regards to Agatha," he called from the bottom of the stairs up to Wapping. "I'll miss her more than words can say."

"You are severe upon your sister," Larinda said to her uncle as the hackney pulled away from the curb.

He took off his hat and rubbed his hand through his thinning hair. "I must confess to you, Larinda, that sisters are almost as fun to bait as butlers." He looked at Jeannie, a touch of embarrassment in his eyes. "I had no idea I was such a bully."

On a sudden whim, Captain Summers ordered the jehu to take them to the Couched Lion. A discussion with the landlord uncovered no information about a small boy of fourteen years with light hair and gray eyes.

"My lord," the landlord importuned, missing the mark wide, "Your worship, sir, do you have any notion how many boys of that description are hanging about London?"

The captain only nodded and then favored the landlord with his gallow's grin. "Only let them come closer to the docks and I'll lead the press gangs out for them myself."

A short drive through London's less-well-favored streets took them to the posting house for the mail coach. By exerting his considerable personality, the captain was able to keep the driver of the mail coach at bay long enough for Jeannie to scurry about and find some rolls and hard cheese. After a few choice words from the driver and a basilisk stare from the captain, they joined Larinda inside the coach.

Larinda was holding a spot for them and eyeing the other inmates of the damp and smelly coach.

"I must admit, Uncle, this is a new experience," she said as she watched two merchants trade a bottle back and forth between them, passing it across a clergyman stiff with disapproval.

Captain Summers cowered the drinkers with a look that stopped the bottle in midpass and then saw it whisked out of sight. Summers settled himself back, pleased with himself.

"You are a wonder, Captain," Jeannie said.

He did not look at her, but tipped his hat forward. "At sea I am a wonder, my dear. On land, fearsomely misfit. I growl and huff and puff, and you see right through me."

"Thank you for not abandoning Clare," she whispered.

A flush rose on his face. "I almost hate to admit this, but she is charming. I couldn't send her back." He sighed. "And to think I came so close."

Jeannie shivered.

"Jeannie, are you cold?" he asked.

She was not, but she made no objection when he pulled his cloak around her and held her close against his side. Larinda looked at him expectantly, so he pulled her close to him on the other side and made some remark about being "the envy of nations, a sailor's sailor," and told them both to go to sleep, as it would be a long night.

Larinda was soon asleep, her head bobbing on the captain's shoulder until he leaned her against the carriage window. He was still then, and Jeannie thought he slept, too. She sighed and squirmed about.

"Mrs. McVinnie, you must be the very devil to sleep with," he said at last when she poked him in the ribs.

"That is improper," she said, her face red.

"It is merely an observation. Do cease wiggling about like a worm on a line. Here now, cast refinement to the wind and rest your head on my lap."

"I won't," she replied, and then pillowed her cloak on his lap and rested her head upon his thigh. "Perhaps I will, considering that if I do not, you will get all thin about the mouth and remind me that I am crew," she grumbled.

He chuckled, but said nothing. She was almost asleep when he spoke.

"Jeannie, if he is not at Portsmouth, I do not know what to do. I must take the next blockade ship to the Channel Fleet and regain the *Venture*. It will fall to you to scout him out. I can make some suggestions and leave you with a note to Lord Wilkins, who has some charge over the army."

"I will manage."

He rested his hand against her cheek. "Of that I have no doubt. I'll leave you with a note to draw upon my account at Pelmsley's in London for any amount."

He leaned back and his hand strayed to her shoulder. "And here I am, going back to sea. I wonder why I do not feel so happy about it this time?"

I could tell you, she thought, but I am too tired. Surely there will be a moment tomorrow, when there isn't a clergyman sitting across the aisle, all ears and bad breath. I'll say yes to your proposal. She sighed. If you even remember having made it . . .

17

THE feeling that morning had come dragged Jeannie out of troubling dreams and laid the foggy harbor of Portsmouth before her eyes. She bit her lips at the pain in her back and looked out the window, breathing in the fog and smelling the tar that permeated the atmosphere.

The captain's eyes were closed, but he did not appear to be sleeping. As she looked at him, he opened his eyes.

"I have spent better nights in prison, or under fire," he said, keeping his voice low so as not to waken Larinda, or the merchants or clergyman across from them, who slept jumbled together like puppies.

Jeannie flexed her back and winced. "You could have made me sit up," she said.

He shook his head. "You were not the source of my discomfort. Far from it." He smiled briefly, an intimate smile meant for no one else, one that put a little heart back in her. "Do you know that you snore?"

"Yes! I have been reminded ever so many times. And I also talk in my sleep," she said, laughter in her voice. "I am a nag and a scold and the veriest harpy when it comes to church attendance."

He laughed then, but sobered immediately, choosing his next words with great deliberation. "And, my dear, did Tom have any bad habits?"

Jeannie was silent then, remembering all of Tom's idiosyncrasies and wondering which one to start with. As she considered the question and how best to answer it, she saw the little light go out of Will Summers' eyes as he retreated inside himself again. She understood then all that his questions had implied, and she was too late with an answer.

"I am sorry," he said, his voice formal even as she hurried to say something and rectify a dreadful situation of her own making. "It really was a vast impertinence on my part. Do forgive me."

"No," she protested as he looked away. "No, Will, it was not impertinent."

Larinda opened her eyes, stretched, and looked about. She swiped at the window with her sleeve, wiping away the accumulated moisture on the pane.

"Uncle, have we arrived at Portsmouth?" she asked.

"We have. Now the hunt for your wretched brother begins."

There was a certain eagerness in his voice that twisted the knife Jeannie had stuck in her own back, as if he were grateful to his niece for waking up and sparing him further pain. Jeannie closed her eyes and kicked herself mentally. Go back to sleep, Larinda, she thought. Close your eyes again and let me have just five minutes more with Will Summers. I will tell him how much I love him, and maybe he will believe me. Please, Larinda.

But Larinda was awake to stay. "What should we do, Uncle? Are there many ships in Portsmouth?"

Captain Summers gave a dry chuckle. "Bless me, Larinda, this is where the Royal Navy calls home. When the fog lifts, you'll see what I mean."

They rode closer as the sun burned away the fog and Larinda saw what he meant.

The bay was filled with ships of all sizes, ships at dry dock, turned on their sides, copper sheathing peeled away like the hide of a great animal, and parts of ships, rows and rows of masts and spars, and everywhere the sound of hammering. Many ships rode at anchor, bobbing light and empty, waiting cargo and crew, or riding heavy in the water, hulls filled and bound for distant ports. And farther out in the magnificent bay, more ships anchored.

"How will we ever find Edward?" Jeannie asked.

Larinda nodded, her eyes filled with apprehension.

"We will first wangle a list of ships from the harbormaster," said Will. "We will search only those vessels ready to slip their moorings, the ones bound for Spain." He patted Larinda's hand. "And we will try to find Bartley MacGregor and see what he knows about all this."

The harbormaster was remarkably unwilling to supply any information, even with the threat of Lord Smeath rolling about like loose cannon on the deck. "Now, if you had something in writing from the gent, Captain, perhaps I could find a list somewhere," he said as he leaned across his desk. "But as it is, I wouldn't take the word of Our Lord Jesus Christ if it wasn't in writing. Begging your pardon, madams, but after all, this is the Royal Navy and we do have standards."

With an oath that caused Larinda to jump and Jeannie to suddenly find a fascination in a wall calendar, the captain dug into his pocket and slapped a handful of coins on the desk. After another moment's pause, a list found its way into his pocket, and the harbormaster returned, dignity intact, to the more pressing matter of a hundredweight of biscuit that weighed only seventy-five pounds.

Captain Summers took the list out into the better light and air of Portsmouth's early morning. "I'd like to flog the lot of them around the fleet, harbormasters and quartermasters," he said under his breath. He ran his finger down the list. "The *Dauntless*, by God! And the *Adventure*, *Polyclitus*, and *Atropos*, bound for the Channel Fleet. And look you, here is the *Minotaur* for the Baltic, and look, *Amaryllis, Melanthion, St. Peter of Lubeck,* and *Samson,* all troop ships for Lisbon. Jeannie, we will find him on board one of those, I'll be bound."

The captain procured two sleeping rooms and a private parlor at the Winston and left Larinda in reluctant possession.

"Uncle, I do not wish to remain here," she said, and she appeared dangerously on the edge of tears.

"No scenes, Larinda," he said. "I am going to sprinkle this wharf with coins, asking the whereabouts of your brother and admonishing them to direct all intelligence to you here at the Winston. You will see to it that any news finds us in the harbor. No argument, my dear. Come, Jeannie."

A waterman was easy to come by, a one-legged man safe from the press gang because of that wooden leg, and smug about it, too.

"The *Melanthion,* and smartly, lad," Summers ordered as he helped Jeannie into the wherry.

The waterman's assurance wilted. "Not with a lady, sir, surely not. There's a new gang of pressed men on board." He made a face. "Didn't I just see them rowed out in chains. Hard cases, Captain."

"Just do as you're told," the captain snapped.

He sat with Jeannie in the thwarts, wrapping his cloak about her to keep off the spray. Jeannie stole a glance at him. His expression was set, and he did not appear like a man in need of any chat. She kept her thought to herself as the waterman and his oarsman put their backs into it. They skimmed across the bay to the great transport riding low in the water.

As they approached the ship, Jeannie felt Captain Summers begin to relax. The tension drained out of his body and his arms went around her. He was at sea again, even if only in a little boat, and at perfect ease with himself.

"A beautiful woman and the ocean," he sighed, his lips close to her ear. "I think I am in heaven."

"But you're not sure," she was prompted to point out.

After a moment of startled silence spent digesting that comment, he pulled her to one side so he could look into her face. "No, I am not sure," he replied slowly.

She looked at him, and now he was embarrassed because he would not meet her eyes. Jeannie touched his cheek and then settled herself against him again so he could be spared the trouble of gazing into her face. She chose her own words carefully, knowing they were spoken too late even as she said them.

"Tom was never on time to anything, in all the years I knew him," she said, looking straight ahead at the helmsman of the little craft, who stood now with a coil of rope in his hand. "He was even-tempered to the point of placidity, and many is the time I had to bite my tongue when he should have scolded the butcher or the gardener and did not. I suppose we would have had some lively fights, had he been around long enough for the newness to have worn off. Setting all that aside, I loved him, Will, even if he was not perfection itself. I love you, too."

Silence. She expected nothing else, so she was not surprised. She sat up straight then and folded her hands in her lap. Ah, well, she thought, this is surely not the time to bring up that rather delicate matter of yesterday's proposal.

"Lay us alongside," the captain was saying to the waterman.

The waterman looked at Jeannie dubiously. "We can call for a boatswain's chair," he offered.

"Not necessary. I'll help the lady. You can surely find something to occupy your attention elsewhere while she goes up over the side."

"Aye, sir," replied the waterman, grinning.

The *Melanthion* rode low in the water, no copper showing.

"She's ready to sail, Jeannie, or almost so. I wonder . . ." He stood up then, pulling his cloak back and exposing his uniform front.

"Why have you brought me along?" she asked point-blank.

He smiled, but it dissolved into no more than a bleak attempt. "I think you know."

Her chin came up. "If you are intending to use this experience on me as you used Caleb Matthews on Edward, you are wide of the mark, sir, and will have no better luck."

"It's more than that," he said. "When we find Edward— and we will, make no mistake—I want you to be with me and make sure that I do the right thing."

The waterman stroked against the current now and the wherry slowed. The helmsman cast a line to a sailor on the *Melanthion*'s deck. The boat slowed as another line was cast off the stern and they were made fast alongside.

"What is the right thing?" she asked.

"That will be for you to say, Jeannie. I have no judgment in this matter."

With that quixotic comment, the captain grabbed hold of the chains on the *Melanthion* and pulled himself up onto the deck. He motioned for Jeannie to follow.

Her eyes on the captain, who seemed so far above the wherry now, she gathered her skirts around her. After a moment spent considering the issue, she realized that any attempt to climb aboard with her hands thus occupied would be unsuccessful. She glanced over her shoulder at the wherryman and his crew, who were looking the other way, intent on some distant occurrence on the Isle of Wight.

Tom, you were wrong about the navy employing no gentlemen, she thought. She forgot her skirts and climbed up the side of the ship, holding out her hand to Will Summers, who pulled her up in one practiced motion.

"Excellent, Mrs. McVinnie," he said. His smile was broader than ever, and he appeared totally relaxed.

She knew why. He was safely in his element again, and she was the stranger. Jeannie gave her skirts a shake and looked about her on the deck. There was scarcely a space not tangled with rope, thick tarry rope, wider than her wrist. As she watched, the confusion of rope and sail seemed to sort itself into an orderly kind of disorder, like a puzzle viewed at from several angles. The *Melanthion* was a transport preparing to get under way and about deadly business in troubled waters. The guns were battened down to the deck, the boarding nets folded carefully, all the trappings of power harnessed, at least for now.

The captain of the *Melanthion* came toward them on the deck, picking his way gracefully through the tangle of cable. He saluted smartly and then extended his hand.

"Sir William," he said as they shook hands, "you honor the *Melanthion.*"

Will inclined his head. "I read in the *Chronicles* that you had assumed command of this vessel, Nicholls. It is promotion overdue."

Captain Nicholls grinned, proud of himself. "Thank you, sir. I consider that high praise." He looked about him with the air of a man determined not to show pride of ownership but bursting with the joy of it anyway. "True, 'tis only a transport, but as you say, it is my command."

The preliminaries disposed of, Captain Summers introduced Jeananie and explained their presence on Nicholls' ship.

Captain Nicholls scratched his head. "I have several new midshipmen," he said, "but none of them fit your description." He laughed. "Other than your part about 'plaguey young chubs!' Lord, Captain Summers, do they grow more green and raw every year, or do I get older?"

Summers nodded. "I am sure we do not age," he said. "But look you here, sir, I would see your newly pressed seamen and any new hands you may have acquired."

"Aye, aye, sir."

Nicholls turned and spoke to the first mate, who stood close by. A word or two, and the mate turned to the boatswain, who blew a blast on his whistle and then another. Jeannie heard the sound of many running bare feet, followed by the more precise stamp of shod marines. Behind them came the pressed seamen, still in chains.

"Order now," snapped the first lieutenant. "You there. Take his name."

A ragged line snaked along the crowded deck of men young and old, the bald, the toothless, the able, the raw, the men in chains who had been coughed up from prisons bound close to the men, still in civilian clothes, who had unwisely ventured out in a seaport town when the press gangs roved.

Captain Summers clapped his hands behind his back and strolled the length of the line. The manacled felons were pale, some hopeful of expression, others resigned to the sure knowledge that they had traded one hell for another.

Will Captain Nicholls ever dare unchain them? Jeannie asked herself as she gazed down the rank. What is to prevent these desperate men from killing him and taking over the ship? How can anyone command such men? It would take . . . She paused and swallowed. It would take one even harder than they.

The pressed men were even less promising, to Jeannie's eyes. Some wore the rough clothes of farm laborers, who even now probably had wives and babes wondering about their fate. Others, paler of face and shifty-eyed, reminded Jeannie of the young cutpurse who had a set upon her outside of the Pantheon Bazaar. Who was to say this was a better life?

And there was another man, darting forward as far as his chain would allow toward Captain Summers, who, to his credit, stopped but did not flinch and regarded the man as he would a dog on a leash. The man was speaking urgently to the captain, even as he fumbled with a bag about his neck. The captain leaned closer, and Jeannie held her breath.

Captain Summers motioned to Captain Nicholls. "I think, sir, you have snabbled a Yankee here."

Nicholls uttered a mighty oath. "I am also short of hands, Summers," he muttered.

"He has an American protection," the captain replied, and held it out to the commander of the *Melanthion*.

Nicholls looked it over, a sour expression on his face. "You can buy these for five pounds in any port," he argued as he looked over his shoulder to the marine corporal. "Cut him out, and be smart about it. And send him back to Portsmouth."

The man looked around in triumph. He rubbed his hands when the chains fell away and went to perch himself on the carronade.

"I wouldn't have such scaff and raff in my command, anyway," Nicholls grumbled.

"Sour grapes. I hear they are good seamen," Summers said. "We will now go below and look about, sir, if you please."

Captain Nicholls frowned and looked from Summers to Jeannie as a flush rose up his already florid face.

"Captain Summers, there are women belowdecks right now, and . . ." He left the sentence unfinished, but raised his eyebrows.

Summers shrugged. "We have to make sure. By your leave, sir?"

"Aye, sir. Do as you chose. I'm sorry, Mrs. McVinnie."

Mystified, Jeannie followed Captain Summers down the narrow companionway, wrinkling her nose and holding her breath against the overpowering stench that rose to meet her. It was the stink of filthy water washing about with the effluvia of men and animals in it, the odor of too many unwashed bodies in too tight a space, mingled with the smell of new canvas and the omnipresent tarred rope.

"Dear me, Will, how do you draw breath down there?" she asked as she pressed her handkerchief to her nose.

"After a while, I don't even notice it," he said. "And I do

spent much of my time on deck. Watch your head now. Well, perhaps you needn't worry about your head.''

She passed easily under the low beams as the captain removed his hat and ducked low. The smell grew worse as they traveled the companionway, peering into small cubicles stuffed with sea chests and slung with hammocks. They reached the forecastle and Jeannie stared about her in amazement.

Women in various stages of undress sat on the deck and dangled from hammocks. No one appeared even slightly inhibited by the unexpected arrival of an officer belowdeck. One of the women, more brazen than the others, darted forward and presented herself to the captain. The others laughed as Jeannie gasped.

''As you were, you bitch,'' said the captain, his face dark, his eyes rock-hard.

The woman held her ground a moment, considering the matter, and was pulled aside by another, who whispered something to her. The woman looked at Will Summers in fright and retreated to a corner beyond the reach of the oil lamps that pitched and tossed.

''Your reputation seems to have preceded you in some way,'' Jeannie said when she found her voice again.

''I won't allow women on my ship in port,'' he said. ''And when I find them, I flog them. I suppose the word has got about. Damned nuisances. Drunkenness, clap, and endless trouble, Jeannie. Look about you now.''

She did as he said, and saw no sign of Edward. She did not peer closely into the hammocks that swayed too vigorously, or into the corners where women laughed low.

They finished their search, and Jeannie returned to the deck with no urging. Captain Nicholls eyed her anxiously. ''You look a bit peaky, Mrs. McVinnie,'' he said, and indicated a hatch cover. ''Sit you down.''

''No,'' she said shortly. ''We have three other transports to look into, do we not, Captain Summers?''

''We do.''

Captain Summers held out his hand to the *Melanthion*'s skipper. ''Do look close at the Scots troops when they board tomorrow, will you? We'll be watching on shore, too, but Edward might be among them.''

''Will do, sir, and good luck to you. Do I heard that Lord

Smeath has relieved you of your London duty and sent you back to sea?''

Summers nodded, no mirth on his face, no light in his eyes. ''I suppose I am still the laughingstock of the Channel Fleet.''

Nicholls had better sense than to smile. ''The word has got about, sir,'' he ventured. ''I expect it will soon be forgotten.''

Captain Summers returned some inaudible reply and saluted Nicholls, who saluted back and took his hand again. ''Happy hunting, sir, and good fortune on the blockade.'' He looked about his transport. ''We depend upon you blockaders to keep the frogs in their little ponds.''

Jeannie clambered down the side of the *Melanthion,* and was lifted, skirt and petticoats flying, into the wherry by its commander, who assured her he had ''daughters a-plenty.'' She merely smiled and sat carefully again, wrapping her cloak about her. Captain Summers joined her in a moment and directed the waterman to row next to the *Samson.* He made no comment to Jeannie, but sat wrapped about in his own cloak, his chin down, his eyes closed.

''It is a grim life,'' Jeannie commented as they neared the *Samson.* ''Not fit for a lad of tender years.''

The captain nodded. ''It is.'' He made no move to touch her, but he leaned nearer. ''A lad grows up fast in the Royal Navy.''

''If he grows up at all,'' was her next objection.

''No one has a safe-conduct, Jeannie,'' was all he said until they gained the deck of the *Samson* and she was introduced to another surprised captain.

And another. And another. A careful search of all four transports turned up no sign of Edward.

The rain began as they completed their search and started back for Portsmouth, which sprawled in the gathering dusk across Portsea Island, winking like a trollop. Jeannie huddled in her cloak and shook her head when Captain Summers offered her the further protection of his own boat cloak.

''You're a stubborn woman,'' he commented as she allowed the wherryman to drape a canvas about her shoulders. It smelled of fish and brine, a veritable perfume after the stink of the ships belowdeck.

''No. I merely wish to think in peace,'' she said as the rain dripped off her face. ''I wish I knew where Edward was. I can only hope he is warm and dry somewhere.''

It was easy then to cry in the dark, with the rain pelting her. No one could hear her sobs above the rain hitting the canvas as she cried for everything she knew she had lost that day, and she wondered how to face Larinda. It was even easier to cry for Captain Summers. I will miss you terribly, she thought. The thought was made more dreadful by the sure knowledge that once she was out of sight, she would be out of mind, too.

Captain Summers paid the waterman such a sum that, as the man knuckled his forehead, he asked the captain where he wanted the boat stowed, now that he had bought it. Summers did not smile as he helped Jeannie out of the boat and onto the wharf. Without any words between them, they trudged up the cobblestoned street and into the light and warmth of the Winston.

Larinda flung open the door to the private parlor when she heard their footsteps on the stairs. The light in her eyes quickly dimmed as Jeannie shook her head.

"You're soaked through," Captain Summers said. "Larinda, find her a blanket to wrap about her when she gets out of those clothes."

"I'll be fine," Jeannie said, and sat down close to the fire, her back to both of them. It was only a sextant, and now Edward was gone. The knowledge sank in, taking root like a barnacle.

Suddenly the room was too small, too crowded. She leapt to her feet and snatched up her cloak again, darting out the door and down the steps as Larinda called to her and the captain said something to Larinda that Jeannie could not hear.

Jeannie walked rapidly away from the Winston, knowing that as she worried and fretted about Edward out on a night like this, she was almost mourning the loss of a lover, this one seduced by the ocean, a power over which she had no more control than the guns at La Coruña. She strode back to the wharf and leaned against the railing. He would marry me if I begged and pleaded enough, she thought, or got myself into his bed and compelled his honor, but he would never be mine.

Hard on the heels of this cold-eyed reality was the worse thought, the knowledge that if he did give himself to her, Captain Summers would be a very happy man. But he would never do that. He had been solitary too long. He lived a life of total power and ultimate responsibility far beyond human limits. He was not a man; he was a tool of the Royal Navy, scarcely different from a topgallant or a binnacle.

I could never do that to Edward, she thought. Not ever.

As she leaned against the wharf railing, Jeannie realized how exhausted she was. She looked down at the water for many minutes. When you can't even remember when was the last night's rest you enjoyed, it is time to pull the covers over your head, Jeannie lass, she told herself.

She stared at the water for a long time and then, with a sigh, heaved herself away from the railing. She was not surprised to see Captain Summers standing at the top of the street. Maybe you do care just a little, she thought as she trudged toward him.

"I wasn't going to throw myself into the murk, Captain," she said, hoping that he could find a measure of humor in the remark.

"I did not suppose that for a minute, Jean," he said. "You have far too much bottom for a silly stunt." He gave her a moment for a rejoinder. When she did not speak, he continued, his tone conversational. "I was merely returning from a walk to the Globe and Anchor, where several officers of the Dumfries Rifles are dug in, writing their wills as they face the prospect of a sea voyage."

Jeannie looked up quickly and took hold of his arm. "Bartley?" she asked. "Was he there?"

He shook his head. "No, Jean, dear, and there lies a bit of a mystery. Colonel Mackey assured me that there has been no communication from Captain MacGregor or the others on that post chaise since they left the Couched Lion. I wonder what has happened."

She looked at him. His eyes were not as hard as they had been on the transport ship. There was even tenderness in his face, and she wondered at it.

"You know, Will, Edward did overhear Bartley say that the Dumfries men were leaving from the Lion at five o'clock," she said. "I wonder, do you think—"

"—that Bartley discovered him and returned him to Wendover Square? I wouldn't doubt it, Jean, and I do believe Bartley is the clue. I wish we could find out, and soon."

He took her hand then, and she surprised herself further by allowing him to and even returning the pressure of his fingers. "I also had a chat with Colonel Mackey."

Her eyes flew to his face in dismay. "No!"

"Yes! He assured me that he would write to Galen this very

night. And to you, Jeannie. I was somewhat insistent.''

She cried then, and he held her close, his hands so tender as he patted her back and the rain poured down again.

"Of course, it will only join the letter from me that Galen McVinnie has likely already received. Now, don't poker up, Jeannie," he declared as she looked up at him. He kissed her nose. "Sometimes people need a little push. Happens you're one of those. You needn't worry about the Dumfries Rifles anymore, my dear. Consider this my parting gift."

They walked hand in hand back to the Winston, stepping back when a post chaise rolled by, splashing mud everywhere, and then running forward, still hand in hand, when a kilted Scot, and another, came out of the carriage.

Jeannie dropped Summers' hand and threw herself into Bartley's arms, grabbing his broad shoulders and shaking him. "Bartley, where is that wretched Edward?"

Bartley stared at her, his mouth open, and then threw back his head and laughed as she shook him again.

"Lord love us, Jeannie my light, if you don't remind me of a terrier," he protested as he chuckled. "Now, mind the pleats, hear?"

"She doesn't have any more regard for my gold leaf," the captain assured him. "But tell us, sir, where in God's holy name is my plaguey nephew?"

Bartley managed to plant a kiss on Jeannie's upturned face before he laughed again and turned her loose. "Come inside! Haven't you two the sense God gave a duck?"

The ran inside the inn and the captain secured the best table in the taproom with a look and a nod.

Bartley watched him, admiration all over his face. "Sir, how you do that I can only speculate. Is there a more fearsome ogre than a sea captain?"

"I doubt it," the captain replied, getting a bit thin about the mouth.

Jeannie recognized the signs. "Bartley, please, where is Edward?"

Bartley took up the tankard of ale that the landlord plunked down in a rousing hurry. "Why, back in Wendover Square, where he belongs. The silly chuff hid himself in the boot of the post chaise and was quite uncovered, literally, when we stopped at Meadow Willingham to take on Jack Farquhar and his duffel.''

He chuckled at the memory. "Such surprise on one laddie's face. I gave him a regular good Presbyterian scold and we took him back to his aunt, who gave him another.'' He took another drink, sighed, and wiped his mouth with the back of his hand. "Made us a bit late. We've got to report to Colonel Mackey on the double quick.''

"He'll have something of a personal nature to tell you, too,'' the captain said quietly.

Bartley made no comment. He drank the rest of the ale, set the tankard down, and cleared his throat.

"Captain Summers, by your leave, may I write to Larinda?''

The thin look about the captain's mouth vanished and was replaced by a grin.

"She's not worth the trouble, Bartley. She'll plague you to death.''

Bartley shook his head, entirely serious. "Nay, none of that, sir. She's worth the trouble. It's only letters I am interested in now, sir. In a year or so, we'll see. Sir?''

"You have my permission,'' Summers said, and shook MacGregor's hand. "My sister will rail and scold, but only remember that I am Larinda's guardian, and I am the one you must please. And by God, I am hard to please.''

"Very well, sir. By your leave, is she upstairs? I'd like a word with her.''

"Go on, Captain. And don't tell me years from now that you weren't sufficiently warned.''

Bartley laughed, tweaked Jeannie's curl, and took the stairs two at a time. He returned at a more sedate pace, his face thoughtful. The other officers and Jeannie waited for him in the taproom. Jeannie stood up and he clasped her in his arms.

"Good-byes are the worst of all, Jeannie McVinnie. I still say Tom was a lucky, lucky man. If you're feeling charitable, drop me a letter once in a while.''

He kissed her, shook Captain Summers' hand, and joined his fellow officers again. He did not look back, and Jeannie, wiping her streaming eyes, could only be grateful.

Summers finished his ale. "You've turned into the veriest

watering pot,'' he observed. ''Well, come on. Morning comes soon enough, and I must be off then.''

Jeannie thought she would never close her eyes that whole night through, especially with Larinda sniffling and blowing her nose and twisting and turning about in the same bed, but she did. When morning came, she felt decidedly optimistic.

Larinda elected to remain at the inn, rather than accompany her uncle back to the dock, where the waterman waited to ferry him to *Atropos*. ''I would only see the Dumfries Rifles preparing to board,'' she explained, ''and I have already had enough tears for one night.''

But she sobbed anyway as she hugged her uncle and told him to take care. ''I shall miss you, Uncle Summers,'' she said. ''I never knew that I loved you before, but I do, I truly do. Be careful, please.''

He kissed her, and Jeannie noted a mist in his own eyes, which were the softest green imaginable. ''Jeannie, buy my totty-headed niece a bushel of cucumbers. Her eyes will be so puffy in London tomorrow that not even Brummell can get her through this London Season.''

Larinda looked at him in surprise. ''Why, Uncle, I had completely forgotten. Jeannie, did you remember?''

Jeannie shook her head. ''I suppose it is only getting under way now. Think of all those invitations, Larinda.'' She sighed.

Larinda was silent a moment, deep in thought. ''I think I will take Edward home to Suffolk. Aunt Agatha can come if she chooses. Jeannie, you may come with us, of course. In fact, I wish it more than anything.''

''I would love to, but I cannot. I am taking Clare home to Kirkcudbrightshire. I have some . . .'' She stopped and looked at Captain Summers. ''Some little business to take care of there.''

''Bravo, Jeannie,'' he said, and offered her his arm. ''Come now, and smartly, smartly. Your last official act as my impressed crew will be to support me to the dock.''

They walked arm in arm to the wharf, where yesterday's wherryman waited. Jeannie screwed up her courage.

''Captain, I need to tell you something . . .''

''Jeannie, I must speak . . .''

They both broke off, laughing.

The captain bowed. "As a gentleman, I should let you go first, but I will not in this instance." He stopped short of the dock and took both her hands. "Jeannie, I am withdrawing my proposal of marriage." The stricken look in her eyes made him falter. "Jeannie, don't!"

"But I love you," she quavered, and leaned her forehead against his chest.

"I love you, too," he said, tightening his grip on her hands. "You'd only be hurt if I married you, because I will not give up the sea."

"I know that," she said, her voice muffled against his cloak.

"Jeannie, it won't do. You deserve a happier life than I could give you."

She could not look him in the face. "May I at least write?"

"Best not, Jeannie dear. Better you just forget."

He started toward the dock again. "There still remains the matter of Edward's future," he said, his voice husky, as if he struggled as much as she.

Her head came up. "I have made my decision," she said. "When I return to Wendover Square, I shall personally escort him to Deptford Hard. Didn't you say there was a captain friend of yours there who was bound for the West Indies?"

"Jeannie," the captain said, and it said the world.

She forced a smile to her face and hoped that her voice was light. "One Jeannie McVinnie sent you to sea. No reason why this one should deny your nephew." She held her hands out in front of her. "He would only run away over and over, as you did. Let us not waste his time, my darling."

In answer, the captain reached inside his uniform coat and drew out a letter. She took it from him, noting that it was addressed to Captain Russell Jones, *Calliope*, Deptford Hard.

"You had planned this all along, hadn't you?" she asked, her voice filled with wonder.

"Only if it was your idea. I was prepared to tear it up."

He kissed her cheek and then pulled himself away from her before she could take his arm again. He continued walking backward toward the wherry. "Let us merely say that I know you well, Jeannie my crew, and maybe myself a little better. God keep you. Would that I could."

18

JEANNIE heard the postman's whistle in front of Galen's house as she and Clare hurried down the street toward St. Giles. She thought a moment about returning, but realized there was no need. Edward had written a rambling narrative, fresh with tales of Jamaica and the Leeward Islands, that they had received only yesterday. Larinda had sent a hurried letter the week before to say that Bartley was chafing behind Wellington's barricades at Lisbon. There had even been a hurried scrawl from Brummell. Captain Summers never wrote.

"Clare, whatever it is will keep," she said as they hurried briskly along. "We will not get many more lovely days like this, now that September is here."

Soon the rains of autumn will pelt down in earnest, to be succeeded by the sleet and snow of winter. Another year would come and go, and she would remain indoors and face the challenge of entertaining a lively four-year-old. It was a challenge she welcomed. She would teach Clare her alphabet, and by spring, she could add her letters to the ones Jeannie sent every week to the *Venture*, care of the White Fleet, Channel.

The apples at Dardwell Head were still too green, but Andrew Maxwell stopped his work long enough to give them two anyway, with the admonition to eat them slowly or suffer the consequences. Jeannie smiled at him. Andrew's wife had died last year. She was glad to see a little light coming back into his eyes again. She could tell him a great deal about death. I can tell you, Andrew, that one day you will wake up and the pain will be only a dull ache. You'll never forget, but at least it won't hurt.

Andrew had walked her home from church last week. It had been on the tip of her tongue to invite him in to dinner, but something had stopped her. Perhaps this next week. Or the one after.

Their walk took them to the abbey ruins, where they watched the ocean in silence. Soon it would be cold and windy on the blockade, with mountainous seas and spray that stung the eyes and scoured the face. And turned men into hard creatures. Jeannie set her lips in a firm line and took Clare's hand again.

They stopped by habit at St. Giles churchyard. Clare had gathered the last bit of heather on the way, which she spread around the grave and then tugged at a weed she had missed last week.

Jeannie stood in front of the marker and felt all over again that stir of contentment that had been her first reaction when Galen had walked her there. It had been a week after she had returned from Portsmouth, pulled her chair close to his, and told him, in her own halting words, what had really happened to her that dreadful winter after La Coruña.

He had sat beside her in shocked silence, and she held her breath, wondering about his heart. After a long moment of silence, he rested his hand on hers.

"Ah, Jean, what time we waste. I knew about my heart. How could I not know? And Tom knew, too. It was to be my last campaign. You shouldn't have had to keep such a secret from me." He thought a minute more and asked her one question.

"I would have named him Kevin," she had answered, her voice scarcely audible above the crackle of the fire. She hesitated. "Kevin William, actually."

"Are there Williams in your family?"

"No. It's just a favorite name of mine, Galen, that's all."

And then a week later, they had strolled to the cemetery, and there was Kevin William's name carved on Tom's stone in companionable association.

"They'll keep each other company better that way," Galen had said.

After he said that, she had looked down at the stone and then felt the dull ache finally leave her.

And here was Clare now, brushing away a little mud that had splashed on the stone during yesterday's squall. Tom and Kevin McVinnie, father and son, remembered now. After a moment of silence, Jeannie held out her hand to Clare, thinking to herself that she would invite Andrew Maxwell to dinner on Sunday.

The house was welcoming and warm. Mary claimed her little charge and took her upstairs to change shoes. Galen called to Jeannie from the front parlor.

There was a letter for her, propped on the mantel. For a moment her heart leapt about in her breast and then resumed its normal rhythm. It was Larinda's handwriting.

She picked it up. "We heard from Larinda last week," she mused out loud. "I wonder." Jeannie looked at Galen in sudden alarm. "Oh, you don't think Bartley or Edward—"

She ripped open the letter, and a newspaper clipping fluttered down. She snatched it before it became part of the fuel in the fireplace, and sat by Galen, smoothing it on her knee. Her hand brushed it once, twice, and then she held her breath.

The word *Venture* leapt out at her. She sucked in her breath and held closer the scrap with its tiny printing.

When her breath started to come in little gasps, Galen looked up in alarm from the letter he was writing. He grabbed her arm and shook her. "Jeannie? Jeannie!"

Without a word, she handed him the clipping and leaned back in her chair, her whole body numb.

"Good God," Galen said quietly. "Jeannie, I am so sorry. Ah, Jean!"

She sat in absolute silence until the quiet began to scream at her. "Galen, it says 'all hands.' No survivors? Not one?"

He sighed. "That's what it means, Jeannie. The Channel's a tricky place."

"But he's a good captain . . ." Her voice trailed off.

"And the ships are small, my dear, so small." He waited for her to speak. When she remained silent, he took hold of her hand. "I'll tell Clare, my dear, if you wish."

Jeannie shook her head. "No. Not now. Maybe not even next week. It can wait."

She sat another moment, listening to the clock tick. "That clock is so loud," she said finally. By the time she had crossed the room to turn it around, she knew what she had to do, and quickly, before it was too late to do one last good deed for Captain Summers.

"Galen, I'm taking the mail coach to London immediately," she said.

It didn't sound like her voice, so high and strained and out of breath, as though she and Clare had run all the way from the cemetery.

"Jeannie, no," Galen said. "What can you do there? And isn't Larinda in Suffolk?"

"I'm not going to Larinda," she said. "There is someone I must see." Jeannie passed her hand in front of her eyes when Galen opened his mouth to protest. "And don't argue with me, my dear. I have to go. Tonight, if I can pack in time. I haven't a minute to spare."

The mail coach was already lumbering down McDermott Street as she threw some clothes in a bag. As the horn blew and the whip cracked, she took the clothes out and folded them more carefully. Tomorrow would do well enough. She knew that she would lie awake all night staring at the ceiling, but she had done that before on countless occasions and she knew she would get through it.

As she packed, she came across the captain's emerald. With hands that trembled, she held it up to the light and admired the flaw that zigzagged through it. She would save it for Clare. There was no way of knowing the conditions of Captain Summers' will. When Clare needed it, the necklace would be there for her.

If any of her fellow travelers had thought to make conversation with her on that interminable journey from Scotland to London, the thought died quickly. Her face white and set, her eyes boring into the back coach wall, Jeannie had kept her own counsel.

London was robed in the glory of early autumn when the mail coach came to its final stop. It was only a moment's business to retrieve her bag and step briskly into the street to hail a hackney.

If the driver seemed surprised to see a woman alone, he did not show it.

"Yes, ma'am," he said, and tipped his hat to her. "Where'll ye be bound for on this glorious afternoon?"

"Greenwich, please," she said. She had thought the word so many times in the last few days of travel that it was a relief to speak it out loud finally. "Greenwich," she said again, savoring the sound of it. "The Royal Naval Hospital, if you please, and do be quick about it."

The jehu appeared disposed to argue. ''That's a long, long way, ma'am.''

"I know," she said quietly, "but I have come all the way from Scotland and I will not be put off by a jarvey who argues with me.''

Without another word, he helped her in and they set off. She had several glimpses of the river, and then they were across the bridge and on a higher road that took them past Deptford Hard in such a way that she could not see the ships at anchor. It was a mercy from God that she could only be grateful for, even as she ached with exhaustion and realized, to her surprise, that she had not eaten for several days.

Foolish of me, she thought. For Clare's sake I must remember to put food in my mouth, chew, and swallow. I shall likely have to remind myself of that every now and again, but I will get through this, I will. Didn't he say I had far too much bottom to do silly things?

They glimpsed the Thames again as Greenwich grew closer, and she was thankful all over that she had not come by water. She would only have thought of the captain, and Edward and Clare, and it would have been too much, even for a woman with so much bottom.

The sun was setting as she paid the jarvey; then, on second thought, she asked him to wait. She squared her shoulders and climbed the steps into Christopher Wren's beautiful building.

Her heart failed her in the high-domed entry. There were sailors everywhere, and she felt her thoughts dragged backward to Portsmouth again. As she watched them, she decided that she would emigrate to the interior of Canada and never run the risk of seeing a sailor again. The thought was improbable in the extreme, but it put the heart back in her.

She climbed the stairs slowly, rehearsing in her mind for the thousandth time what she would say to Caleb Matthews. It would be hard indeed to tell him that William Summers was dead, but far, far better that he should hear it from her rather than have it read to him when the next *Naval Chronicles* was delivered. Or even if by chance, the article was overlooked, better that he should know straight up rather then spend the rest of his life wondering why his captain never came back.

And when she had done the thing, she would ask the sisters

how much she would need to send each month to continue Caleb Matthews few luxuries. It would strain her widow's pension, she was sure, but any sacrifice was worth it. The gesture was the smallest thing she could do in memory of her dear Will Summers, and she would not neglect her duty.

"I am still crew, sir," she whispered as she faced the door.

Do I knock? she wondered. It hardly mattered. She opened the door slowly, steeling herself for the ordeal ahead and wishing again that she had taken the time to eat something. Her head felt as though it would separate from her body.

The ward was the same as she remembered, only the play of light across the beds different. The room was wreathed in shadows, and it was that time of early night when the frugal put off lighting the evening candles. If the Royal Navy was anything, it was frugal. In another few minutes, the sisters would glide about, lighting tallow candles for the benefit of those with sight and saving pence elsewhere. There would be no candles for Caleb Matthews.

Dinner was over, but the odors remained, and her mouth watered. Oh, I am so hungry, she thought.

She walked the length of the ward, and then she saw Caleb propped against his pillow, paying close attention to the man who sat upon his cot.

Jeannie felt a prickle of gratitude in her heart. Thank God there were others who cared about Caleb Matthews. It was good to know that he would not be alone. Of course, she would still find a way to see him at least once a year and bring Edward when the lad came home from the West Indies station.

She stopped. I should not intrude, she thought. Only look how intently Caleb is listening, leaning forward. I can stand here a moment more. Why is it that bad news always keeps?

She stayed where she was, watching Caleb and his visitor, conversing in the dark. In a few moments, the sisters came into the hall with their candles. One by one, they lighted their way down the ward until Caleb remained in shadow. And then the sister brought a branch of candles and the visitor turned to move them closer.

Jeannie stared and swallowed hard. There was no mistaking that profile. She had memorized it that last night on the wharf in Portsmouth. William Summers sat beside Caleb Matthews, engaged in animated conversation. As she watched in wide-eyed, openmouthed shock, he ran his fingers through his hair and glanced her way.

Jeannie only remembered the look of amazement on his face as she sank to the floor, unconscious.

Jeannie twitched her nose against the smell of ammonia. She moved her hand to make it go away, and then she heard the murmur of deep voices and smelled that smell again. She waved her hand at it, and the ammonia went away. In another moment, her forehead felt cool and damp.

Her ear throbbed with a life of its own. She put her hand to it and felt a rising lump.

"I know what I am doing here, Jeannie my love, but you?" Summers felt her temple and she winced. "I'm sorry I wasn't quicker. I thought you were the sister."

Jeannie opened her eyes and stared up into Will Summers' dear face.

She was comfortably ensconced in his arms. He smelled wonderfully of bay rum and metal polish and brine. She reached up her hand and touched his face, just to make sure that he was real and that her wits hadn't gone wandering.

He kissed her hands and his eyes filled with tears as it suddenly occurred to him why she was there. "You wanted to tell Caleb, didn't you?" he asked, his voice a whisper, the tears on his cheeks. "You saw that monstrous clipping and you wanted to spare him pain. Jeannie, I'm not even remotely worthy of that."

She shook her head, groaned, and closed her eyes. "Of course you're not," she agreed. "But I love you anyway."

"She's a rum one, Captain," said Caleb Matthews.

"Even more than I knew, Caleb," he murmured. "Jeannie, we came off the blockade two days ago. There's still so much wrong with the *Venture*, even with that new mast. We're being drydocked for four months."

"I really don't understand any of this," she said. "You're not dead."

"Not yet, and I haven't any plans along those lines. Quite the contrary, my dearest, dearest Jeannie McVinnie."

She traced the outline of his mouth with her finger. "Please don't think I am being forward, my love, but will you marry me?''

"Aye, aye. But, Jeannie, I am supposed to do the proposing."

"And you are remarkably poor about it," she reminded him. She sat up carefully in his arms and removed the cold cloth from her forehead. "Caleb, how are you? I'm sorry to have created all this huggle-muggle."

Caleb only grinned.

Jeannie smiled back and kissed the captain. "There, now," she said as his arms went around her waist. "I have taken care of all the needfuls, as you would say. You have agreed to marry me, and you're quite, quite alive. Now tell me, sir, how does this come about?"

He kissed her. "Do you recall those other ships anchored at Spithead that were preparing for blockade duty?" he asked.

Jeannie thought a moment, her hand to the bump on her temple. "You went out on the *Atropos,* I think. The *Amaryllis,* the . . . Oh, the *Adventure!*"

He nodded. "It caused no end of trouble on the Channel station, I can assure you! It was the *Adventure* that broached in a following sea and went down, not the *Venture.*"

"No survivors? That's what that infamous article said."

"Well, there were survivors, and that may have caused part of the confusion. The *Venture* was close by and took them off." He looked at Caleb. "A tricky piece of sailing, but then, you trained me to sail ever so close to the wind, Caleb. We were able to take off some of the crew. Not the captain or his officers, regrettably."

"But you didn't write, you didn't even explain to Larinda," she said.

He shook his head. "We had no idea that the newspaper had latched on to that infernal piece of misinformation." He tightened his grip on her waist. "When we disembarked at Portsmouth, I met some of my brother officers at the Winston and they showed me that article. I hadn't heard of it, naturally, and we had a good laugh."

He laughed then, too, a shaky sound that went straight to Jeannie's heart. "And then it struck me that everyone I held dear must think me dead. God, what a moment. I overturned the whist table and nearly got run over by the mail coach I was trying to flag down." He rested his chin on her shoulder. "I suppose my friends will chuckle about that for years to come. I will not."

He stared at the darkening window until he had command over his voice again. "This had to be my first stop, Jeannie. You of all people understand that. Kirkcudbrightshire was to be my second." He rubbed his cheek against hers. "I'm no bargain, dear," he began.

She put her fingers over his lips. "You're not going to get out of this proposal, Captain," she said. "I have a witness. Certainly you are no bargain." She laughed and then put her hand to her ear again. "What one of us is?"

"I'm not giving up the sea."

"Did I ask you to?" Jeannie reached over and touched Caleb's stump of an arm. "Caleb, it seems to me that I had better leg-shackle myself to this man immediately before he thinks of a thousand more reasons to cry off."

Caleb nodded. "I didn't train him that way, Mrs. McVinnie. I always taught him to say, 'No excuse, sir,' and take his medicine."

Jeannie smiled and nestled herself against the captain again. "Not every wife is willing to tolerate a mistress as I am. I know I do not hold a candle to the sea, my dear, but there may be some little compensation to marriage with me."

"I thought as much. I have four months to plague you with my company all hours of the day and night." He kissed her. "In fact, I think that the only activity that won't require your presence will be dropping a line in one of Galen's trout streams."

"Really, sir," she murmured, suddenly shy.

"Yes, rreally. How do you roll your rrs that way? I shall study the matter at my leisure."

She rested her hand against his chest. "It will be too cold for fishing. I fear you must remain indoors."

"Oh, too bad, too bad!" He took her hand and ran his fingers over her knuckles. "You might as well know this, too. Lord Smeath has interfered in my life again and I have new orders."

She groaned. "Not London! I can't depend on the Beau doing us a favor ever again after last Season! And besides, who needs a London Season?"

"No, no," he assured her. "Lord Bag of Guts is posting me

to the West Indies station, where I will have every opportunity to oversee Edward, who, by the way, is getting along famously on the *Calliope,* according to Captain Jones.'' He nudged her. ''There is a promotion, too, and the station promises to be a lively one, with the frogs to watch, and freebooters as well.'

''Oh.''

''All you can say is 'oh' and look at me in that dense way?'' he demanded, and then peered closer at her solemn face. ''But you do not see the whole picture, do you, my dear?''

She shook her head.

He paused a moment to kiss her again and then another time.

''Really, Jeannie, for one infirm, you are a wonder. I shall lose my train of thought entirely. Kingston is a grand old town. I'd consider it a fine thing if I could see your lovely face there on the dock, and maybe in a few years, other little faces, every time we come back into port.''

''Jamaica?'' she asked.

''Aye, and don't look at me in that silly fashion. I am beginning to fear that you twaddled your brains when you threw yourself on the floor. Jeannie you can share my hammock all the way to Jamaica.''

''I thought you flogged women on board your ship,'' she reminded him.

''I will make an exception in your case. Jeannie, I love you. It took me too long to figure it out, but I do love you.'' He helped her to her feet. ''Caleb, you must excuse us. I have to make a visit to the Inns and procure a special license. If Jeannie marries me tomorrow morning, and smartly, too, it might be soon enough. Of course, this means you will be impressed for life.''

Jeannie's eyes misted over. She touched Caleb and looked at her captain. ''Is there a chaplain here?'' she asked. ''Could we not be married here tomorrow morning?''

It was the captain's turn to wipe his eyes. ''We can, and we will. And then we'll spend a night or two in Suffolk on our way north. I have an estate there, did you know?''

She shook her head.

''It marches next to Edward's property. You probably aren't even aware that for these past five months and more, it has been deeded to you.''

''Will,'' she murmured.

"I think it is time you looked over your property. It's good land, if you like land, but you probably won't mind relinquishing it to your oldest son someday, should he be silly enough to want it."

"There's no guarantee that he will be a landsman, my dear."

The captain's arms went around her again. "There's no guarantee of anything, Jeannie Summers, but we knew that when we started this."

"Aye, Captain."